Princeless

Book 1:
SAVE YOURSELF

DELUXE EDITION

Bryan Seaton: Publisher
Kevin Freeman: President
Dave Dwonch: Creative Director
Shawn Gabborin: Editor In Chief
Jamal Igle: Vice-President of Marketing
Vito Delsante: Director of Marketing
Jim Dietz: Social Media Director
Nicole DAndria: Script Editor
Chad Cicconi: The Patriarchy
Colleen Boyd: Submissions Editor

This book is dedicated to my mom,
who taught me that women can be heroes..
My wife and her sisters,
who inspired me to write characters as amazing as they are..
And my daughter,
for whom I had to make comics better.

-Jeremy Whitley

Princeless Book 1: Issues 1-4.
Written by Jeremy Whitley. Illustrated by M.Goodwin
and DE Belton (Mr. Froggy)

"The Thing in the Dungeon"
Written by Jeremy Whitley. Illustrated by Nancy King

"The Merry Adventures of Young Prince Ashe Part 1"
Written by Jeremy Whitley Illustrated by Quinne Larsen

"The Runaway Prince"
Written by Jeremy Whitley. Illustrated by Kelly Lawrence

"The Smiths"
Written by Jeremy Whitley. Illustrated by Jules Rivera

"Princeless X Skullkickers"
Written by Jim Zub. Illustrated by M. Goodwin

Covers by Mia Goodwin, Super Ugly, and Jules Rivera

Pinups by Emily Martin, Sarah Leuver, Nancy King, Elsa Kroese,
Tressa Bowling, Laura Guzzo, Janet Wade, and Autumn Crossman

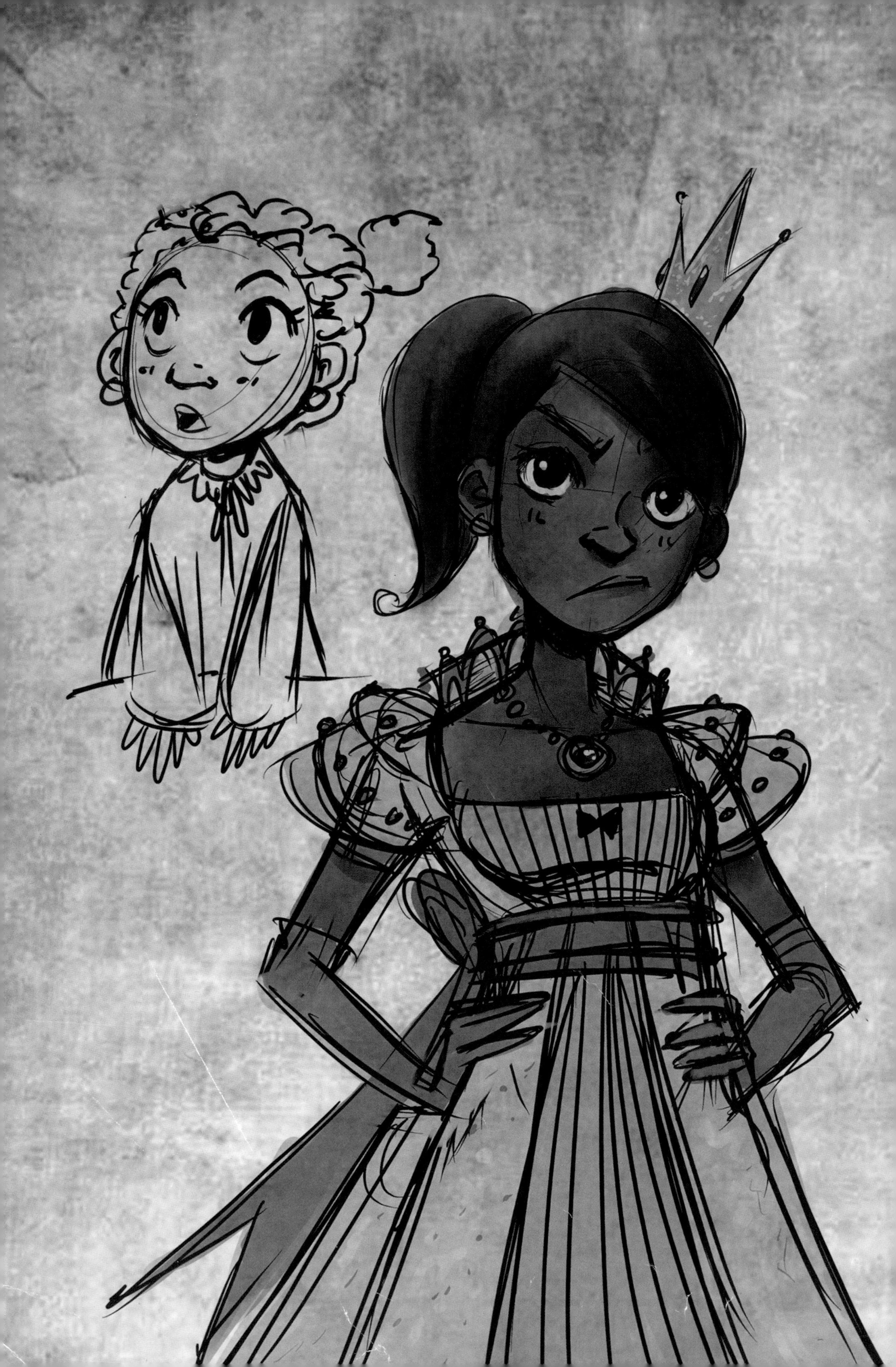

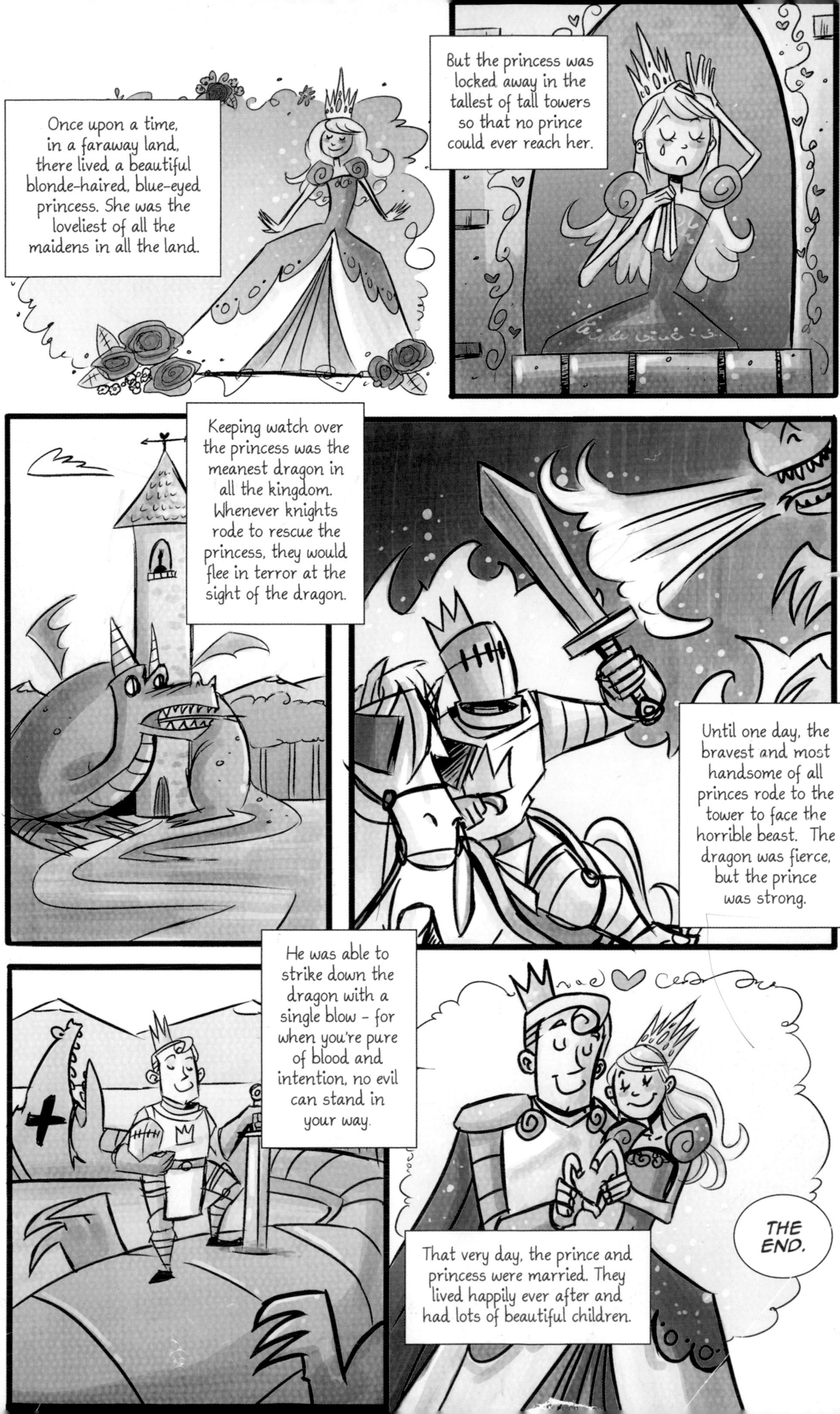
Once upon a time, in a faraway land, there lived a beautiful blonde-haired, blue-eyed princess. She was the loveliest of all the maidens in all the land.
But the princess was locked away in the tallest of tall towers so that no prince could ever reach her.
Keeping watch over the princess was the meanest dragon in all the kingdom. Whenever knights rode to rescue the princess, they would flee in terror at the sight of the dragon.
Until one day, the bravest and most handsome of all princes rode to the tower to face the horrible beast. The dragon was fierce, but the prince was strong.
He was able to strike down the dragon with a single blow - for when you're pure of blood and intention, no evil can stand in your way.
That very day, the prince and princess were married. They lived happily ever after and had lots of beautiful children.
THE END.

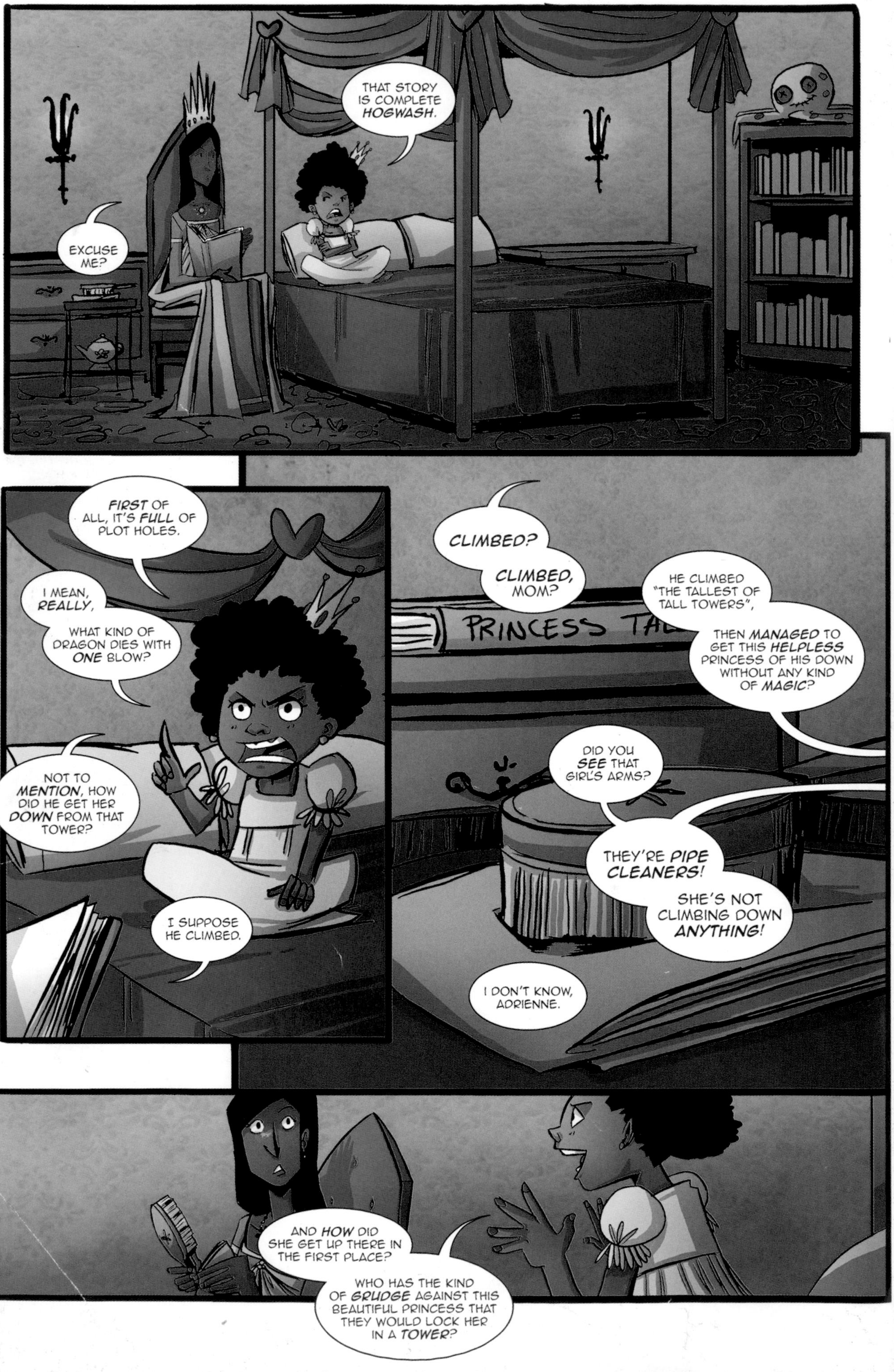

THAT STORY IS COMPLETE HOGWASH.
EXCUSE ME?
FIRST OF ALL, IT'S FULL OF PLOT HOLES.
I MEAN, REALLY,
WHAT KIND OF DRAGON DIES WITH ONE BLOW?
NOT TO MENTION, HOW DID HE GET HER DOWN FROM THAT TOWER?
I SUPPOSE HE CLIMBED.
CLIMBED?
CLIMBED, MOM?
PRINCESS TAL
HE CLIMBED "THE TALLEST OF TALL TOWERS",
THEN MANAGED TO GET THIS HELPLESS PRINCESS OF HIS DOWN WITHOUT ANY KIND OF MAGIC?
DID YOU SEE THAT GIRL'S ARMS?
THEY'RE PIPE CLEANERS!
SHE'S NOT CLIMBING DOWN ANYTHING!
I DON'T KNOW, ADRIENNE.
AND HOW DID SHE GET UP THERE IN THE FIRST PLACE?
WHO HAS THE KIND OF GRUDGE AGAINST THIS BEAUTIFUL PRINCESS THAT THEY WOULD LOCK HER IN A TOWER?

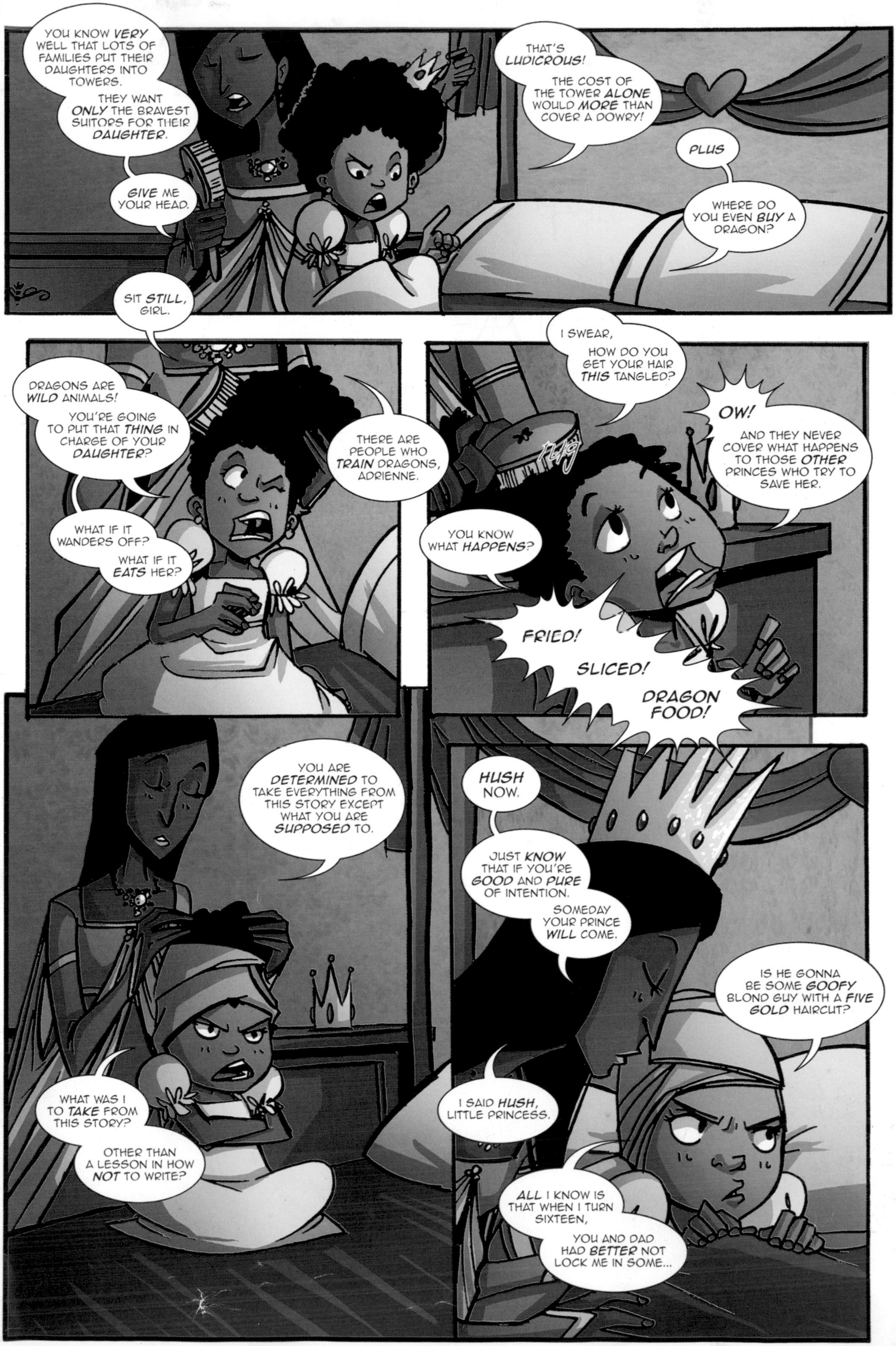
YOU KNOW VERY WELL THAT LOTS OF FAMILIES PUT THEIR DAUGHTERS INTO TOWERS.
THEY WANT ONLY THE BRAVEST SUITORS FOR THEIR DAUGHTER.
GIVE ME YOUR HEAD.
THAT'S LUDICROUS!
THE COST OF THE TOWER ALONE WOULD MORE THAN COVER A DOWRY!
PLUS
WHERE DO YOU EVEN BUY A DRAGON?
SIT STILL, GIRL.
DRAGONS ARE WILD ANIMALS!
YOU'RE GOING TO PUT THAT THING IN CHARGE OF YOUR DAUGHTER?
WHAT IF IT WANDERS OFF?
WHAT IF IT EATS HER?
THERE ARE PEOPLE WHO TRAIN DRAGONS, ADRIENNE.
I SWEAR,
HOW DO YOU GET YOUR HAIR THIS TANGLED?
tug
OW!
AND THEY NEVER COVER WHAT HAPPENS TO THOSE OTHER PRINCES WHO TRY TO SAVE HER.
YOU KNOW WHAT HAPPENS?
FRIED!
SLICED!
DRAGON FOOD!
YOU ARE DETERMINED TO TAKE EVERYTHING FROM THIS STORY EXCEPT WHAT YOU ARE SUPPOSED TO.
WHAT WAS I TO TAKE FROM THIS STORY?
OTHER THAN A LESSON IN HOW NOT TO WRITE?
HUSH NOW.
JUST KNOW THAT IF YOU'RE GOOD AND PURE OF INTENTION.
SOMEDAY YOUR PRINCE WILL COME.
IS HE GONNA BE SOME GOOFY BLOND GUY WITH A FIVE GOLD HAIRCUT?
I SAID HUSH, LITTLE PRINCESS.
ALL I KNOW IS THAT WHEN I TURN SIXTEEN,
YOU AND DAD HAD BETTER NOT LOCK ME IN SOME...

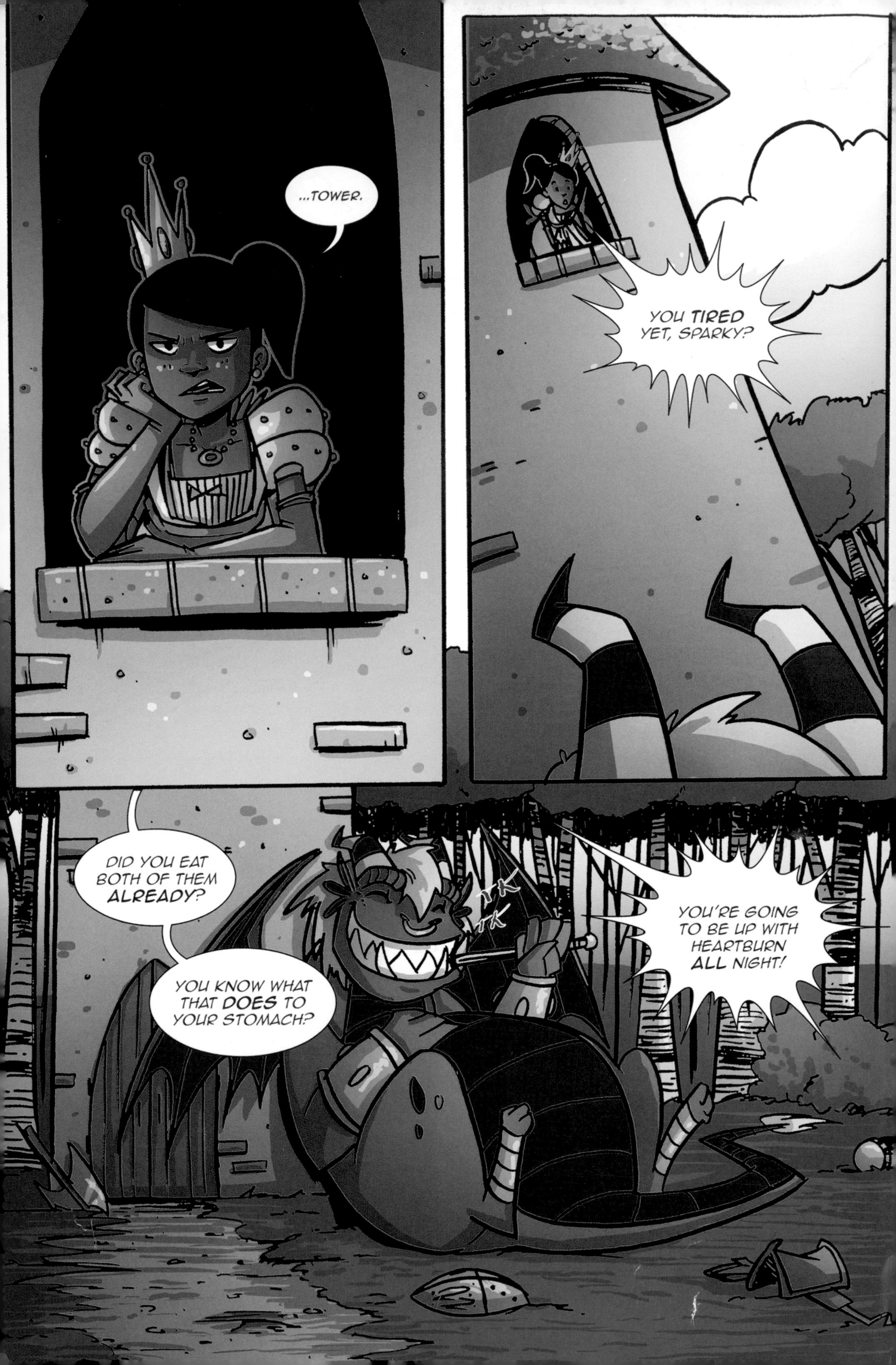
...TOWER.
YOU TIRED YET, SPARKY?
DID YOU EAT BOTH OF THEM ALREADY?
YOU KNOW WHAT THAT DOES TO YOUR STOMACH?
YOU'RE GOING TO BE UP WITH HEARTBURN ALL NIGHT!

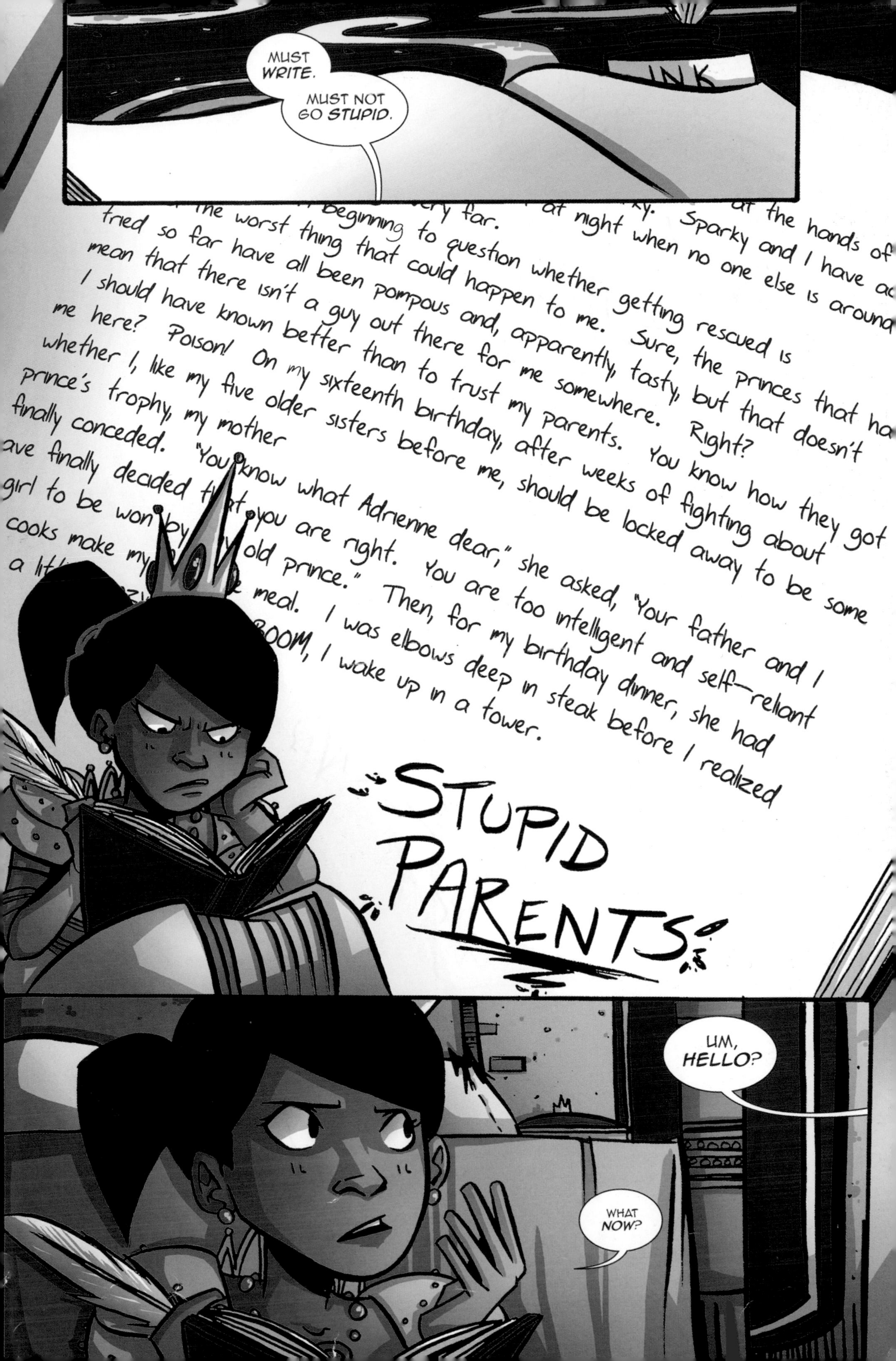
MUST WRITE.
MUST NOT GO STUPID.
INK
at the hands of
ky. Sparky and I have ac
at night when no one else is aroun
very far.
beginning to question whether getting rescued is
the worst thing that could happen to me. Sure, the princes that ha
tried so far have all been pompous and, apparently, tasty, but that doesn't
mean that there isn't a guy out there for me somewhere. Right?
I should have known better than to trust my parents. You know how they got
me here? Poison! On my sixteenth birthday, after weeks of fighting about
whether I, like my five older sisters before me, should be locked away to be some
prince's trophy, my mother
finally conceded. "You know what Adrienne dear," she asked, "Your father and I
ave finally decided that you are right. You are too intelligent and self-reliant
girl to be won by old prince." Then, for my birthday dinner, she had
cooks make my meal. I was elbows deep in steak before I realized
OOM, I wake up in a tower.
STUPID PARENTS!
UM, HELLO?
WHAT NOW?

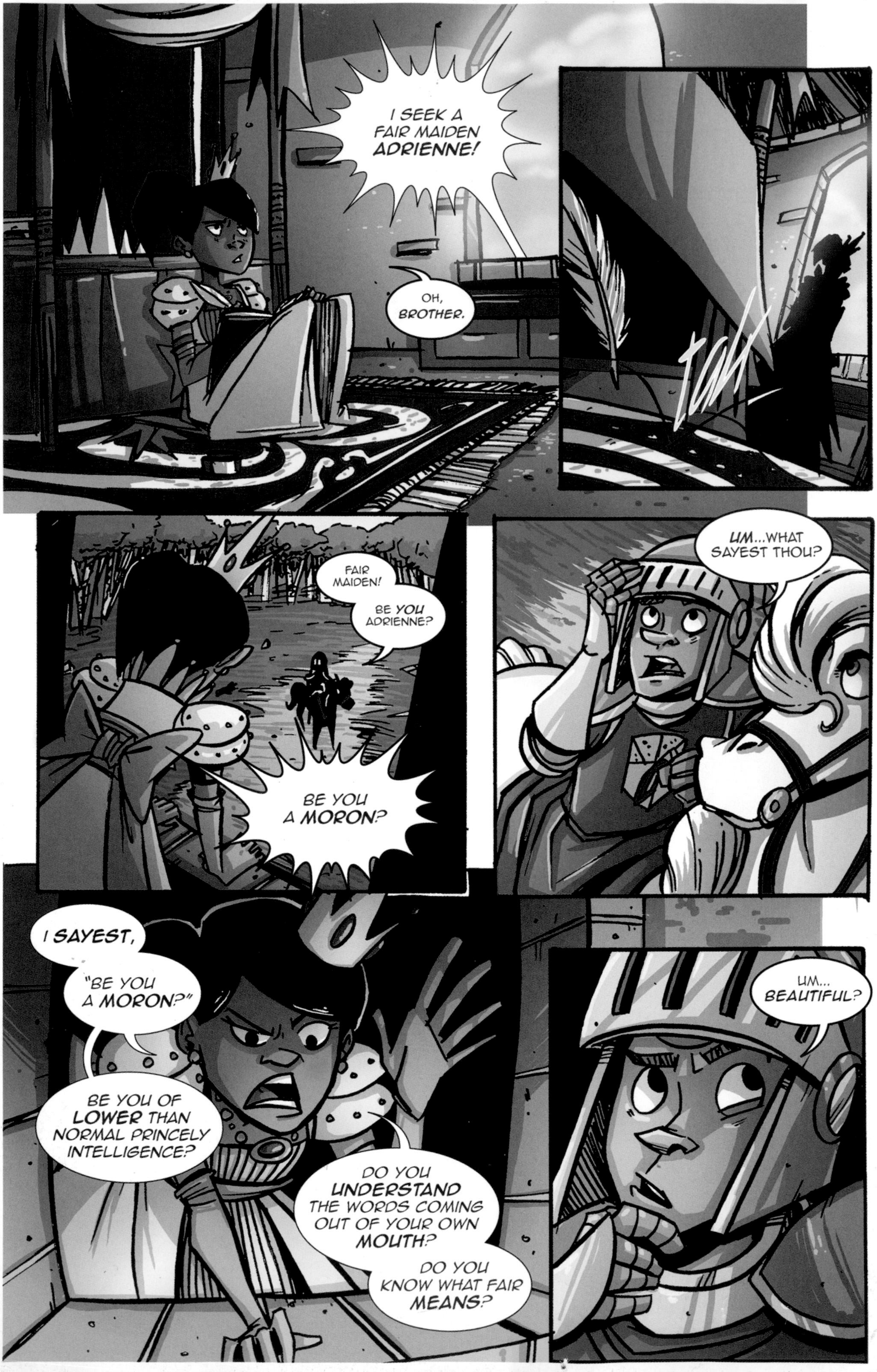
I SEEK A FAIR MAIDEN **ADRIENNE!**
OH, BROTHER.
tak
FAIR MAIDEN!
BE *YOU* ADRIENNE?
BE YOU A **MORON**?
UM...WHAT SAYEST THOU?
I **SAYEST**,
"BE YOU A **MORON**?"
BE YOU OF **LOWER** THAN NORMAL PRINCELY INTELLIGENCE?
DO YOU **UNDERSTAND** THE WORDS COMING OUT OF YOUR OWN **MOUTH**?
DO YOU KNOW WHAT FAIR **MEANS**?
UM... **BEAUTIFUL**?

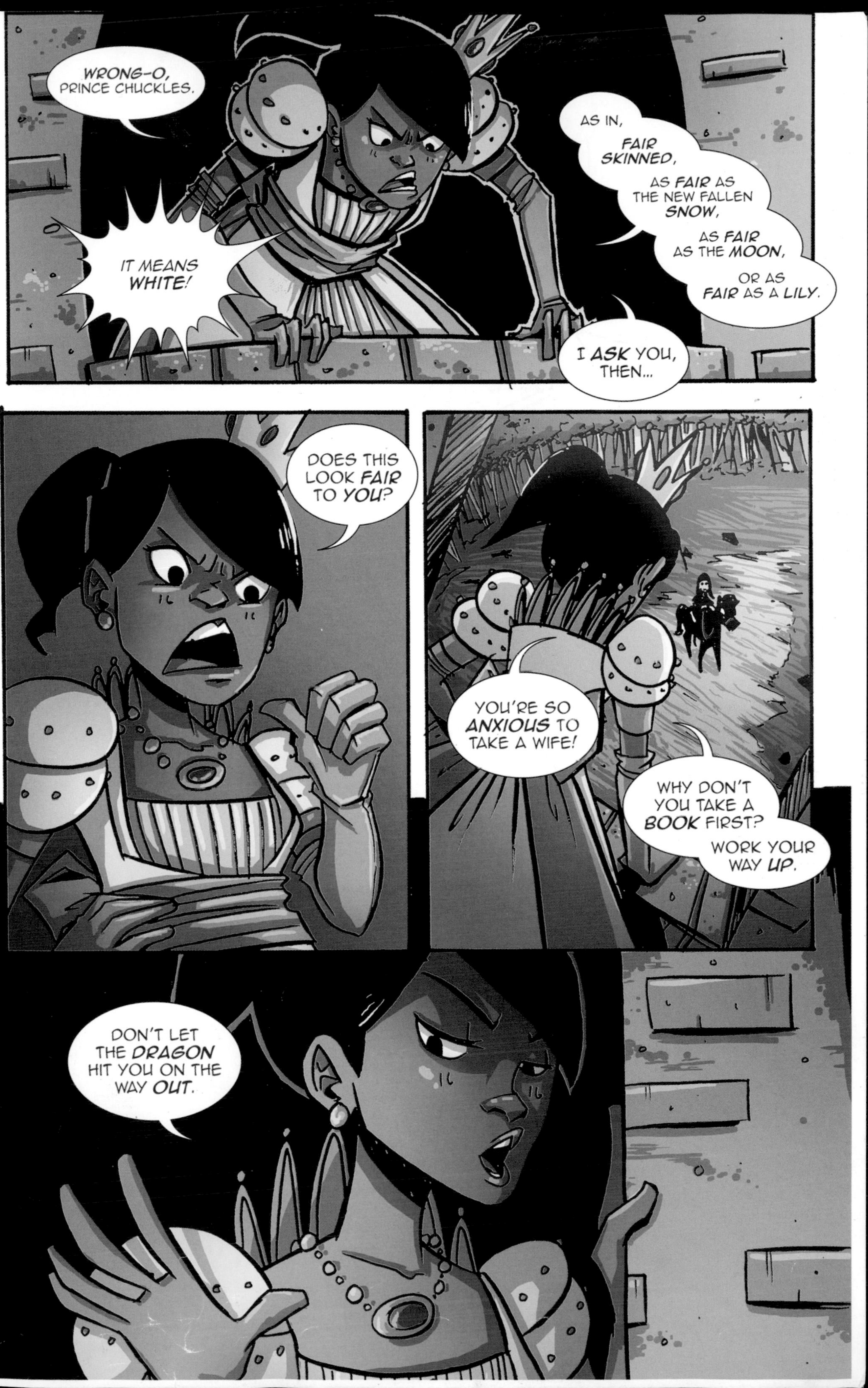
WRONG-O, PRINCE CHUCKLES.
IT MEANS WHITE!
AS IN, FAIR SKINNED,
AS FAIR AS THE NEW FALLEN SNOW,
AS FAIR AS THE MOON,
OR AS FAIR AS A LILY.
I ASK YOU, THEN...
DOES THIS LOOK FAIR TO YOU?
YOU'RE SO ANXIOUS TO TAKE A WIFE!
WHY DON'T YOU TAKE A BOOK FIRST?
WORK YOUR WAY UP.
DON'T LET THE DRAGON HIT YOU ON THE WAY OUT.

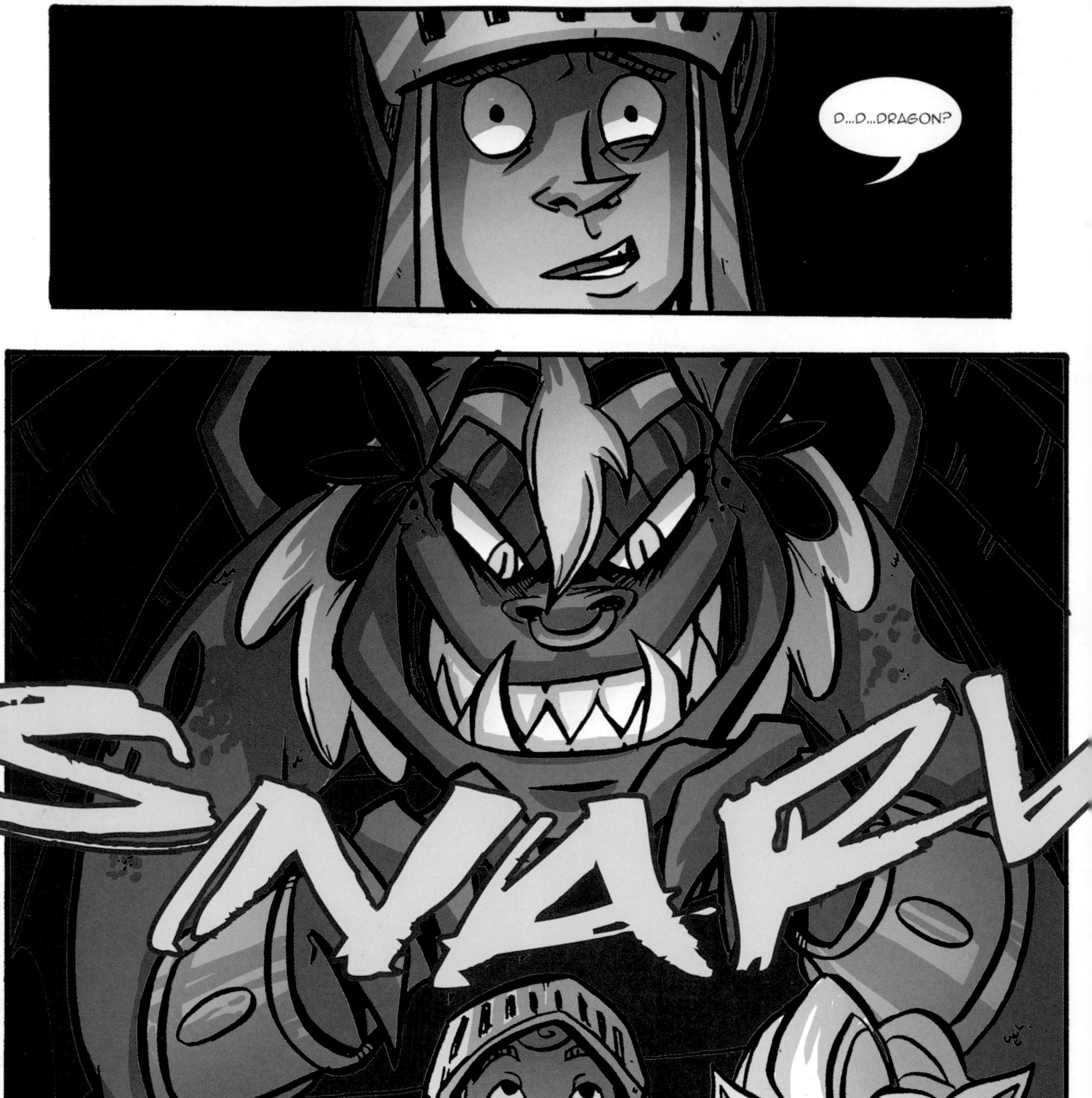
D...D...DRAGON?
SNARL

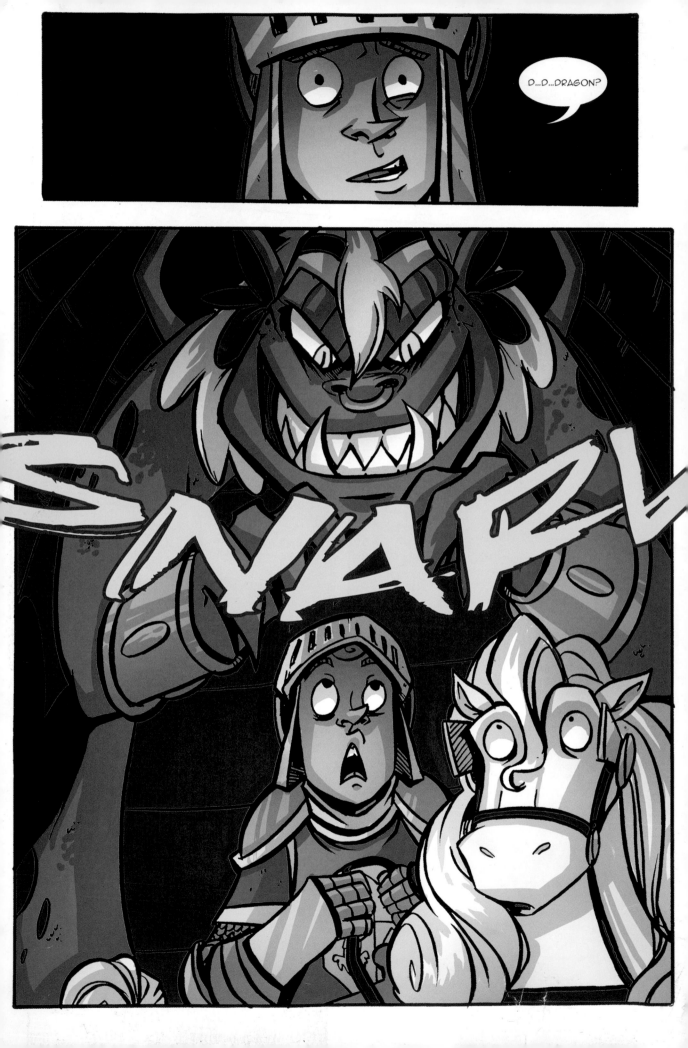

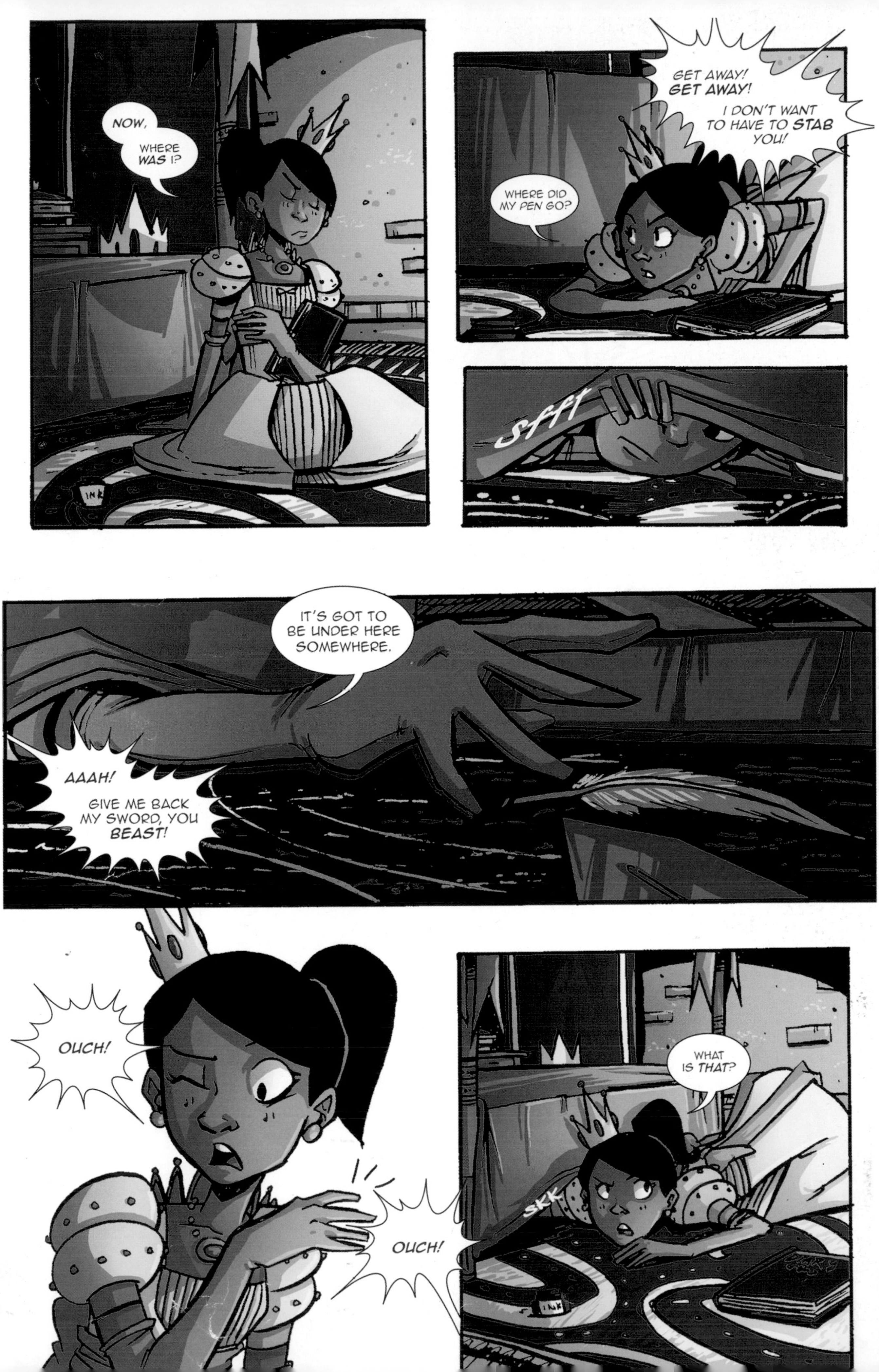
NOW,
WHERE WAS I?
GET AWAY! GET AWAY!
I DON'T WANT TO HAVE TO STAB YOU!
WHERE DID MY PEN GO?
SFFT
IT'S GOT TO BE UNDER HERE SOMEWHERE.
AAAH!
GIVE ME BACK MY SWORD, YOU BEAST!
OUCH!
OUCH!
SKK
WHAT IS THAT?
INK

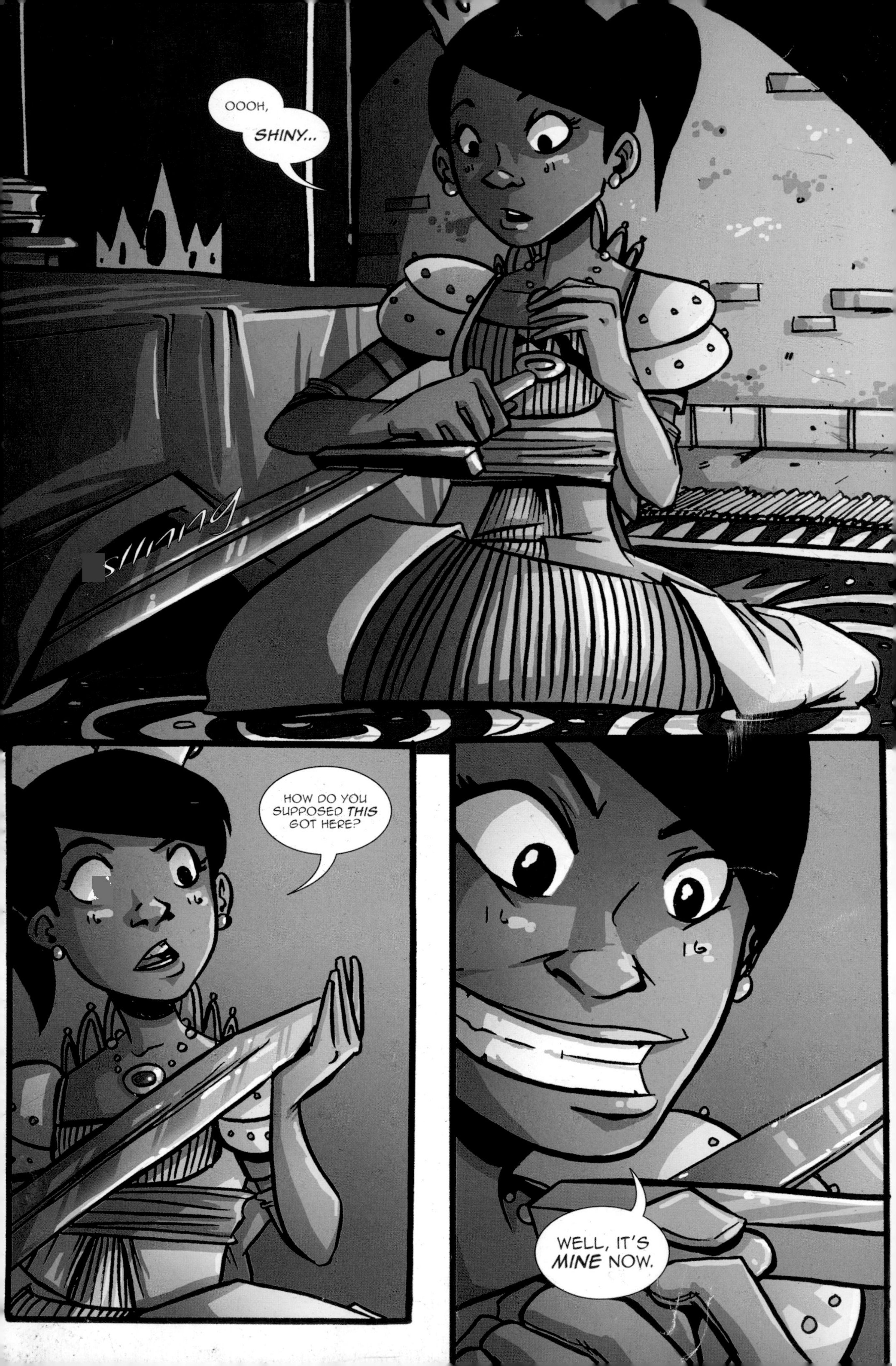
OOOH, SHINY...
HOW DO YOU SUPPOSED THIS GOT HERE?
WELL, IT'S MINE NOW.

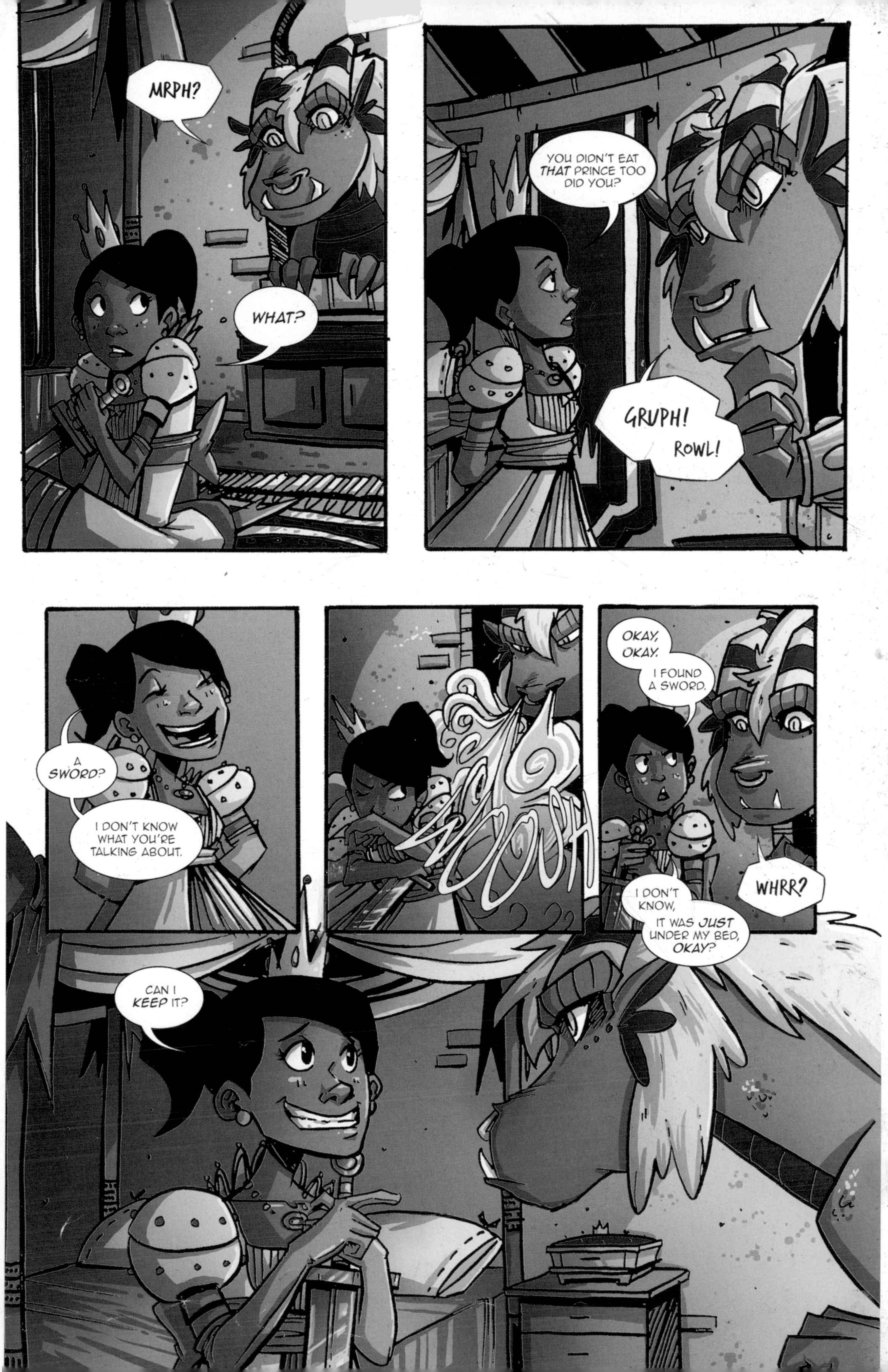
MRPH?
WHAT?
YOU DIDN'T EAT *THAT* PRINCE TOO DID YOU?
GRUPH!
ROWL!
A *SWORD*?
I DON'T KNOW WHAT YOU'RE TALKING ABOUT.
WOOOSH
OKAY, OKAY.
I FOUND A SWORD.
WHRR?
I DON'T KNOW,
IT WAS *JUST* UNDER MY BED, *OKAY*?
CAN I *KEEP* IT?

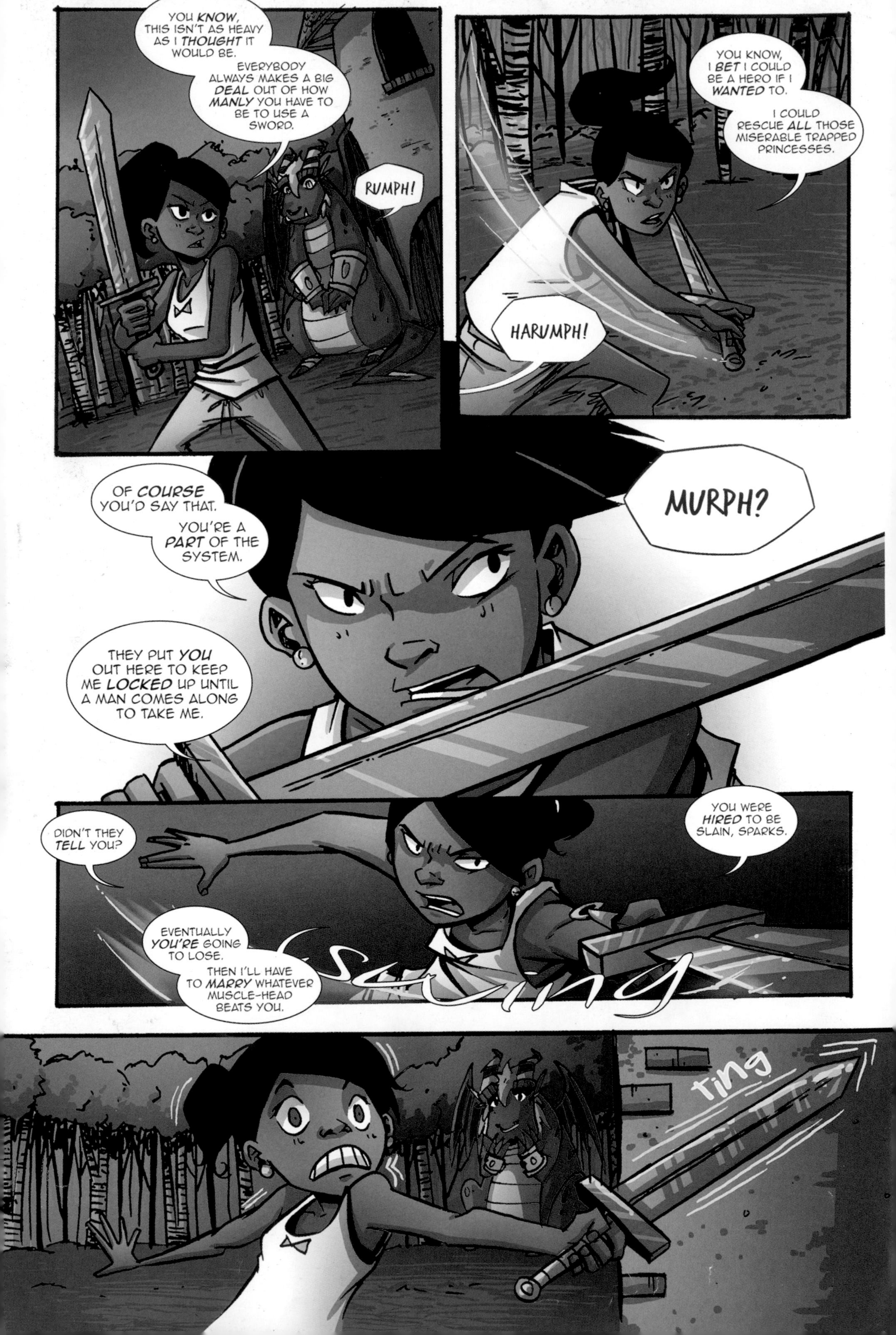
YOU KNOW, THIS ISN'T AS HEAVY AS I THOUGHT IT WOULD BE.
EVERYBODY ALWAYS MAKES A BIG DEAL OUT OF HOW MANLY YOU HAVE TO BE TO USE A SWORD.
RUMPH!
YOU KNOW, I BET I COULD BE A HERO IF I WANTED TO.
I COULD RESCUE ALL THOSE MISERABLE TRAPPED PRINCESSES.
HARUMPH!
OF COURSE YOU'D SAY THAT.
YOU'RE A PART OF THE SYSTEM.
MURPH?
THEY PUT YOU OUT HERE TO KEEP ME LOCKED UP UNTIL A MAN COMES ALONG TO TAKE ME.
DIDN'T THEY TELL YOU?
YOU WERE HIRED TO BE SLAIN, SPARKS.
EVENTUALLY YOU'RE GOING TO LOSE.
THEN I'LL HAVE TO MARRY WHATEVER MUSCLE-HEAD BEATS YOU.
swing
ting

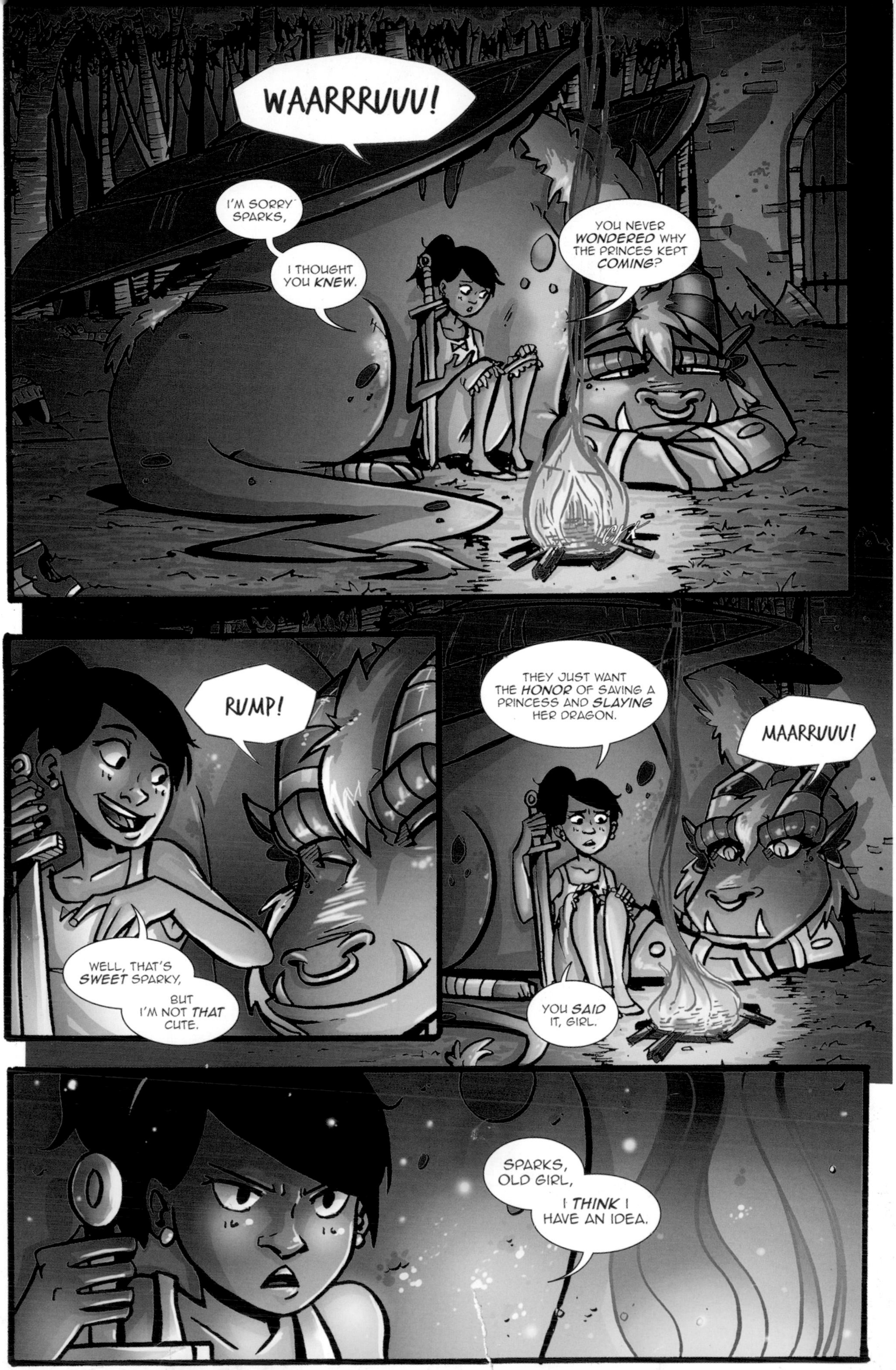

WAARRRUUU!
I'M SORRY SPARKS,
I THOUGHT YOU KNEW.
YOU NEVER WONDERED WHY THE PRINCES KEPT COMING?
RUMP!
WELL, THAT'S SWEET SPARKY,
BUT I'M NOT THAT CUTE.
THEY JUST WANT THE HONOR OF SAVING A PRINCESS AND SLAYING HER DRAGON.
MAARRUUU!
YOU SAID IT, GIRL.
SPARKS, OLD GIRL,
I THINK I HAVE AN IDEA.

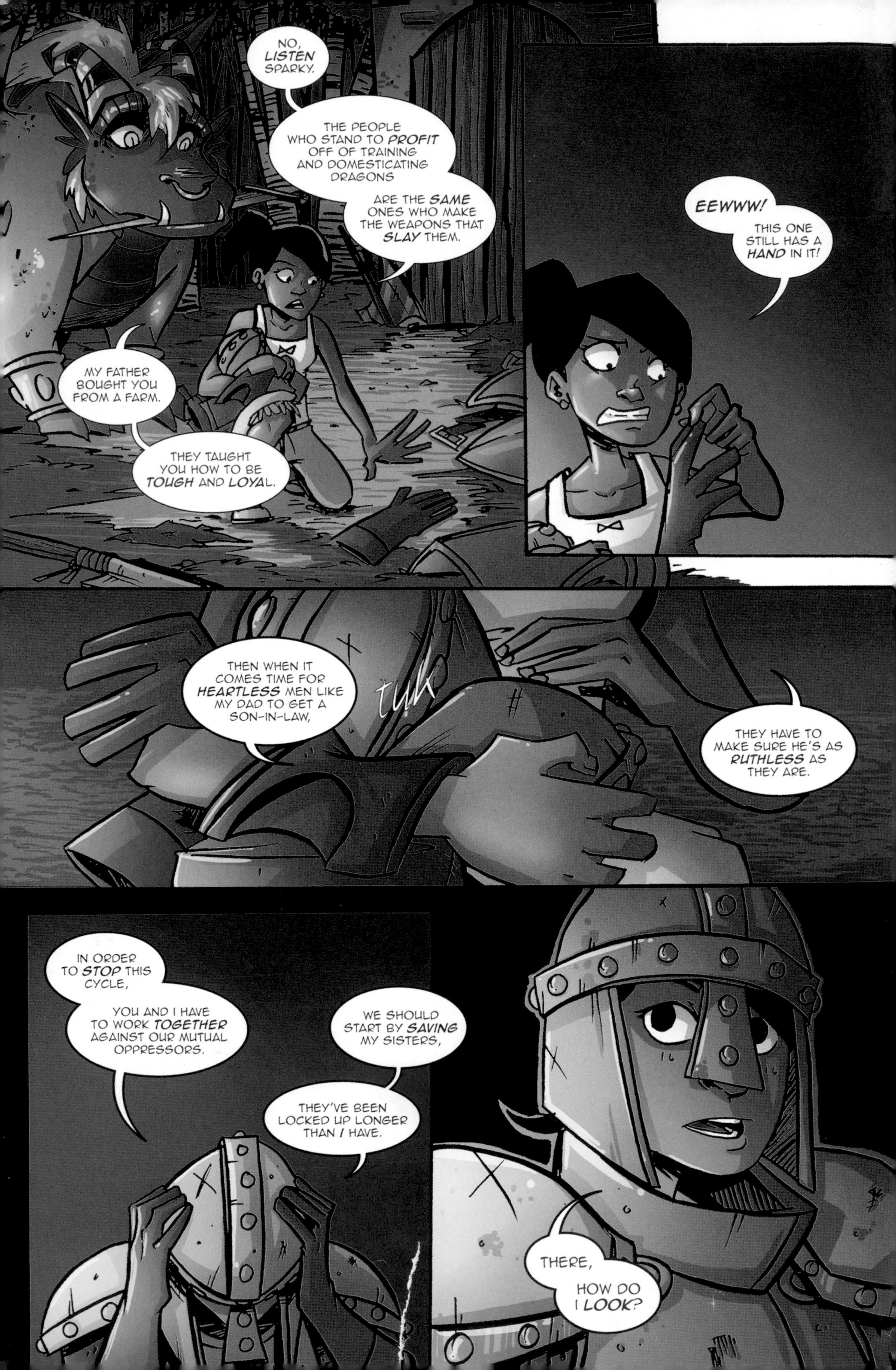
NO, LISTEN SPARKY.
THE PEOPLE WHO STAND TO PROFIT OFF OF TRAINING AND DOMESTICATING DRAGONS
ARE THE SAME ONES WHO MAKE THE WEAPONS THAT SLAY THEM.
MY FATHER BOUGHT YOU FROM A FARM.
THEY TAUGHT YOU HOW TO BE TOUGH AND LOYAL.
EEWWW!
THIS ONE STILL HAS A HAND IN IT!
THEN WHEN IT COMES TIME FOR HEARTLESS MEN LIKE MY DAD TO GET A SON-IN-LAW,
tuk
THEY HAVE TO MAKE SURE HE'S AS RUTHLESS AS THEY ARE.
IN ORDER TO STOP THIS CYCLE,
YOU AND I HAVE TO WORK TOGETHER AGAINST OUR MUTUAL OPPRESSORS.
WE SHOULD START BY SAVING MY SISTERS,
THEY'VE BEEN LOCKED UP LONGER THAN I HAVE.
THERE,
HOW DO I LOOK?

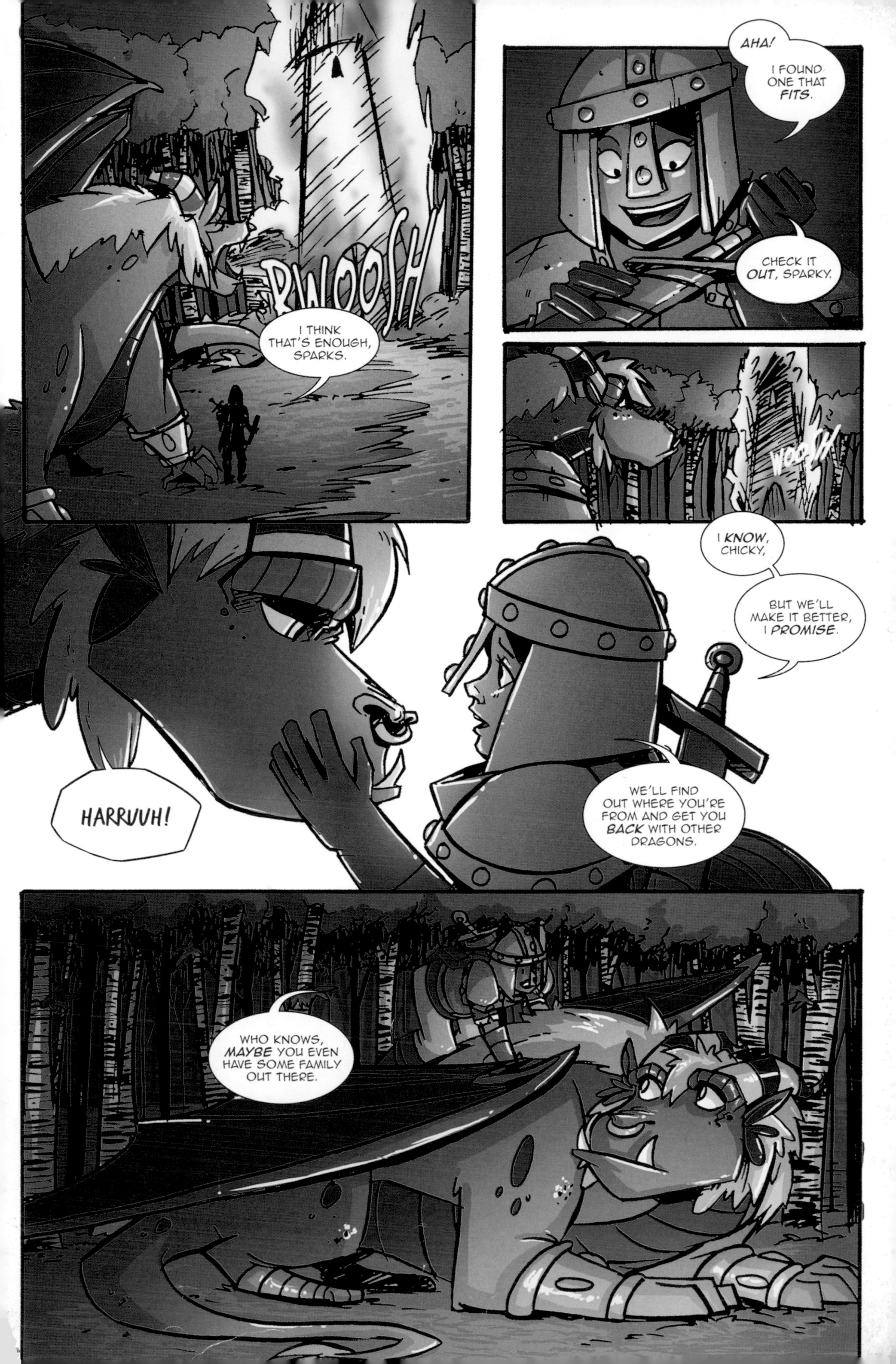
BWOOSH
I THINK THAT'S ENOUGH, SPARKS.
AHA!
I FOUND ONE THAT *FITS*.
CHECK IT *OUT*, SPARKY.
WOOSH
I *KNOW*, CHICKY,
BUT WE'LL MAKE IT BETTER, I *PROMISE*.
HARRUUH!
WE'LL FIND OUT WHERE YOU'RE FROM AND GET YOU *BACK* WITH OTHER DRAGONS.
WHO KNOWS, *MAYBE* YOU EVEN HAVE SOME FAMILY OUT THERE.

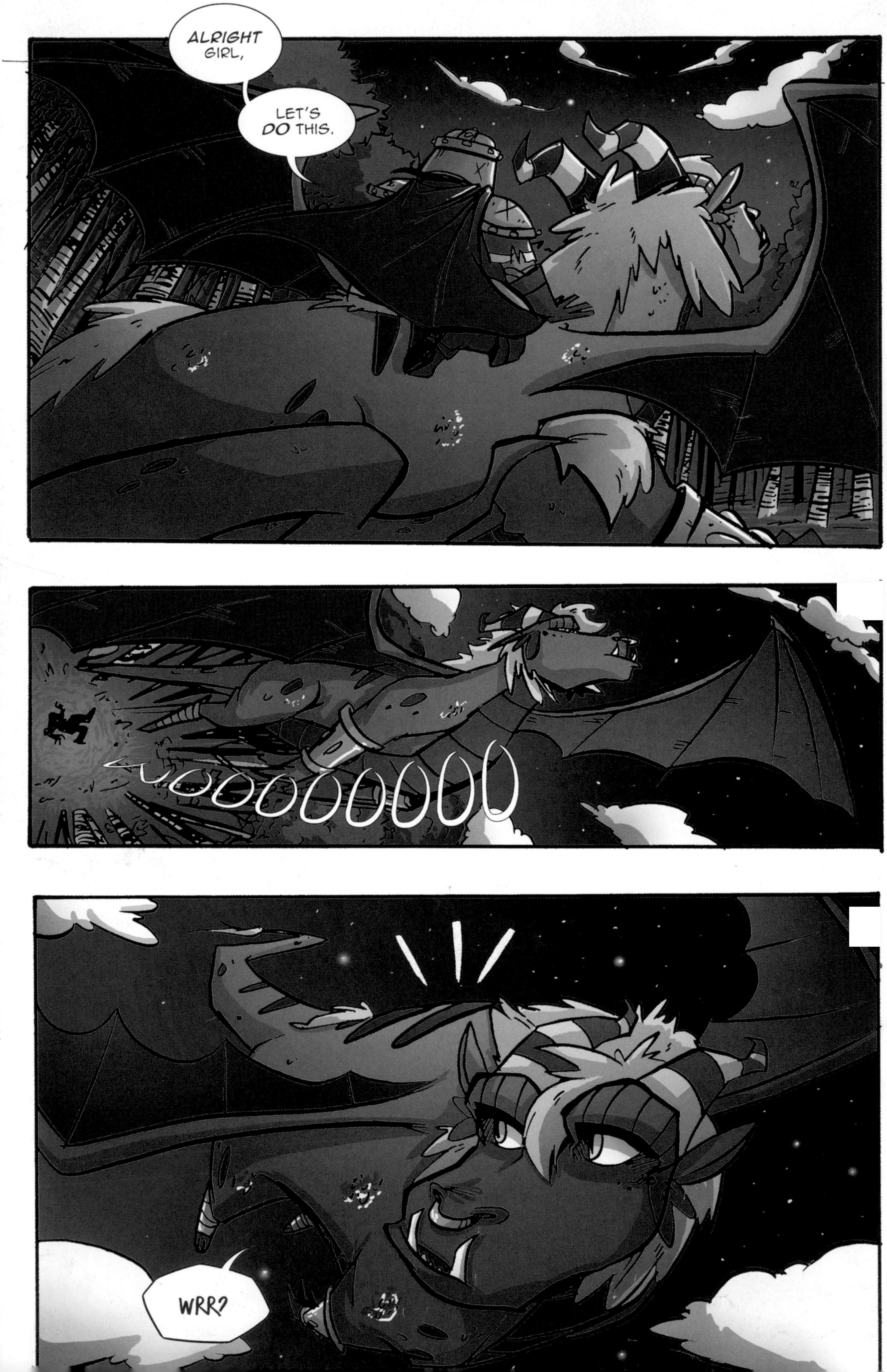
ALRIGHT GIRL,
LET'S DO THIS.
WOOOOOOOOO
WRR?

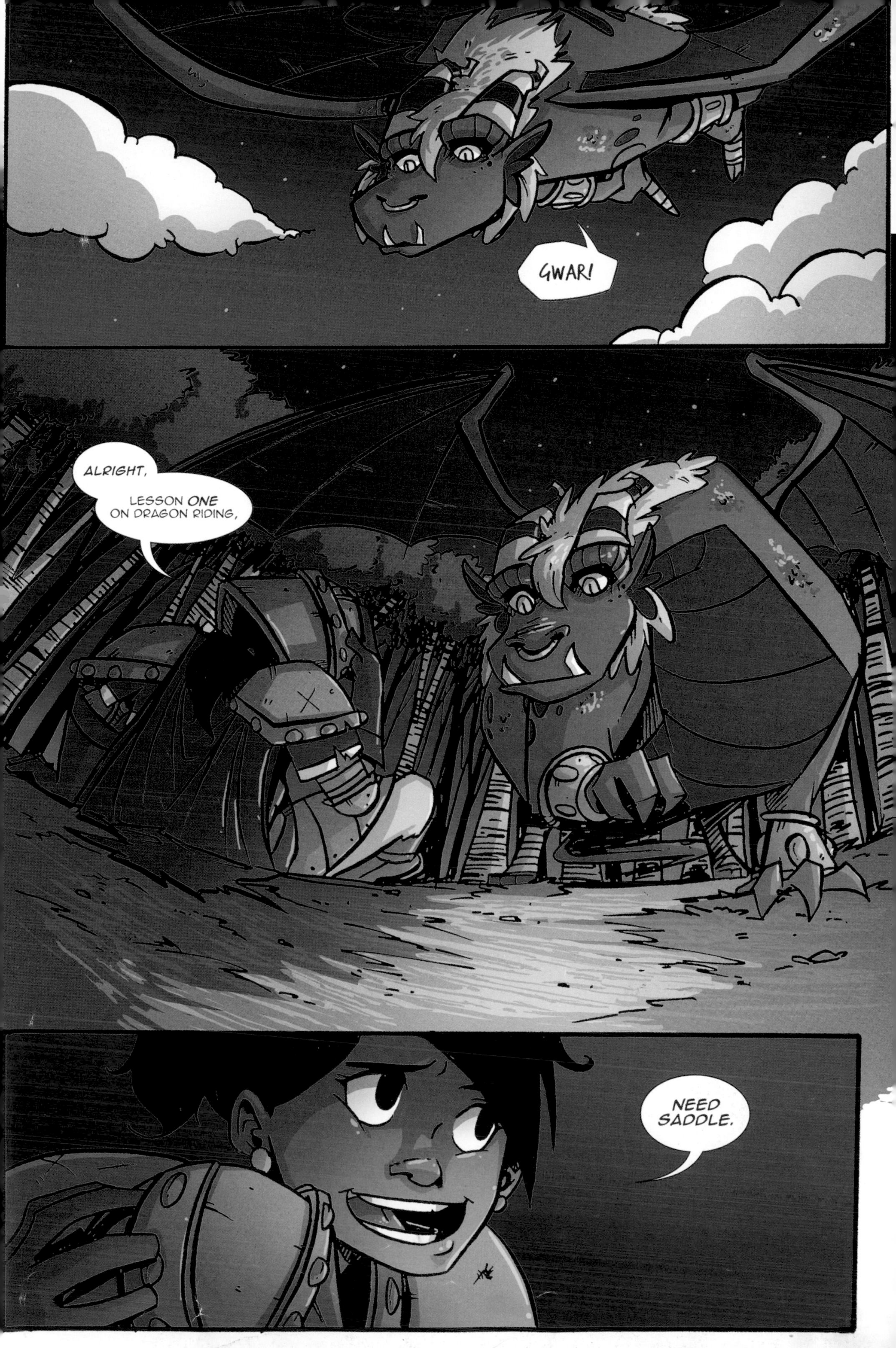
GWAR!
ALRIGHT,
LESSON ONE ON DRAGON RIDING,
NEED SADDLE.

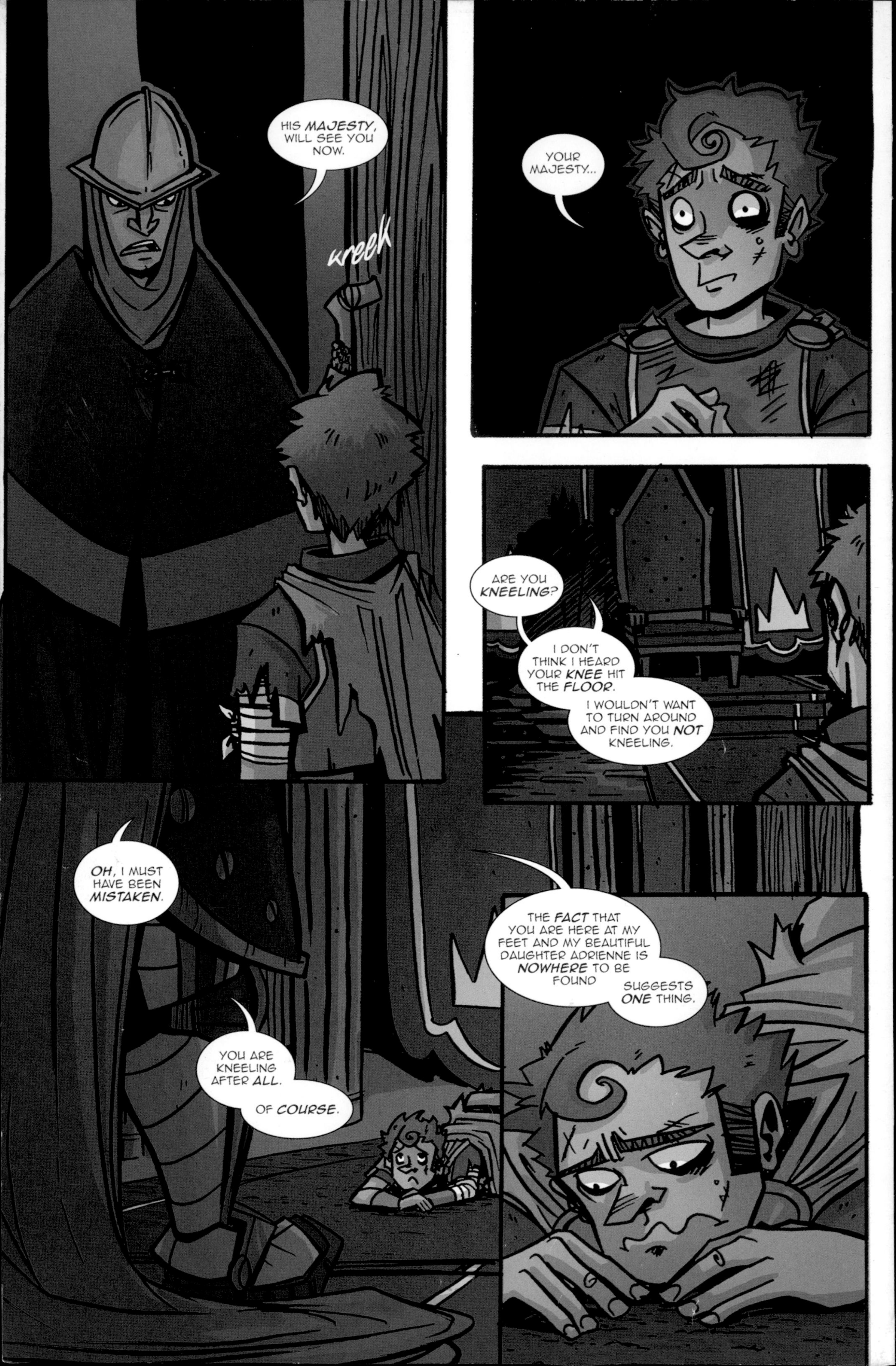
HIS MAJESTY, WILL SEE YOU NOW.
kreek
YOUR MAJESTY...
ARE YOU KNEELING?
I DON'T THINK I HEARD YOUR KNEE HIT THE FLOOR.
I WOULDN'T WANT TO TURN AROUND AND FIND YOU NOT KNEELING.
OH, I MUST HAVE BEEN MISTAKEN.
YOU ARE KNEELING AFTER ALL.
OF COURSE.
THE FACT THAT YOU ARE HERE AT MY FEET AND MY BEAUTIFUL DAUGHTER ADRIENNE IS NOWHERE TO BE FOUND
SUGGESTS ONE THING.

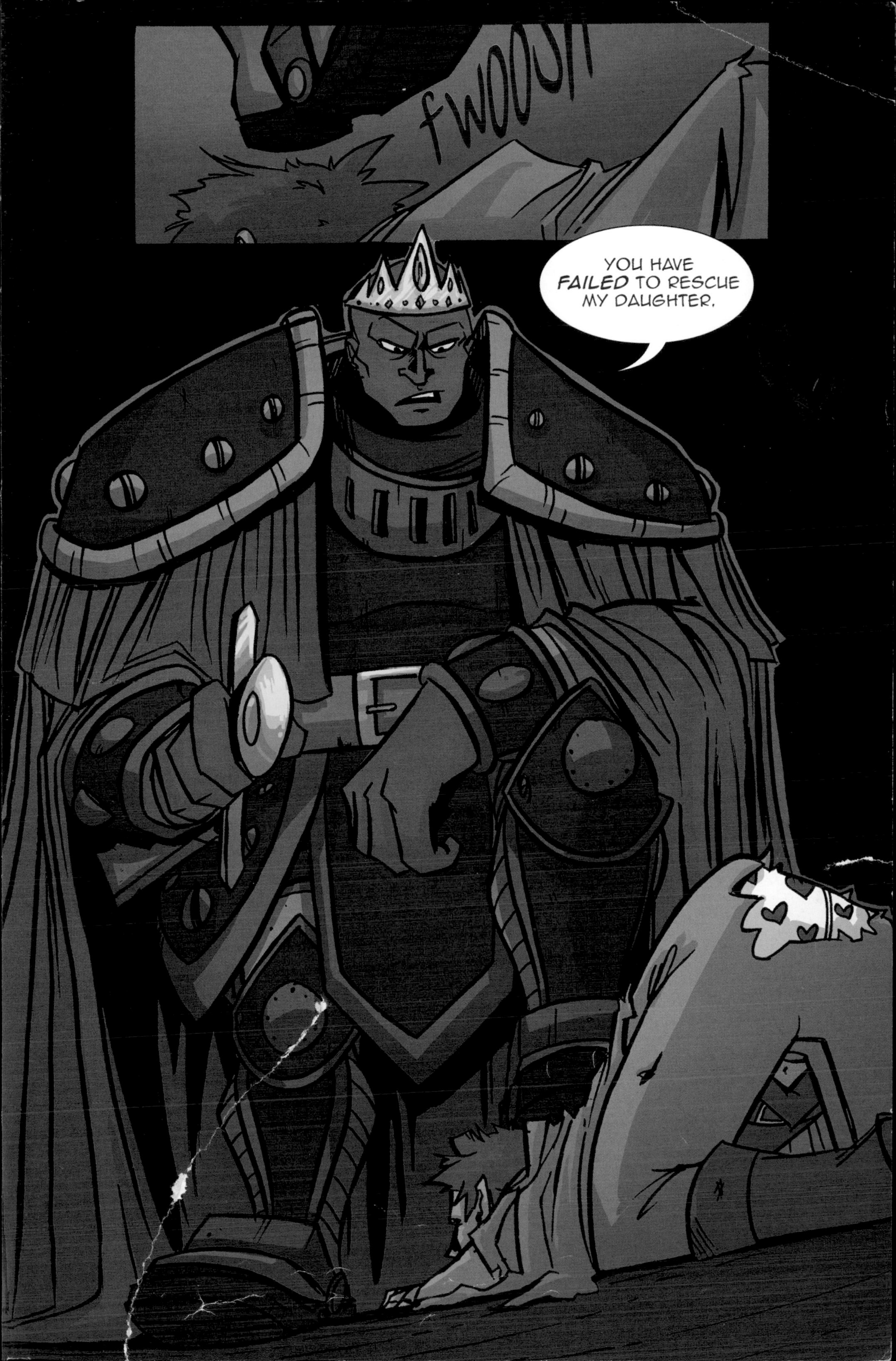
FWOOSH
YOU HAVE **FAILED** TO RESCUE MY DAUGHTER.

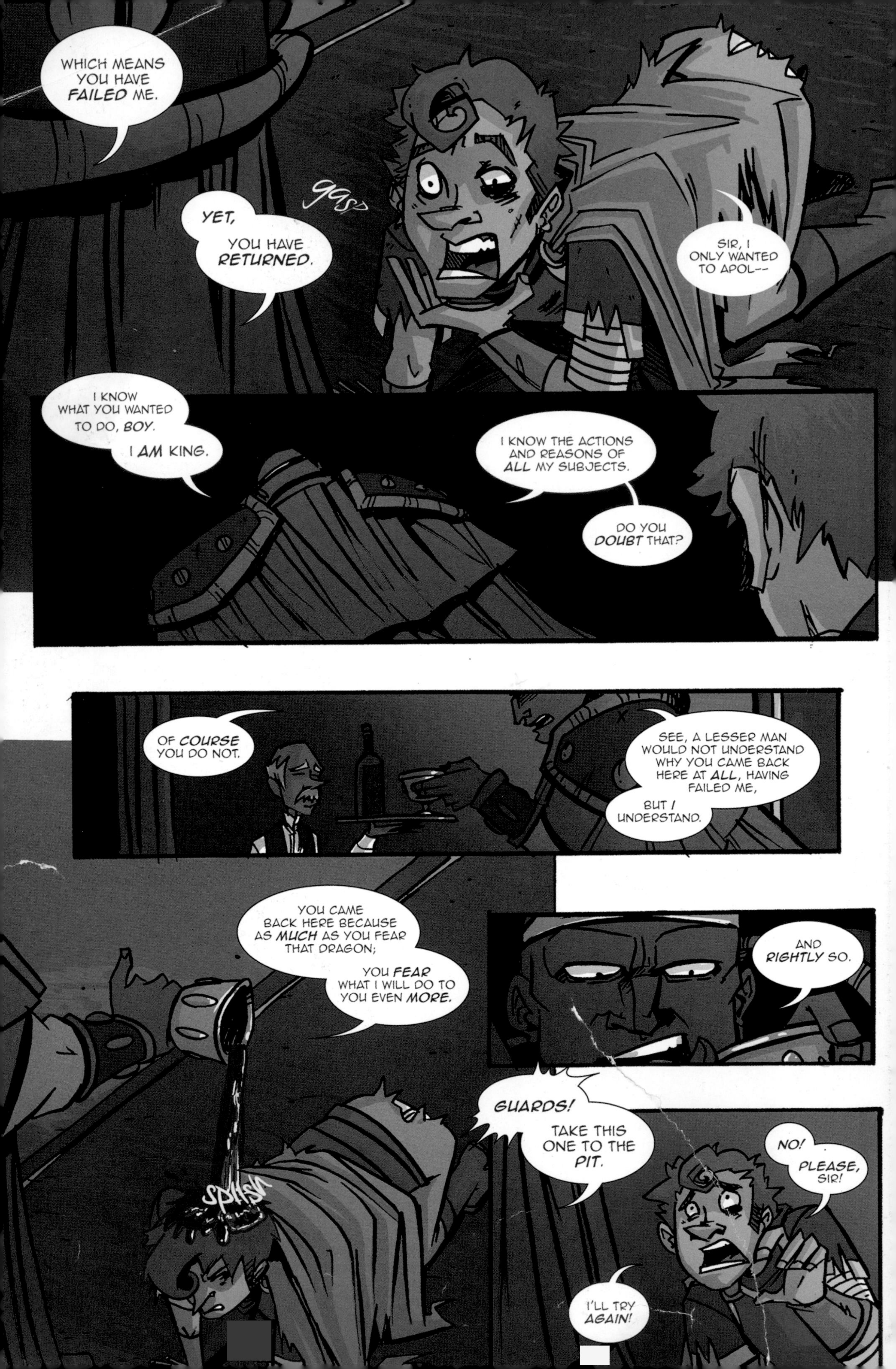
WHICH MEANS YOU HAVE FAILED ME.
YET, YOU HAVE RETURNED.
gasp
SIR, I ONLY WANTED TO APOL--
I KNOW WHAT YOU WANTED TO DO, BOY.
I AM KING.
I KNOW THE ACTIONS AND REASONS OF ALL MY SUBJECTS.
DO YOU DOUBT THAT?
OF COURSE YOU DO NOT.
SEE, A LESSER MAN WOULD NOT UNDERSTAND WHY YOU CAME BACK HERE AT ALL, HAVING FAILED ME,
BUT I UNDERSTAND.
YOU CAME BACK HERE BECAUSE AS MUCH AS YOU FEAR THAT DRAGON;
YOU FEAR WHAT I WILL DO TO YOU EVEN MORE.
AND RIGHTLY SO.
GUARDS!
TAKE THIS ONE TO THE PIT.
splsh
NO!
PLEASE, SIR!
I'LL TRY AGAIN!

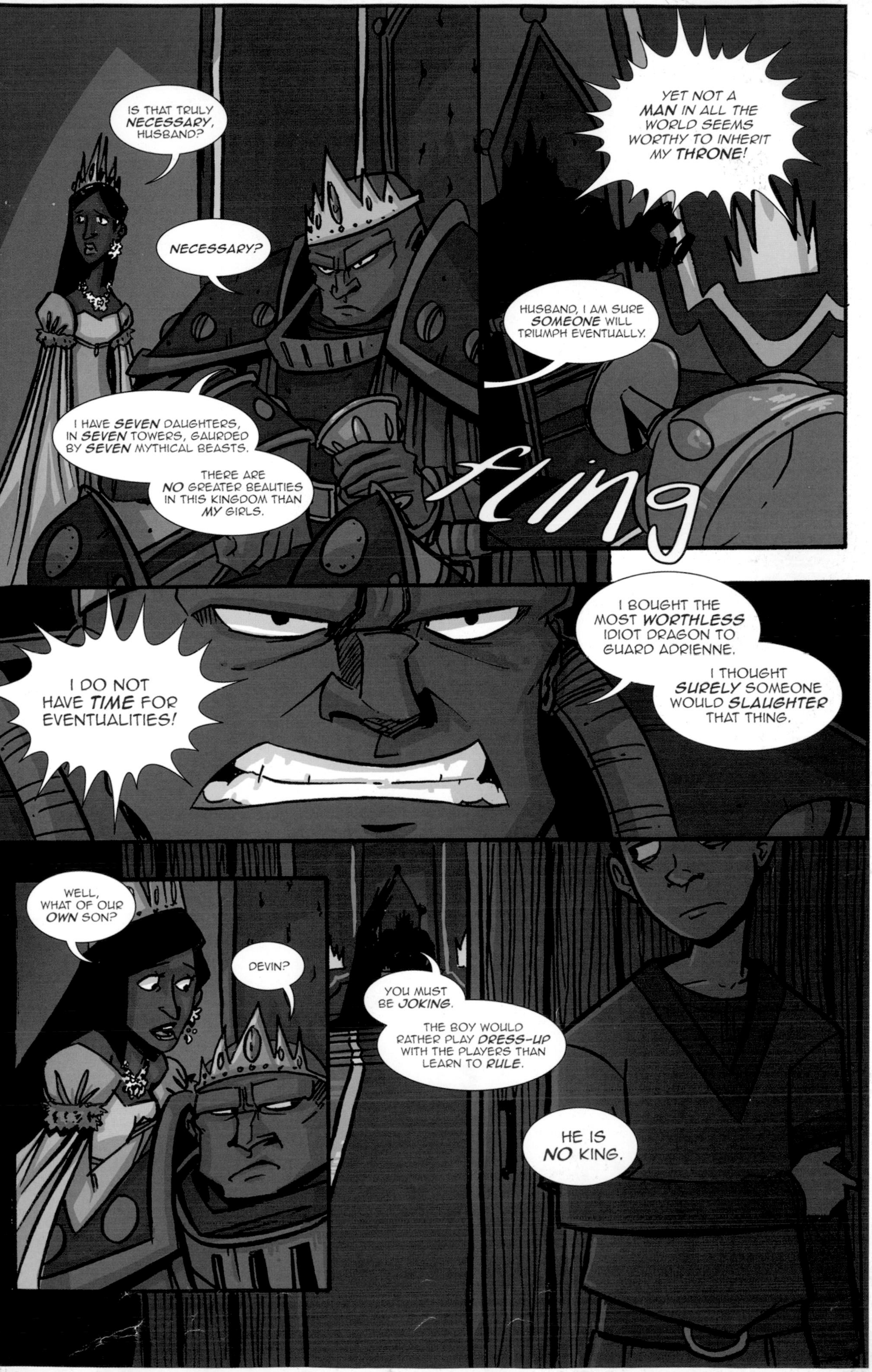
IS THAT TRULY NECESSARY, HUSBAND?
NECESSARY?
I HAVE SEVEN DAUGHTERS, IN SEVEN TOWERS, GAURDED BY SEVEN MYTHICAL BEASTS.
THERE ARE NO GREATER BEAUTIES IN THIS KINGDOM THAN MY GIRLS.
YET NOT A MAN IN ALL THE WORLD SEEMS WORTHY TO INHERIT MY THRONE!
HUSBAND, I AM SURE SOMEONE WILL TRIUMPH EVENTUALLY.
fling
I DO NOT HAVE TIME FOR EVENTUALITIES!
I BOUGHT THE MOST WORTHLESS IDIOT DRAGON TO GUARD ADRIENNE.
I THOUGHT SURELY SOMEONE WOULD SLAUGHTER THAT THING.
WELL, WHAT OF OUR OWN SON?
DEVIN?
YOU MUST BE JOKING.
THE BOY WOULD RATHER PLAY DRESS-UP WITH THE PLAYERS THAN LEARN TO RULE.
HE IS NO KING.

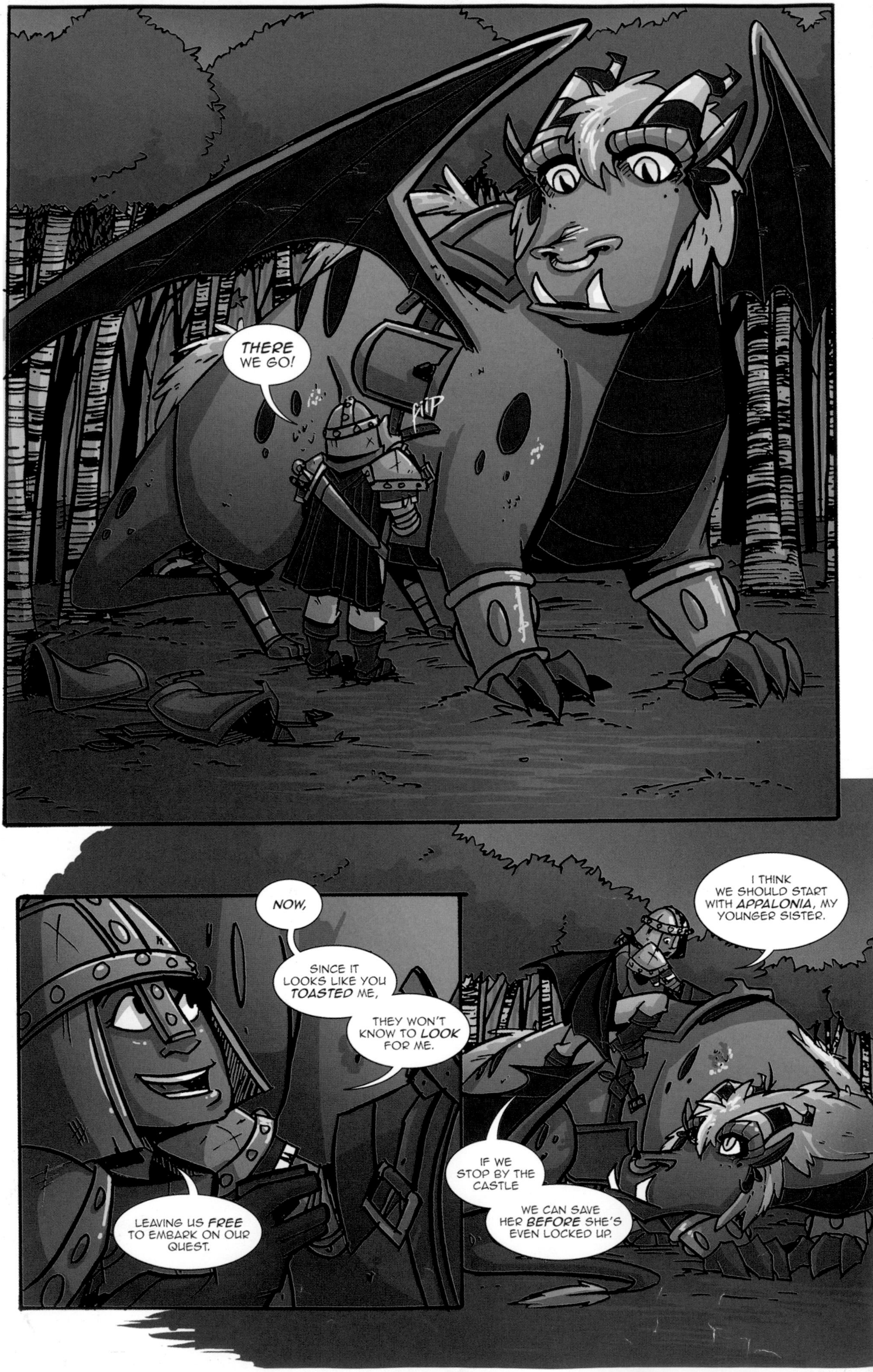
THERE WE GO!
NOW,
SINCE IT LOOKS LIKE YOU TOASTED ME,
THEY WON'T KNOW TO LOOK FOR ME.
LEAVING US FREE TO EMBARK ON OUR QUEST.
I THINK WE SHOULD START WITH APPALONIA, MY YOUNGER SISTER.
IF WE STOP BY THE CASTLE
WE CAN SAVE HER BEFORE SHE'S EVEN LOCKED UP.

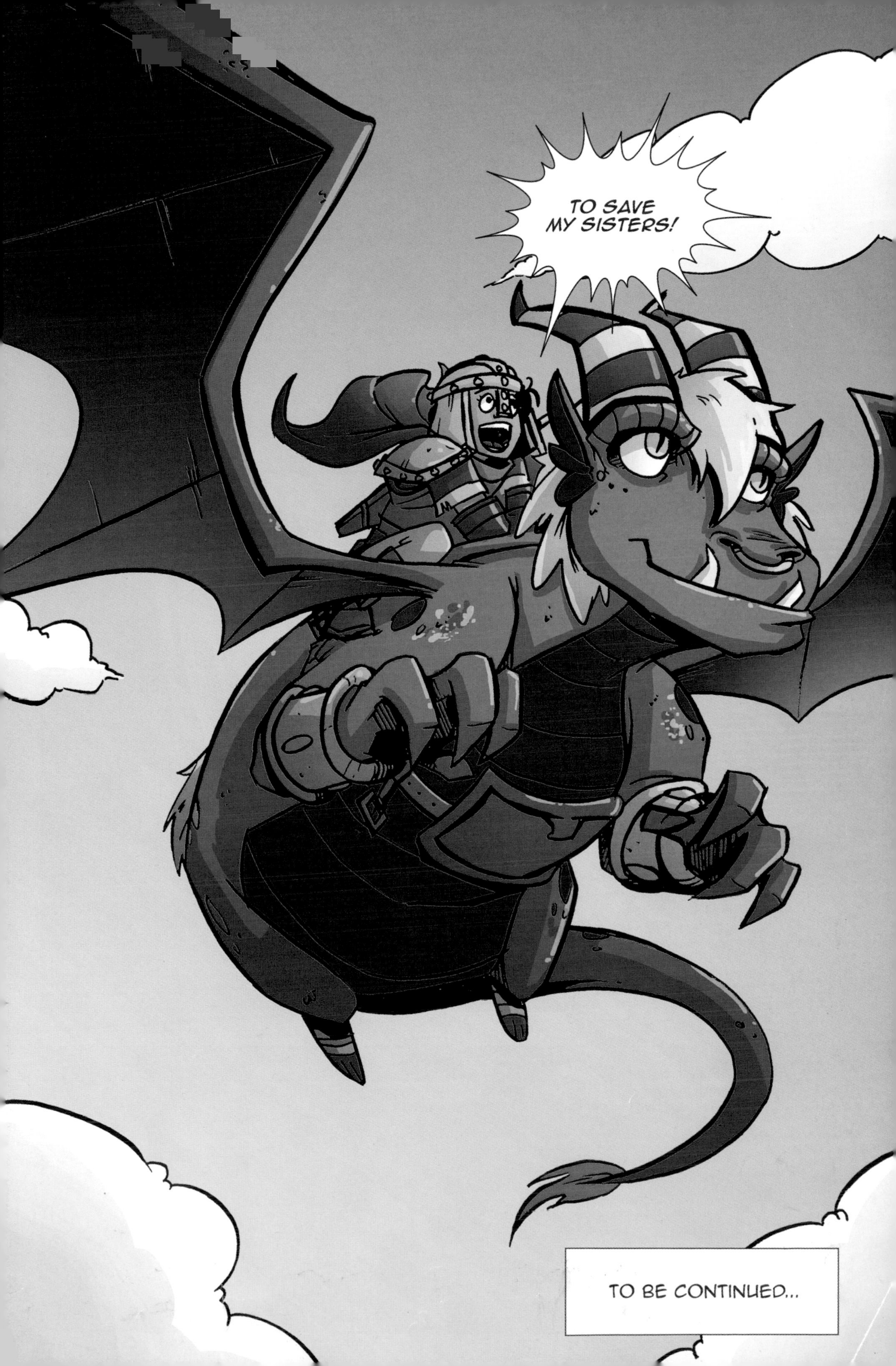
TO SAVE MY SISTERS!
TO BE CONTINUED...

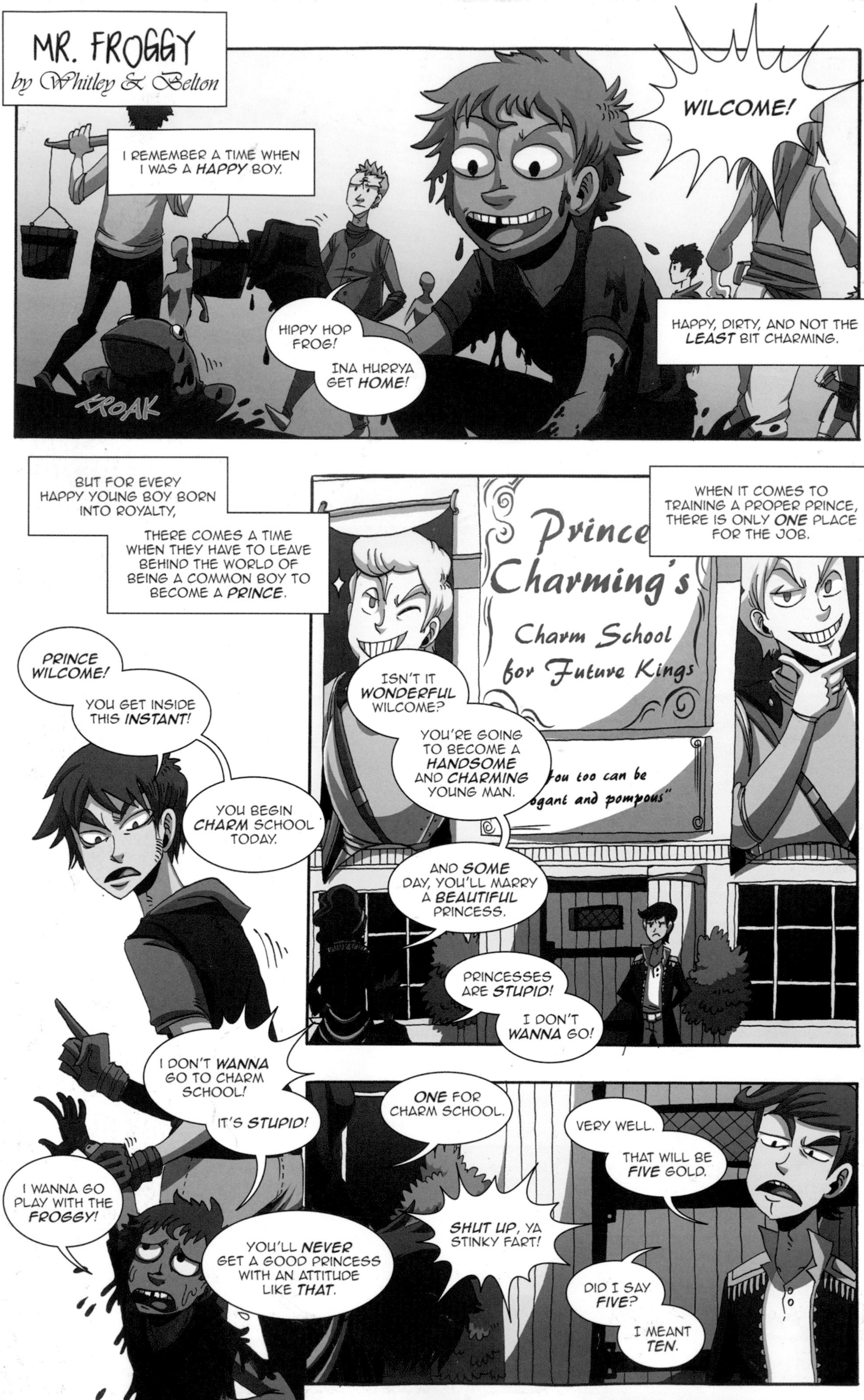
MR. FROGGY
by Whitley & Belton
I REMEMBER A TIME WHEN I WAS A HAPPY BOY.
WILCOME!
HIPPY HOP FROG!
INA HURRYA GET HOME!
KROAK
HAPPY, DIRTY, AND NOT THE LEAST BIT CHARMING.
BUT FOR EVERY HAPPY YOUNG BOY BORN INTO ROYALTY,
THERE COMES A TIME WHEN THEY HAVE TO LEAVE BEHIND THE WORLD OF BEING A COMMON BOY TO BECOME A PRINCE.
WHEN IT COMES TO TRAINING A PROPER PRINCE, THERE IS ONLY ONE PLACE FOR THE JOB.
Prince Charming's
Charm School for Future Kings
PRINCE WILCOME!
YOU GET INSIDE THIS INSTANT!
YOU BEGIN CHARM SCHOOL TODAY.
ISN'T IT WONDERFUL WILCOME?
YOU'RE GOING TO BECOME A HANDSOME AND CHARMING YOUNG MAN.
AND SOME DAY, YOU'LL MARRY A BEAUTIFUL PRINCESS.
PRINCESSES ARE STUPID!
I DON'T WANNA GO!
I DON'T WANNA GO TO CHARM SCHOOL!
IT'S STUPID!
I WANNA GO PLAY WITH THE FROGGY!
YOU'LL NEVER GET A GOOD PRINCESS WITH AN ATTITUDE LIKE THAT.
ONE FOR CHARM SCHOOL.
VERY WELL.
THAT WILL BE FIVE GOLD.
SHUT UP, YA STINKY FART!
DID I SAY FIVE?
I MEANT TEN.

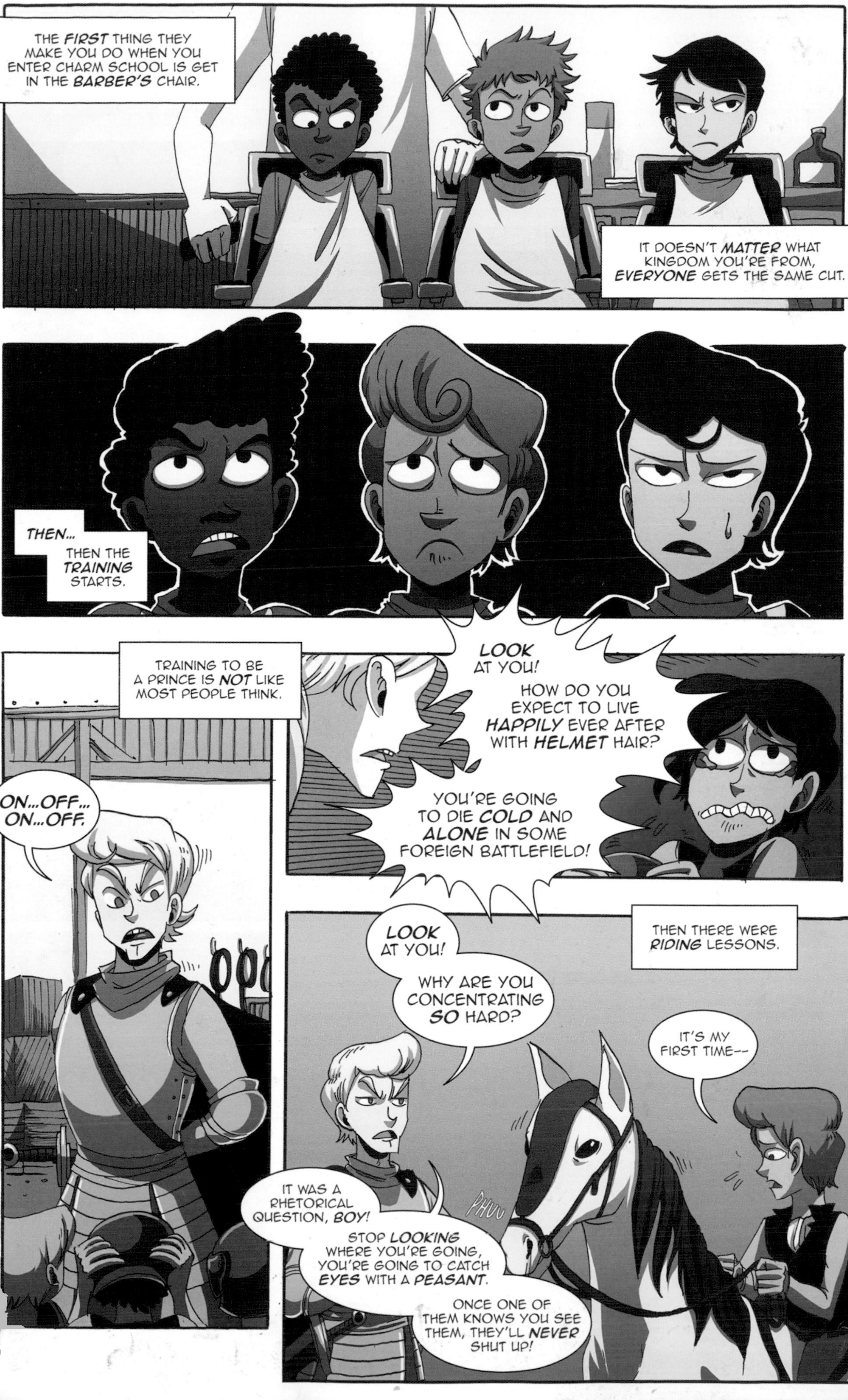
THE FIRST THING THEY MAKE YOU DO WHEN YOU ENTER CHARM SCHOOL IS GET IN THE BARBER'S CHAIR.
IT DOESN'T MATTER WHAT KINGDOM YOU'RE FROM, EVERYONE GETS THE SAME CUT.
THEN...
THEN THE TRAINING STARTS.
TRAINING TO BE A PRINCE IS NOT LIKE MOST PEOPLE THINK.
ON...OFF... ON...OFF.
LOOK AT YOU!
HOW DO YOU EXPECT TO LIVE HAPPILY EVER AFTER WITH HELMET HAIR?
YOU'RE GOING TO DIE COLD AND ALONE IN SOME FOREIGN BATTLEFIELD!
THEN THERE WERE RIDING LESSONS.
LOOK AT YOU!
WHY ARE YOU CONCENTRATING SO HARD?
IT'S MY FIRST TIME--
IT WAS A RHETORICAL QUESTION, BOY!
PHUU
STOP LOOKING WHERE YOU'RE GOING, YOU'RE GOING TO CATCH EYES WITH A PEASANT.
ONCE ONE OF THEM KNOWS YOU SEE THEM, THEY'LL NEVER SHUT UP!

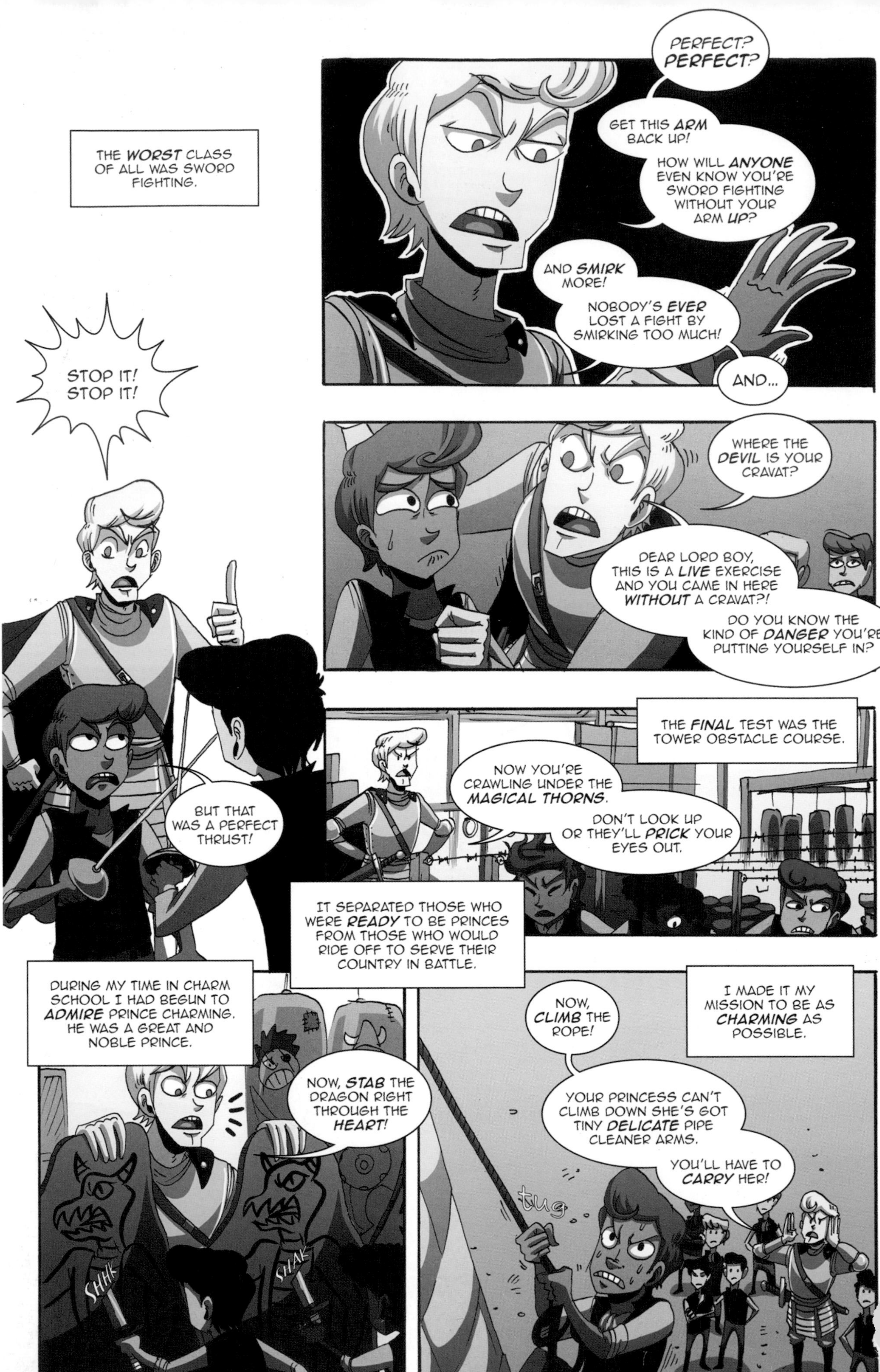
THE WORST CLASS OF ALL WAS SWORD FIGHTING.
PERFECT? PERFECT?
GET THIS ARM BACK UP!
HOW WILL ANYONE EVEN KNOW YOU'RE SWORD FIGHTING WITHOUT YOUR ARM UP?
AND SMIRK MORE!
NOBODY'S EVER LOST A FIGHT BY SMIRKING TOO MUCH!
AND...
STOP IT! STOP IT!
BUT THAT WAS A PERFECT THRUST!
WHERE THE DEVIL IS YOUR CRAVAT?
DEAR LORD BOY, THIS IS A LIVE EXERCISE AND YOU CAME IN HERE WITHOUT A CRAVAT?!
DO YOU KNOW THE KIND OF DANGER YOU'RE PUTTING YOURSELF IN?
THE FINAL TEST WAS THE TOWER OBSTACLE COURSE.
NOW YOU'RE CRAWLING UNDER THE MAGICAL THORNS.
DON'T LOOK UP OR THEY'LL PRICK YOUR EYES OUT.
IT SEPARATED THOSE WHO WERE READY TO BE PRINCES FROM THOSE WHO WOULD RIDE OFF TO SERVE THEIR COUNTRY IN BATTLE.
DURING MY TIME IN CHARM SCHOOL I HAD BEGUN TO ADMIRE PRINCE CHARMING. HE WAS A GREAT AND NOBLE PRINCE.
NOW, STAB THE DRAGON RIGHT THROUGH THE HEART!
SHHK
SHAK
I MADE IT MY MISSION TO BE AS CHARMING AS POSSIBLE.
NOW, CLIMB THE ROPE!
YOUR PRINCESS CAN'T CLIMB DOWN SHE'S GOT TINY DELICATE PIPE CLEANER ARMS.
YOU'LL HAVE TO CARRY HER!
tug

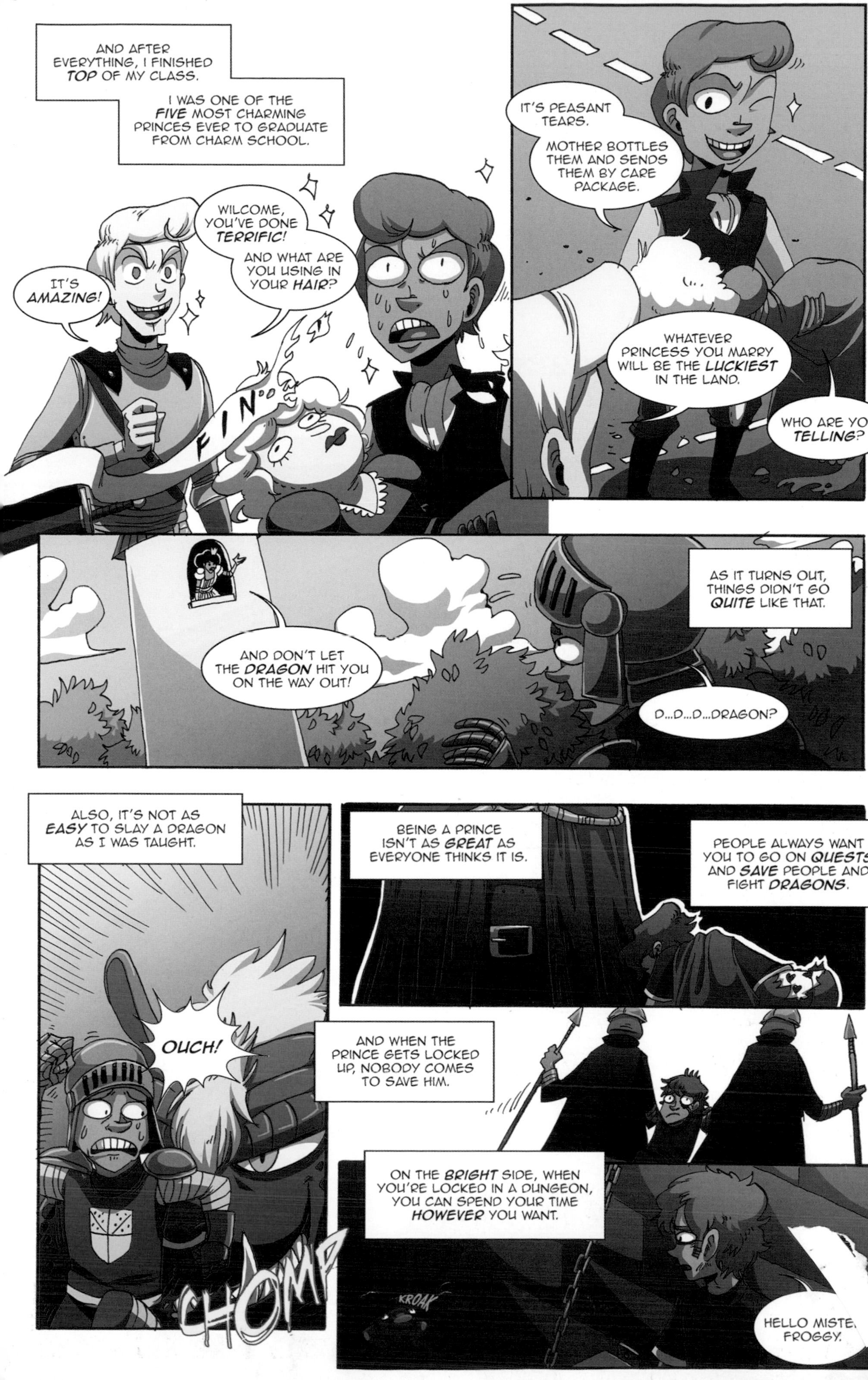
AND AFTER EVERYTHING, I FINISHED TOP OF MY CLASS.
I WAS ONE OF THE FIVE MOST CHARMING PRINCES EVER TO GRADUATE FROM CHARM SCHOOL.
IT'S AMAZING!
WILCOME, YOU'VE DONE TERRIFIC!
AND WHAT ARE YOU USING IN YOUR HAIR?
FIN
IT'S PEASANT TEARS.
MOTHER BOTTLES THEM AND SENDS THEM BY CARE PACKAGE.
WHATEVER PRINCESS YOU MARRY WILL BE THE LUCKIEST IN THE LAND.
WHO ARE YOU TELLING?
AS IT TURNS OUT, THINGS DIDN'T GO QUITE LIKE THAT.
AND DON'T LET THE DRAGON HIT YOU ON THE WAY OUT!
D...D...D...DRAGON?
ALSO, IT'S NOT AS EASY TO SLAY A DRAGON AS I WAS TAUGHT.
OUCH!
CHOMP
BEING A PRINCE ISN'T AS GREAT AS EVERYONE THINKS IT IS.
PEOPLE ALWAYS WANT YOU TO GO ON QUESTS AND SAVE PEOPLE AND FIGHT DRAGONS.
AND WHEN THE PRINCE GETS LOCKED UP, NOBODY COMES TO SAVE HIM.
ON THE BRIGHT SIDE, WHEN YOU'RE LOCKED IN A DUNGEON, YOU CAN SPEND YOUR TIME HOWEVER YOU WANT.
KROAK
HELLO MISTE FROGGY.

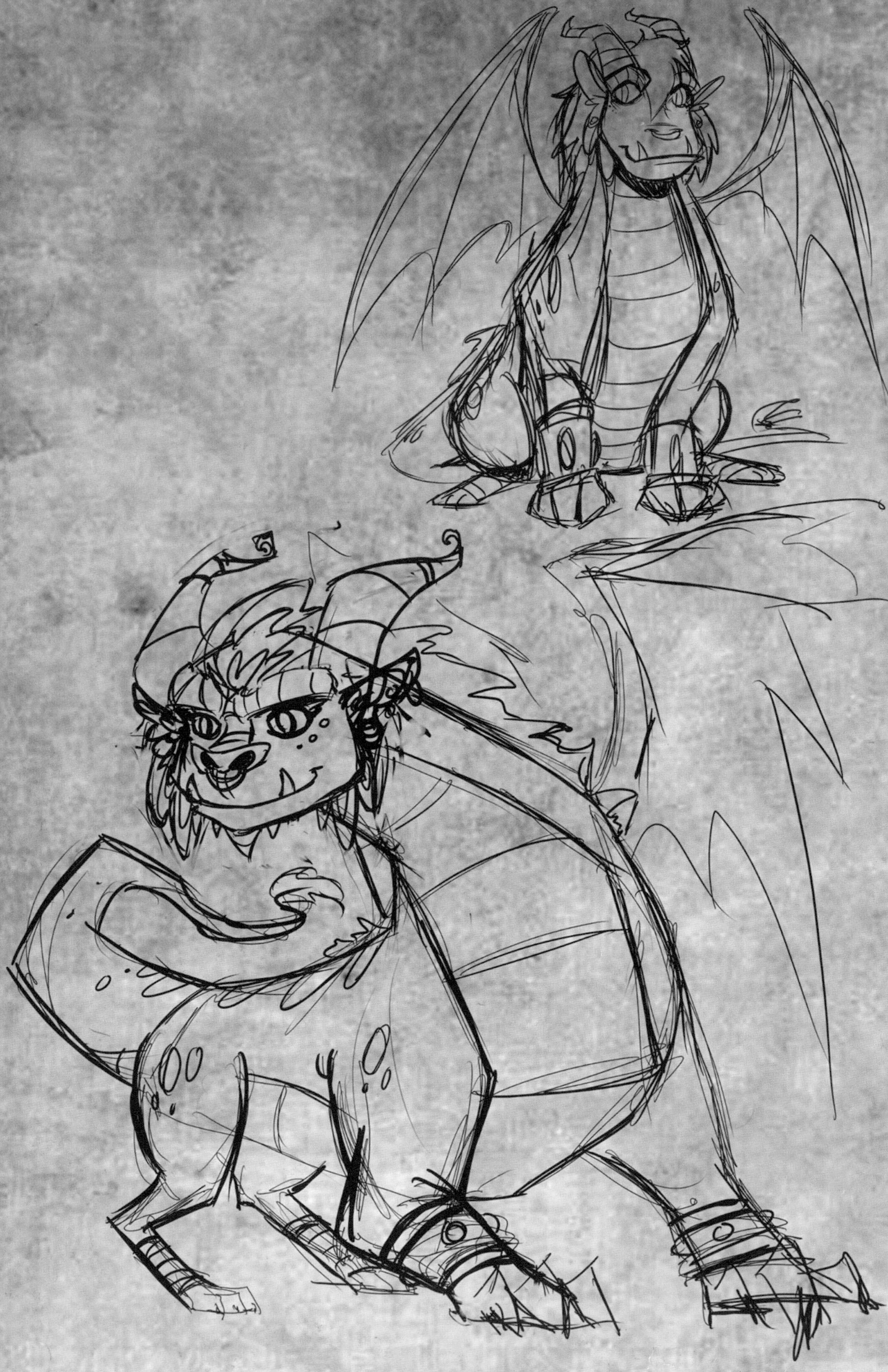

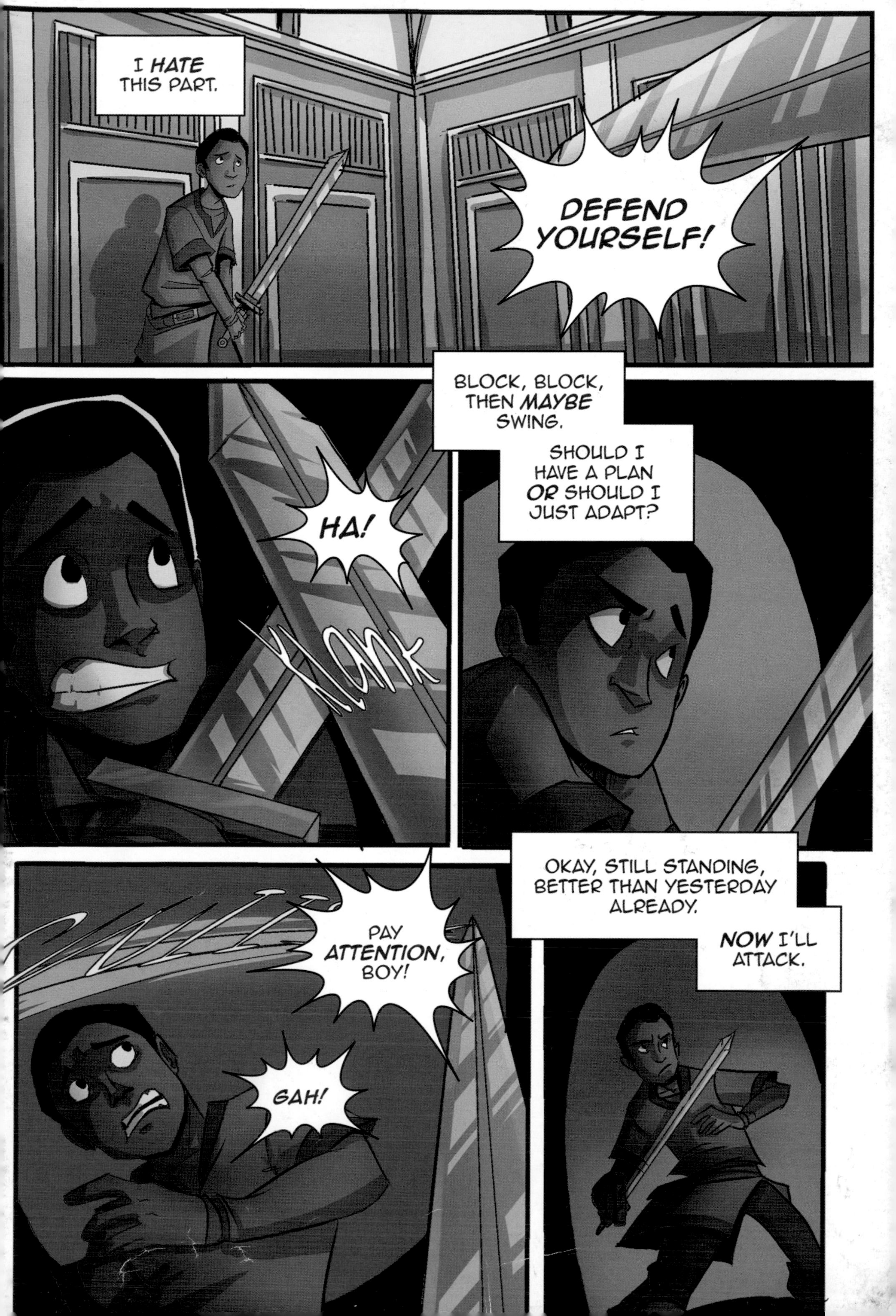
I *HATE* THIS PART.
DEFEND YOURSELF!
BLOCK, BLOCK, THEN *MAYBE* SWING.
HA!
KLANK
SHOULD I HAVE A PLAN *OR* SHOULD I JUST ADAPT?
PAY *ATTENTION*, BOY!
GAH!
OKAY, STILL STANDING, BETTER THAN YESTERDAY ALREADY.
NOW I'LL ATTACK.

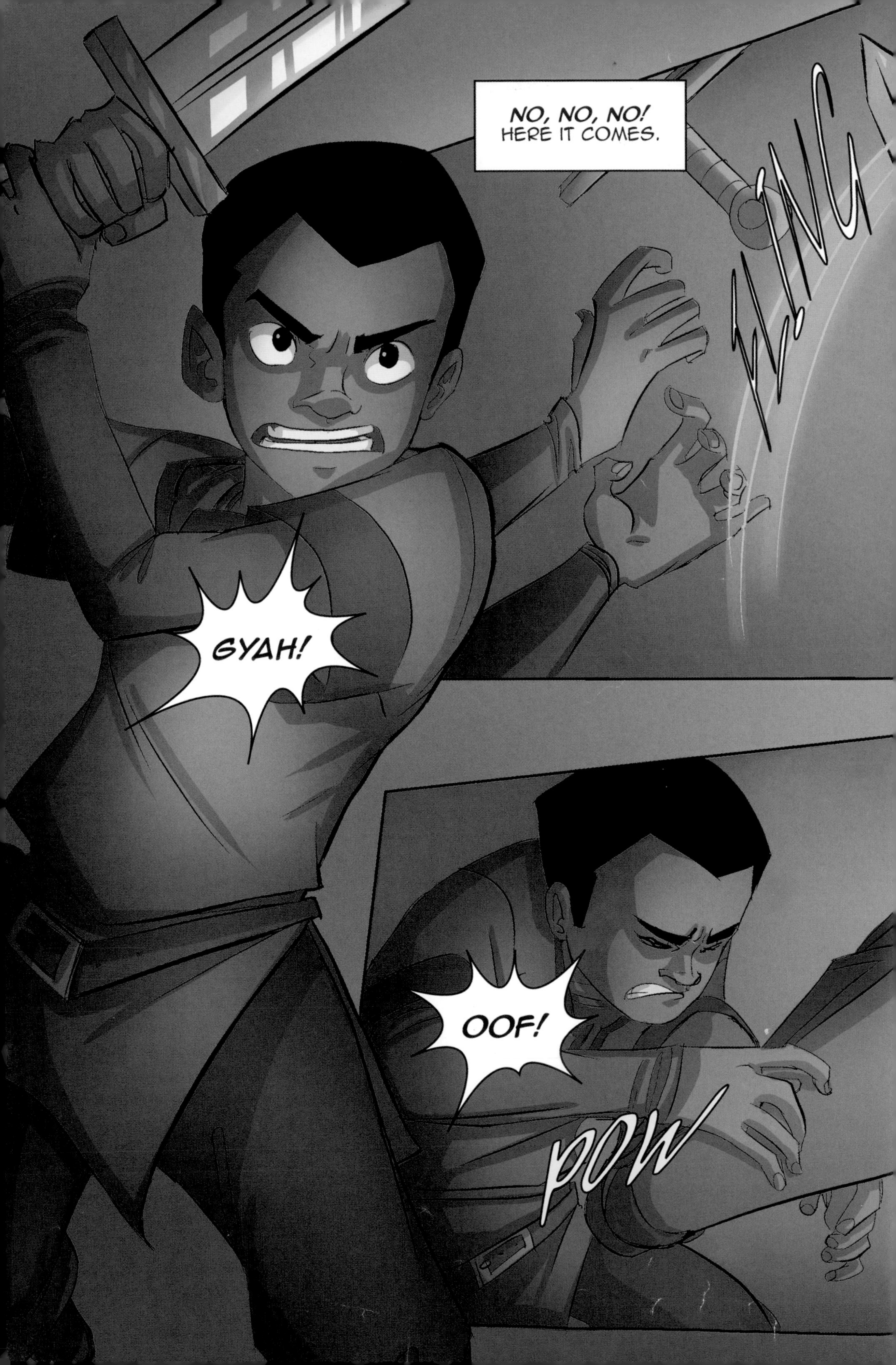
NO, NO, NO!
HERE IT COMES.
KLING
GYAH!
OOF!
POW

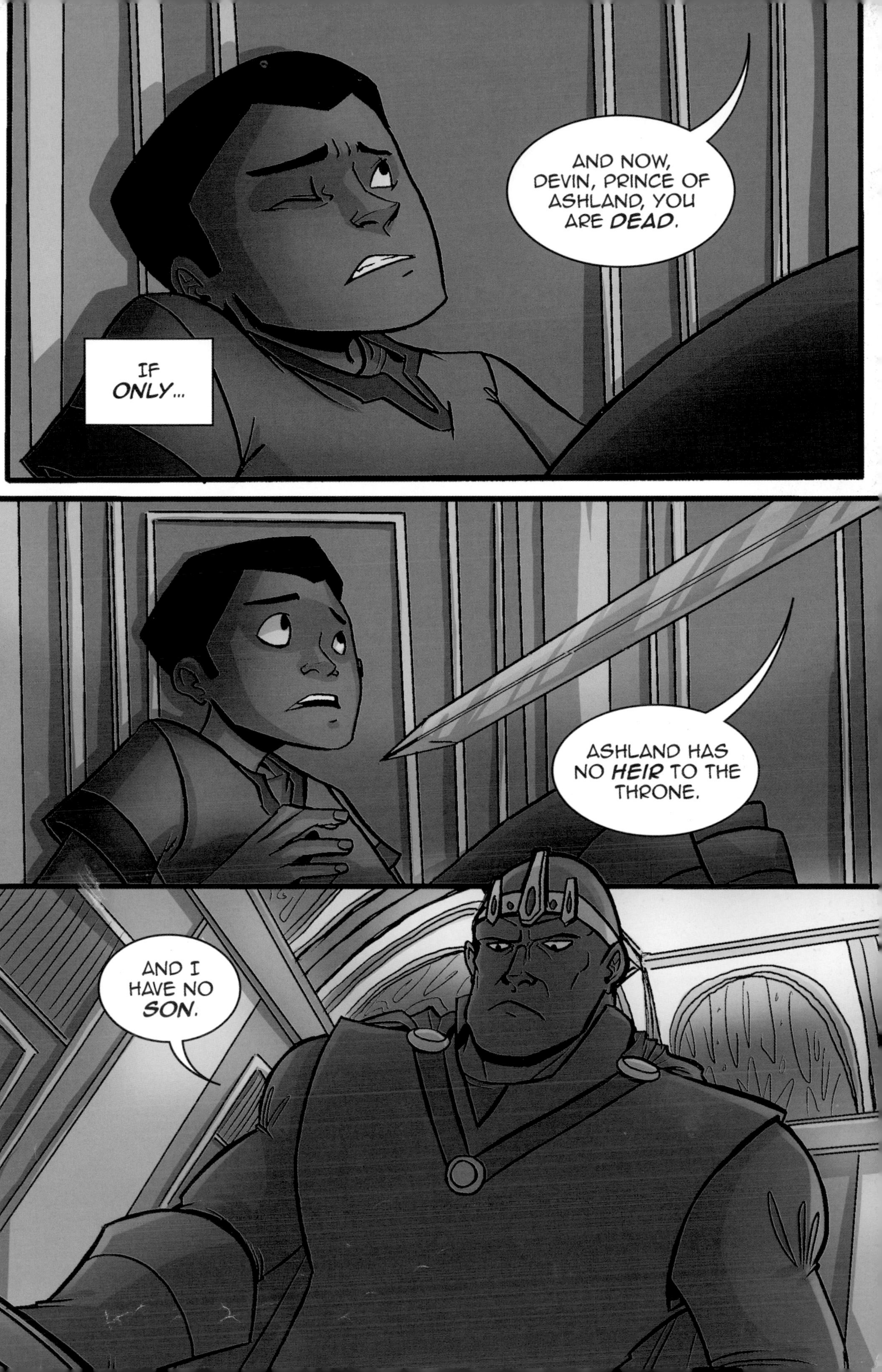
AND NOW, DEVIN, PRINCE OF ASHLAND, YOU ARE DEAD.
IF ONLY...
ASHLAND HAS NO HEIR TO THE THRONE.
AND I HAVE NO SON.

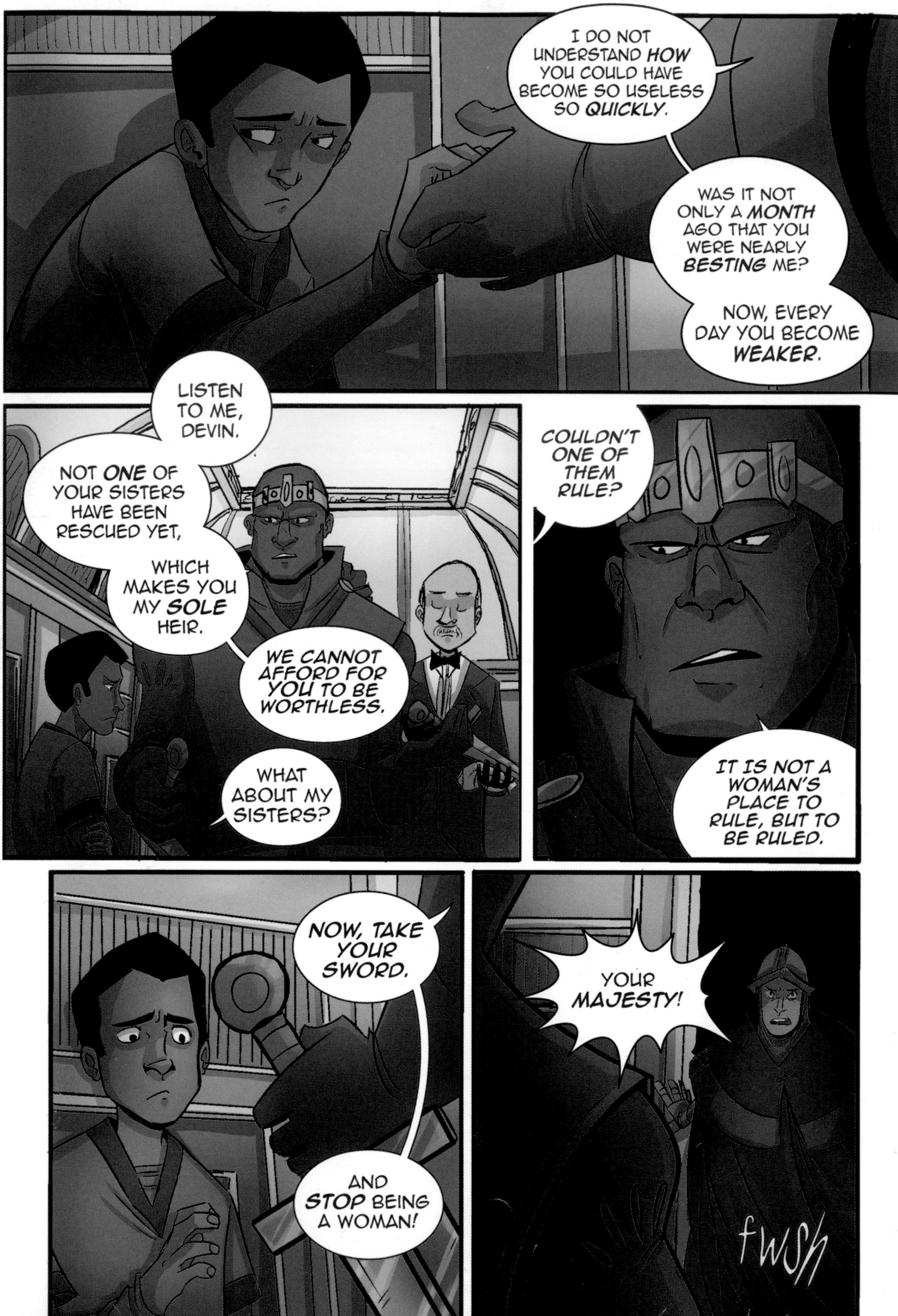

I DO NOT UNDERSTAND HOW YOU COULD HAVE BECOME SO USELESS SO QUICKLY.
WAS IT NOT ONLY A MONTH AGO THAT YOU WERE NEARLY BESTING ME?
NOW, EVERY DAY YOU BECOME WEAKER.
LISTEN TO ME, DEVIN.
NOT ONE OF YOUR SISTERS HAVE BEEN RESCUED YET,
WHICH MAKES YOU MY SOLE HEIR.
WE CANNOT AFFORD FOR YOU TO BE WORTHLESS.
WHAT ABOUT MY SISTERS?
COULDN'T ONE OF THEM RULE?
IT IS NOT A WOMAN'S PLACE TO RULE, BUT TO BE RULED.
NOW, TAKE YOUR SWORD.
AND STOP BEING A WOMAN!
YOUR MAJESTY!
fwsh

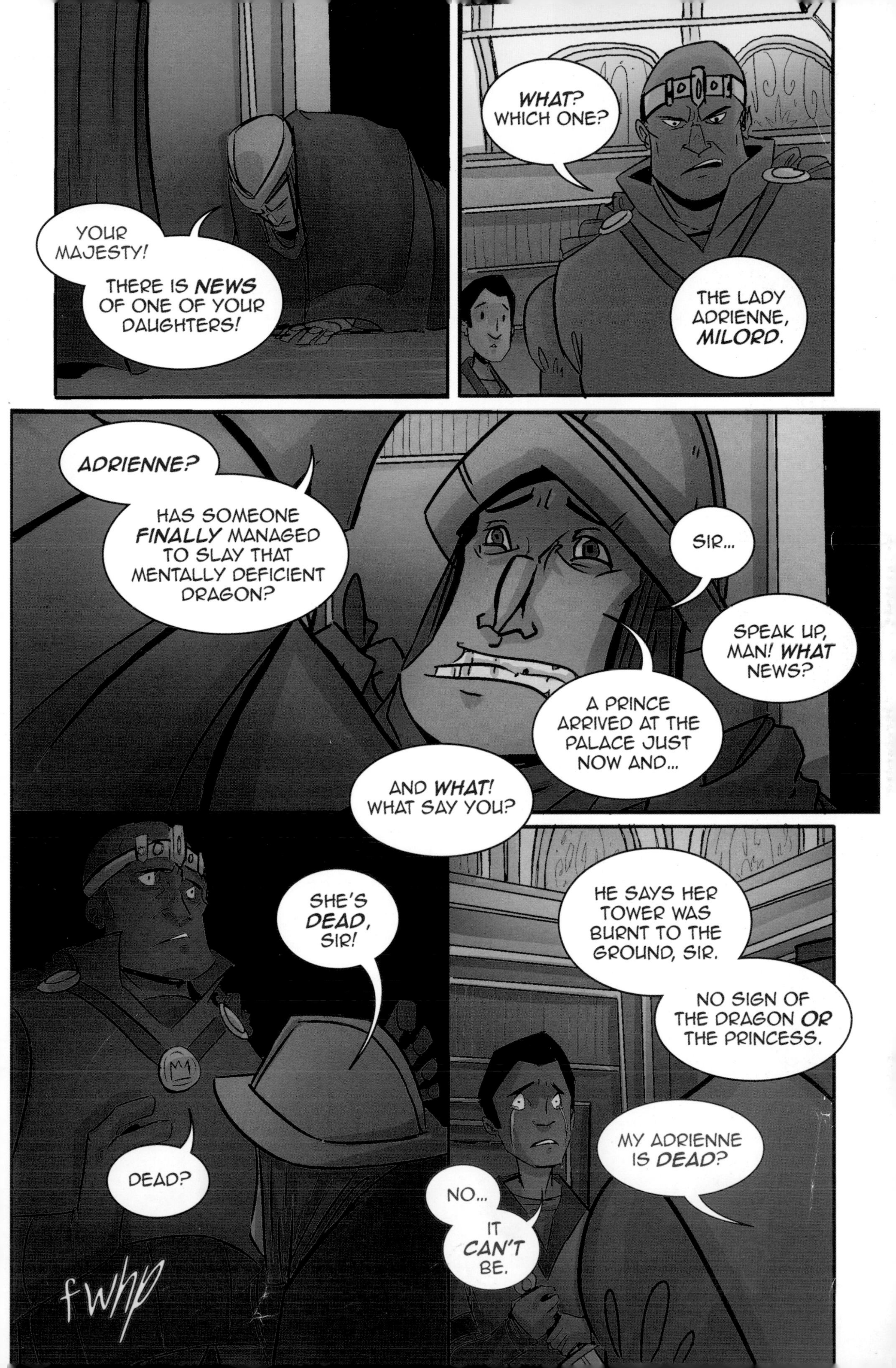
YOUR MAJESTY!
THERE IS NEWS OF ONE OF YOUR DAUGHTERS!
WHAT? WHICH ONE?
THE LADY ADRIENNE, MILORD.
ADRIENNE?
HAS SOMEONE FINALLY MANAGED TO SLAY THAT MENTALLY DEFICIENT DRAGON?
SIR...
SPEAK UP, MAN! WHAT NEWS?
A PRINCE ARRIVED AT THE PALACE JUST NOW AND...
AND WHAT! WHAT SAY YOU?
SHE'S DEAD, SIR!
DEAD?
HE SAYS HER TOWER WAS BURNT TO THE GROUND, SIR.
NO SIGN OF THE DRAGON OR THE PRINCESS.
MY ADRIENNE IS DEAD?
NO...
IT CAN'T BE.
fwhp

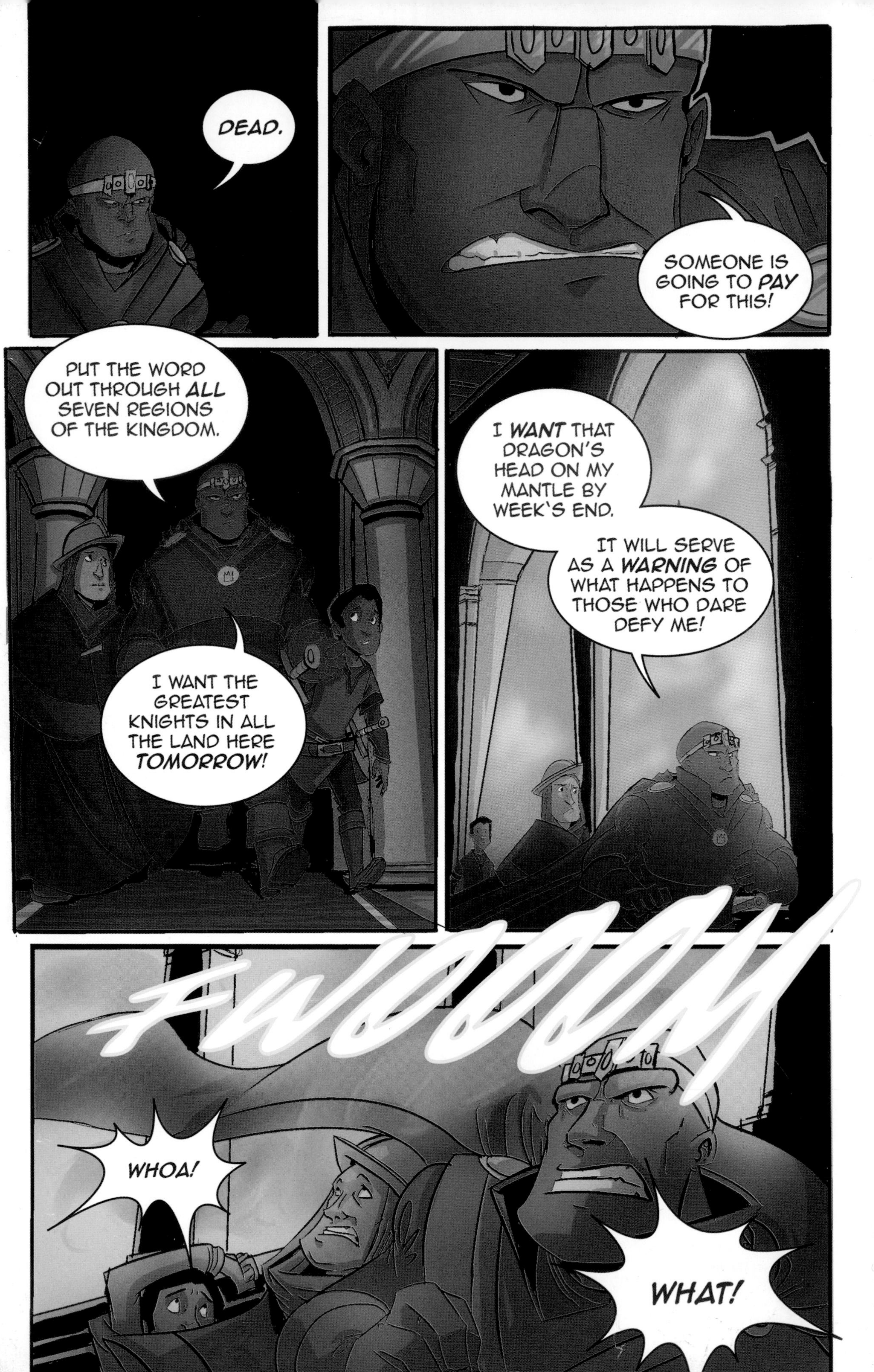
DEAD.
SOMEONE IS GOING TO PAY FOR THIS!
PUT THE WORD OUT THROUGH ALL SEVEN REGIONS OF THE KINGDOM.
I WANT THE GREATEST KNIGHTS IN ALL THE LAND HERE TOMORROW!
I WANT THAT DRAGON'S HEAD ON MY MANTLE BY WEEK'S END.
IT WILL SERVE AS A WARNING OF WHAT HAPPENS TO THOSE WHO DARE DEFY ME!
FWOOOM
WHOA!
WHAT!

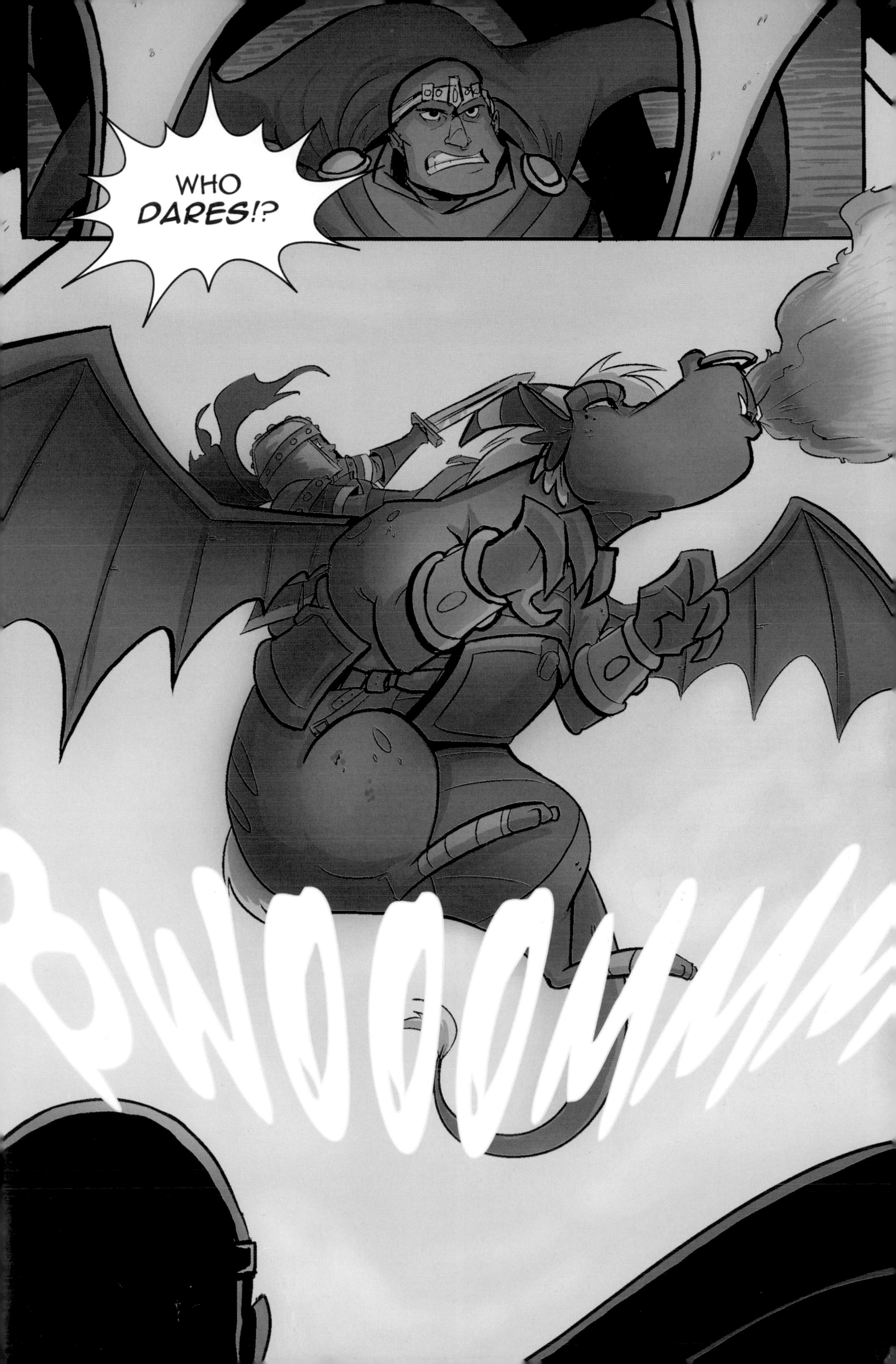
WHO DARES!?

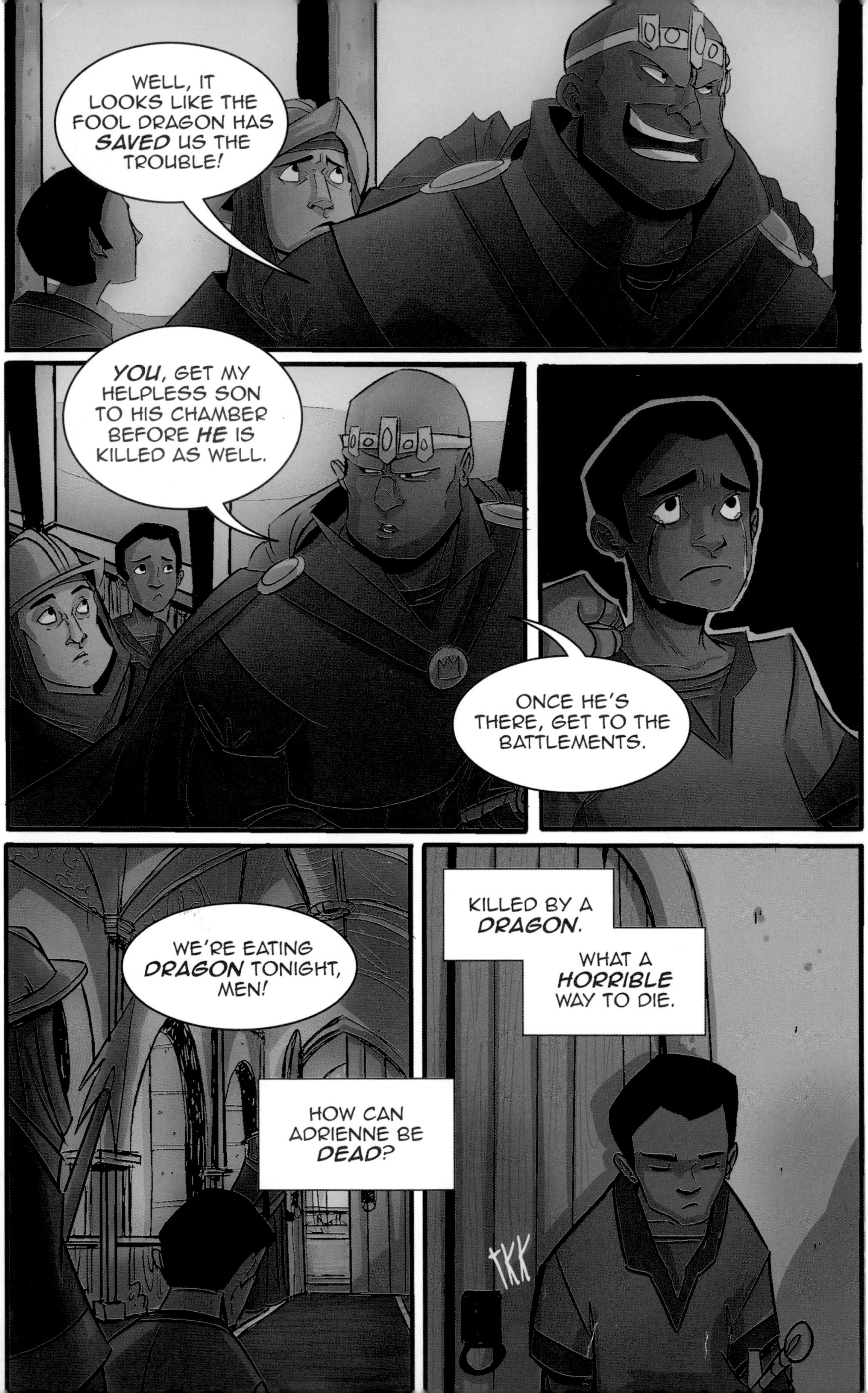
WELL, IT LOOKS LIKE THE FOOL DRAGON HAS SAVED US THE TROUBLE!
YOU, GET MY HELPLESS SON TO HIS CHAMBER BEFORE HE IS KILLED AS WELL.
ONCE HE'S THERE, GET TO THE BATTLEMENTS.
WE'RE EATING DRAGON TONIGHT, MEN!
HOW CAN ADRIENNE BE DEAD?
KILLED BY A DRAGON.
WHAT A HORRIBLE WAY TO DIE.
TKK

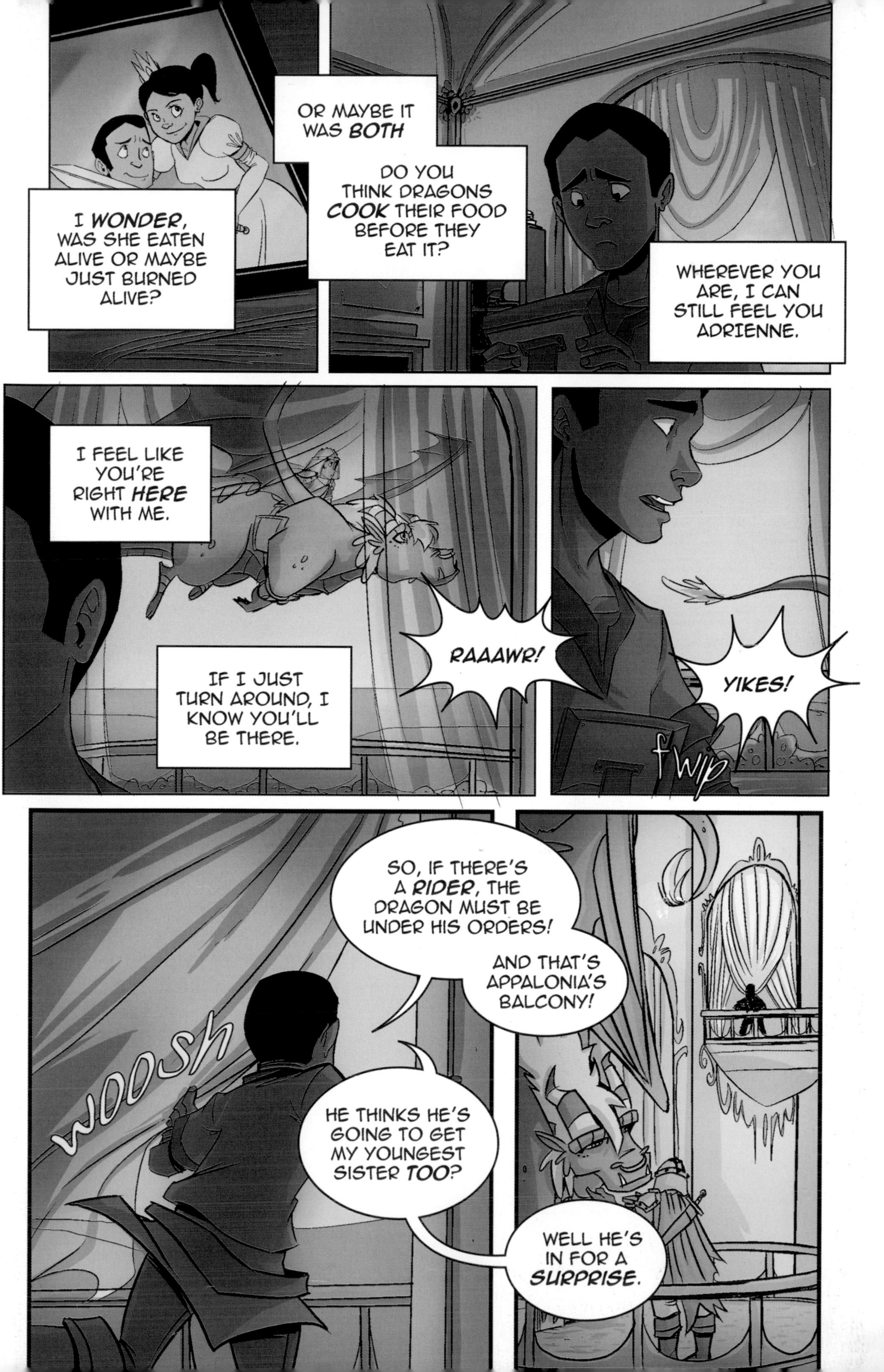
I WONDER, WAS SHE EATEN ALIVE OR MAYBE JUST BURNED ALIVE?
OR MAYBE IT WAS BOTH
DO YOU THINK DRAGONS COOK THEIR FOOD BEFORE THEY EAT IT?
WHEREVER YOU ARE, I CAN STILL FEEL YOU ADRIENNE.
I FEEL LIKE YOU'RE RIGHT HERE WITH ME.
IF I JUST TURN AROUND, I KNOW YOU'LL BE THERE.
RAAAWR!
YIKES!
fwip
SO, IF THERE'S A RIDER, THE DRAGON MUST BE UNDER HIS ORDERS!
AND THAT'S APPALONIA'S BALCONY!
WOOSH
HE THINKS HE'S GOING TO GET MY YOUNGEST SISTER TOO?
WELL HE'S IN FOR A SURPRISE.

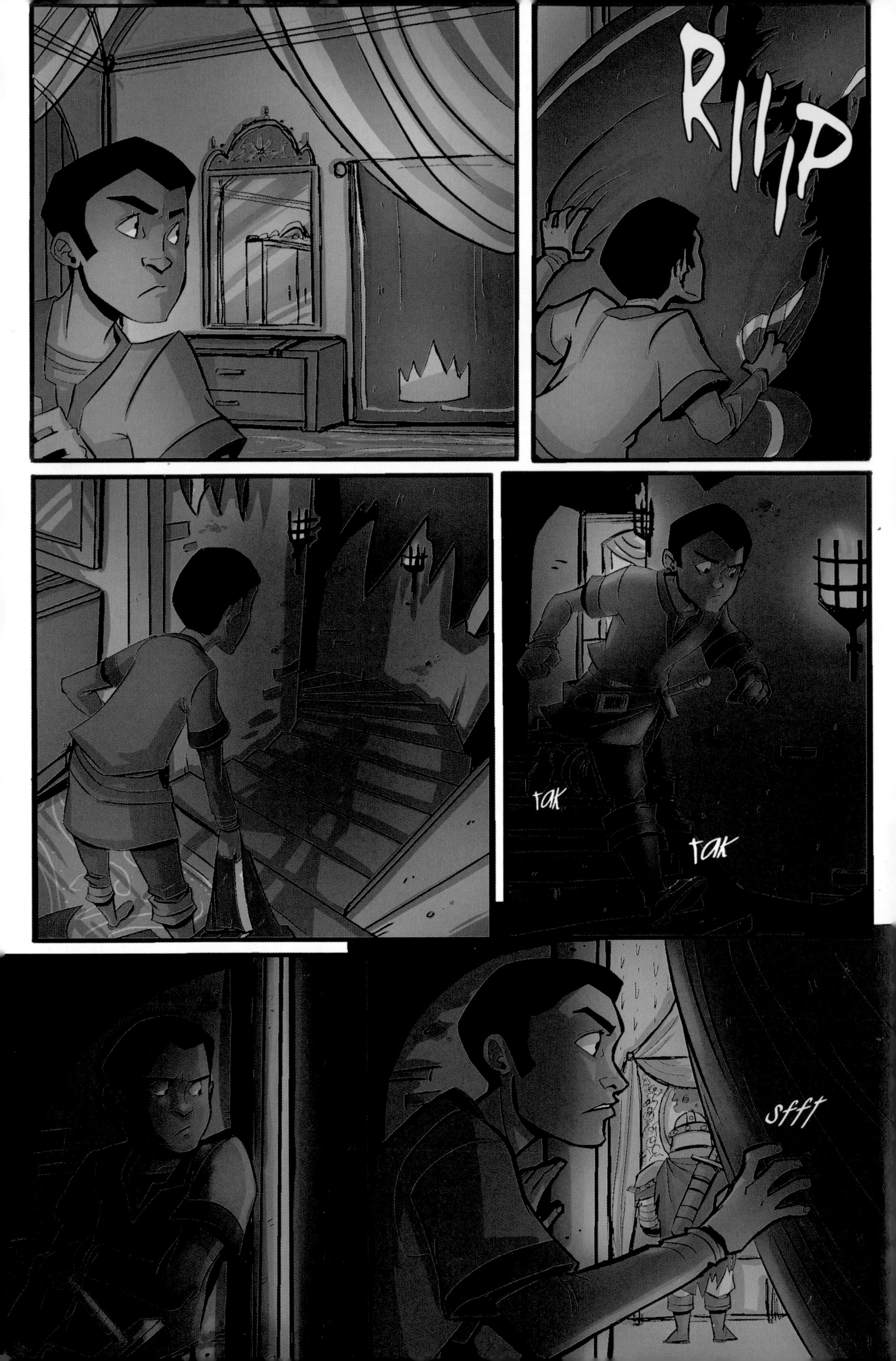
RIIP
tak
tak
sfft

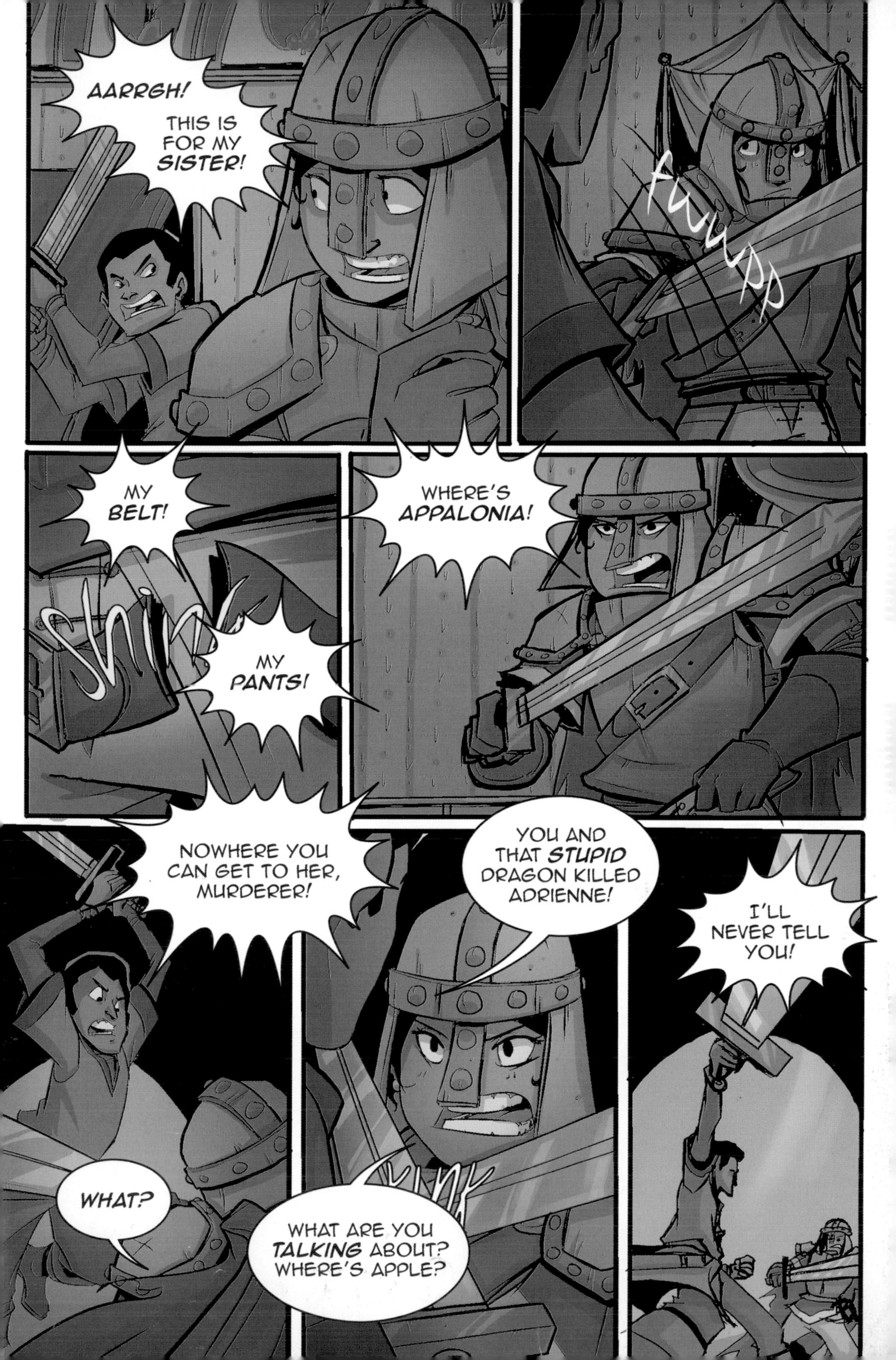
AARRGH!
THIS IS FOR MY *SISTER!*
FWWPP
MY *BELT!*
SHINK
MY *PANTS!*
WHERE'S *APPALONIA!*
NOWHERE YOU CAN GET TO HER, MURDERER!
YOU AND THAT *STUPID* DRAGON KILLED ADRIENNE!
WHAT?
WHAT ARE YOU *TALKING* ABOUT? WHERE'S APPLE?
I'LL NEVER TELL YOU!

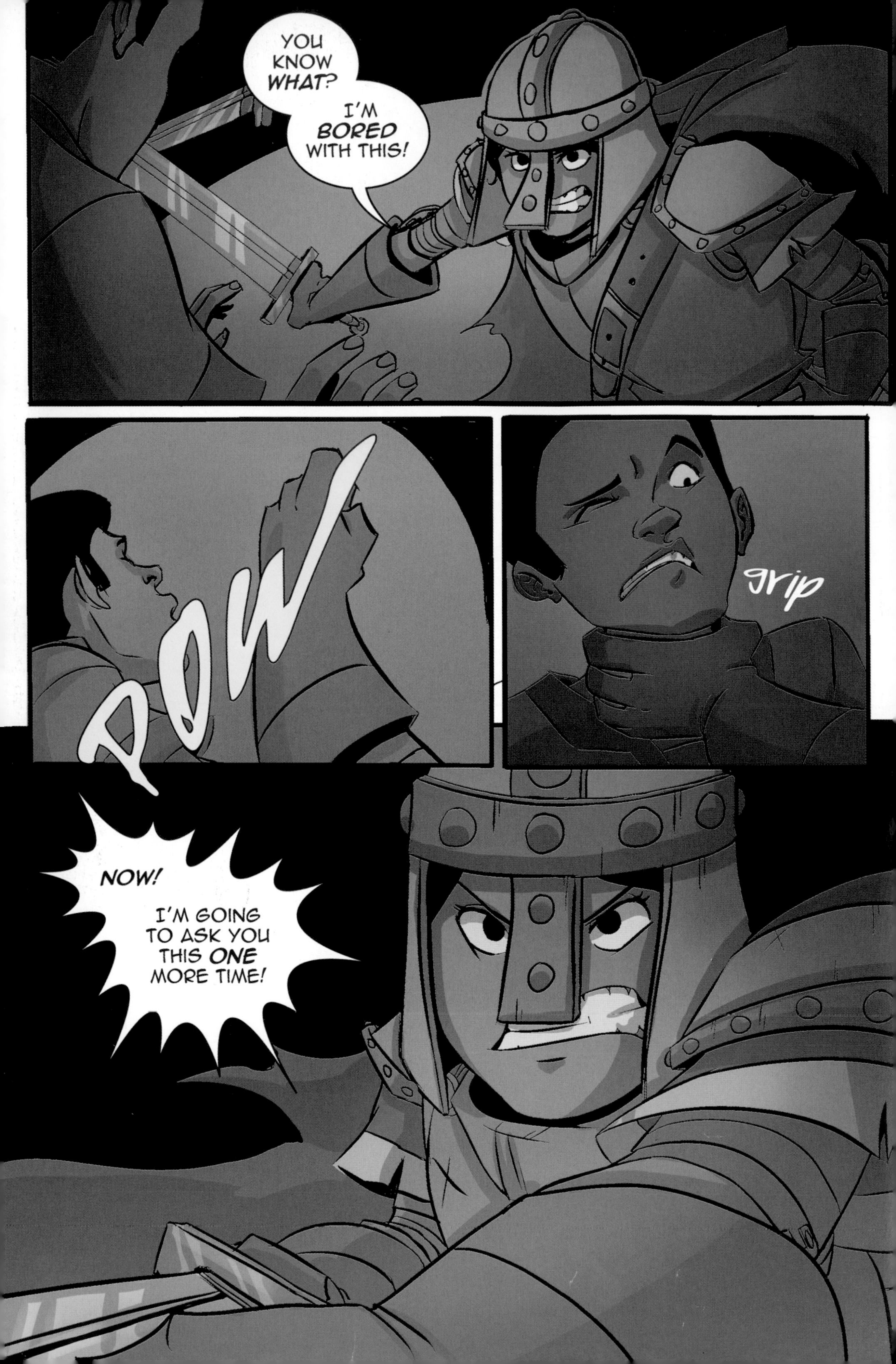

YOU KNOW WHAT?
I'M BORED WITH THIS!
POW
grip
NOW!
I'M GOING TO ASK YOU THIS ONE MORE TIME!

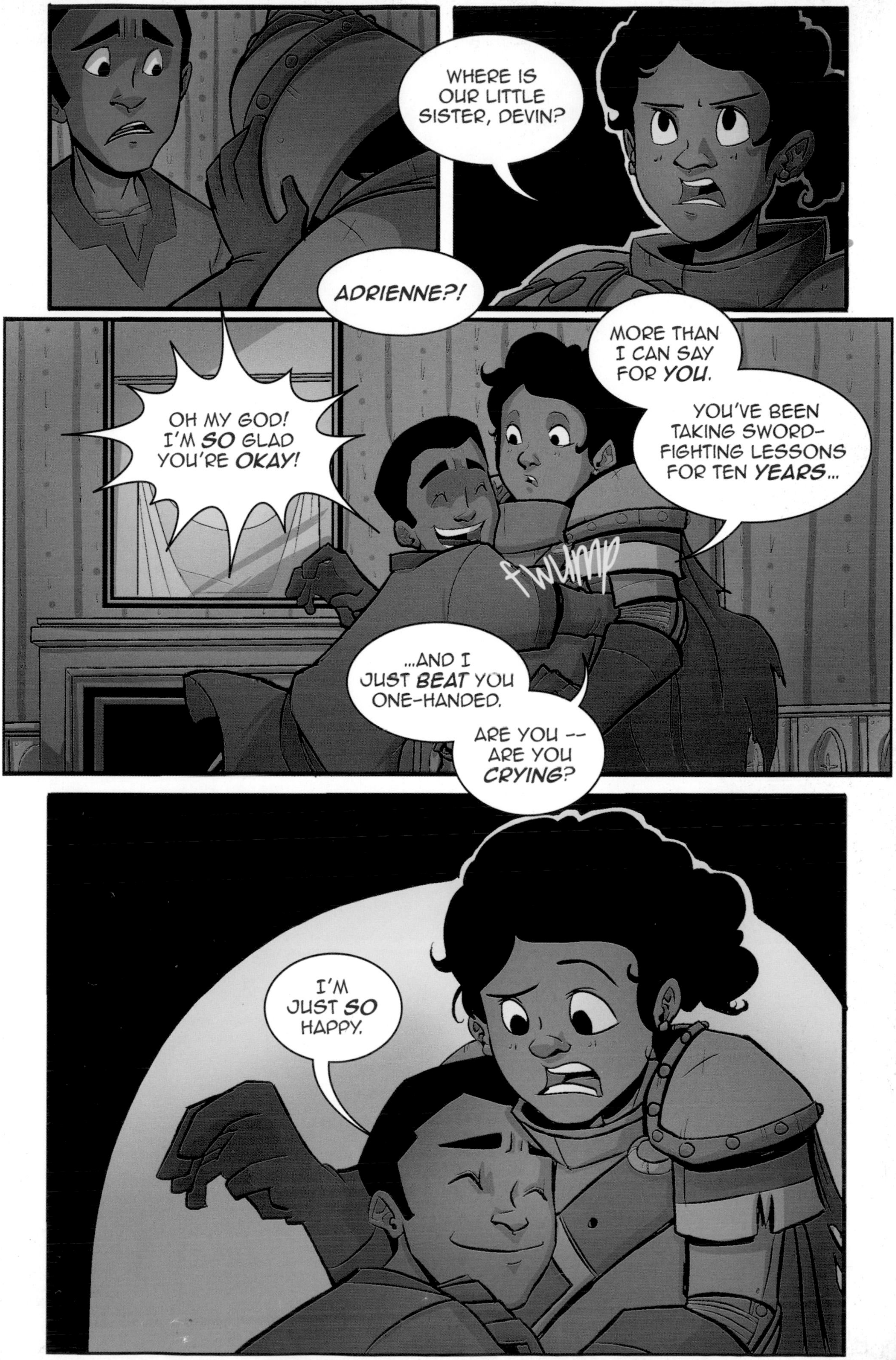
WHERE IS OUR LITTLE SISTER, DEVIN?
ADRIENNE?!
OH MY GOD! I'M SO GLAD YOU'RE OKAY!
MORE THAN I CAN SAY FOR YOU.
YOU'VE BEEN TAKING SWORD-FIGHTING LESSONS FOR TEN YEARS...
fwump
...AND I JUST BEAT YOU ONE-HANDED.
ARE YOU -- ARE YOU CRYING?
I'M JUST SO HAPPY.

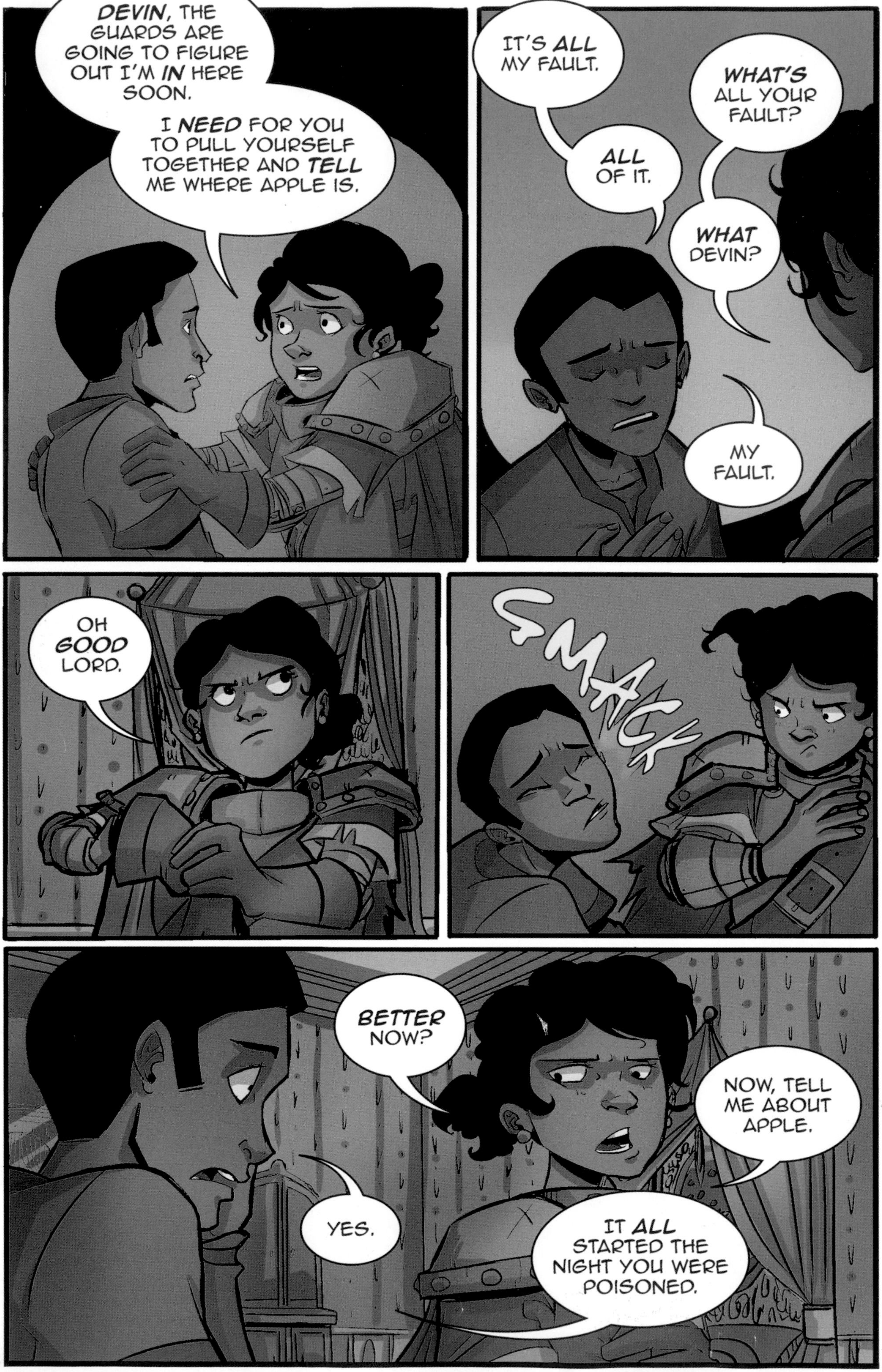
DEVIN, THE GUARDS ARE GOING TO FIGURE OUT I'M IN HERE SOON.
I NEED FOR YOU TO PULL YOURSELF TOGETHER AND TELL ME WHERE APPLE IS.
IT'S ALL MY FAULT.
WHAT'S ALL YOUR FAULT?
ALL OF IT.
WHAT DEVIN?
MY FAULT.
OH GOOD LORD.
SMACK
BETTER NOW?
YES.
NOW, TELL ME ABOUT APPLE.
IT ALL STARTED THE NIGHT YOU WERE POISONED.

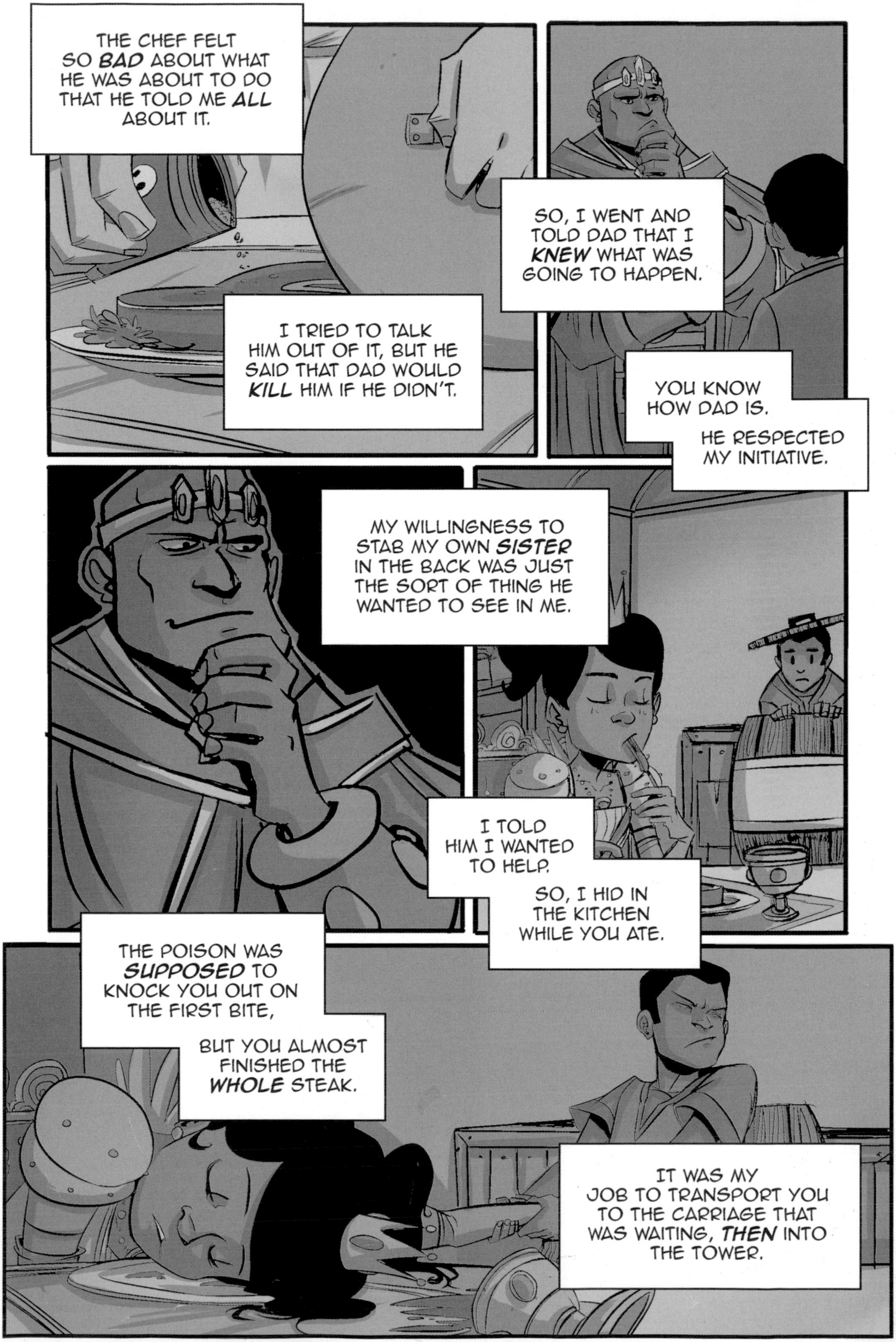
THE CHEF FELT SO BAD ABOUT WHAT HE WAS ABOUT TO DO THAT HE TOLD ME ALL ABOUT IT.
I TRIED TO TALK HIM OUT OF IT, BUT HE SAID THAT DAD WOULD KILL HIM IF HE DIDN'T.
SO, I WENT AND TOLD DAD THAT I KNEW WHAT WAS GOING TO HAPPEN.
YOU KNOW HOW DAD IS.
HE RESPECTED MY INITIATIVE.
MY WILLINGNESS TO STAB MY OWN SISTER IN THE BACK WAS JUST THE SORT OF THING HE WANTED TO SEE IN ME.
I TOLD HIM I WANTED TO HELP.
SO, I HID IN THE KITCHEN WHILE YOU ATE.
THE POISON WAS SUPPOSED TO KNOCK YOU OUT ON THE FIRST BITE,
BUT YOU ALMOST FINISHED THE WHOLE STEAK.
IT WAS MY JOB TO TRANSPORT YOU TO THE CARRIAGE THAT WAS WAITING, THEN INTO THE TOWER.

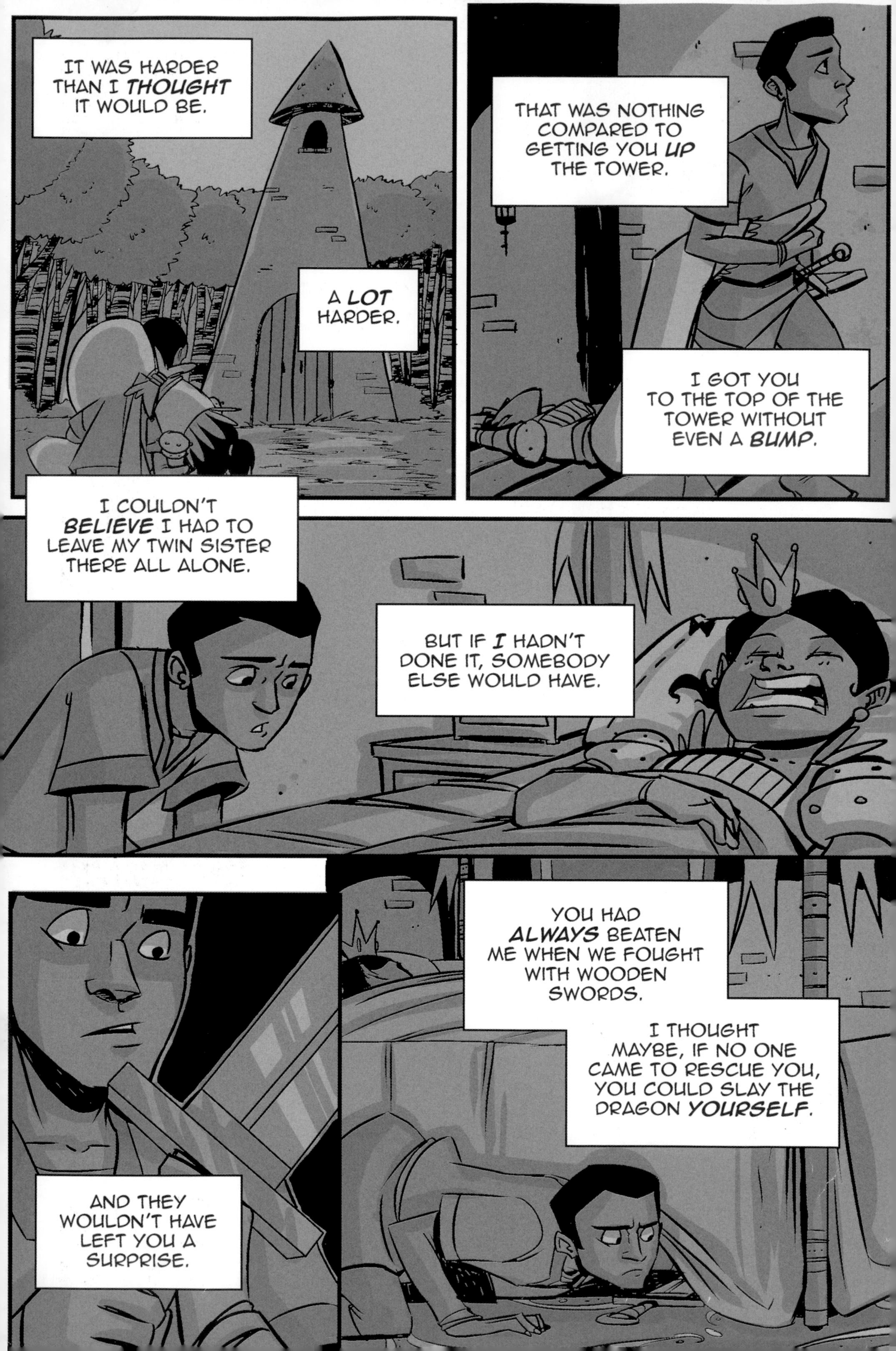
IT WAS HARDER THAN I *THOUGHT* IT WOULD BE.
A *LOT* HARDER.
THAT WAS NOTHING COMPARED TO GETTING YOU *UP* THE TOWER.
I GOT YOU TO THE TOP OF THE TOWER WITHOUT EVEN A *BUMP*.
I COULDN'T *BELIEVE* I HAD TO LEAVE MY TWIN SISTER THERE ALL ALONE.
BUT IF *I* HADN'T DONE IT, SOMEBODY ELSE WOULD HAVE.
AND THEY WOULDN'T HAVE LEFT YOU A SURPRISE.
YOU HAD *ALWAYS* BEATEN ME WHEN WE FOUGHT WITH WOODEN SWORDS.
I THOUGHT MAYBE, IF NO ONE CAME TO RESCUE YOU, YOU COULD SLAY THE DRAGON *YOURSELF*.

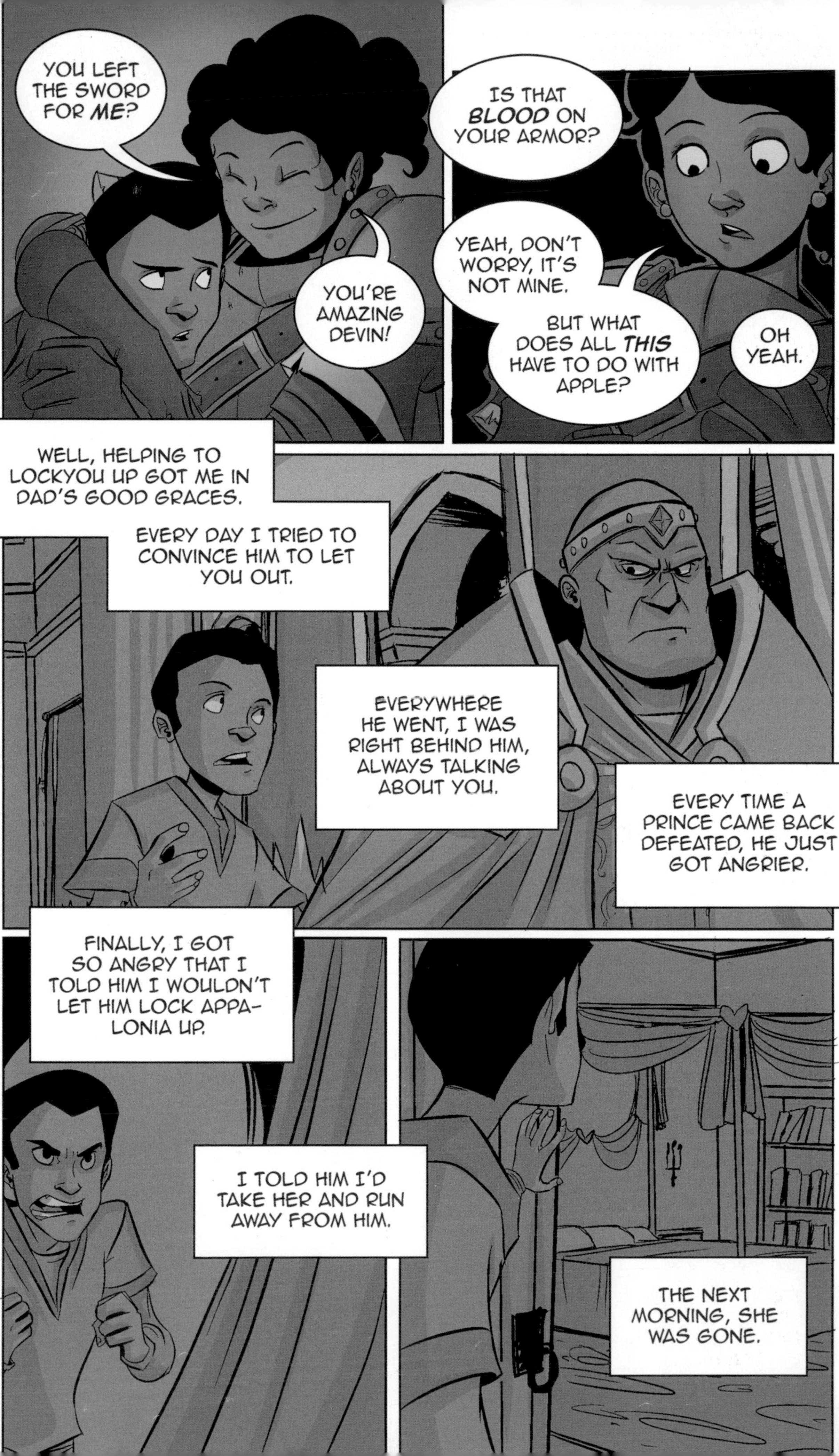
YOU LEFT THE SWORD FOR *ME*?
YOU'RE AMAZING DEVIN!
IS THAT *BLOOD* ON YOUR ARMOR?
YEAH, DON'T WORRY, IT'S NOT MINE.
BUT WHAT DOES ALL *THIS* HAVE TO DO WITH APPLE?
OH YEAH.
WELL, HELPING TO LOCKYOU UP GOT ME IN DAD'S GOOD GRACES.
EVERY DAY I TRIED TO CONVINCE HIM TO LET YOU OUT.
EVERYWHERE HE WENT, I WAS RIGHT BEHIND HIM, ALWAYS TALKING ABOUT YOU.
EVERY TIME A PRINCE CAME BACK DEFEATED, HE JUST GOT ANGRIER.
FINALLY, I GOT SO ANGRY THAT I TOLD HIM I WOULDN'T LET HIM LOCK APPA-LONIA UP.
I TOLD HIM I'D TAKE HER AND RUN AWAY FROM HIM.
THE NEXT MORNING, SHE WAS GONE.

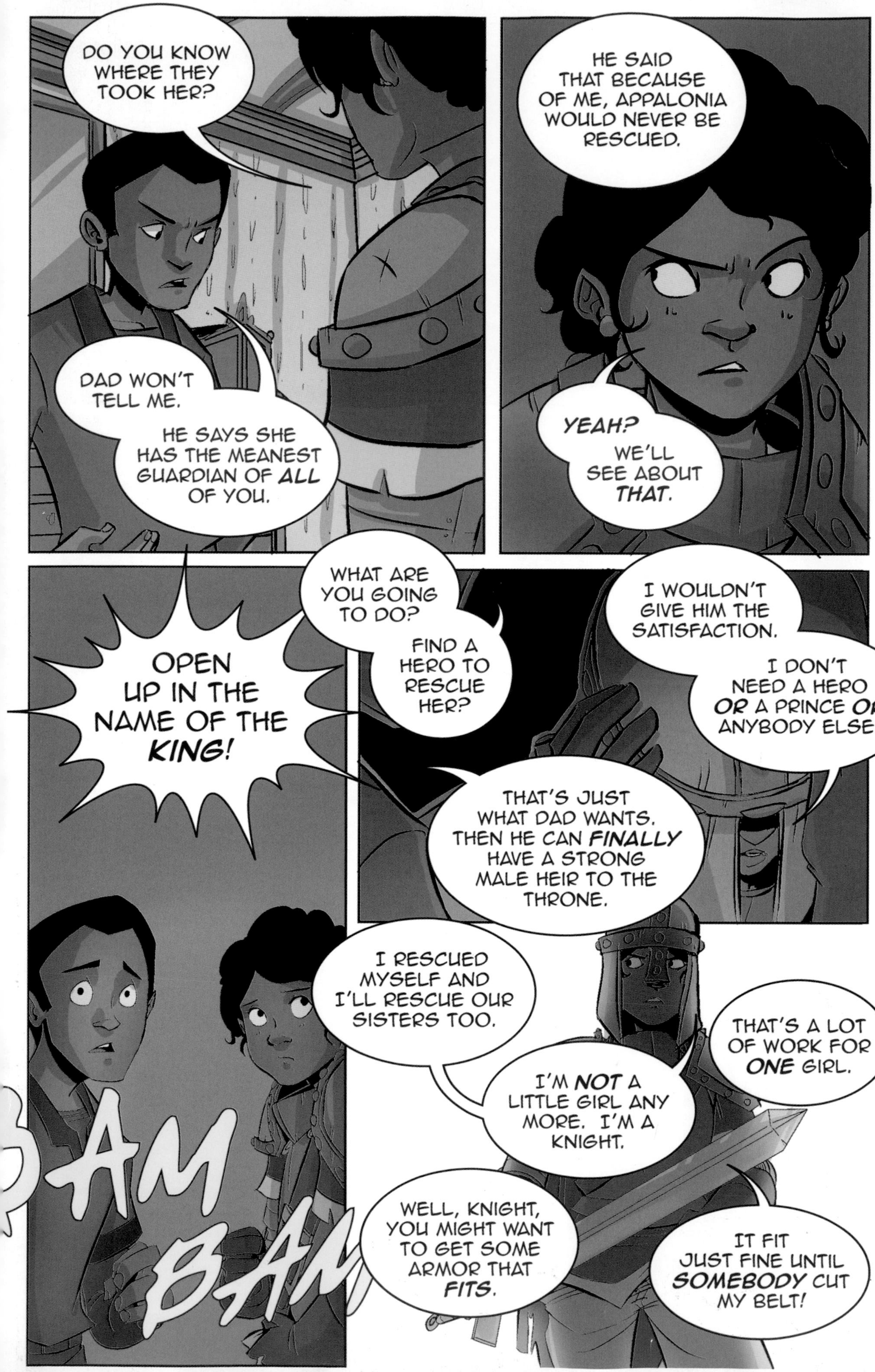
DO YOU KNOW WHERE THEY TOOK HER?
DAD WON'T TELL ME.
HE SAYS SHE HAS THE MEANEST GUARDIAN OF ALL OF YOU.
HE SAID THAT BECAUSE OF ME, APPALONIA WOULD NEVER BE RESCUED.
YEAH?
WE'LL SEE ABOUT THAT.
WHAT ARE YOU GOING TO DO?
FIND A HERO TO RESCUE HER?
I WOULDN'T GIVE HIM THE SATISFACTION.
I DON'T NEED A HERO OR A PRINCE OR ANYBODY ELSE!
THAT'S JUST WHAT DAD WANTS. THEN HE CAN FINALLY HAVE A STRONG MALE HEIR TO THE THRONE.
OPEN UP IN THE NAME OF THE KING!
I RESCUED MYSELF AND I'LL RESCUE OUR SISTERS TOO.
THAT'S A LOT OF WORK FOR ONE GIRL.
I'M NOT A LITTLE GIRL ANY MORE. I'M A KNIGHT.
WELL, KNIGHT, YOU MIGHT WANT TO GET SOME ARMOR THAT FITS.
IT FIT JUST FINE UNTIL SOMEBODY CUT MY BELT!

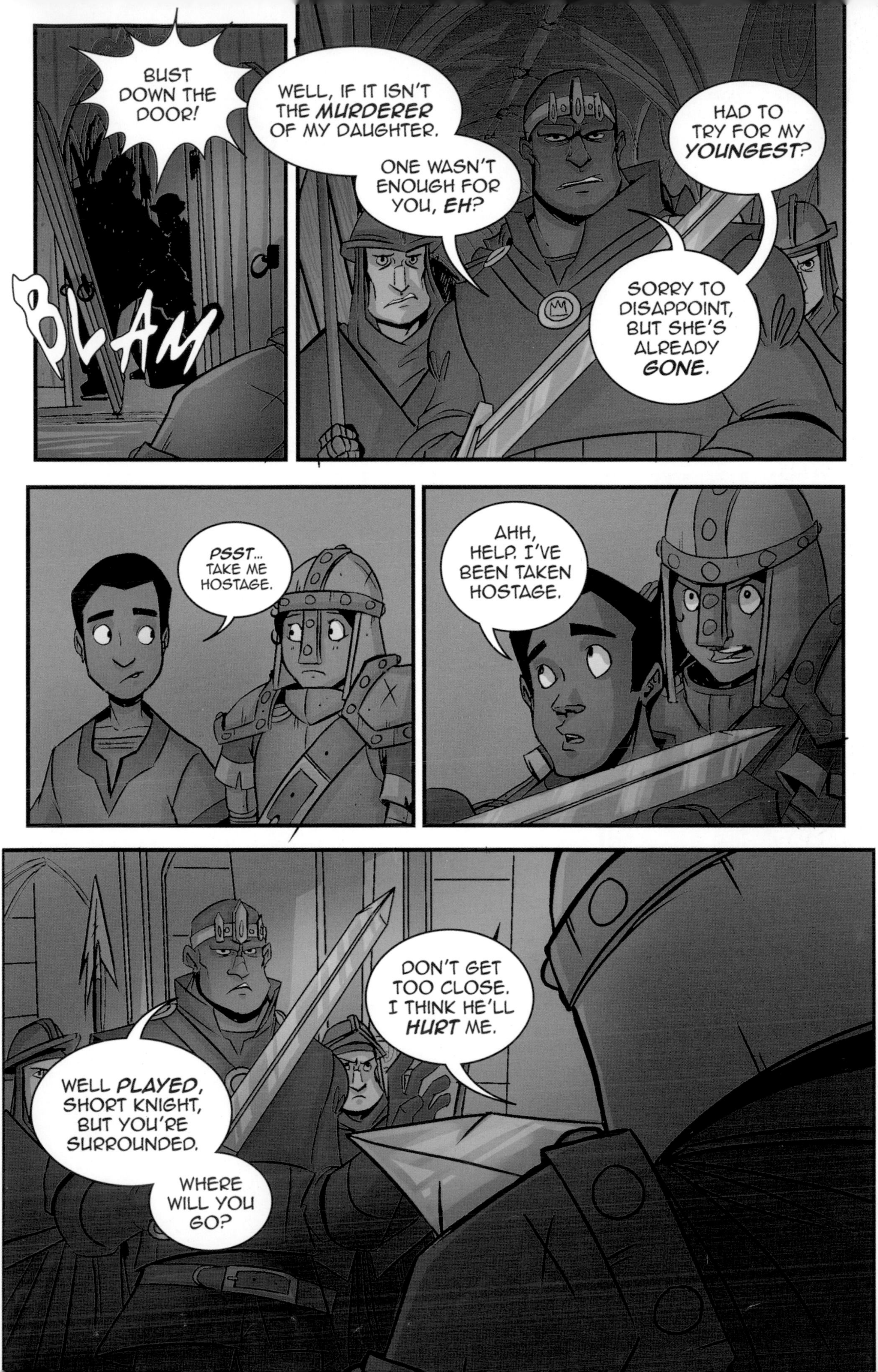
BUST DOWN THE DOOR!
BLAM
WELL, IF IT ISN'T THE MURDERER OF MY DAUGHTER.
ONE WASN'T ENOUGH FOR YOU, EH?
HAD TO TRY FOR MY YOUNGEST?
SORRY TO DISAPPOINT, BUT SHE'S ALREADY GONE.
PSST... TAKE ME HOSTAGE.
AHH, HELP. I'VE BEEN TAKEN HOSTAGE.
DON'T GET TOO CLOSE. I THINK HE'LL HURT ME.
WELL PLAYED, SHORT KNIGHT, BUT YOU'RE SURROUNDED.
WHERE WILL YOU GO?

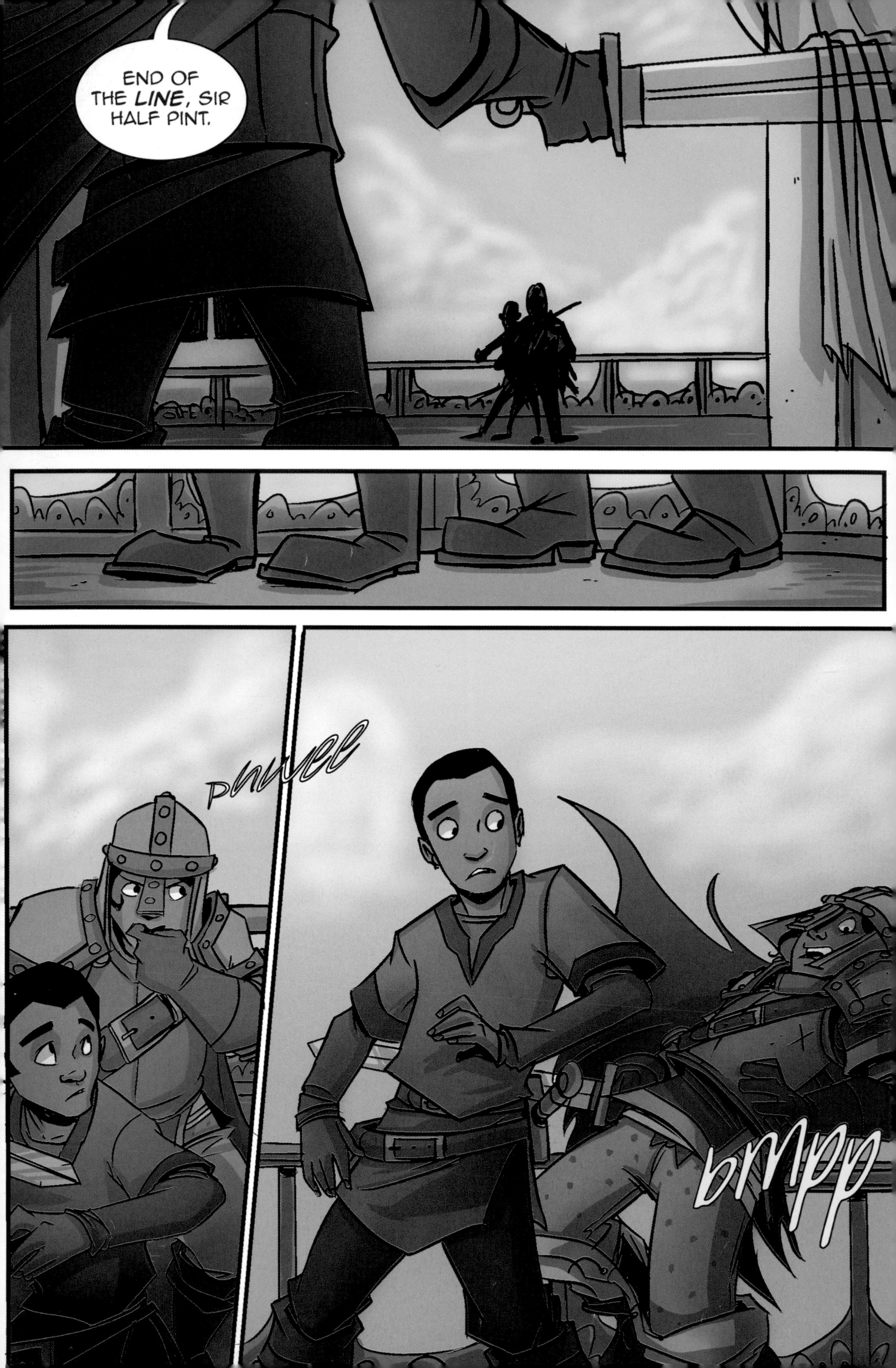
END OF THE LINE, SIR HALF PINT.
phweel
brnpp

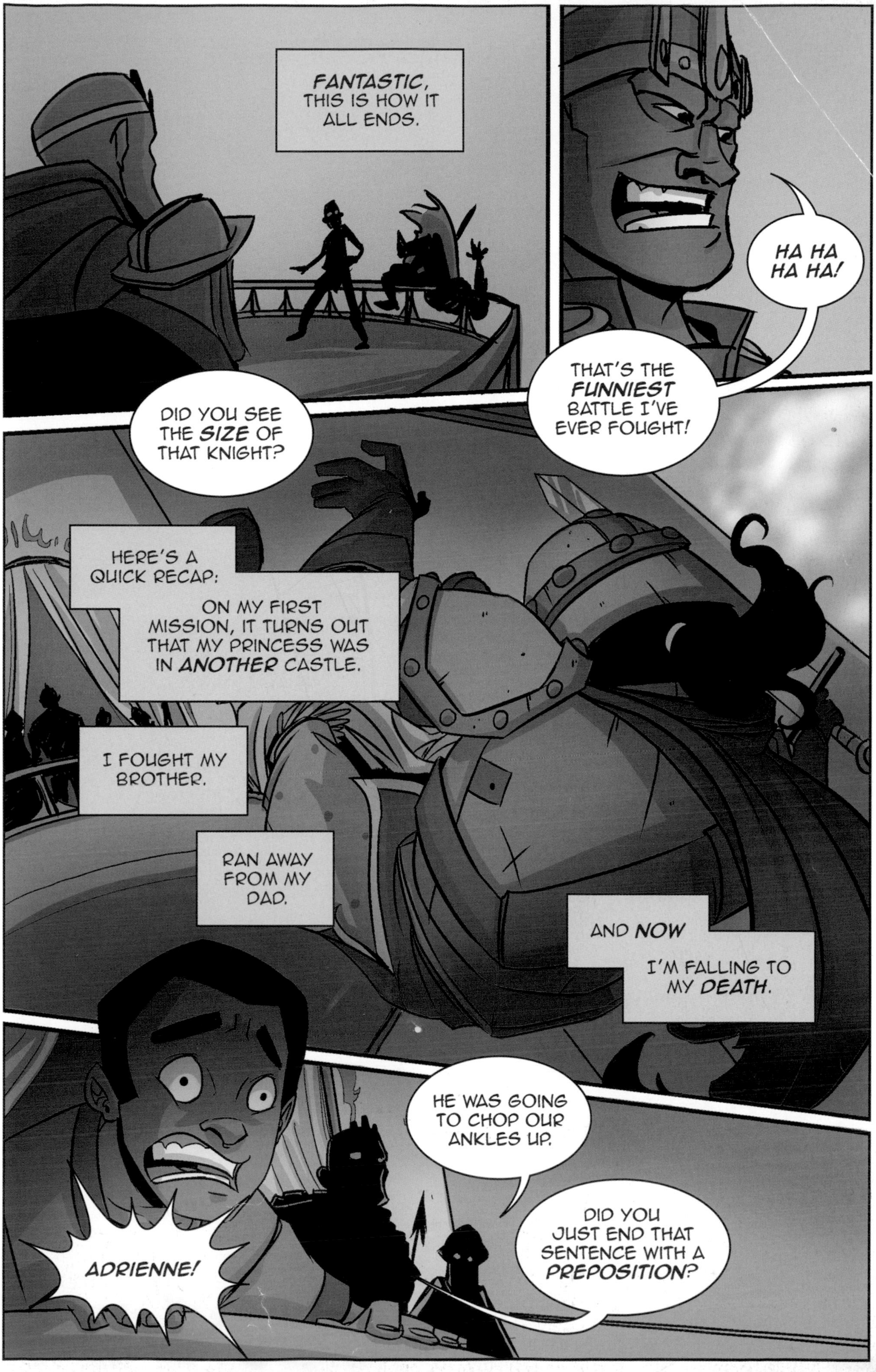

FANTASTIC, THIS IS HOW IT ALL ENDS.
HA HA HA HA!
THAT'S THE ***FUNNIEST*** BATTLE I'VE EVER FOUGHT!
DID YOU SEE THE ***SIZE*** OF THAT KNIGHT?
HERE'S A QUICK RECAP:
ON MY FIRST MISSION, IT TURNS OUT THAT MY PRINCESS WAS IN ***ANOTHER*** CASTLE.
I FOUGHT MY BROTHER.
RAN AWAY FROM MY DAD.
AND ***NOW***
I'M FALLING TO MY ***DEATH***.
ADRIENNE!
HE WAS GOING TO CHOP OUR ANKLES UP.
DID YOU JUST END THAT SENTENCE WITH A ***PREPOSITION***?

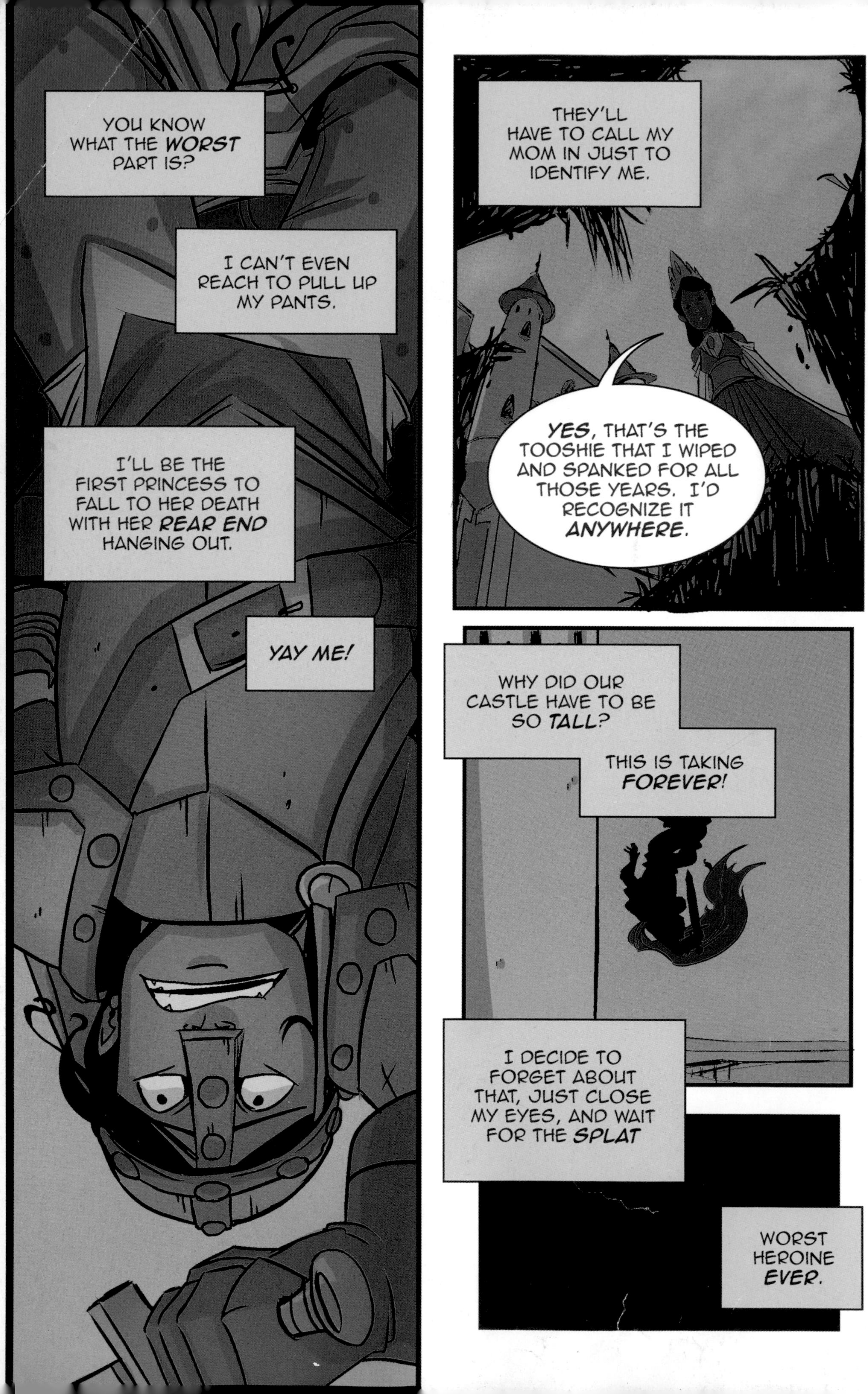
YOU KNOW WHAT THE *WORST* PART IS?
I CAN'T EVEN REACH TO PULL UP MY PANTS.
I'LL BE THE FIRST PRINCESS TO FALL TO HER DEATH WITH HER *REAR END* HANGING OUT.
YAY ME!
THEY'LL HAVE TO CALL MY MOM IN JUST TO IDENTIFY ME.
YES, THAT'S THE TOOSHIE THAT I WIPED AND SPANKED FOR ALL THOSE YEARS. I'D RECOGNIZE IT *ANYWHERE*.
WHY DID OUR CASTLE HAVE TO BE SO *TALL*?
THIS IS TAKING *FOREVER*!
I DECIDE TO FORGET ABOUT THAT, JUST CLOSE MY EYES, AND WAIT FOR THE *SPLAT*
WORST HEROINE *EVER*.

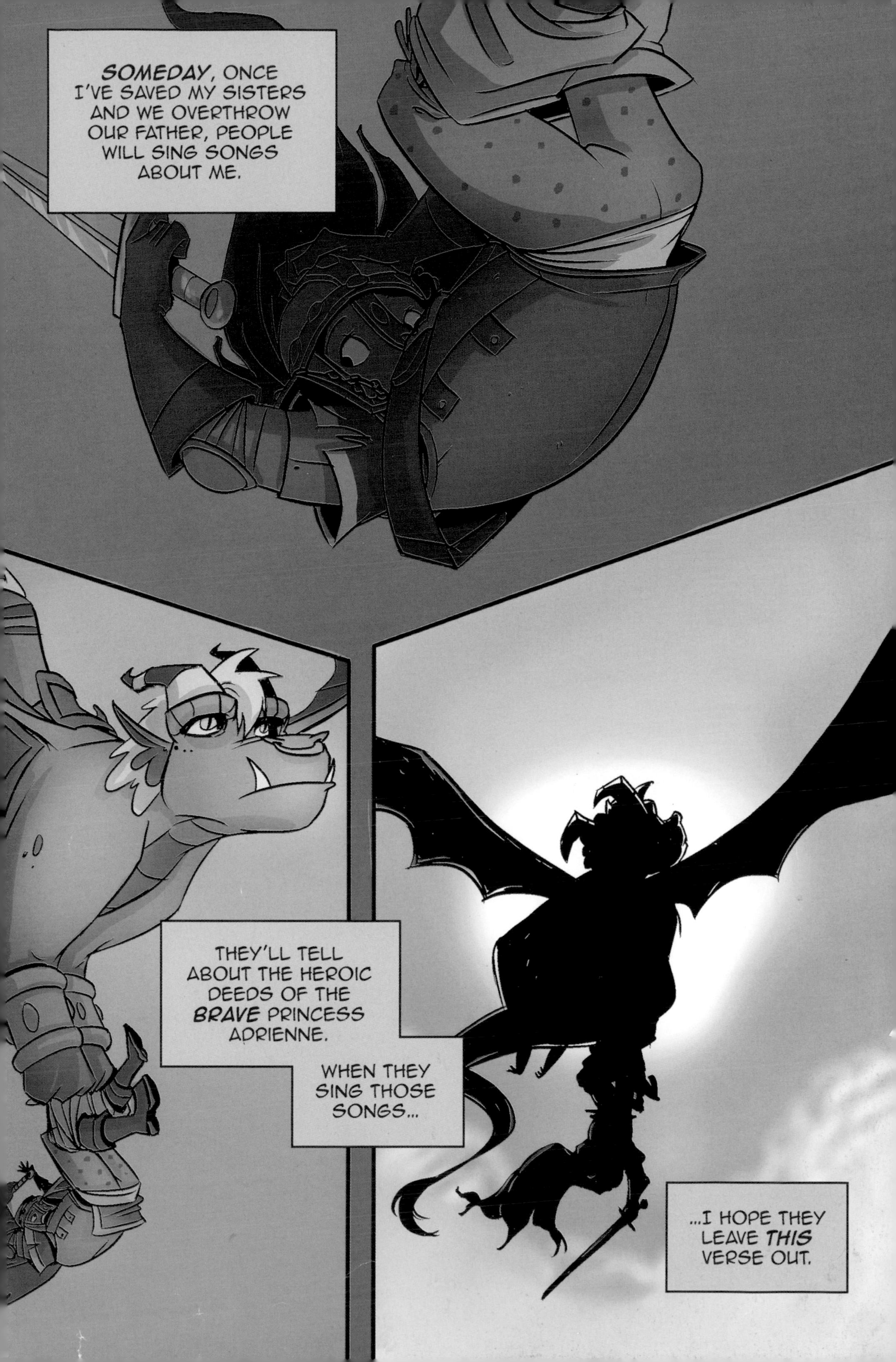
SOMEDAY, ONCE I'VE SAVED MY SISTERS AND WE OVERTHROW OUR FATHER, PEOPLE WILL SING SONGS ABOUT ME.
THEY'LL TELL ABOUT THE HEROIC DEEDS OF THE BRAVE PRINCESS ADRIENNE.
WHEN THEY SING THOSE SONGS...
...I HOPE THEY LEAVE THIS VERSE OUT.

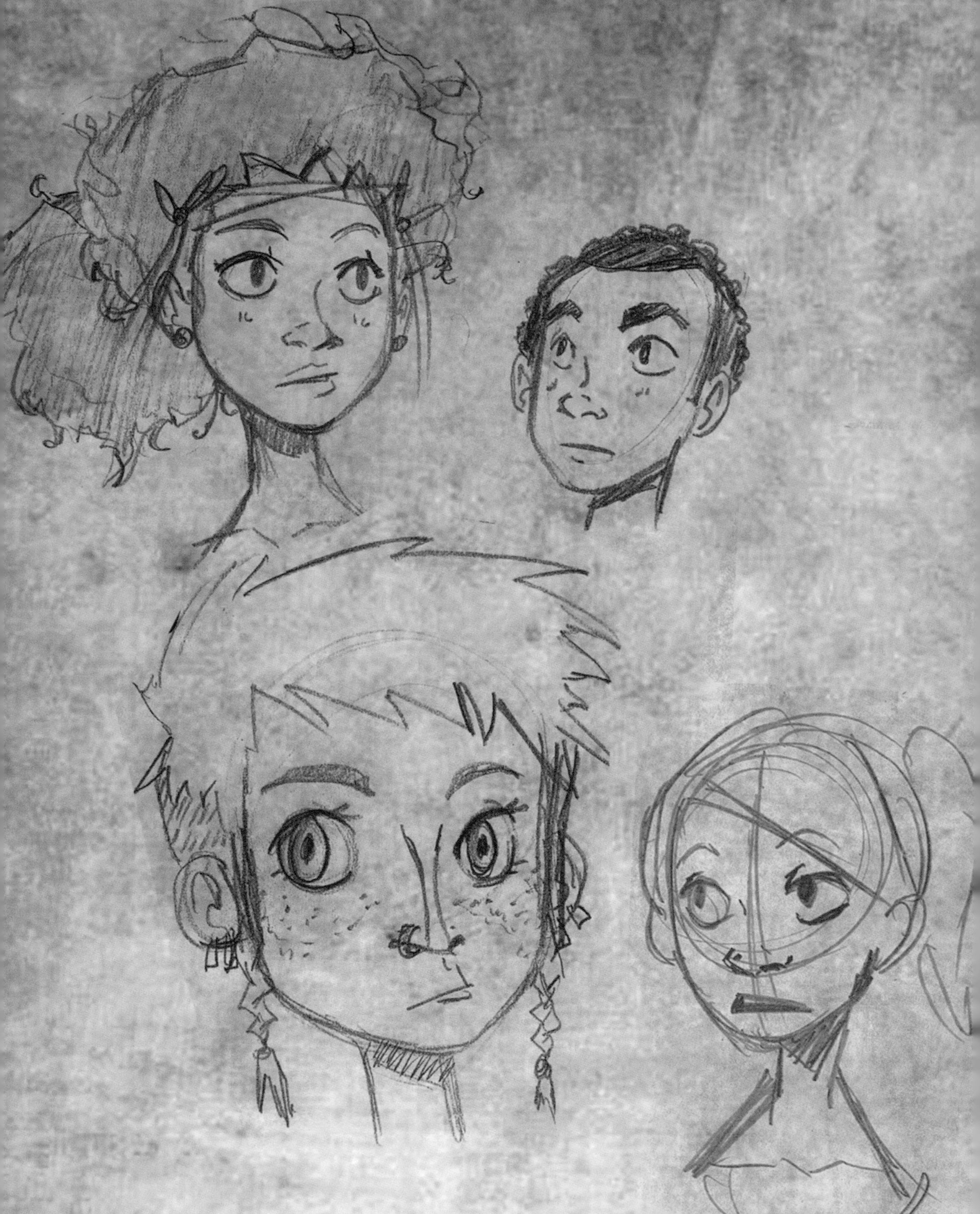

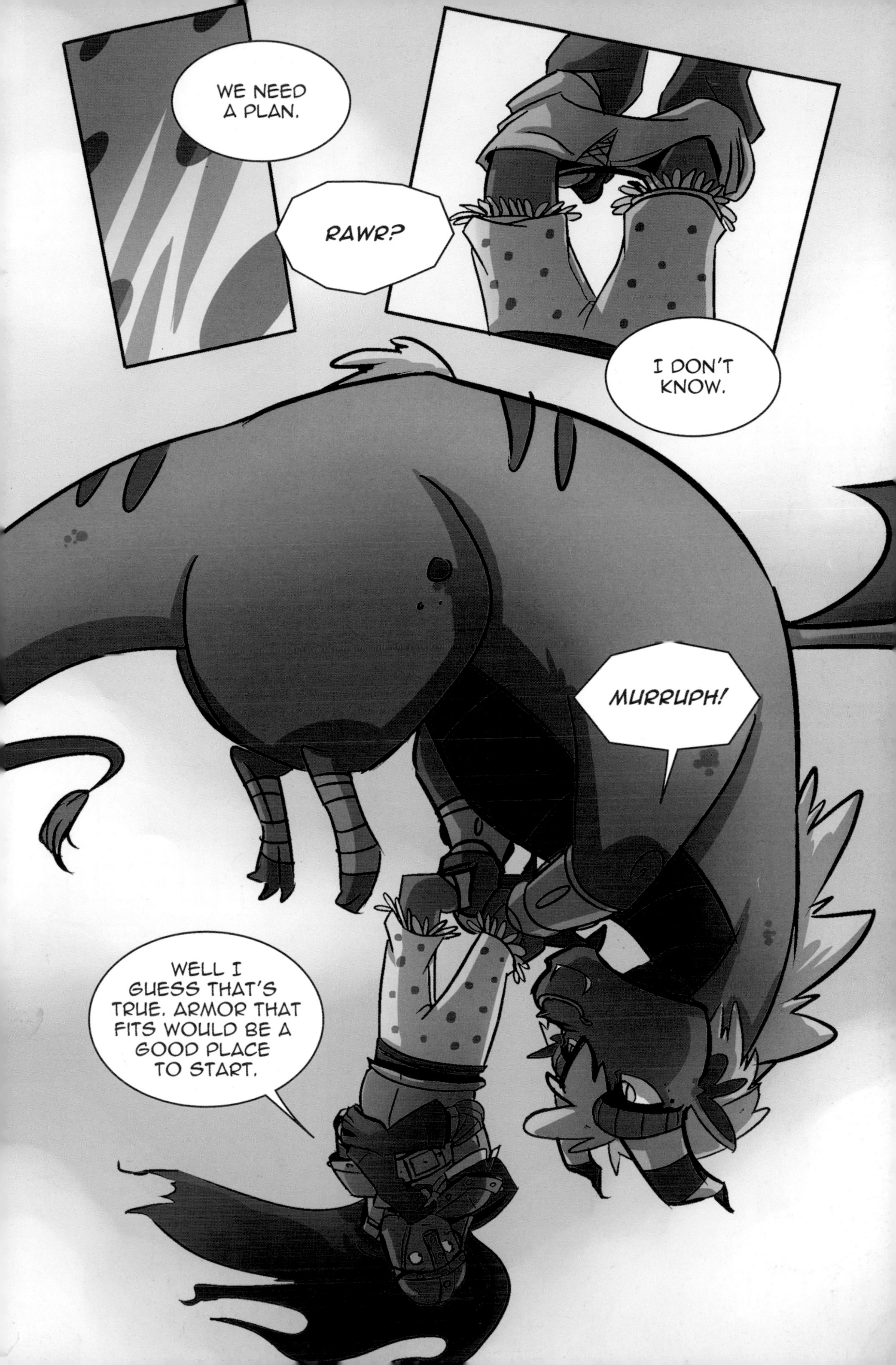
WE NEED A PLAN.
RAWR?
I DON'T KNOW.
MURRUPH!
WELL I GUESS THAT'S TRUE. ARMOR THAT FITS WOULD BE A GOOD PLACE TO START.

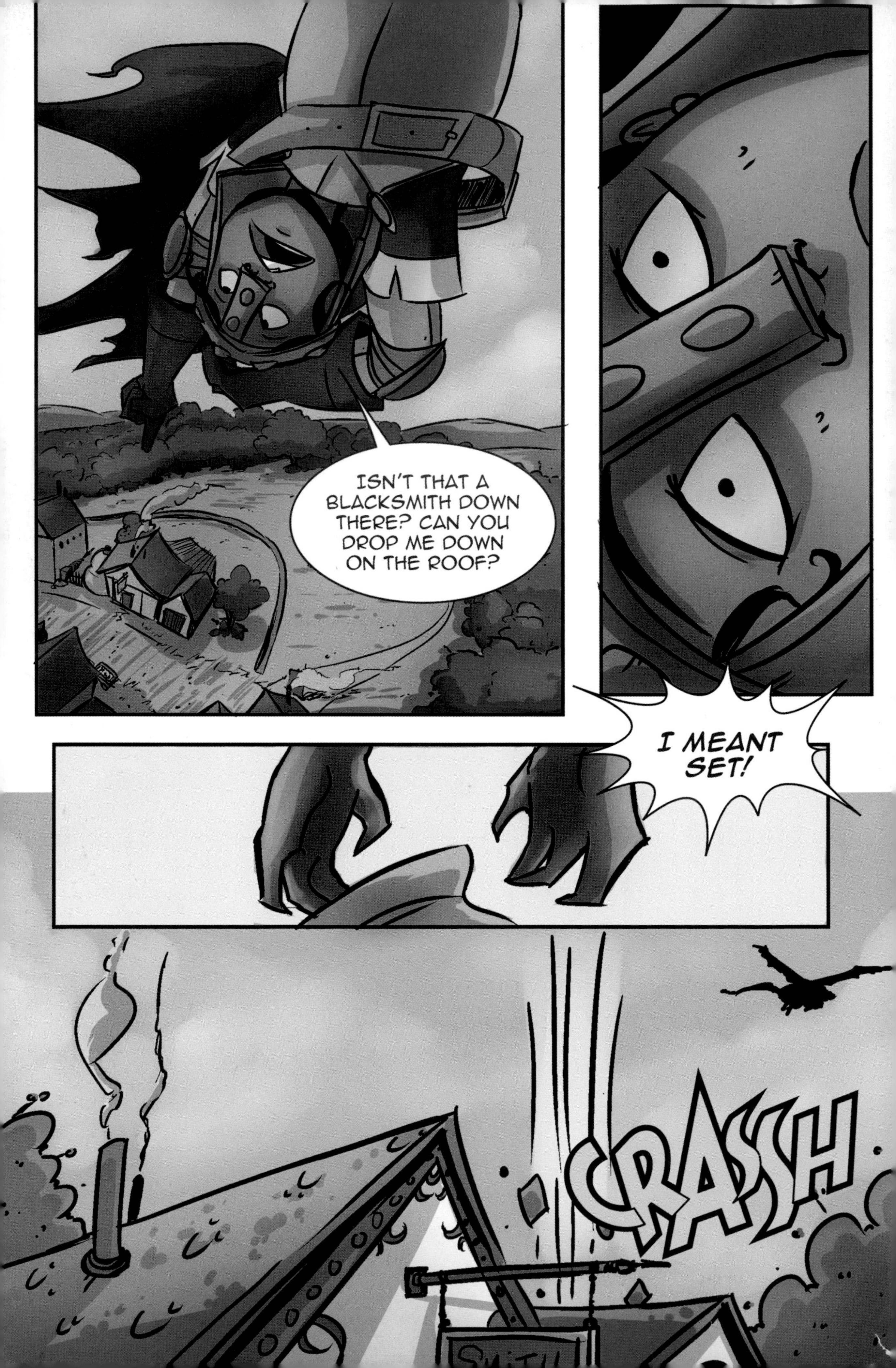
ISN'T THAT A BLACKSMITH DOWN THERE? CAN YOU DROP ME DOWN ON THE ROOF?
I MEANT SET!
CRASH

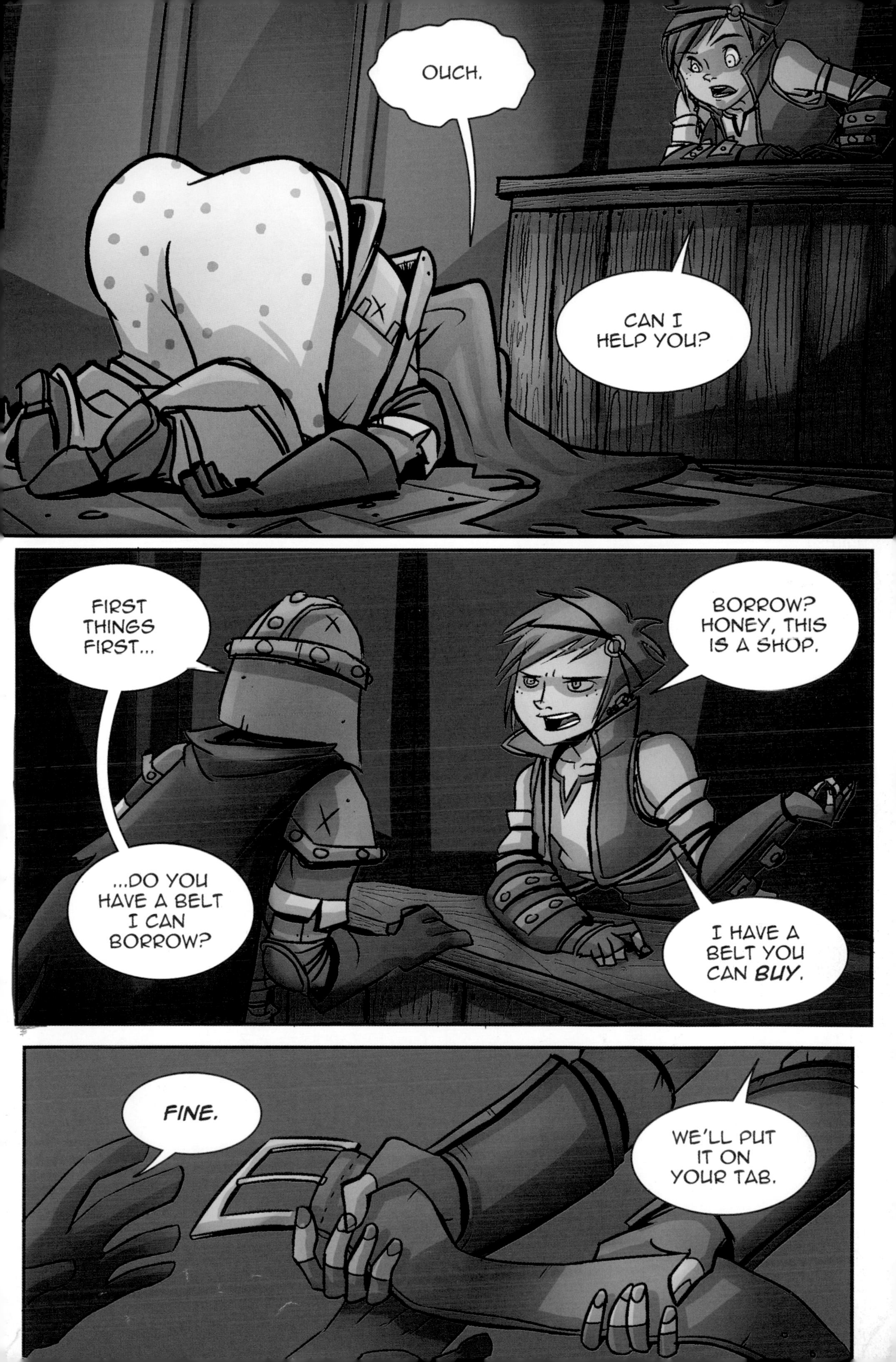
OUCH.
CAN I HELP YOU?
FIRST THINGS FIRST...
BORROW? HONEY, THIS IS A SHOP.
...DO YOU HAVE A BELT I CAN BORROW?
I HAVE A BELT YOU CAN *BUY*.
FINE.
WE'LL PUT IT ON YOUR TAB.

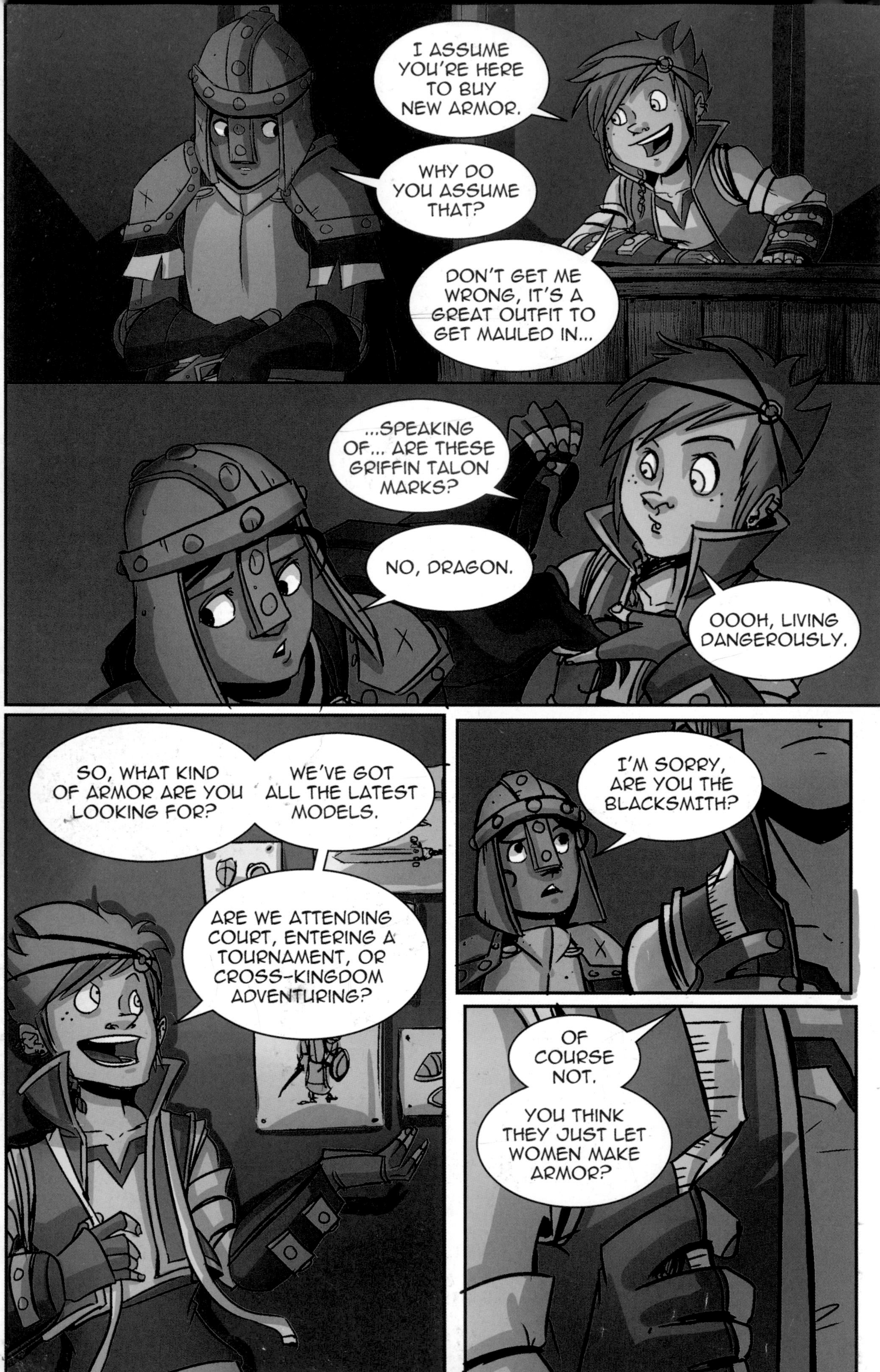
I ASSUME YOU'RE HERE TO BUY NEW ARMOR.
WHY DO YOU ASSUME THAT?
DON'T GET ME WRONG, IT'S A GREAT OUTFIT TO GET MAULED IN...
...SPEAKING OF... ARE THESE GRIFFIN TALON MARKS?
NO, DRAGON.
OOOH, LIVING DANGEROUSLY.
SO, WHAT KIND OF ARMOR ARE YOU LOOKING FOR?
WE'VE GOT ALL THE LATEST MODELS.
ARE WE ATTENDING COURT, ENTERING A TOURNAMENT, OR CROSS-KINGDOM ADVENTURING?
I'M SORRY, ARE YOU THE BLACKSMITH?
OF COURSE NOT.
YOU THINK THEY JUST LET WOMEN MAKE ARMOR?

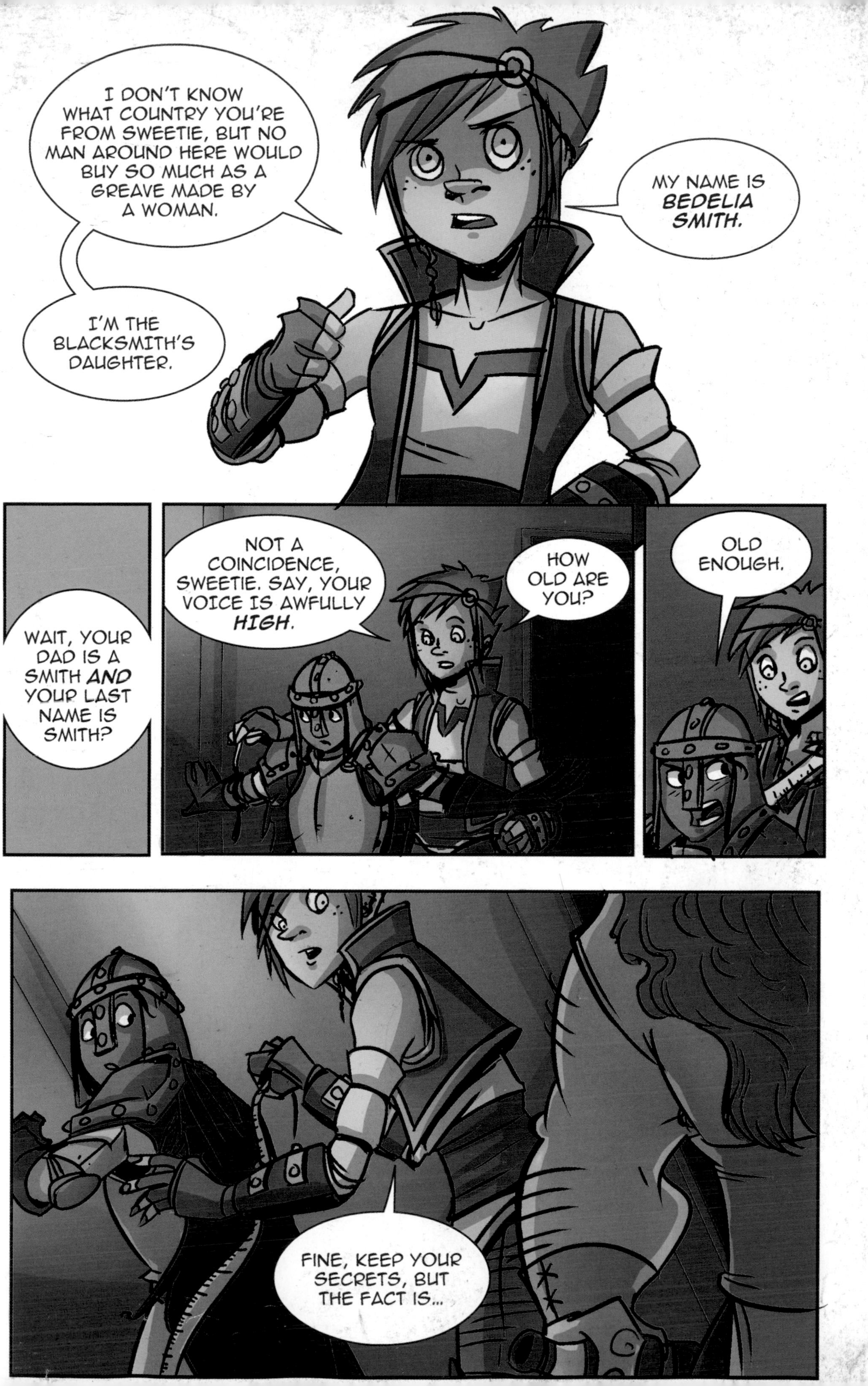
I DON'T KNOW WHAT COUNTRY YOU'RE FROM SWEETIE, BUT NO MAN AROUND HERE WOULD BUY SO MUCH AS A GREAVE MADE BY A WOMAN.
I'M THE BLACKSMITH'S DAUGHTER.
MY NAME IS BEDELIA SMITH.
WAIT, YOUR DAD IS A SMITH AND YOUR LAST NAME IS SMITH?
NOT A COINCIDENCE, SWEETIE. SAY, YOUR VOICE IS AWFULLY HIGH.
HOW OLD ARE YOU?
OLD ENOUGH.
FINE, KEEP YOUR SECRETS, BUT THE FACT IS...

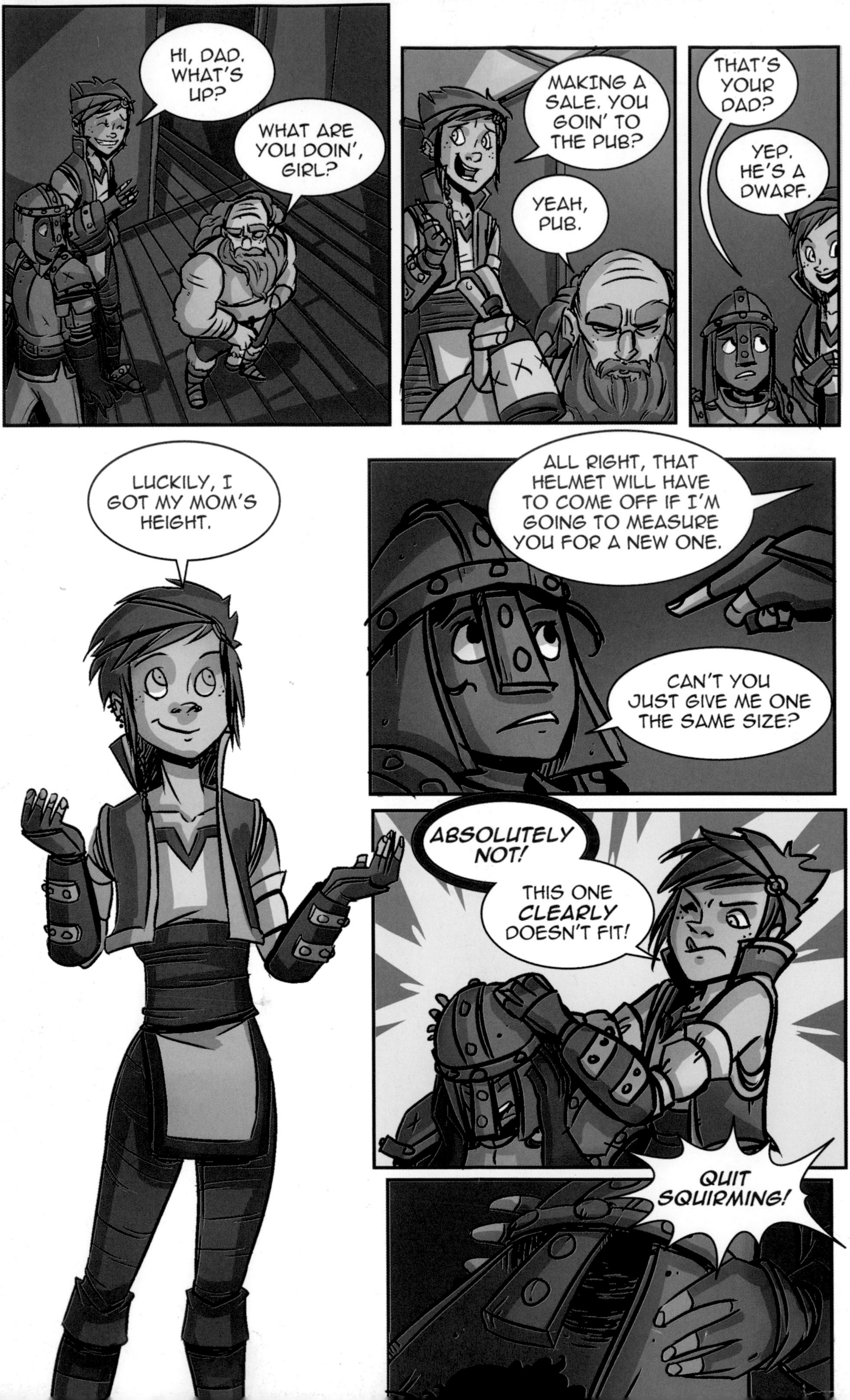
HI, DAD. WHAT'S UP?
WHAT ARE YOU DOIN', GIRL?
MAKING A SALE. YOU GOIN' TO THE PUB?
YEAH, PUB.
THAT'S YOUR DAD?
YEP. HE'S A DWARF.
LUCKILY, I GOT MY MOM'S HEIGHT.
ALL RIGHT, THAT HELMET WILL HAVE TO COME OFF IF I'M GOING TO MEASURE YOU FOR A NEW ONE.
CAN'T YOU JUST GIVE ME ONE THE SAME SIZE?
ABSOLUTELY NOT!
THIS ONE CLEARLY DOESN'T FIT!
QUIT SQUIRMING!

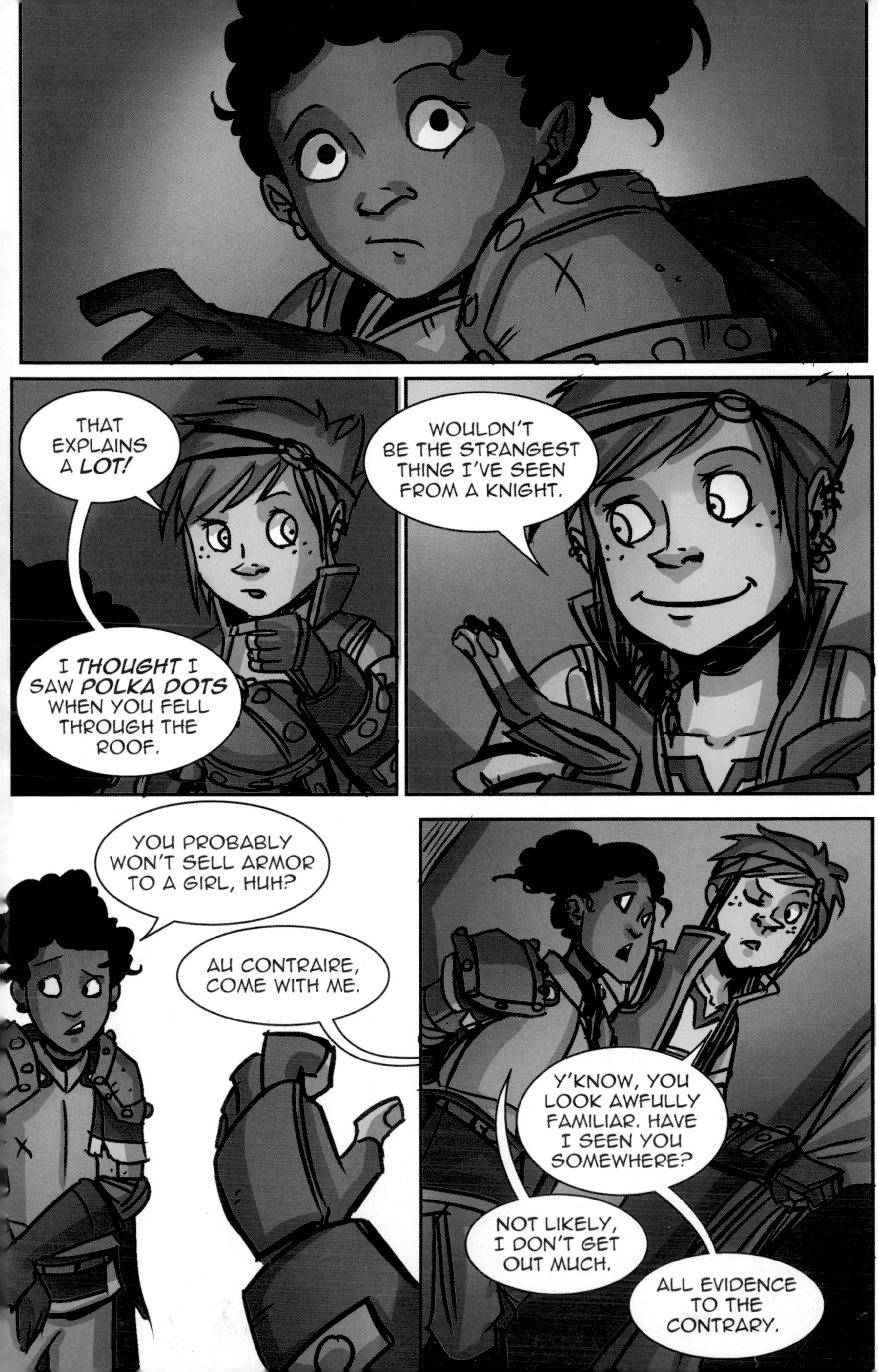
THAT EXPLAINS A *LOT!*
I *THOUGHT* I SAW *POLKA DOTS* WHEN YOU FELL THROUGH THE ROOF.
WOULDN'T BE THE STRANGEST THING I'VE SEEN FROM A KNIGHT.
YOU PROBABLY WON'T SELL ARMOR TO A GIRL, HUH?
AU CONTRAIRE, COME WITH ME.
Y'KNOW, YOU LOOK AWFULLY FAMILIAR. HAVE I SEEN YOU SOMEWHERE?
NOT LIKELY, I DON'T GET OUT MUCH.
ALL EVIDENCE TO THE CONTRARY.

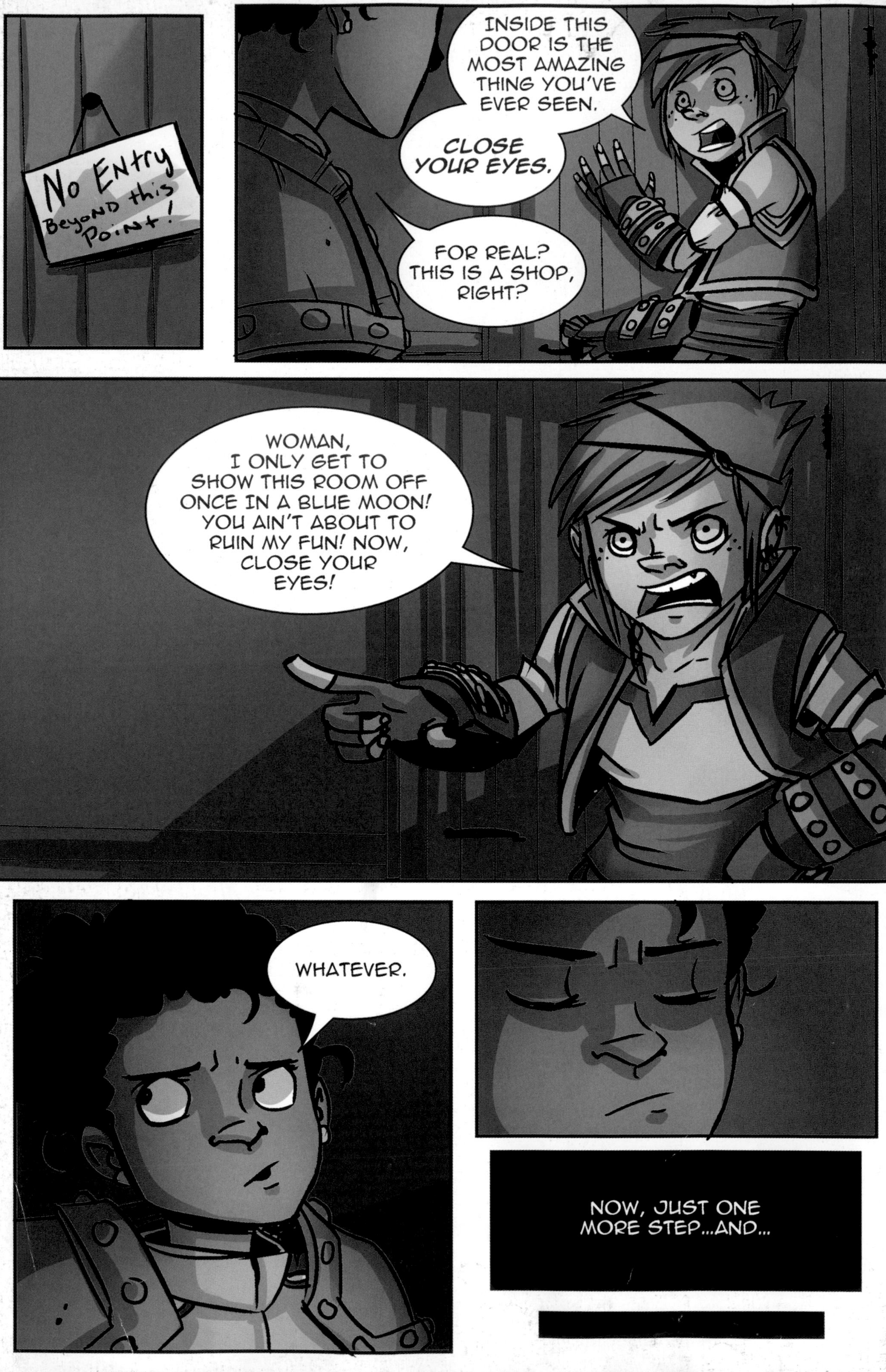
No Entry Beyond this Point!
INSIDE THIS DOOR IS THE MOST AMAZING THING YOU'VE EVER SEEN.
CLOSE YOUR EYES.
FOR REAL? THIS IS A SHOP, RIGHT?
WOMAN, I ONLY GET TO SHOW THIS ROOM OFF ONCE IN A BLUE MOON! YOU AIN'T ABOUT TO RUIN MY FUN! NOW, CLOSE YOUR EYES!
WHATEVER.
NOW, JUST ONE MORE STEP...AND...

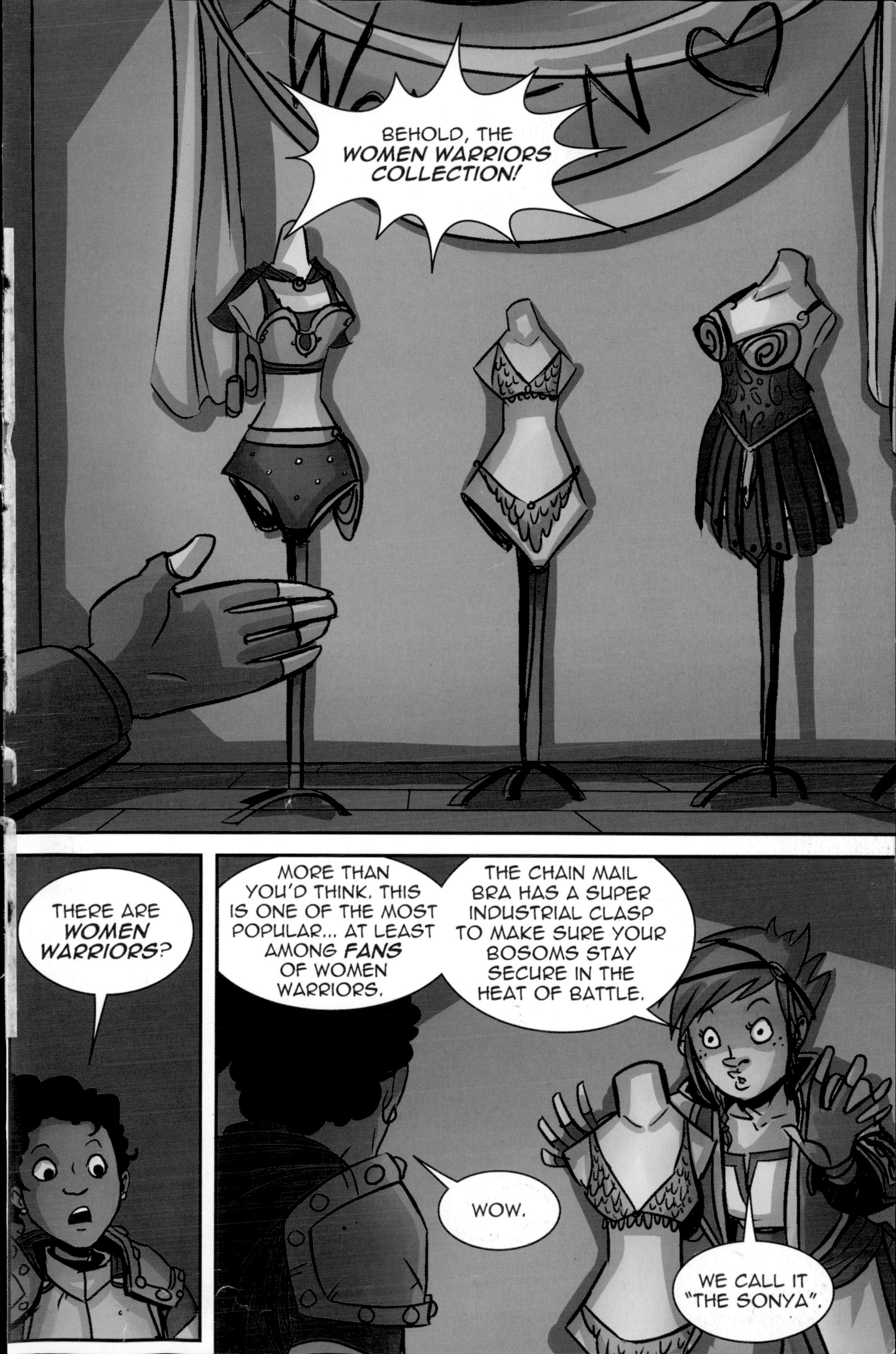
BEHOLD, THE *WOMEN WARRIORS* COLLECTION!
THERE ARE *WOMEN WARRIORS*?
MORE THAN YOU'D THINK. THIS IS ONE OF THE MOST POPULAR... AT LEAST AMONG *FANS* OF WOMEN WARRIORS.
THE CHAIN MAIL BRA HAS A SUPER INDUSTRIAL CLASP TO MAKE SURE YOUR BOSOMS STAY SECURE IN THE HEAT OF BATTLE.
WOW.
WE CALL IT "THE SONYA".

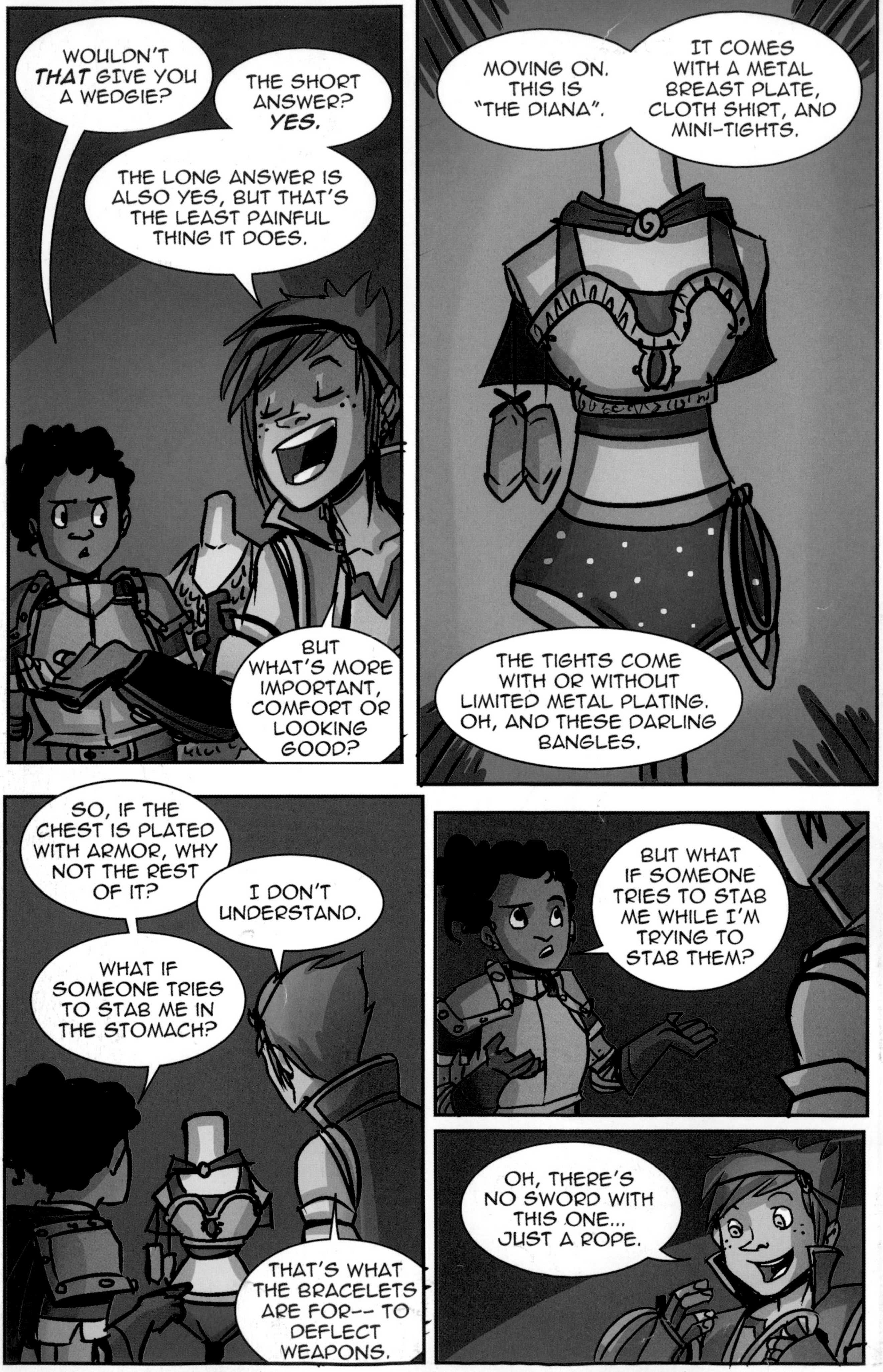
WOULDN'T *THAT* GIVE YOU A WEDGIE?
THE SHORT ANSWER? *YES.*
THE LONG ANSWER IS ALSO YES, BUT THAT'S THE LEAST PAINFUL THING IT DOES.
BUT WHAT'S MORE IMPORTANT, COMFORT OR LOOKING GOOD?
MOVING ON. THIS IS "THE DIANA".
IT COMES WITH A METAL BREAST PLATE, CLOTH SHIRT, AND MINI-TIGHTS.
THE TIGHTS COME WITH OR WITHOUT LIMITED METAL PLATING. OH, AND THESE DARLING BANGLES.
SO, IF THE CHEST IS PLATED WITH ARMOR, WHY NOT THE REST OF IT?
I DON'T UNDERSTAND.
WHAT IF SOMEONE TRIES TO STAB ME IN THE STOMACH?
THAT'S WHAT THE BRACELETS ARE FOR-- TO DEFLECT WEAPONS.
BUT WHAT IF SOMEONE TRIES TO STAB ME WHILE I'M TRYING TO STAB THEM?
OH, THERE'S NO SWORD WITH THIS ONE... JUST A ROPE.

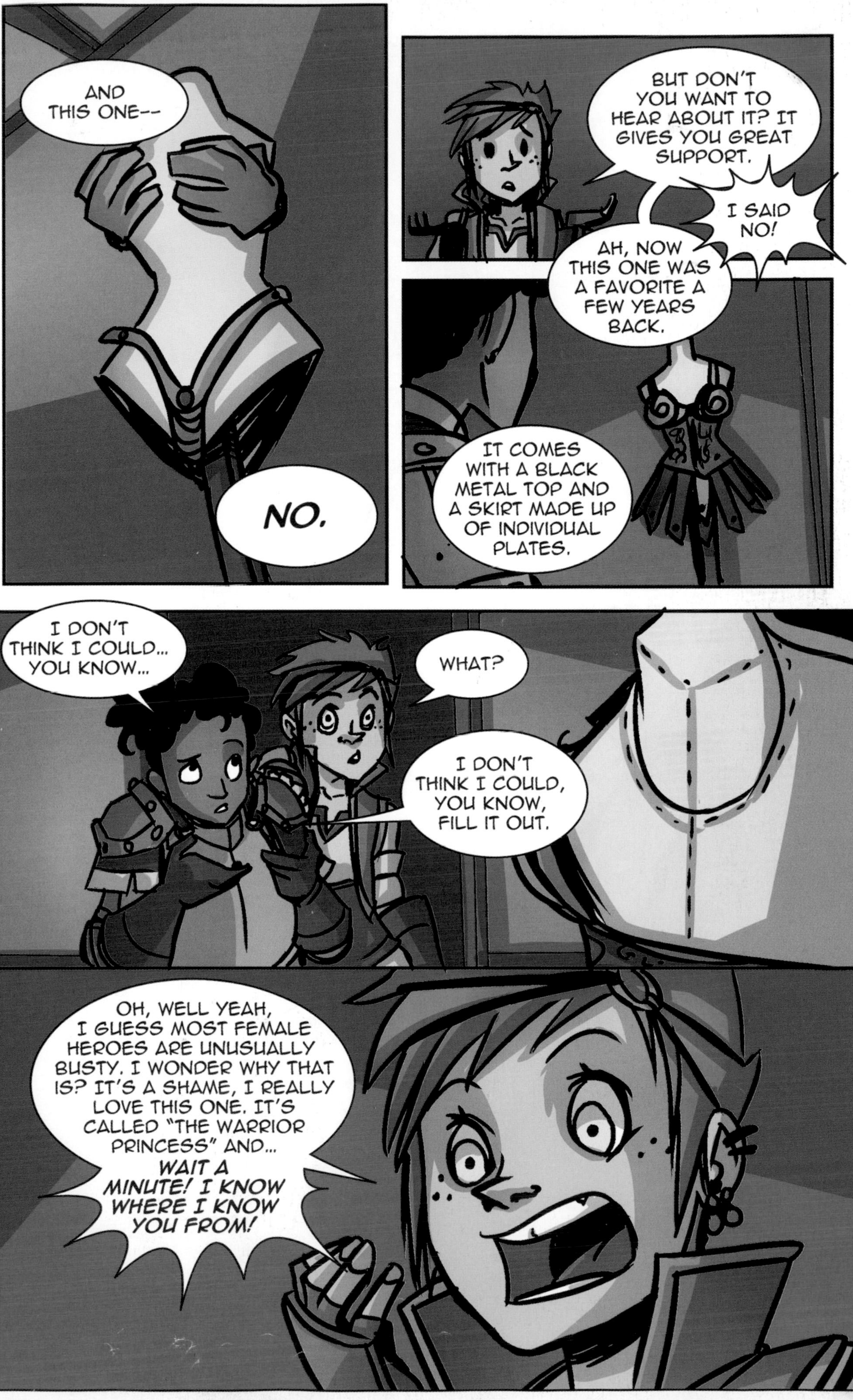
AND THIS ONE--
NO.
BUT DON'T YOU WANT TO HEAR ABOUT IT? IT GIVES YOU GREAT SUPPORT.
I SAID NO!
AH, NOW THIS ONE WAS A FAVORITE A FEW YEARS BACK.
IT COMES WITH A BLACK METAL TOP AND A SKIRT MADE UP OF INDIVIDUAL PLATES.
I DON'T THINK I COULD... YOU KNOW...
WHAT?
I DON'T THINK I COULD, YOU KNOW, FILL IT OUT.
OH, WELL YEAH, I GUESS MOST FEMALE HEROES ARE UNUSUALLY BUSTY. I WONDER WHY THAT IS? IT'S A SHAME, I REALLY LOVE THIS ONE. IT'S CALLED "THE WARRIOR PRINCESS" AND... *WAIT A MINUTE! I KNOW WHERE I KNOW YOU FROM!*

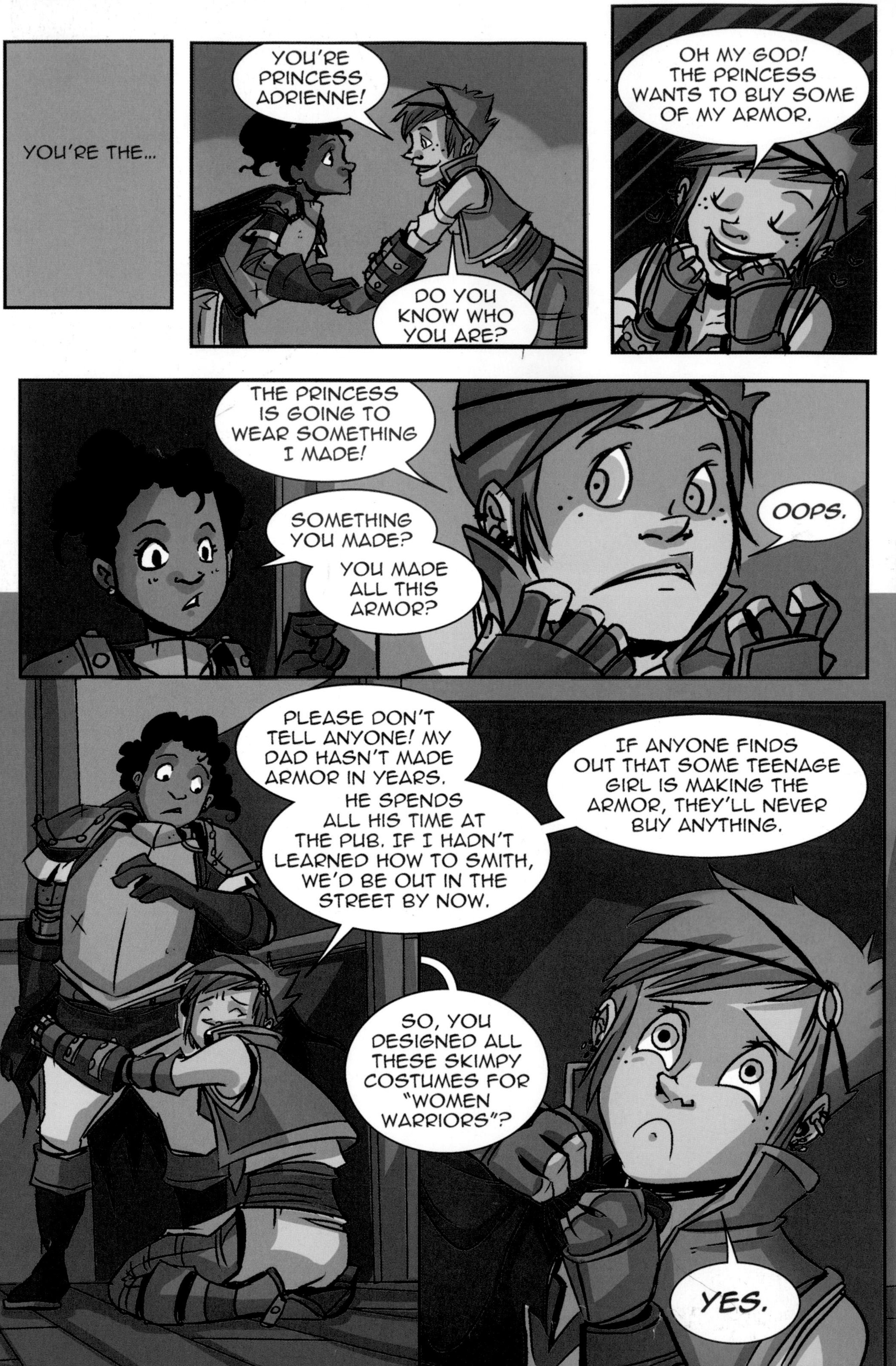
YOU'RE THE...
YOU'RE PRINCESS ADRIENNE!
DO YOU KNOW WHO YOU ARE?
OH MY GOD! THE PRINCESS WANTS TO BUY SOME OF MY ARMOR.
THE PRINCESS IS GOING TO WEAR SOMETHING I MADE!
SOMETHING YOU MADE?
YOU MADE ALL THIS ARMOR?
OOPS.
PLEASE DON'T TELL ANYONE! MY DAD HASN'T MADE ARMOR IN YEARS.
HE SPENDS ALL HIS TIME AT THE PUB. IF I HADN'T LEARNED HOW TO SMITH, WE'D BE OUT IN THE STREET BY NOW.
IF ANYONE FINDS OUT THAT SOME TEENAGE GIRL IS MAKING THE ARMOR, THEY'LL NEVER BUY ANYTHING.
SO, YOU DESIGNED ALL THESE SKIMPY COSTUMES FOR "WOMEN WARRIORS"?
YES.

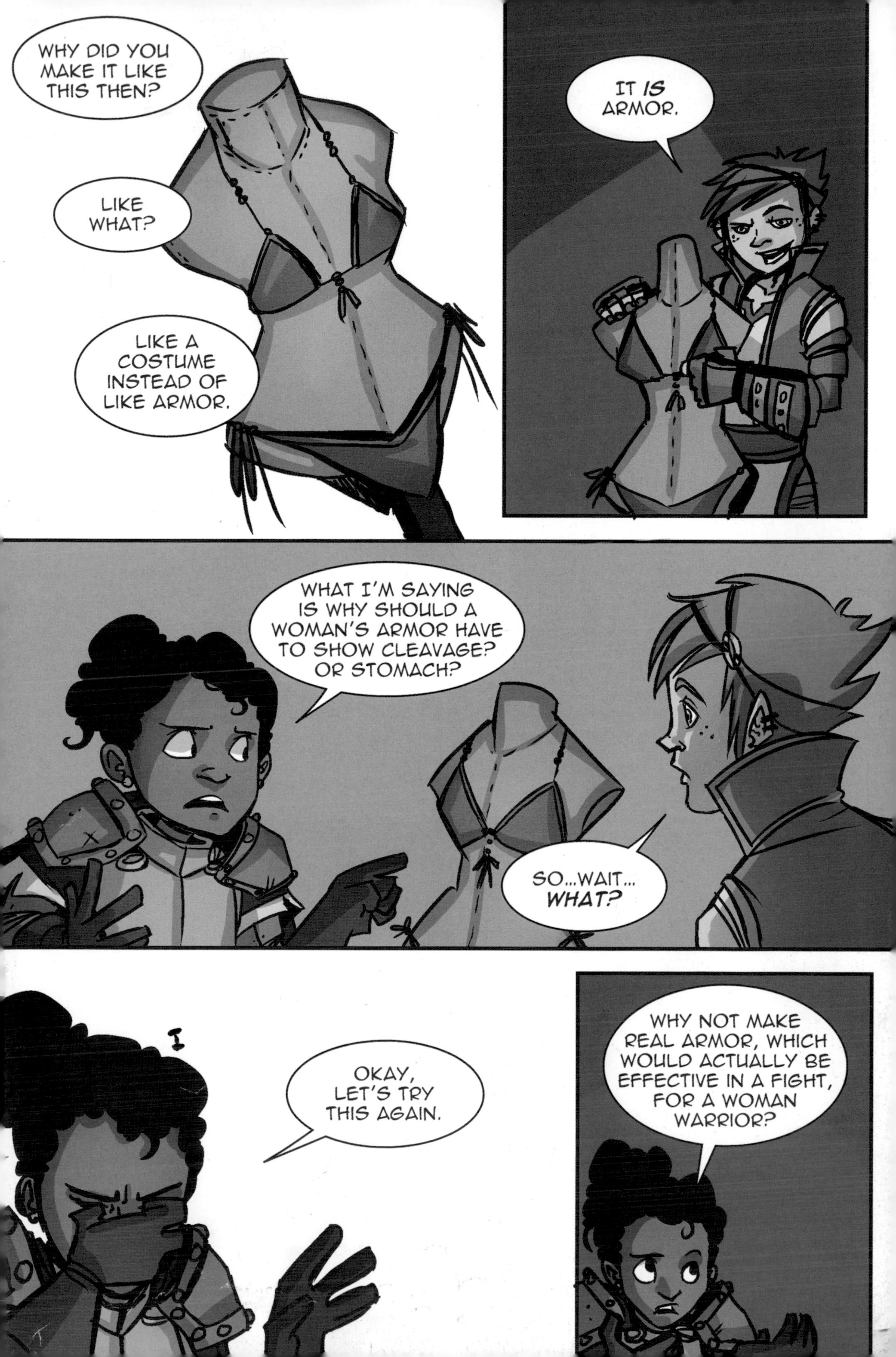
WHY DID YOU MAKE IT LIKE THIS THEN?
LIKE WHAT?
LIKE A COSTUME INSTEAD OF LIKE ARMOR.
IT *IS* ARMOR.
WHAT I'M SAYING IS WHY SHOULD A WOMAN'S ARMOR HAVE TO SHOW CLEAVAGE? OR STOMACH?
SO...WAIT... *WHAT?*
OKAY, LET'S TRY THIS AGAIN.
WHY NOT MAKE REAL ARMOR, WHICH WOULD ACTUALLY BE EFFECTIVE IN A FIGHT, FOR A WOMAN WARRIOR?

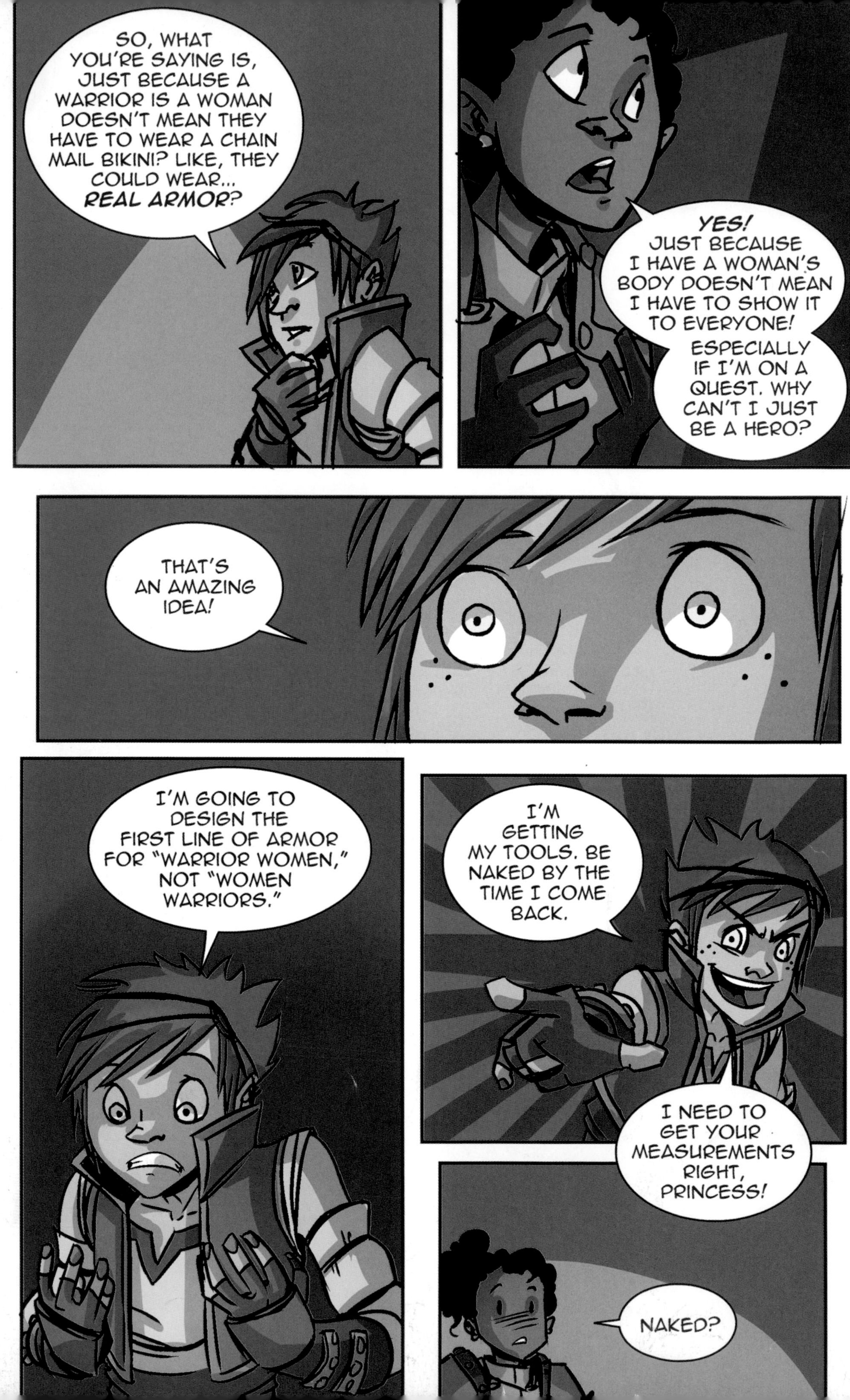
SO, WHAT YOU'RE SAYING IS, JUST BECAUSE A WARRIOR IS A WOMAN DOESN'T MEAN THEY HAVE TO WEAR A CHAIN MAIL BIKINI? LIKE, THEY COULD WEAR... REAL ARMOR?
YES! JUST BECAUSE I HAVE A WOMAN'S BODY DOESN'T MEAN I HAVE TO SHOW IT TO EVERYONE!
ESPECIALLY IF I'M ON A QUEST. WHY CAN'T I JUST BE A HERO?
THAT'S AN AMAZING IDEA!
I'M GOING TO DESIGN THE FIRST LINE OF ARMOR FOR "WARRIOR WOMEN," NOT "WOMEN WARRIORS."
I'M GETTING MY TOOLS. BE NAKED BY THE TIME I COME BACK.
I NEED TO GET YOUR MEASUREMENTS RIGHT, PRINCESS!
NAKED?

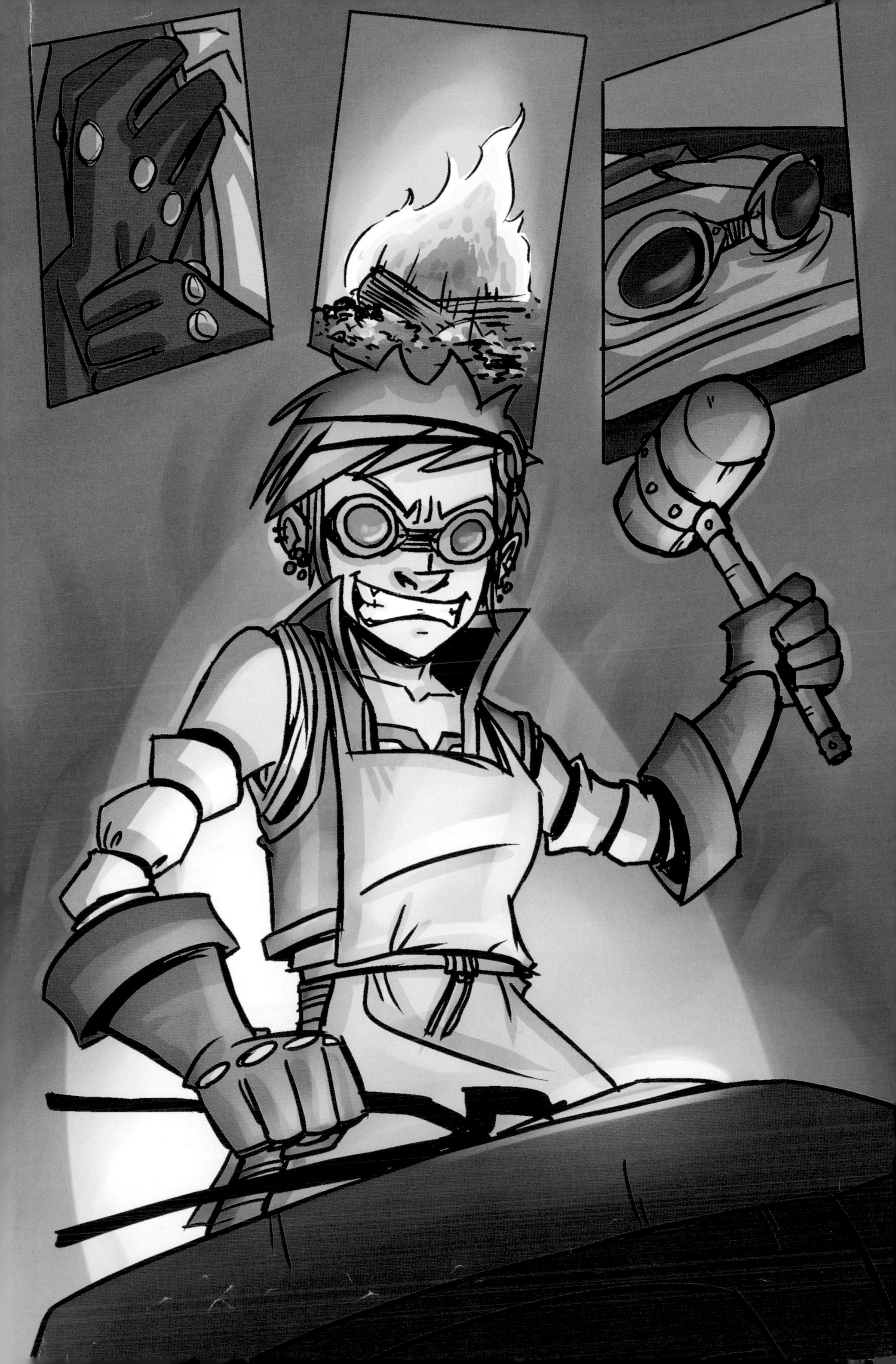

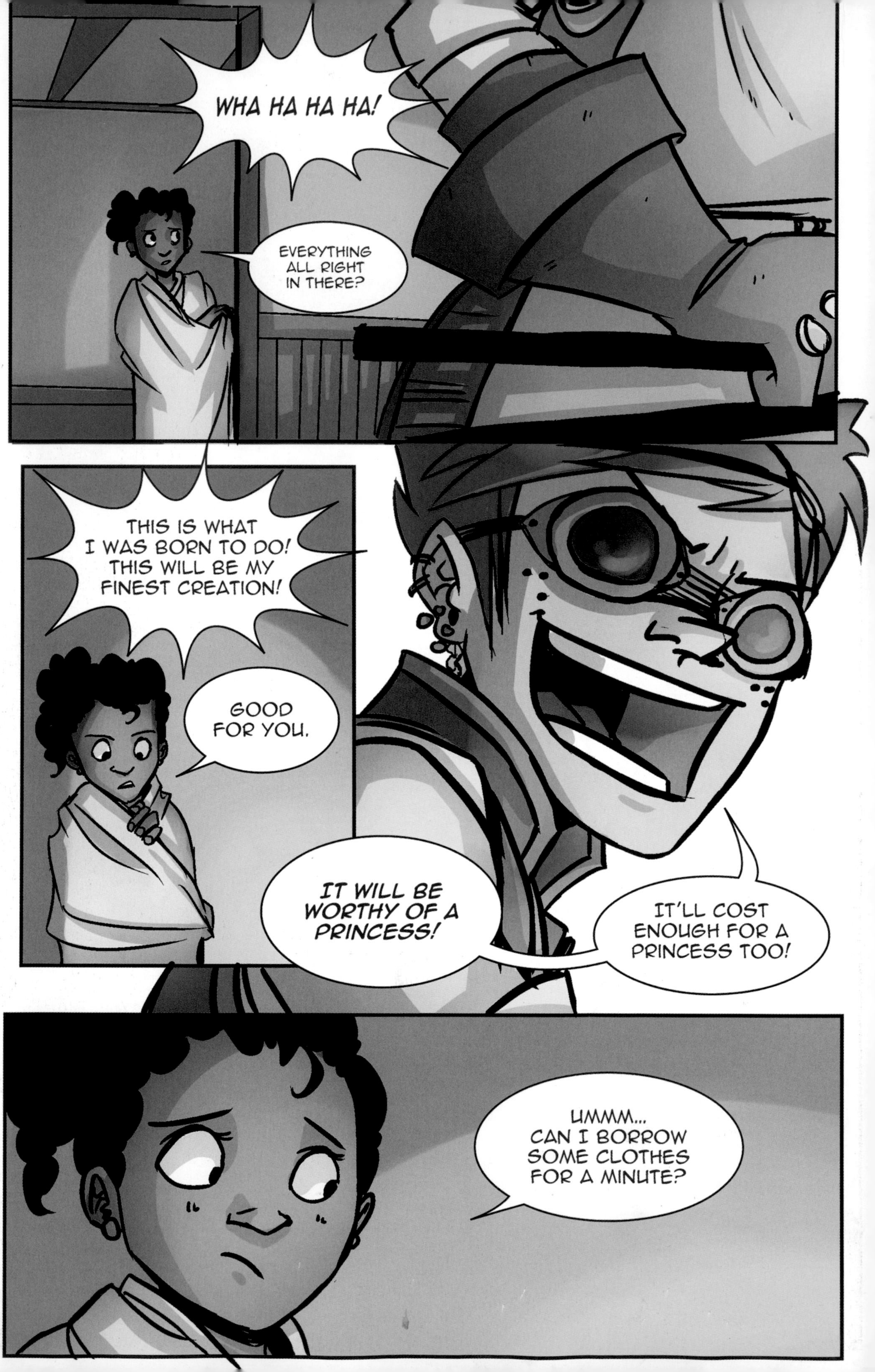
WHA HA HA HA!
EVERYTHING ALL RIGHT IN THERE?
THIS IS WHAT I WAS BORN TO DO! THIS WILL BE MY FINEST CREATION!
GOOD FOR YOU.
IT WILL BE WORTHY OF A PRINCESS!
IT'LL COST ENOUGH FOR A PRINCESS TOO!
UMMM... CAN I BORROW SOME CLOTHES FOR A MINUTE?

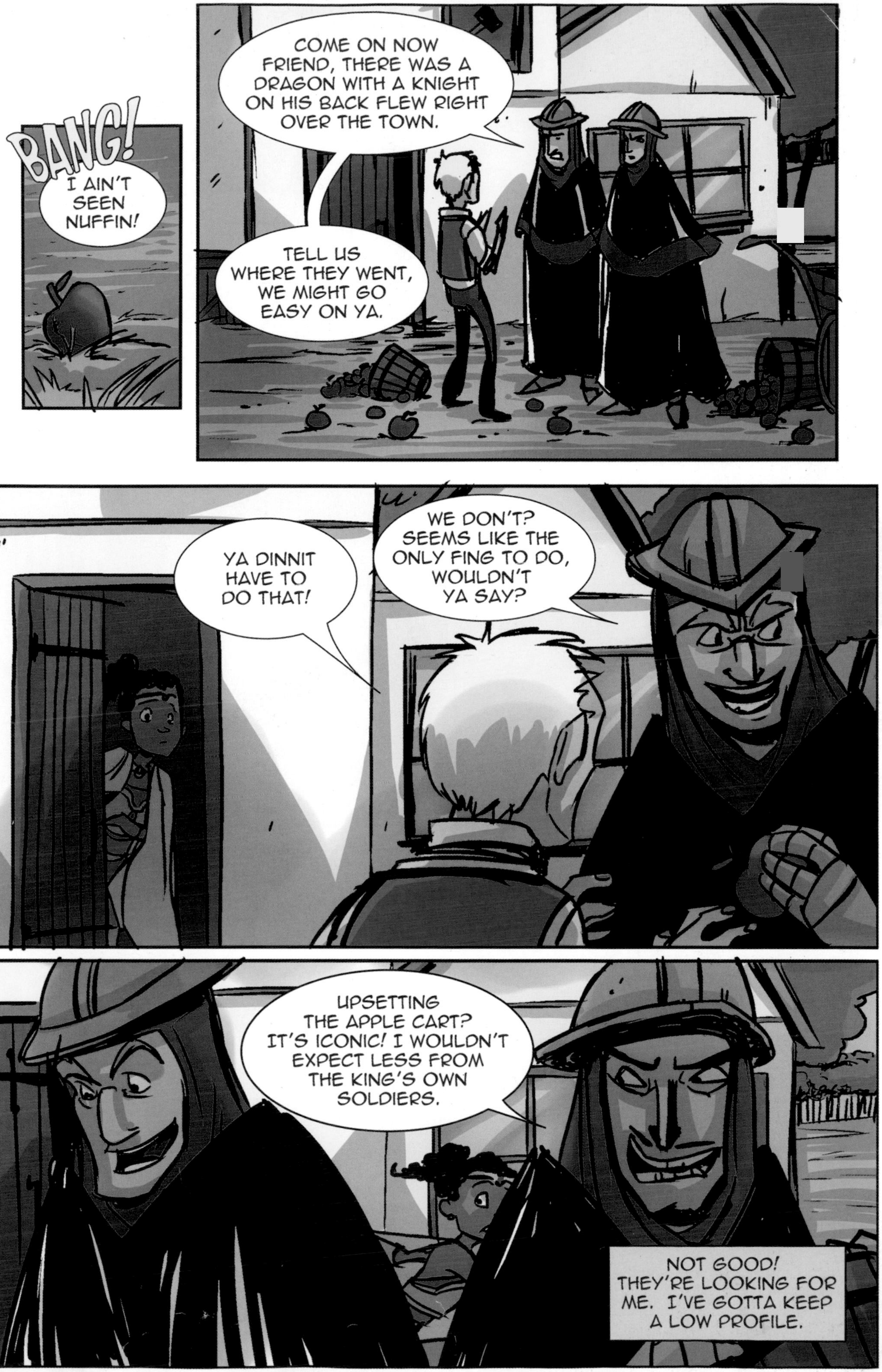
BANG!
I AIN'T SEEN NUFFIN!
COME ON NOW FRIEND, THERE WAS A DRAGON WITH A KNIGHT ON HIS BACK FLEW RIGHT OVER THE TOWN.
TELL US WHERE THEY WENT, WE MIGHT GO EASY ON YA.
YA DINNIT HAVE TO DO THAT!
WE DON'T? SEEMS LIKE THE ONLY FING TO DO, WOULDN'T YA SAY?
UPSETTING THE APPLE CART? IT'S ICONIC! I WOULDN'T EXPECT LESS FROM THE KING'S OWN SOLDIERS.
NOT GOOD! THEY'RE LOOKING FOR ME. I'VE GOTTA KEEP A LOW PROFILE.

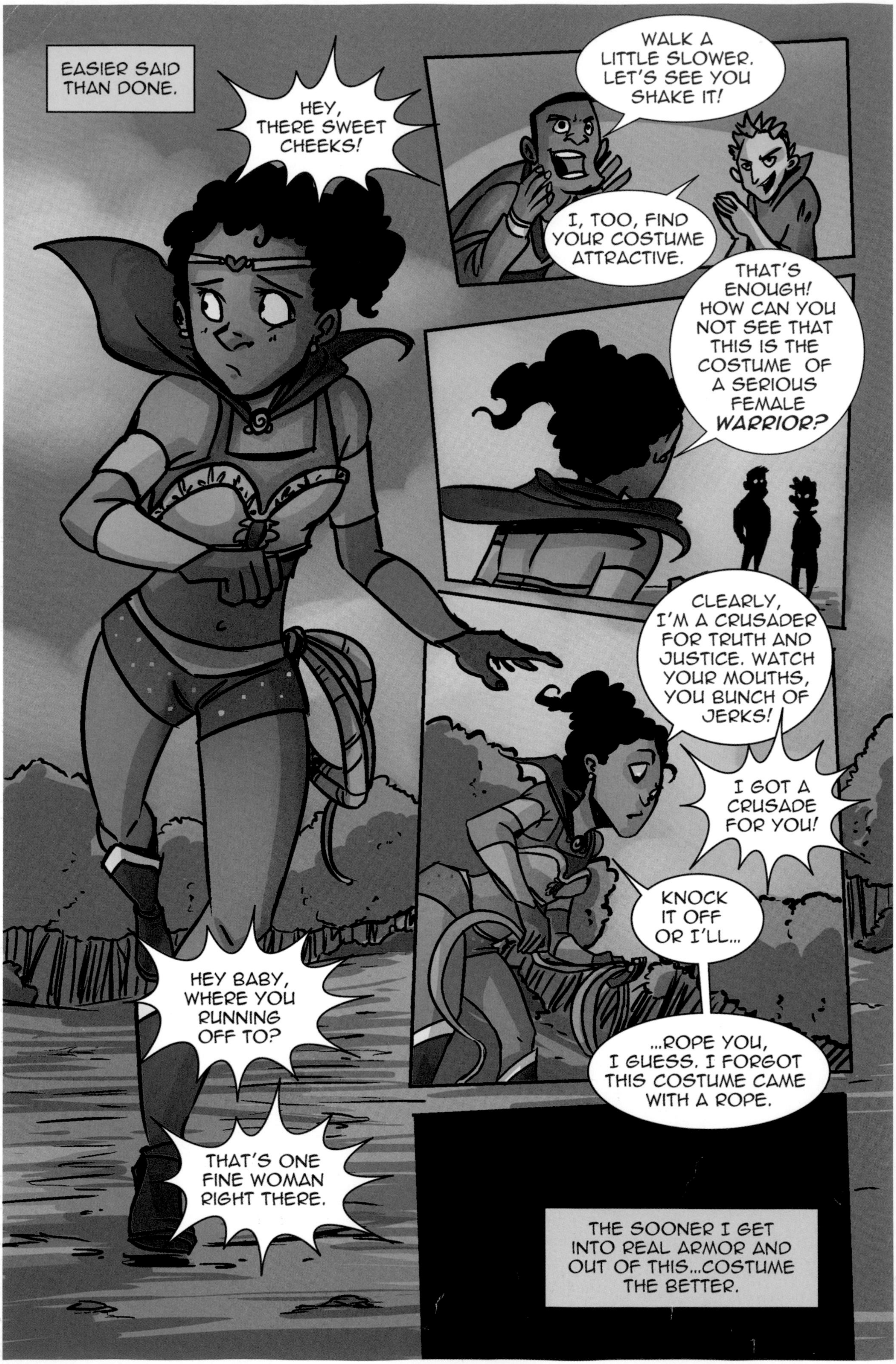
EASIER SAID THAN DONE.
HEY, THERE SWEET CHEEKS!
WALK A LITTLE SLOWER. LET'S SEE YOU SHAKE IT!
I, TOO, FIND YOUR COSTUME ATTRACTIVE.
THAT'S ENOUGH! HOW CAN YOU NOT SEE THAT THIS IS THE COSTUME OF A SERIOUS FEMALE WARRIOR?
CLEARLY, I'M A CRUSADER FOR TRUTH AND JUSTICE. WATCH YOUR MOUTHS, YOU BUNCH OF JERKS!
I GOT A CRUSADE FOR YOU!
KNOCK IT OFF OR I'LL...
...ROPE YOU, I GUESS. I FORGOT THIS COSTUME CAME WITH A ROPE.
HEY BABY, WHERE YOU RUNNING OFF TO?
THAT'S ONE FINE WOMAN RIGHT THERE.
THE SOONER I GET INTO REAL ARMOR AND OUT OF THIS...COSTUME THE BETTER.

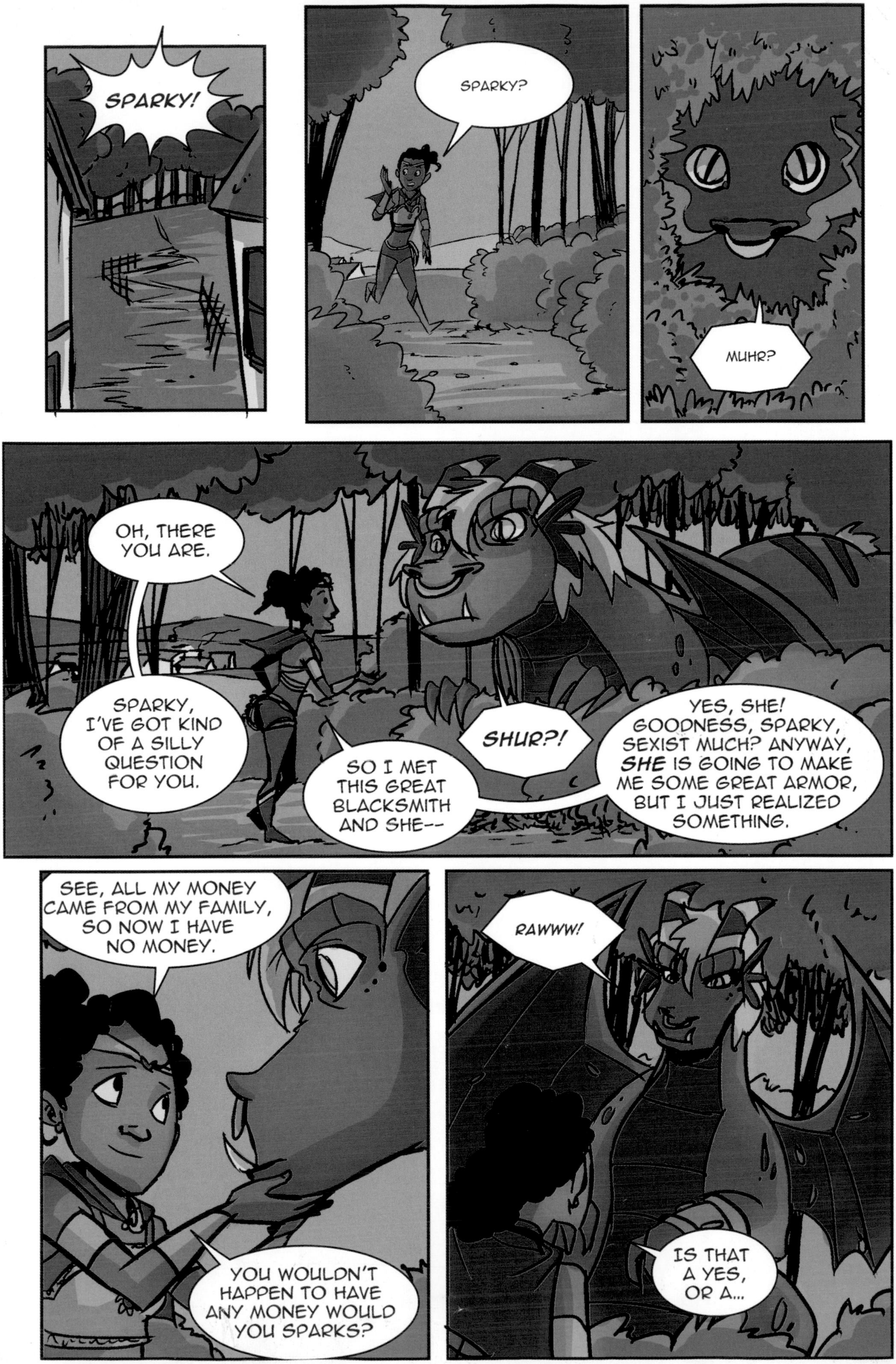
SPARKY!
SPARKY?
MUHR?
OH, THERE YOU ARE.
SPARKY, I'VE GOT KIND OF A SILLY QUESTION FOR YOU.
SO I MET THIS GREAT BLACKSMITH AND SHE--
SHUR?!
YES, SHE! GOODNESS, SPARKY, SEXIST MUCH? ANYWAY, SHE IS GOING TO MAKE ME SOME GREAT ARMOR, BUT I JUST REALIZED SOMETHING.
SEE, ALL MY MONEY CAME FROM MY FAMILY, SO NOW I HAVE NO MONEY.
YOU WOULDN'T HAPPEN TO HAVE ANY MONEY WOULD YOU SPARKS?
RAWWW!
IS THAT A YES, OR A...

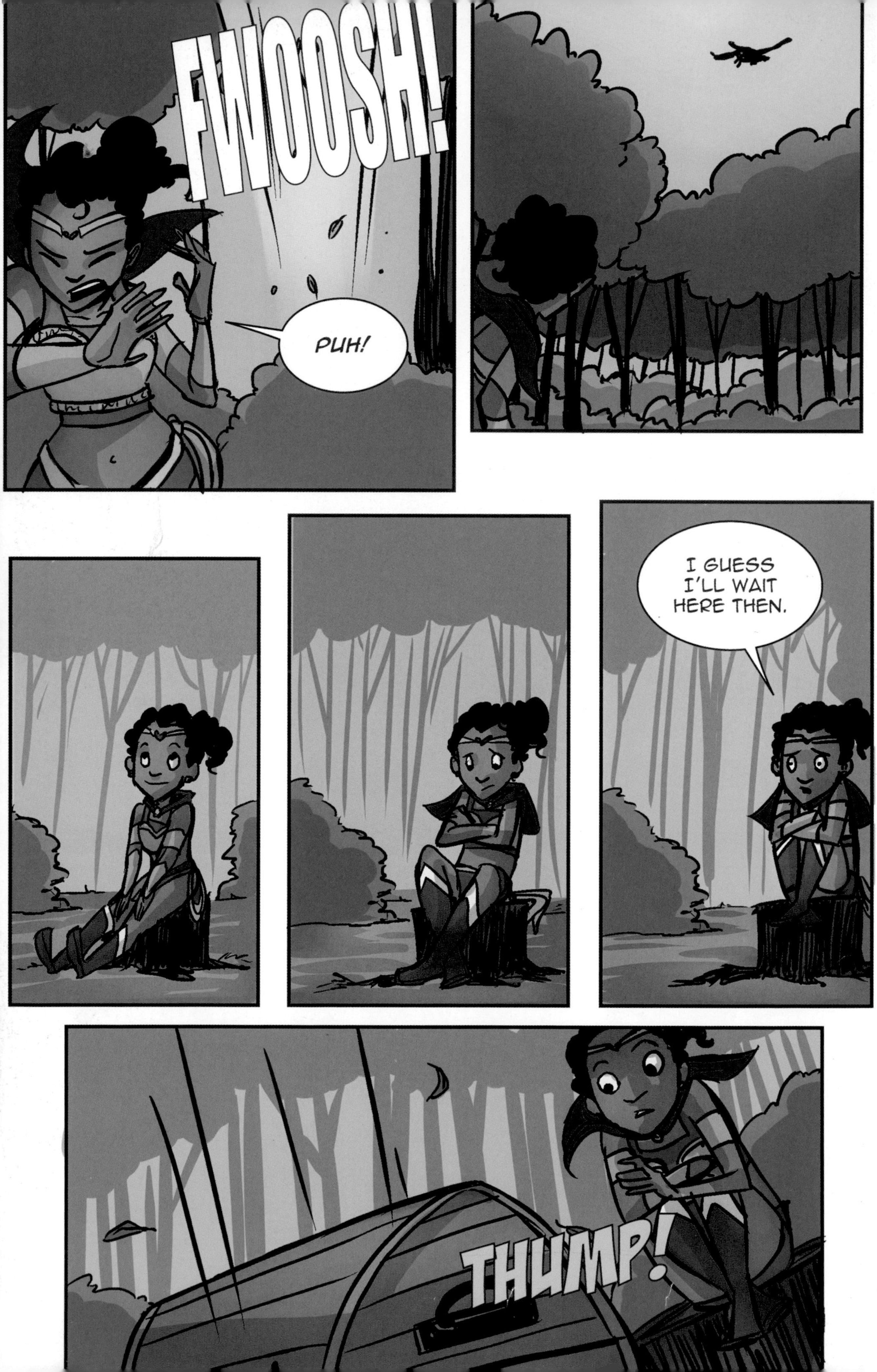
FWOOSH!
PUH!
I GUESS I'LL WAIT HERE THEN.
THUMP!

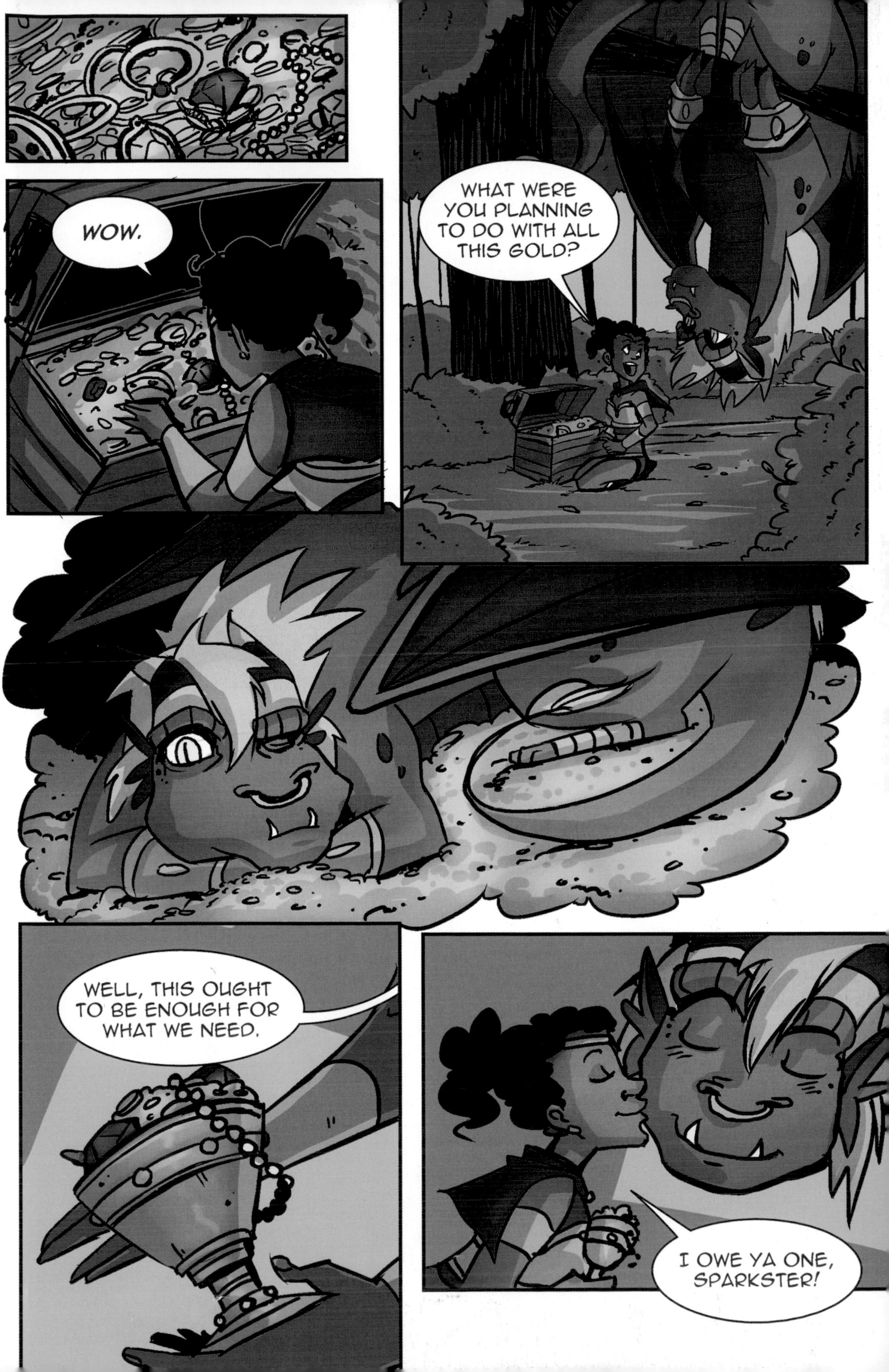
WOW.
WHAT WERE YOU PLANNING TO DO WITH ALL THIS GOLD?
WELL, THIS OUGHT TO BE ENOUGH FOR WHAT WE NEED.
I OWE YA ONE, SPARKSTER!

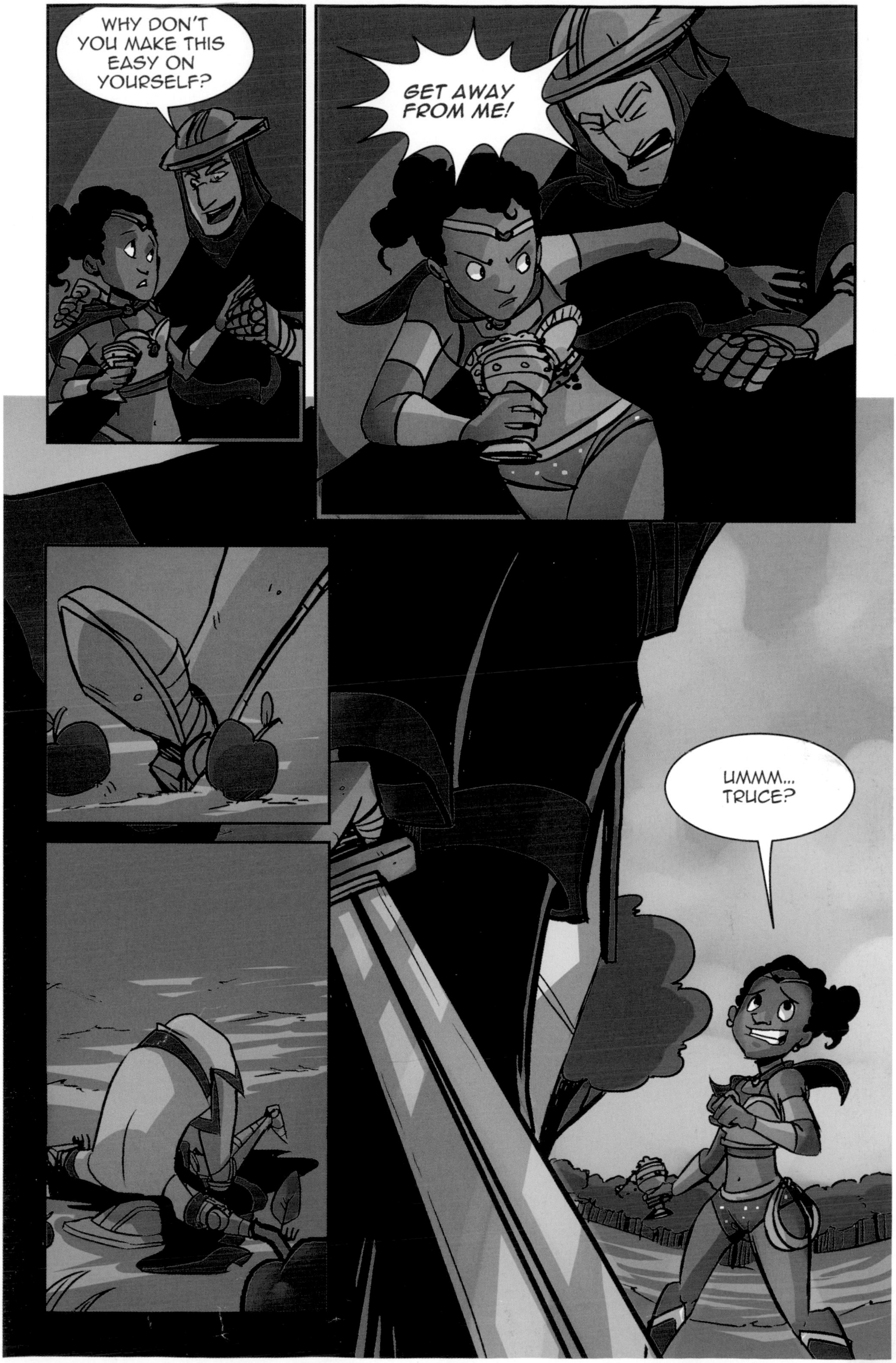
WHY DON'T YOU MAKE THIS EASY ON YOURSELF?
GET AWAY FROM ME!
UMMM... TRUCE?

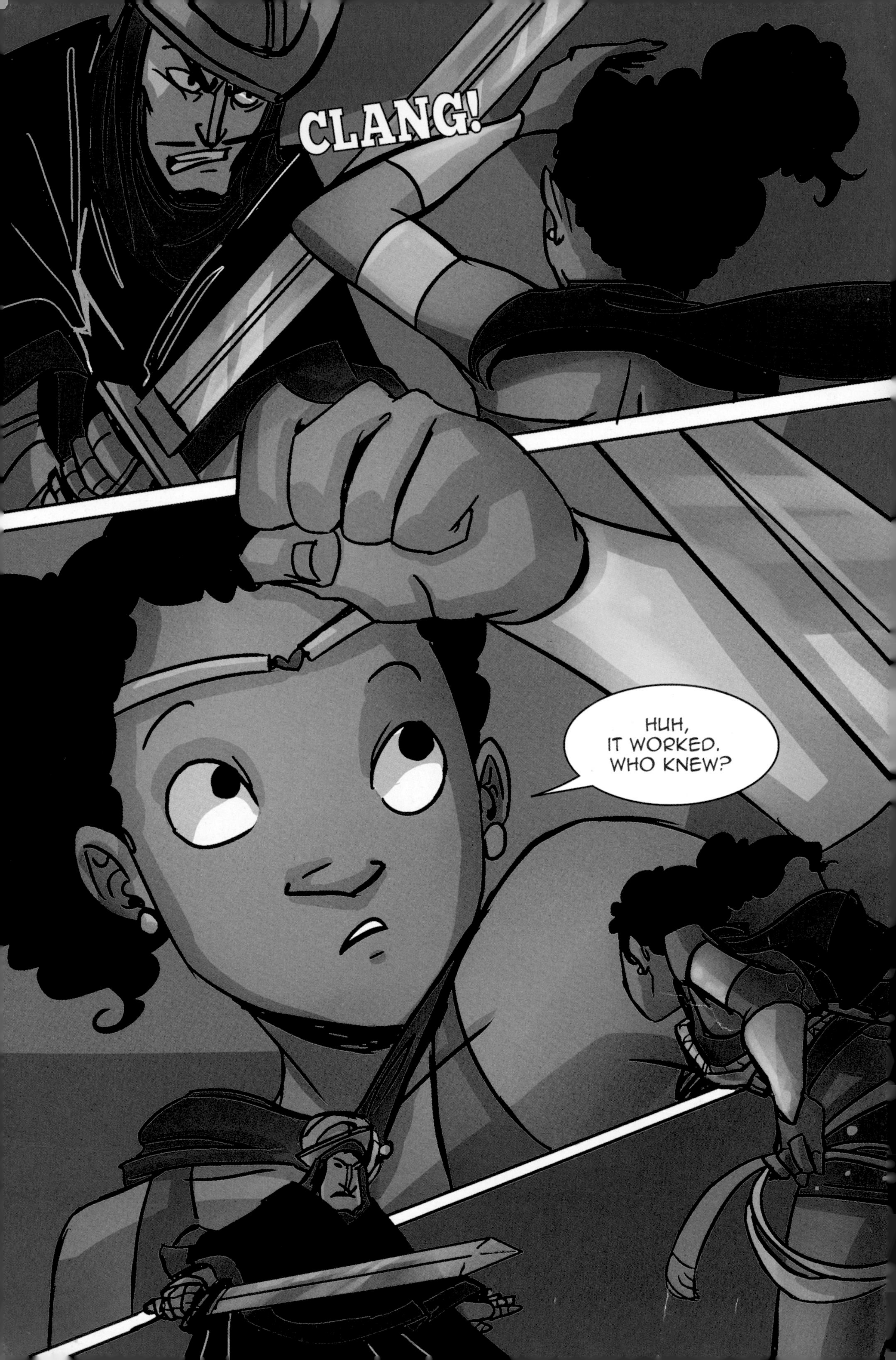
CLANG!
HUH, IT WORKED. WHO KNEW?

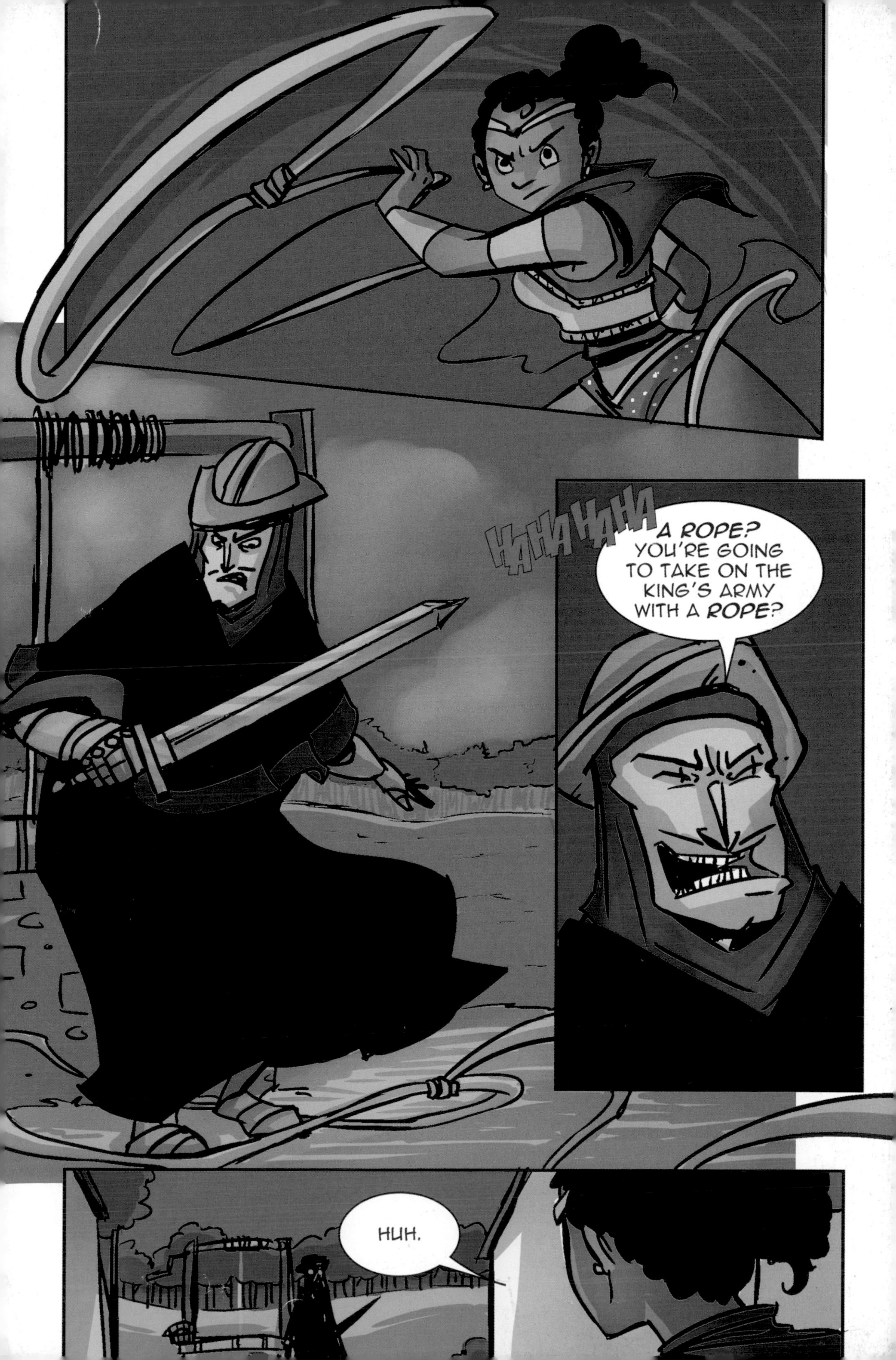
HAHA HAHA
A ROPE? YOU'RE GOING TO TAKE ON THE KING'S ARMY WITH A ROPE?
HUH.

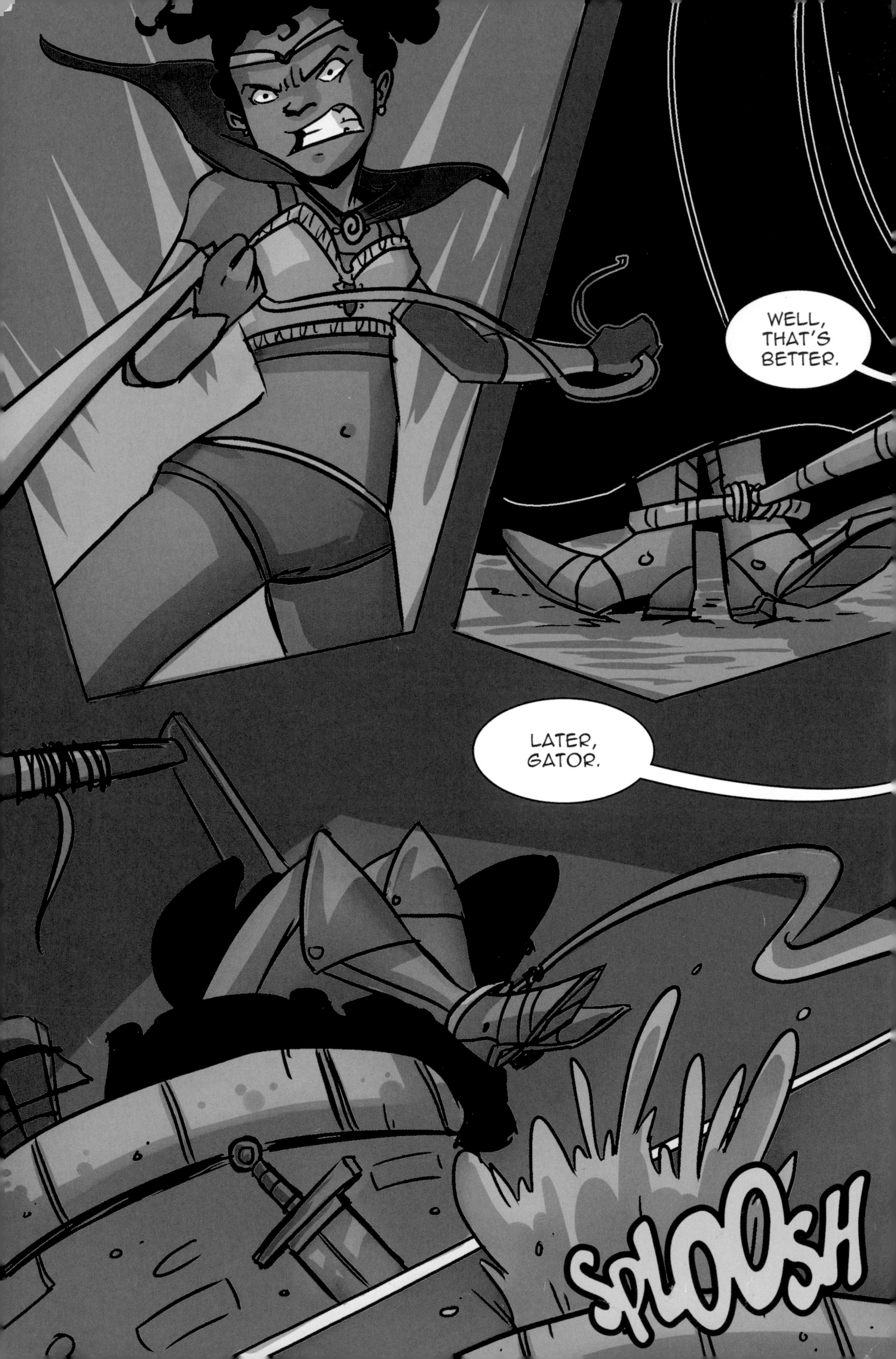
WELL, THAT'S BETTER.
LATER, GATOR.
SPLOOSH

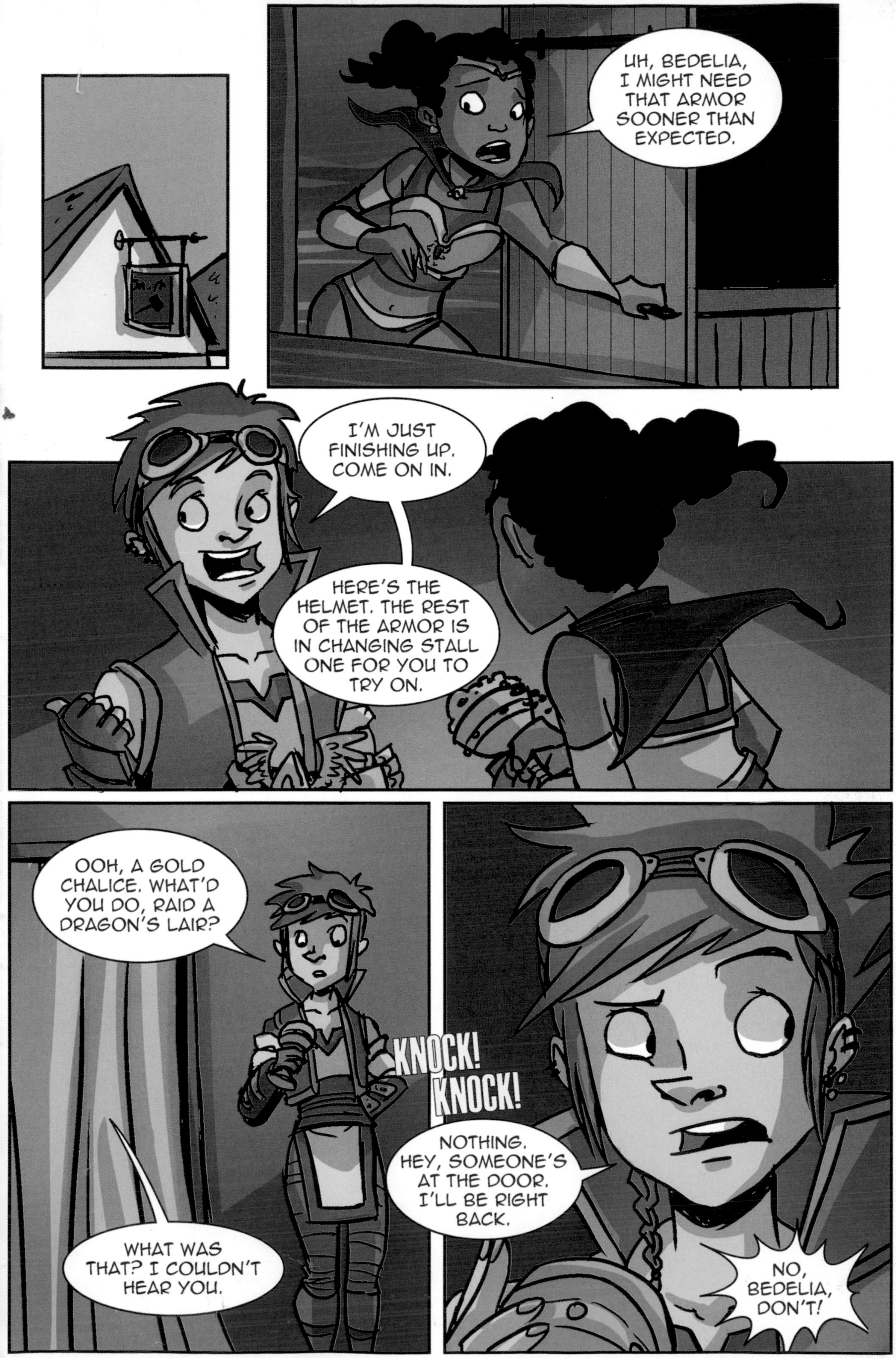
UH, BEDELIA, I MIGHT NEED THAT ARMOR SOONER THAN EXPECTED.
I'M JUST FINISHING UP. COME ON IN.
HERE'S THE HELMET. THE REST OF THE ARMOR IS IN CHANGING STALL ONE FOR YOU TO TRY ON.
OOH, A GOLD CHALICE. WHAT'D YOU DO, RAID A DRAGON'S LAIR?
KNOCK! KNOCK!
WHAT WAS THAT? I COULDN'T HEAR YOU.
NOTHING. HEY, SOMEONE'S AT THE DOOR. I'LL BE RIGHT BACK.
NO, BEDELIA, DON'T!

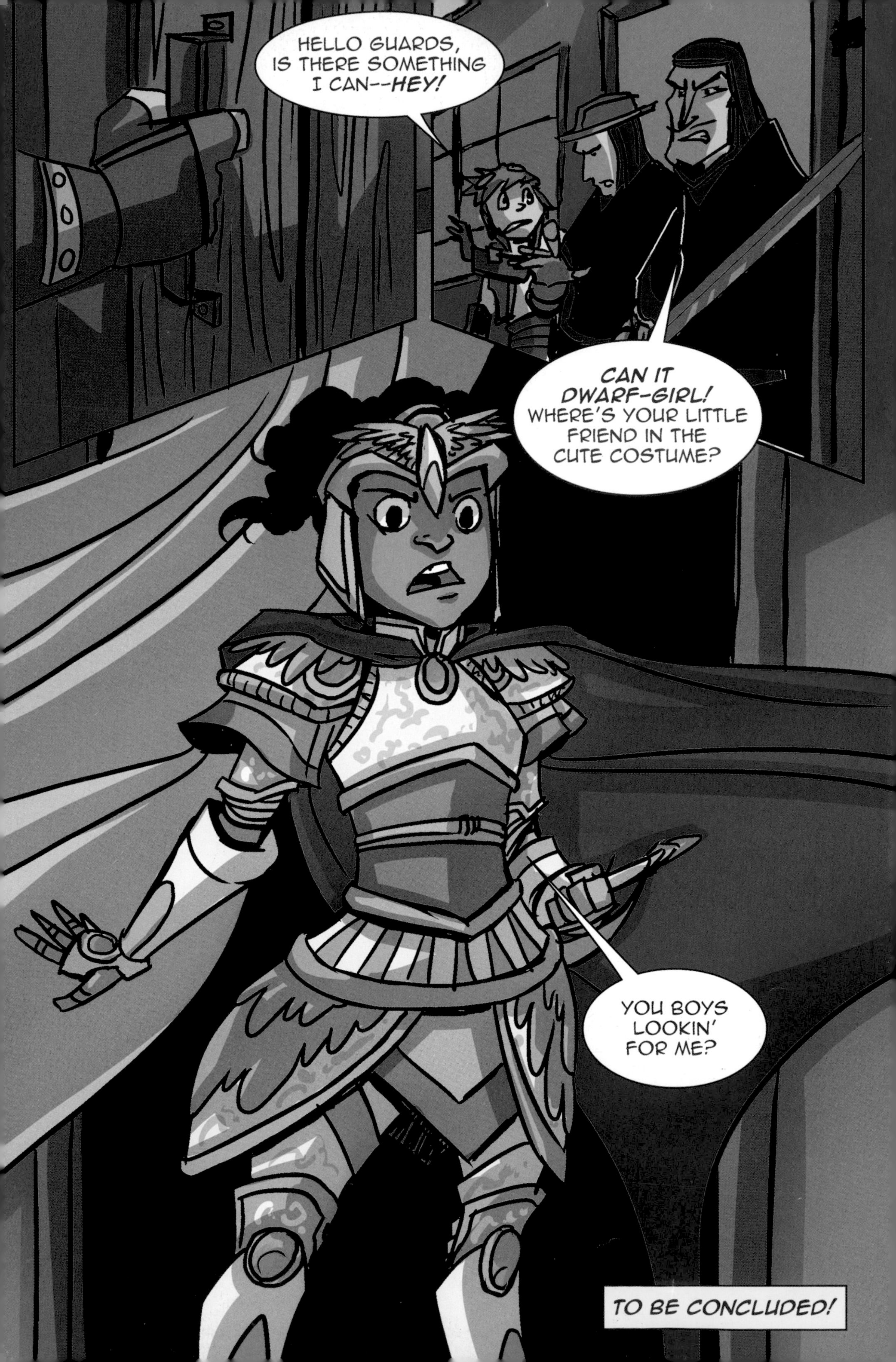
HELLO GUARDS, IS THERE SOMETHING I CAN--HEY!
CAN IT DWARF-GIRL! WHERE'S YOUR LITTLE FRIEND IN THE CUTE COSTUME?
YOU BOYS LOOKIN' FOR ME?
TO BE CONCLUDED!

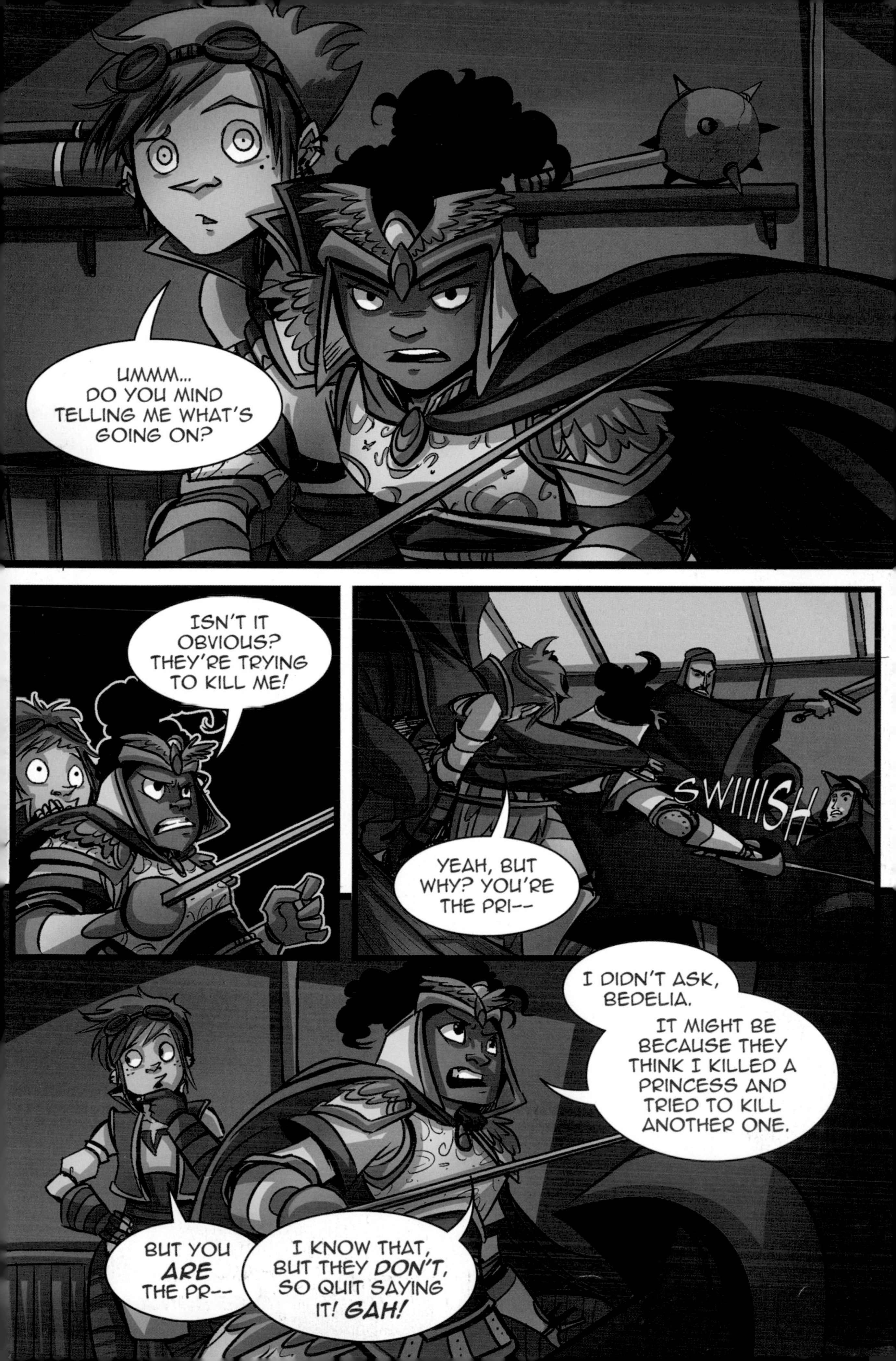
UMMM... DO YOU MIND TELLING ME WHAT'S GOING ON?
ISN'T IT OBVIOUS? THEY'RE TRYING TO KILL ME!
SWIIIISH
YEAH, BUT WHY? YOU'RE THE PRI--
I DIDN'T ASK, BEDELIA.
IT MIGHT BE BECAUSE THEY THINK I KILLED A PRINCESS AND TRIED TO KILL ANOTHER ONE.
BUT YOU *ARE* THE PR--
I KNOW THAT, BUT THEY *DON'T*, SO QUIT SAYING IT! *GAH!*

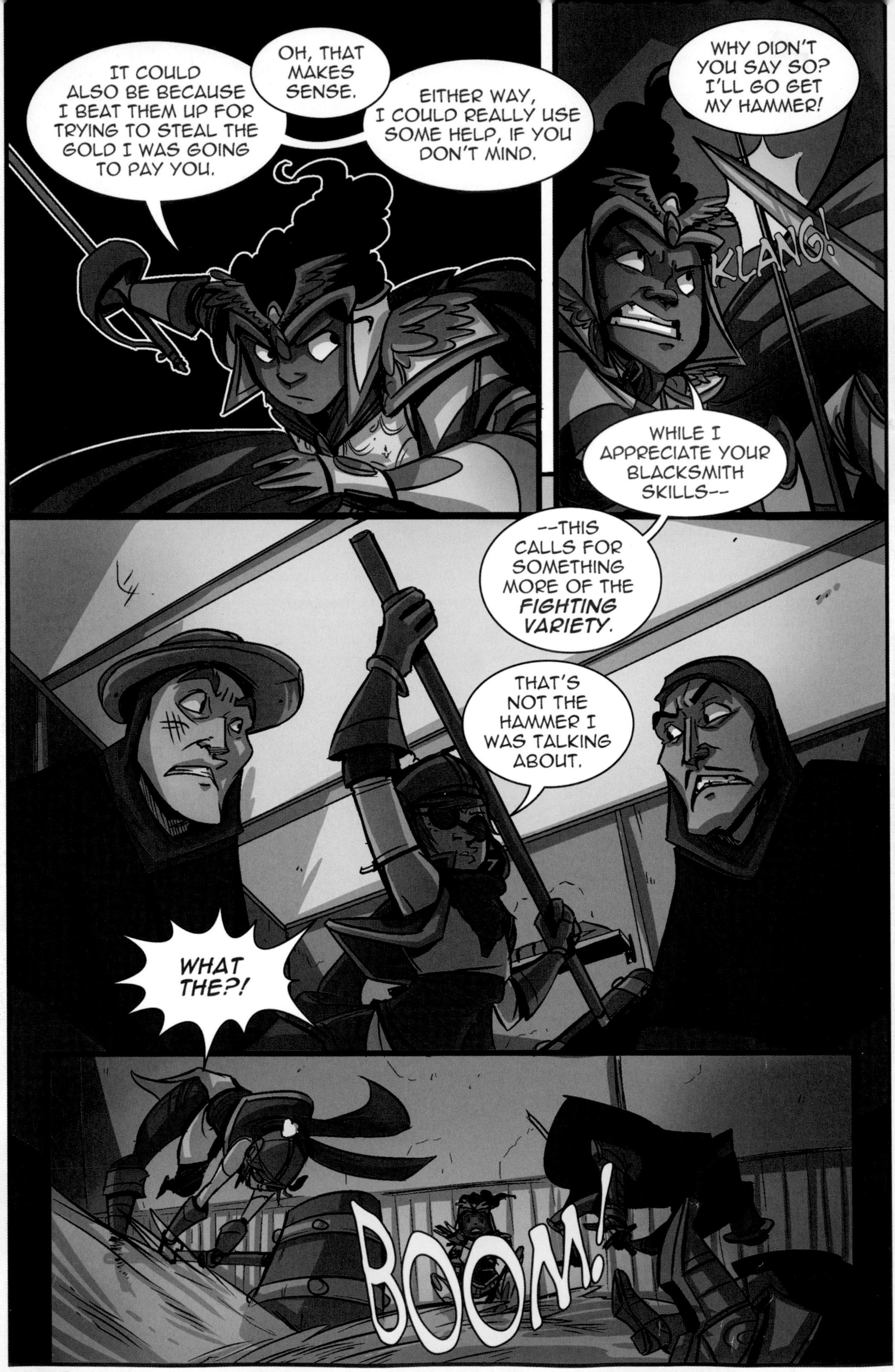
IT COULD ALSO BE BECAUSE I BEAT THEM UP FOR TRYING TO STEAL THE GOLD I WAS GOING TO PAY YOU.
OH, THAT MAKES SENSE.
EITHER WAY, I COULD REALLY USE SOME HELP, IF YOU DON'T MIND.
WHY DIDN'T YOU SAY SO? I'LL GO GET MY HAMMER!
KLANG!
WHILE I APPRECIATE YOUR BLACKSMITH SKILLS--
--THIS CALLS FOR SOMETHING MORE OF THE *FIGHTING VARIETY*.
THAT'S NOT THE HAMMER I WAS TALKING ABOUT.
WHAT THE?!
BOOM!

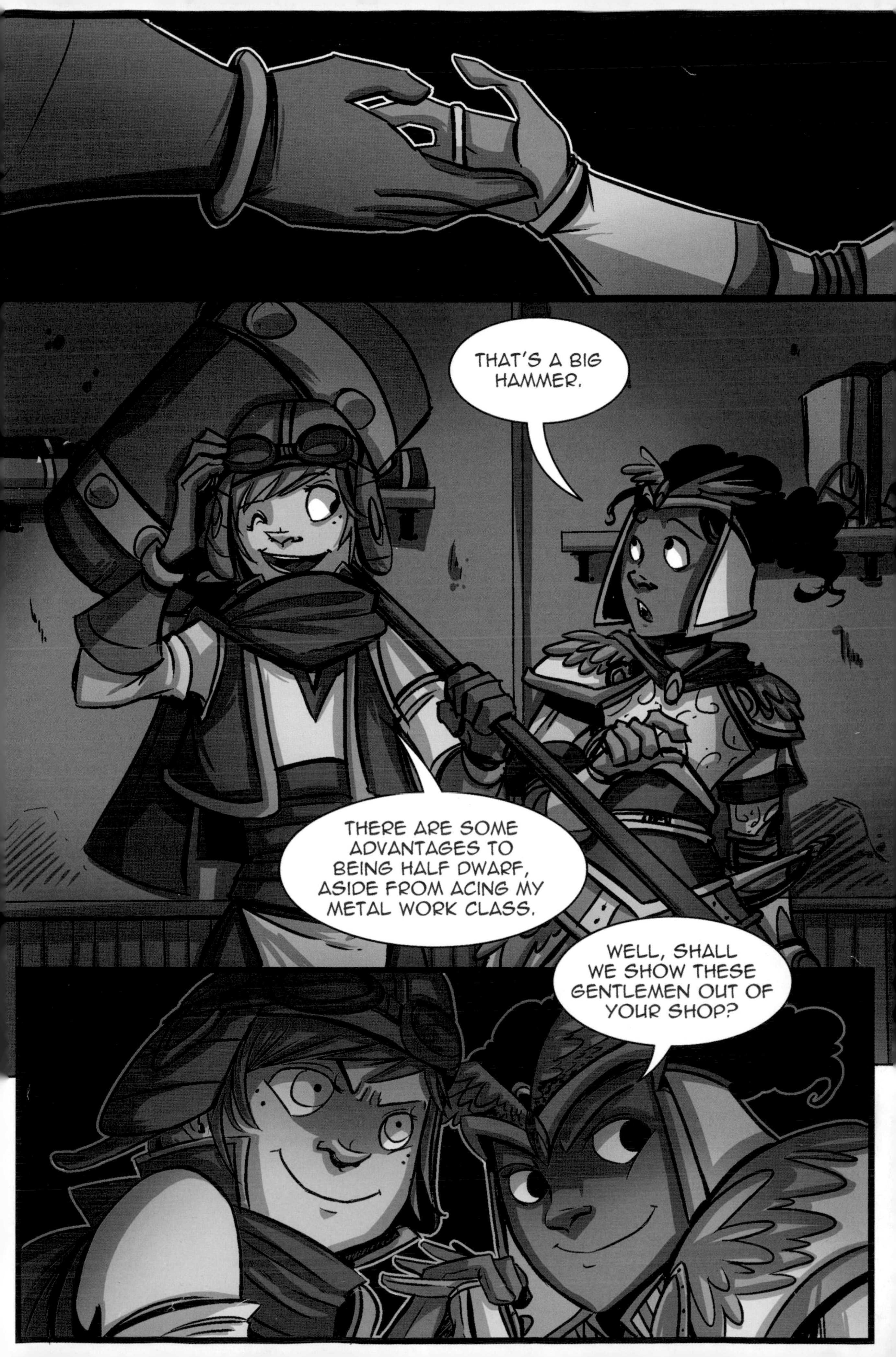
THAT'S A BIG HAMMER.
THERE ARE SOME ADVANTAGES TO BEING HALF DWARF, ASIDE FROM ACING MY METAL WORK CLASS.
WELL, SHALL WE SHOW THESE GENTLEMEN OUT OF YOUR SHOP?

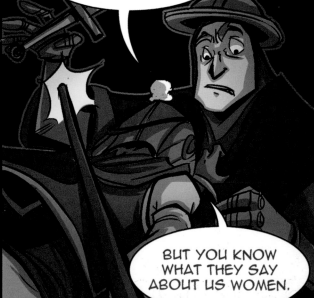

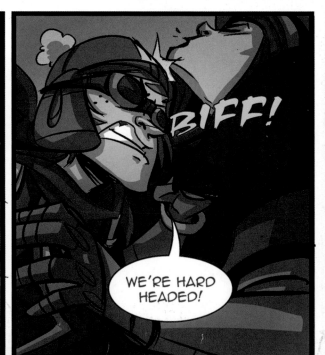

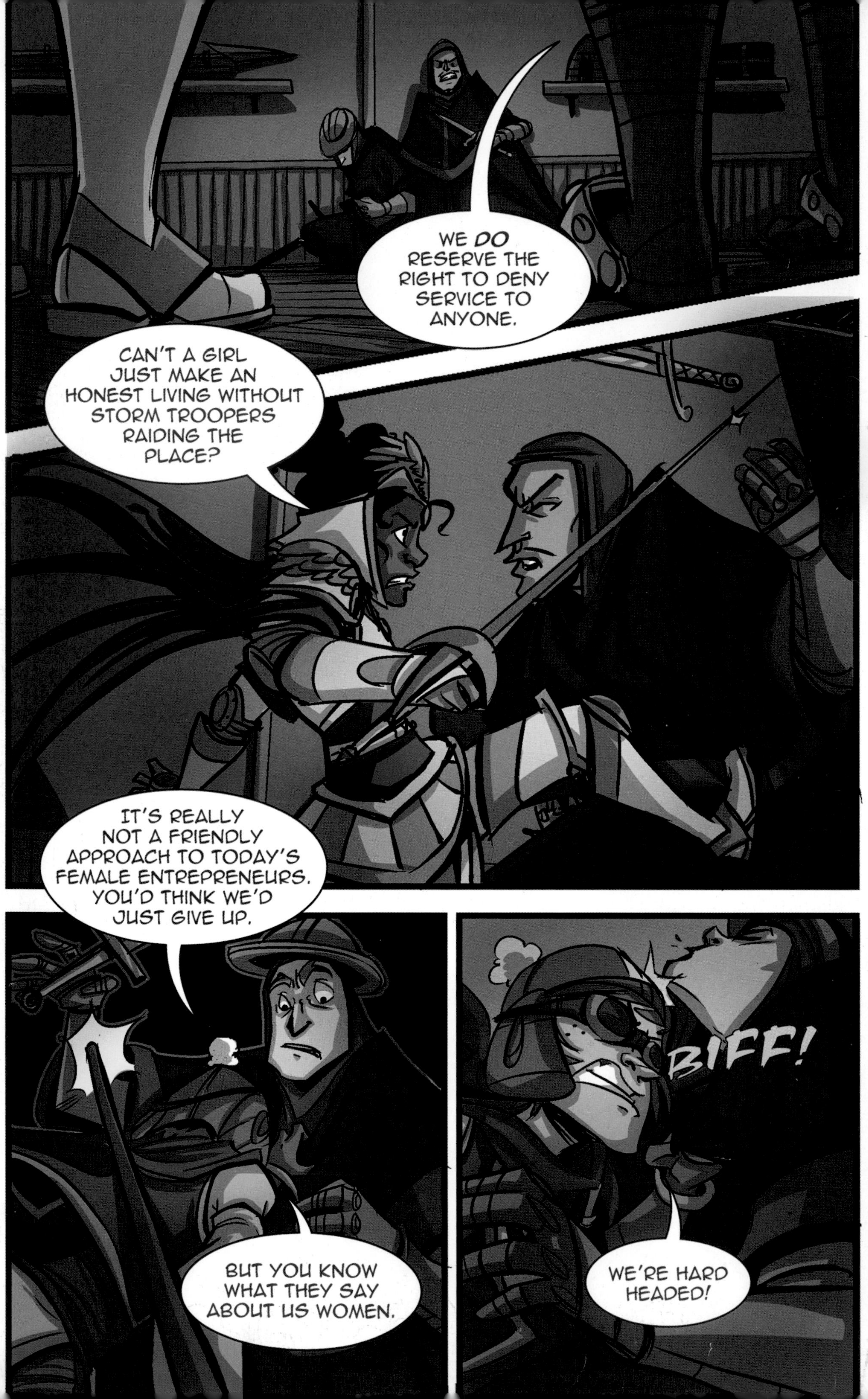
WE DO RESERVE THE RIGHT TO DENY SERVICE TO ANYONE.
CAN'T A GIRL JUST MAKE AN HONEST LIVING WITHOUT STORM TROOPERS RAIDING THE PLACE?
IT'S REALLY NOT A FRIENDLY APPROACH TO TODAY'S FEMALE ENTREPRENEURS. YOU'D THINK WE'D JUST GIVE UP.
BUT YOU KNOW WHAT THEY SAY ABOUT US WOMEN.
BIFF!
WE'RE HARD HEADED!

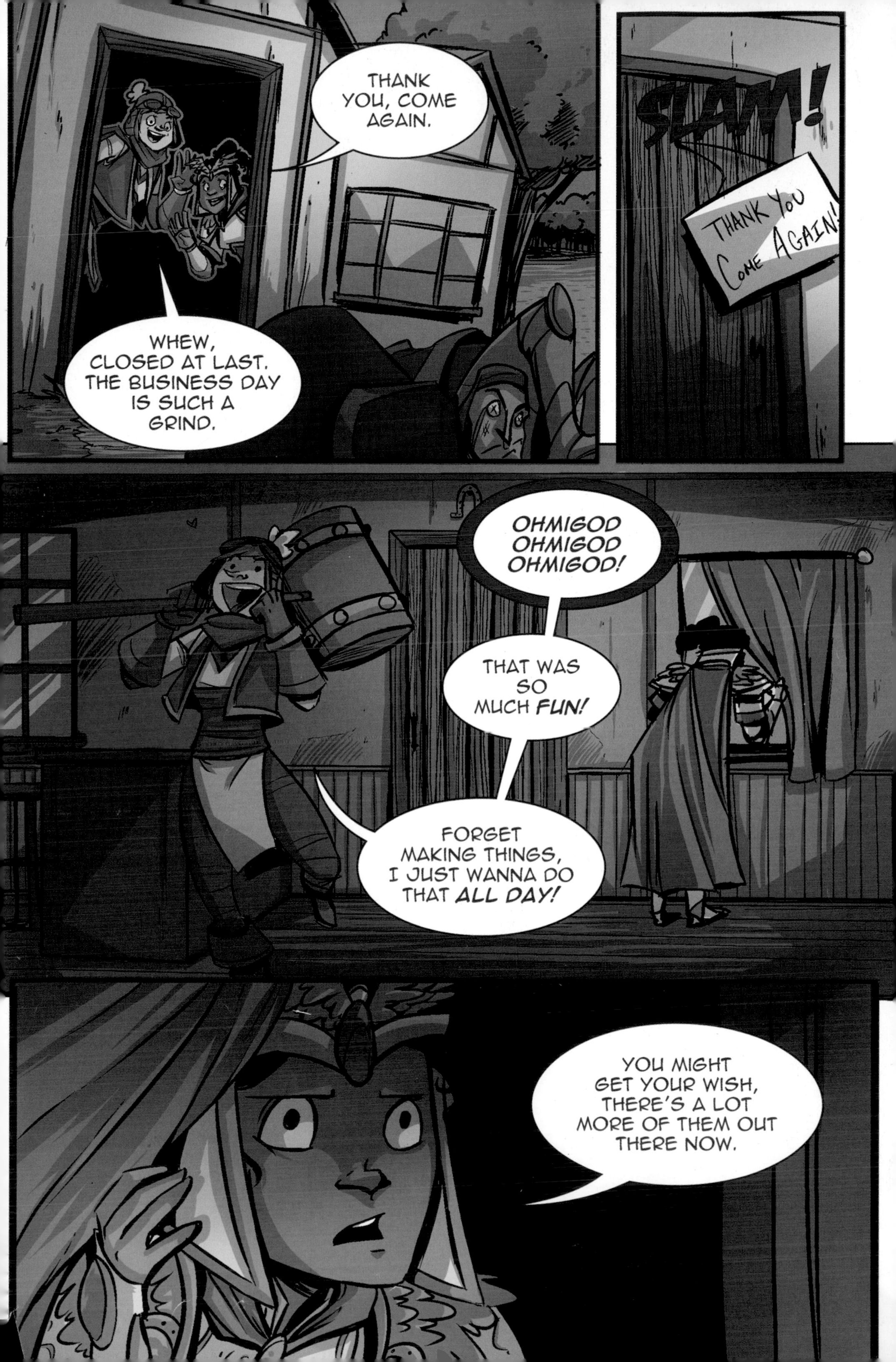
THANK YOU, COME AGAIN.
WHEW, CLOSED AT LAST. THE BUSINESS DAY IS SUCH A GRIND.
SLAM!
THANK YOU COME AGAIN!
OHMIGOD OHMIGOD OHMIGOD!
THAT WAS SO MUCH FUN!
FORGET MAKING THINGS, I JUST WANNA DO THAT ALL DAY!
YOU MIGHT GET YOUR WISH, THERE'S A LOT MORE OF THEM OUT THERE NOW.

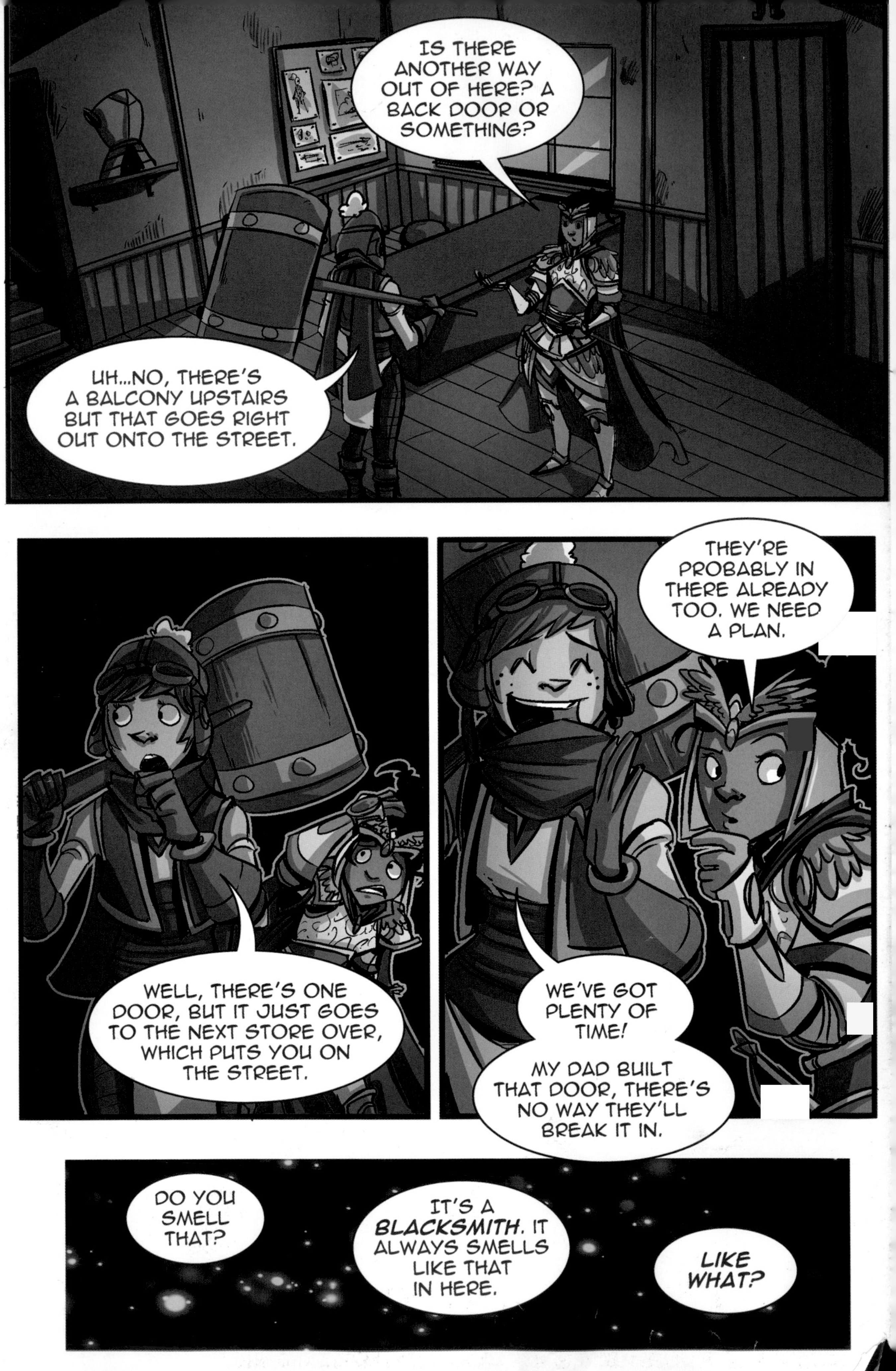
IS THERE ANOTHER WAY OUT OF HERE? A BACK DOOR OR SOMETHING?
UH...NO, THERE'S A BALCONY UPSTAIRS BUT THAT GOES RIGHT OUT ONTO THE STREET.
WELL, THERE'S ONE DOOR, BUT IT JUST GOES TO THE NEXT STORE OVER, WHICH PUTS YOU ON THE STREET.
THEY'RE PROBABLY IN THERE ALREADY TOO. WE NEED A PLAN.
WE'VE GOT PLENTY OF TIME!
MY DAD BUILT THAT DOOR, THERE'S NO WAY THEY'LL BREAK IT IN.
DO YOU SMELL THAT?
IT'S A *BLACKSMITH*. IT ALWAYS SMELLS LIKE THAT IN HERE.
LIKE WHAT?

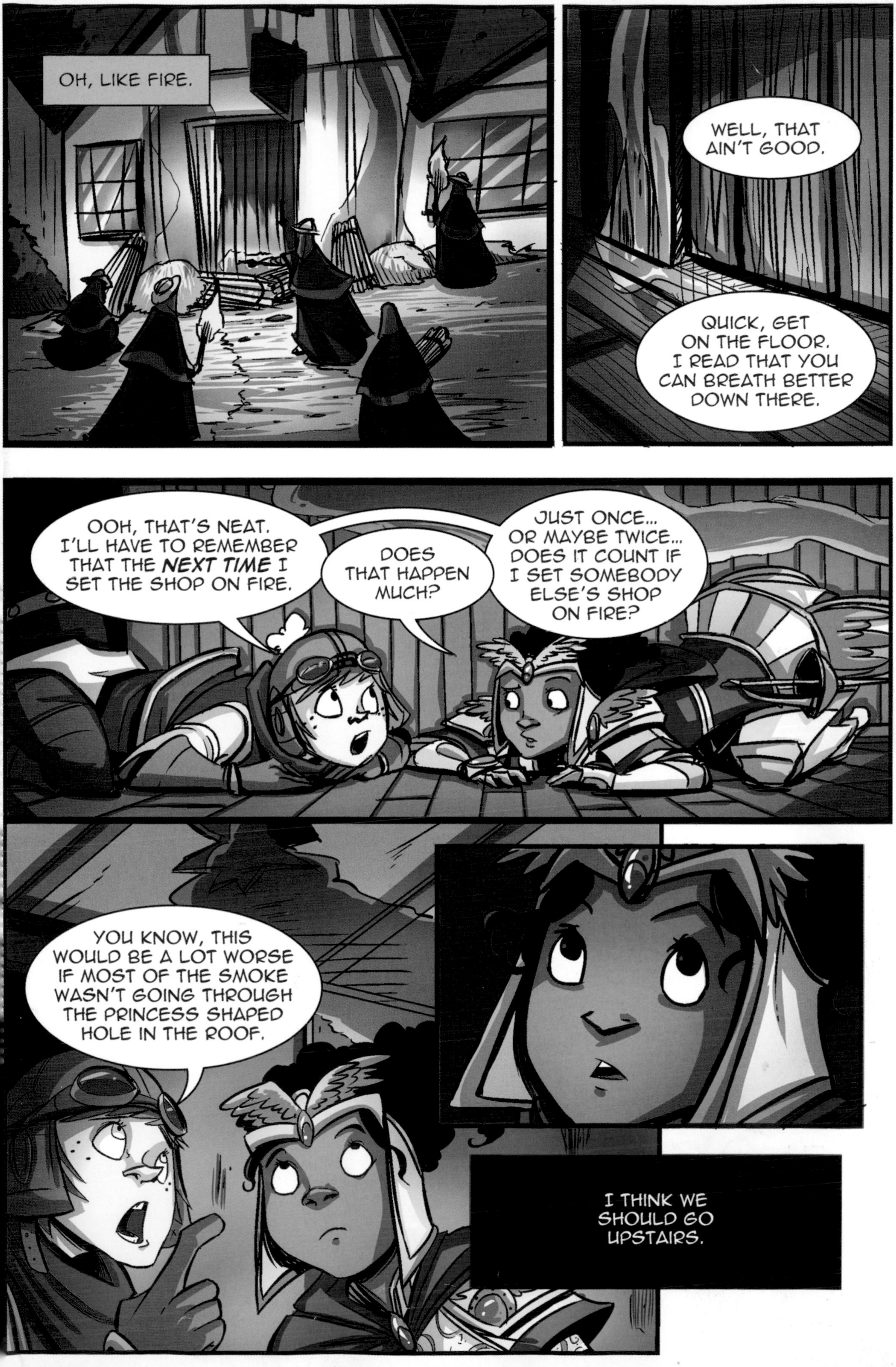
OH, LIKE FIRE.
WELL, THAT AIN'T GOOD.
QUICK, GET ON THE FLOOR. I READ THAT YOU CAN BREATH BETTER DOWN THERE.
OOH, THAT'S NEAT. I'LL HAVE TO REMEMBER THAT THE *NEXT TIME* I SET THE SHOP ON FIRE.
DOES THAT HAPPEN MUCH?
JUST ONCE... OR MAYBE TWICE... DOES IT COUNT IF I SET SOMEBODY ELSE'S SHOP ON FIRE?
YOU KNOW, THIS WOULD BE A LOT WORSE IF MOST OF THE SMOKE WASN'T GOING THROUGH THE PRINCESS SHAPED HOLE IN THE ROOF.
I THINK WE SHOULD GO UPSTAIRS.

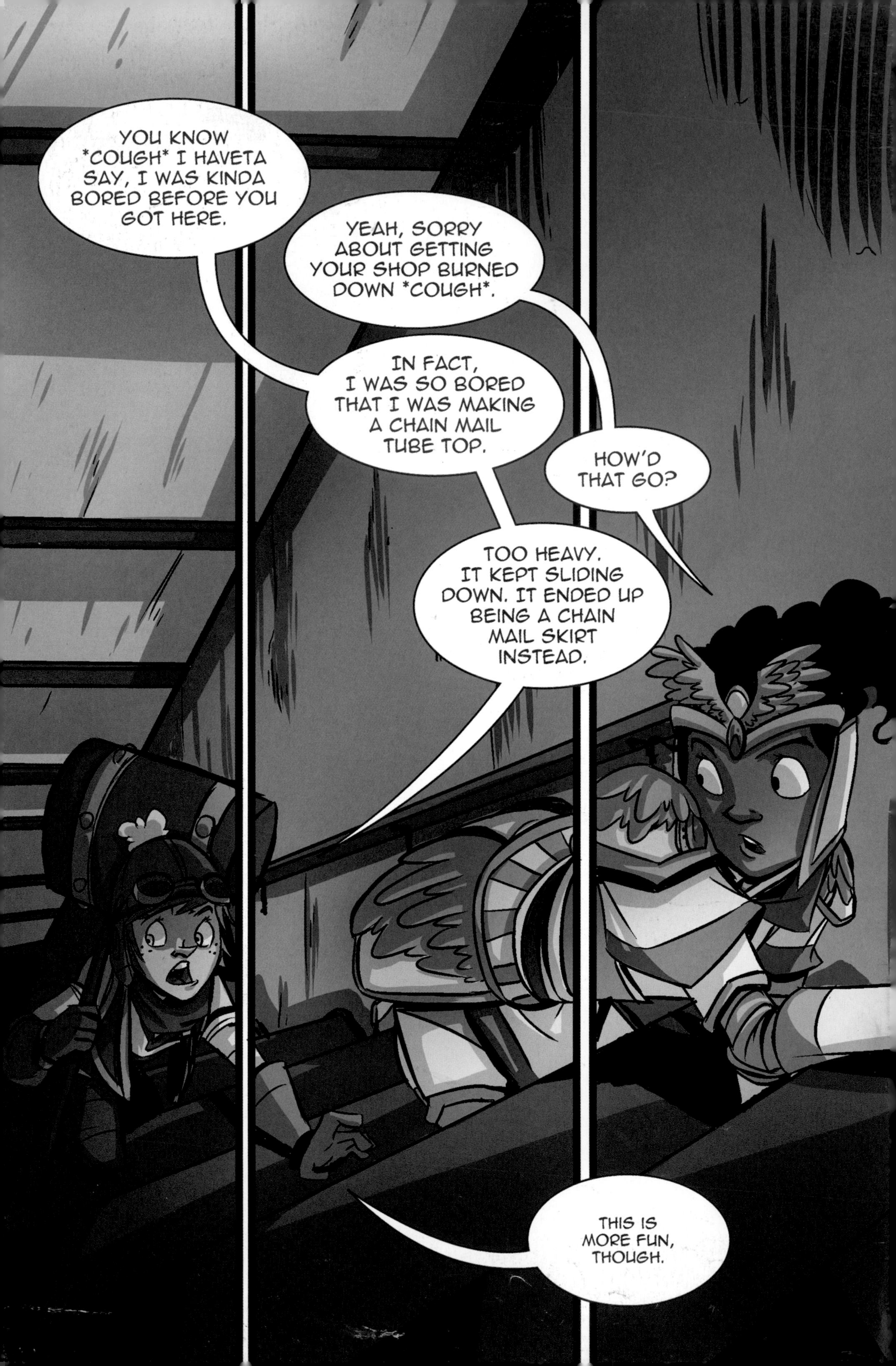
YOU KNOW *COUGH* I HAVETA SAY, I WAS KINDA BORED BEFORE YOU GOT HERE.
YEAH, SORRY ABOUT GETTING YOUR SHOP BURNED DOWN *COUGH*.
IN FACT, I WAS SO BORED THAT I WAS MAKING A CHAIN MAIL TUBE TOP.
HOW'D THAT GO?
TOO HEAVY. IT KEPT SLIDING DOWN. IT ENDED UP BEING A CHAIN MAIL SKIRT INSTEAD.
THIS IS MORE FUN, THOUGH.

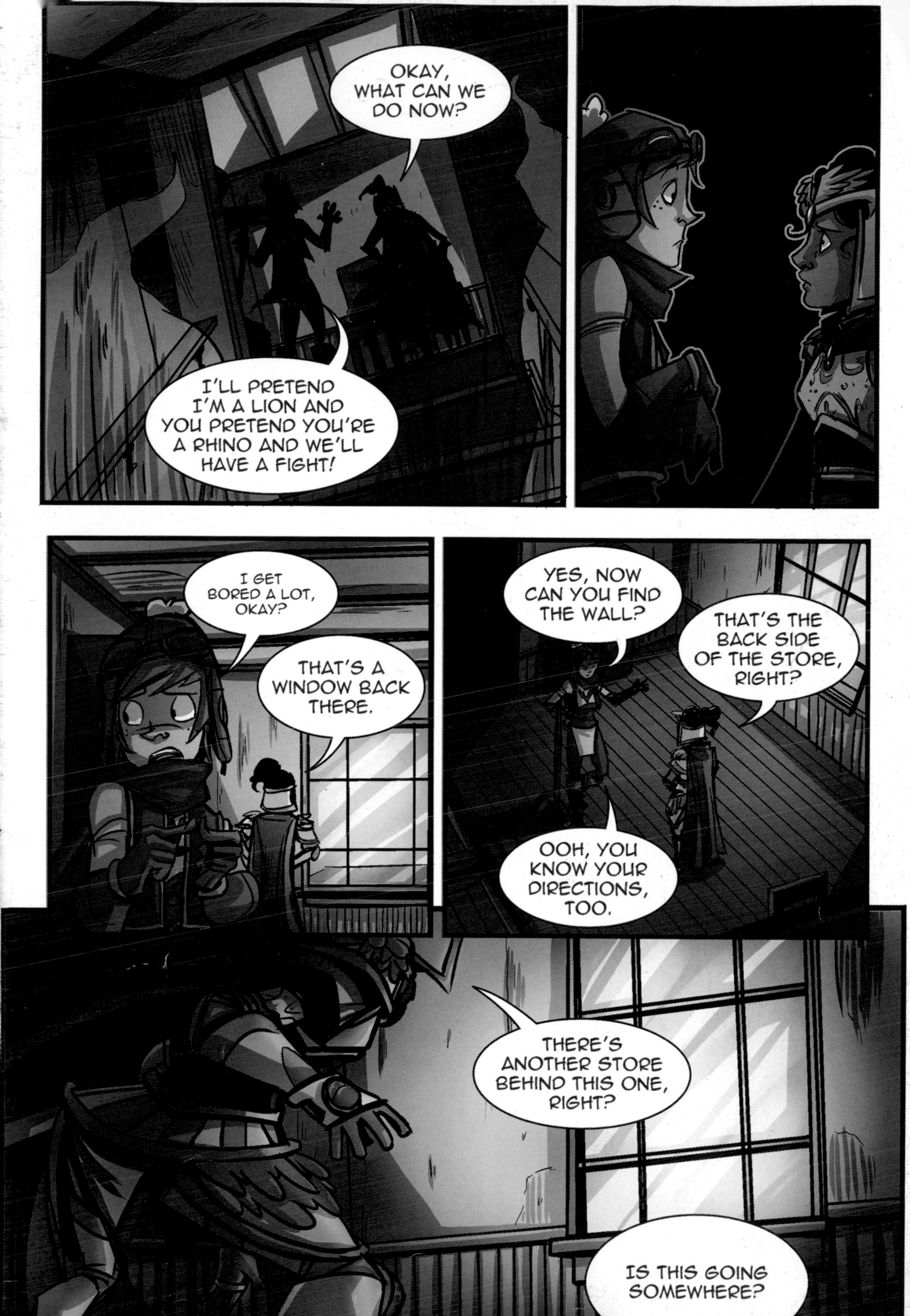
OKAY, WHAT CAN WE DO NOW?
I'LL PRETEND I'M A LION AND YOU PRETEND YOU'RE A RHINO AND WE'LL HAVE A FIGHT!
I GET BORED A LOT, OKAY?
THAT'S A WINDOW BACK THERE.
YES, NOW CAN YOU FIND THE WALL?
THAT'S THE BACK SIDE OF THE STORE, RIGHT?
OOH, YOU KNOW YOUR DIRECTIONS, TOO.
THERE'S ANOTHER STORE BEHIND THIS ONE, RIGHT?
IS THIS GOING SOMEWHERE?

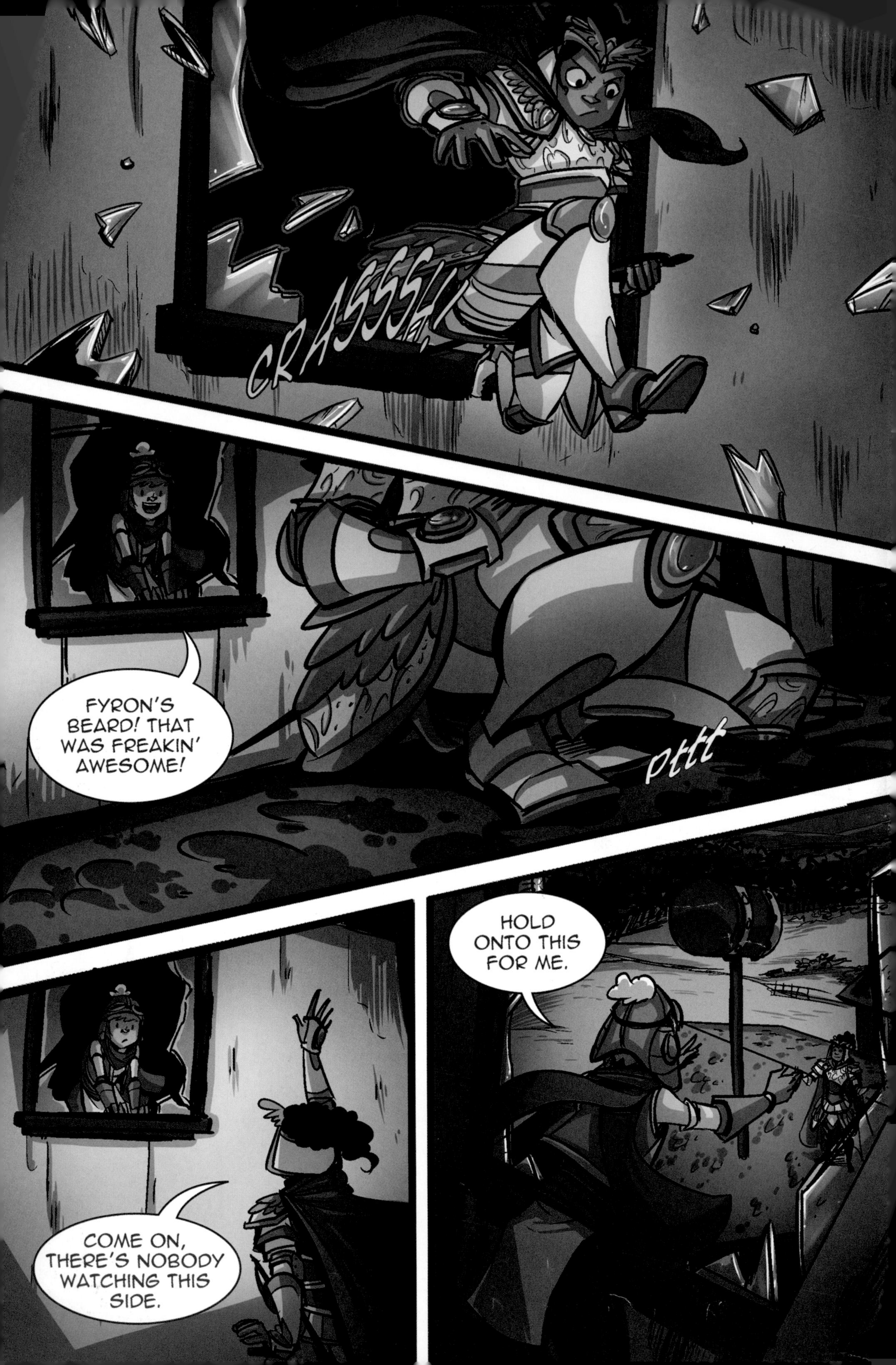
CRASSSH!
FYRON'S BEARD! THAT WAS FREAKIN' AWESOME!
pttt
COME ON, THERE'S NOBODY WATCHING THIS SIDE.
HOLD ONTO THIS FOR ME.

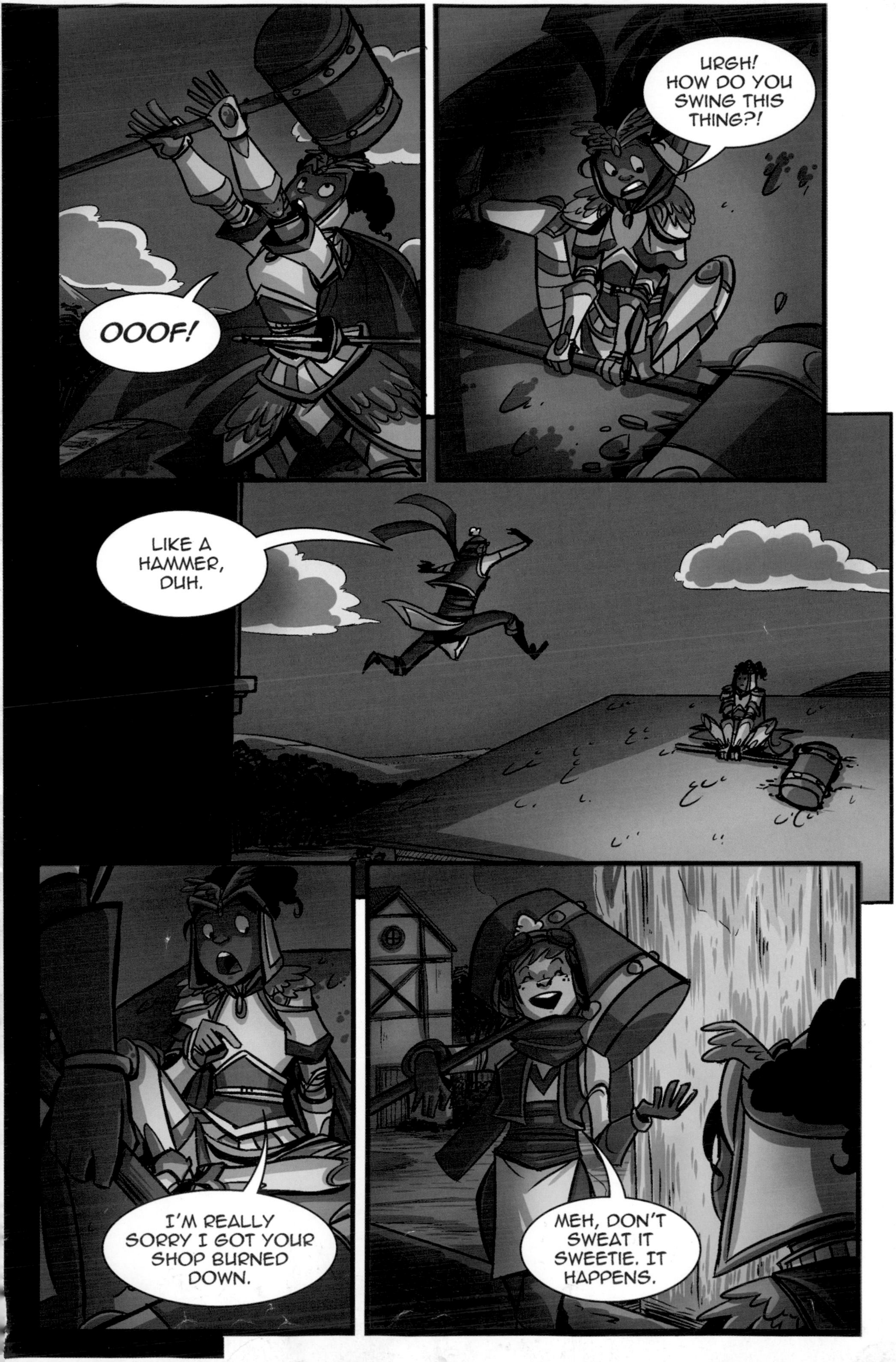
OOOF!
URGH! HOW DO YOU SWING THIS THING?!
LIKE A HAMMER, DUH.
I'M REALLY SORRY I GOT YOUR SHOP BURNED DOWN.
MEH, DON'T SWEAT IT SWEETIE. IT HAPPENS.

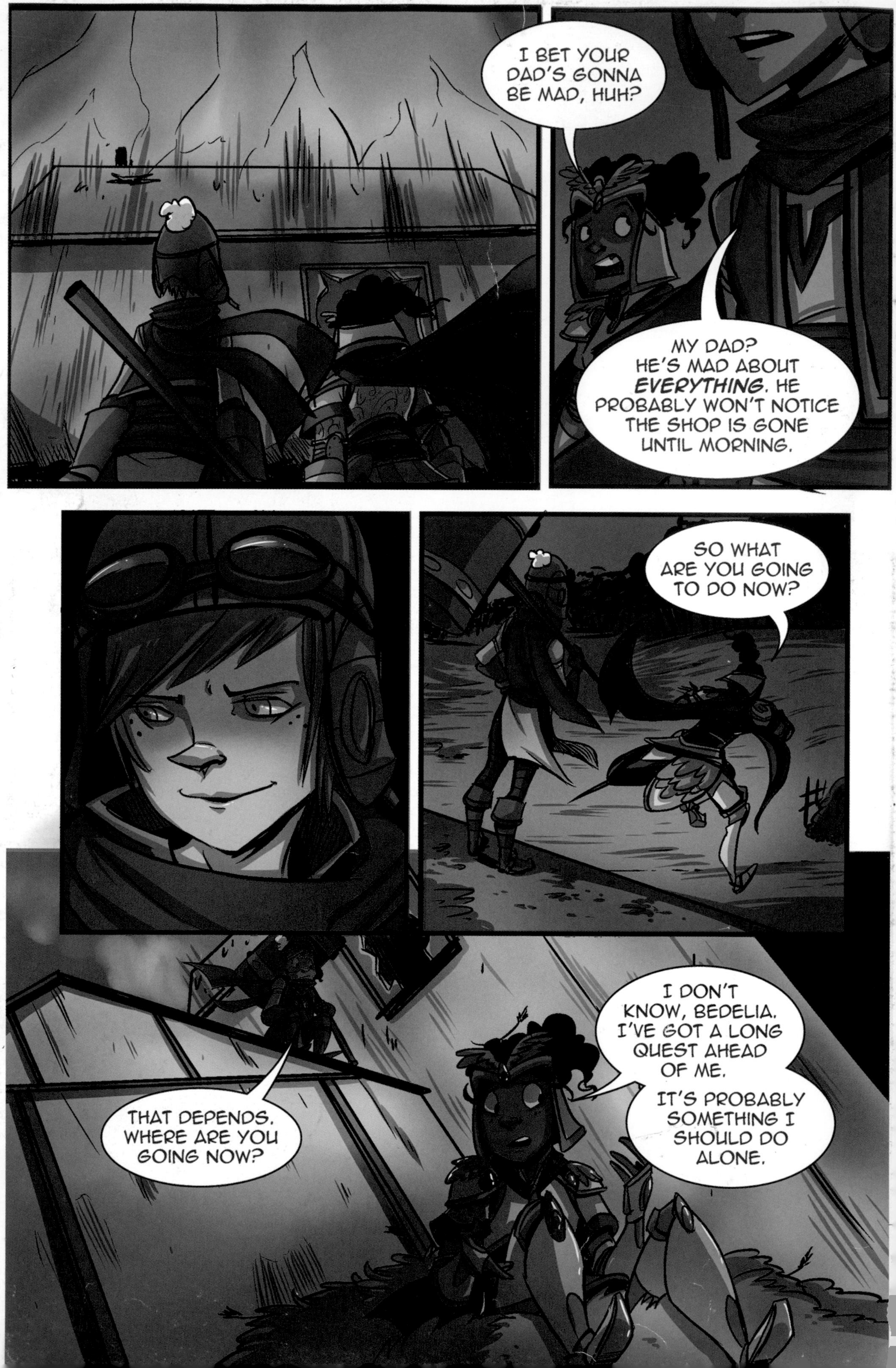
I BET YOUR DAD'S GONNA BE MAD, HUH?
MY DAD? HE'S MAD ABOUT ***EVERYTHING***. HE PROBABLY WON'T NOTICE THE SHOP IS GONE UNTIL MORNING.
SO WHAT ARE YOU GOING TO DO NOW?
I DON'T KNOW, BEDELIA. I'VE GOT A LONG QUEST AHEAD OF ME.
IT'S PROBABLY SOMETHING I SHOULD DO ALONE.
THAT DEPENDS. WHERE ARE YOU GOING NOW?

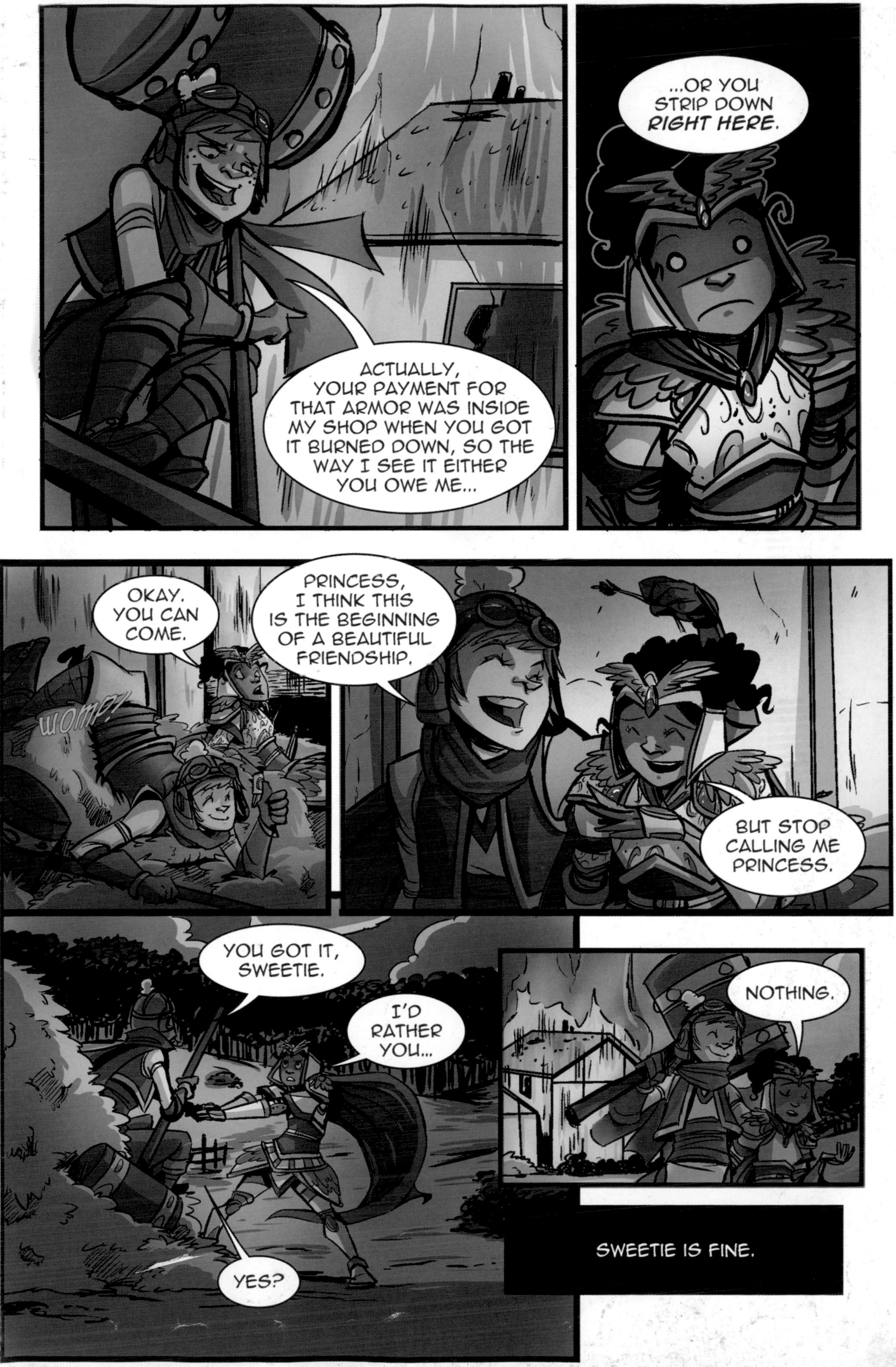
ACTUALLY, YOUR PAYMENT FOR THAT ARMOR WAS INSIDE MY SHOP WHEN YOU GOT IT BURNED DOWN, SO THE WAY I SEE IT EITHER YOU OWE ME...
...OR YOU STRIP DOWN *RIGHT HERE*.
WOMP!
OKAY. YOU CAN COME.
PRINCESS, I THINK THIS IS THE BEGINNING OF A BEAUTIFUL FRIENDSHIP.
BUT STOP CALLING ME PRINCESS.
YOU GOT IT, SWEETIE.
YES?
I'D RATHER YOU...
NOTHING.
SWEETIE IS FINE.

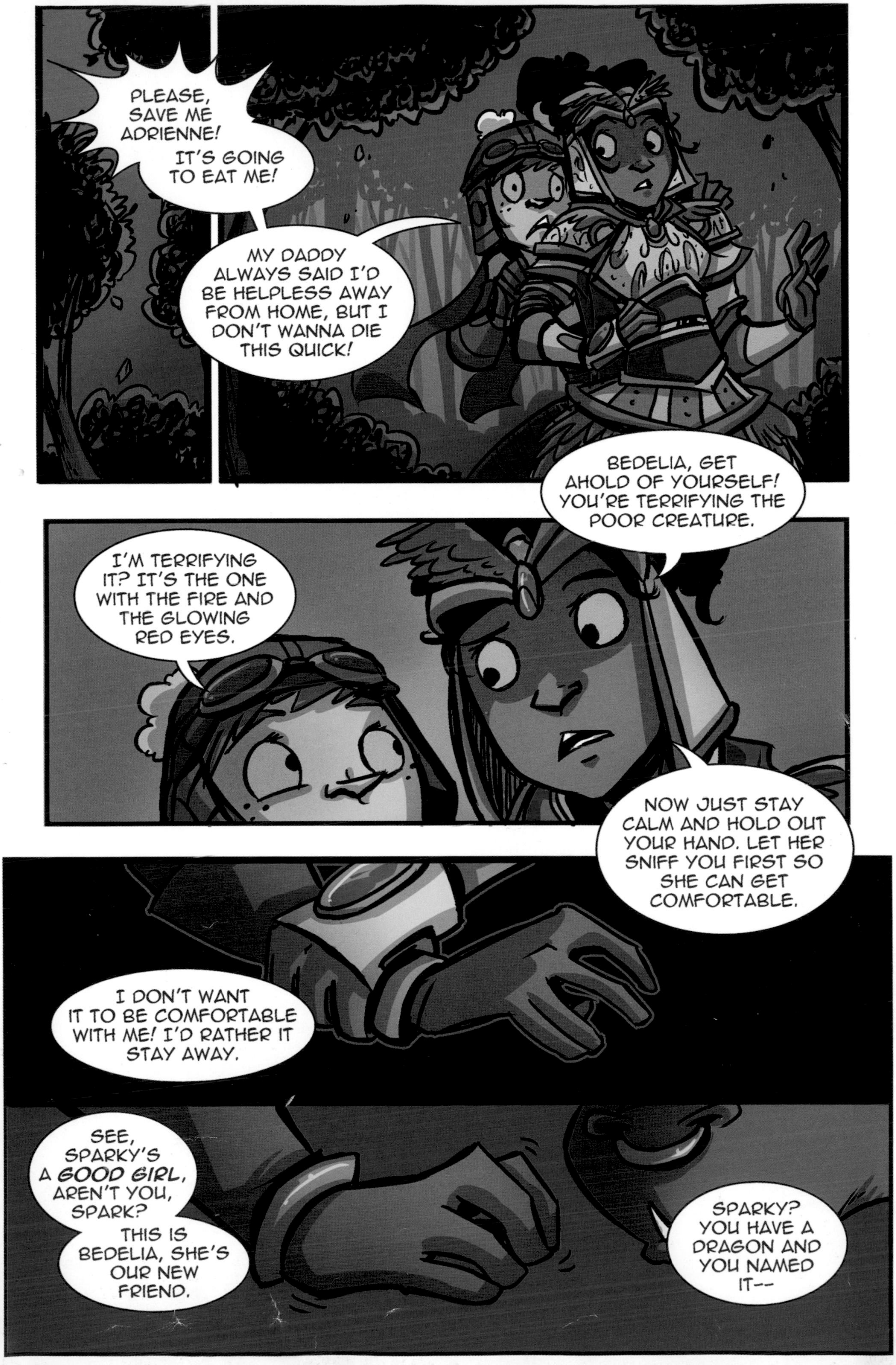
PLEASE, SAVE ME ADRIENNE!
IT'S GOING TO EAT ME!
MY DADDY ALWAYS SAID I'D BE HELPLESS AWAY FROM HOME, BUT I DON'T WANNA DIE THIS QUICK!
BEDELIA, GET AHOLD OF YOURSELF! YOU'RE TERRIFYING THE POOR CREATURE.
I'M TERRIFYING IT? IT'S THE ONE WITH THE FIRE AND THE GLOWING RED EYES.
NOW JUST STAY CALM AND HOLD OUT YOUR HAND. LET HER SNIFF YOU FIRST SO SHE CAN GET COMFORTABLE.
I DON'T WANT IT TO BE COMFORTABLE WITH ME! I'D RATHER IT STAY AWAY.
SEE, SPARKY'S A *GOOD GIRL*, AREN'T YOU, SPARK?
THIS IS BEDELIA, SHE'S OUR NEW FRIEND.
SPARKY? YOU HAVE A DRAGON AND YOU NAMED IT--

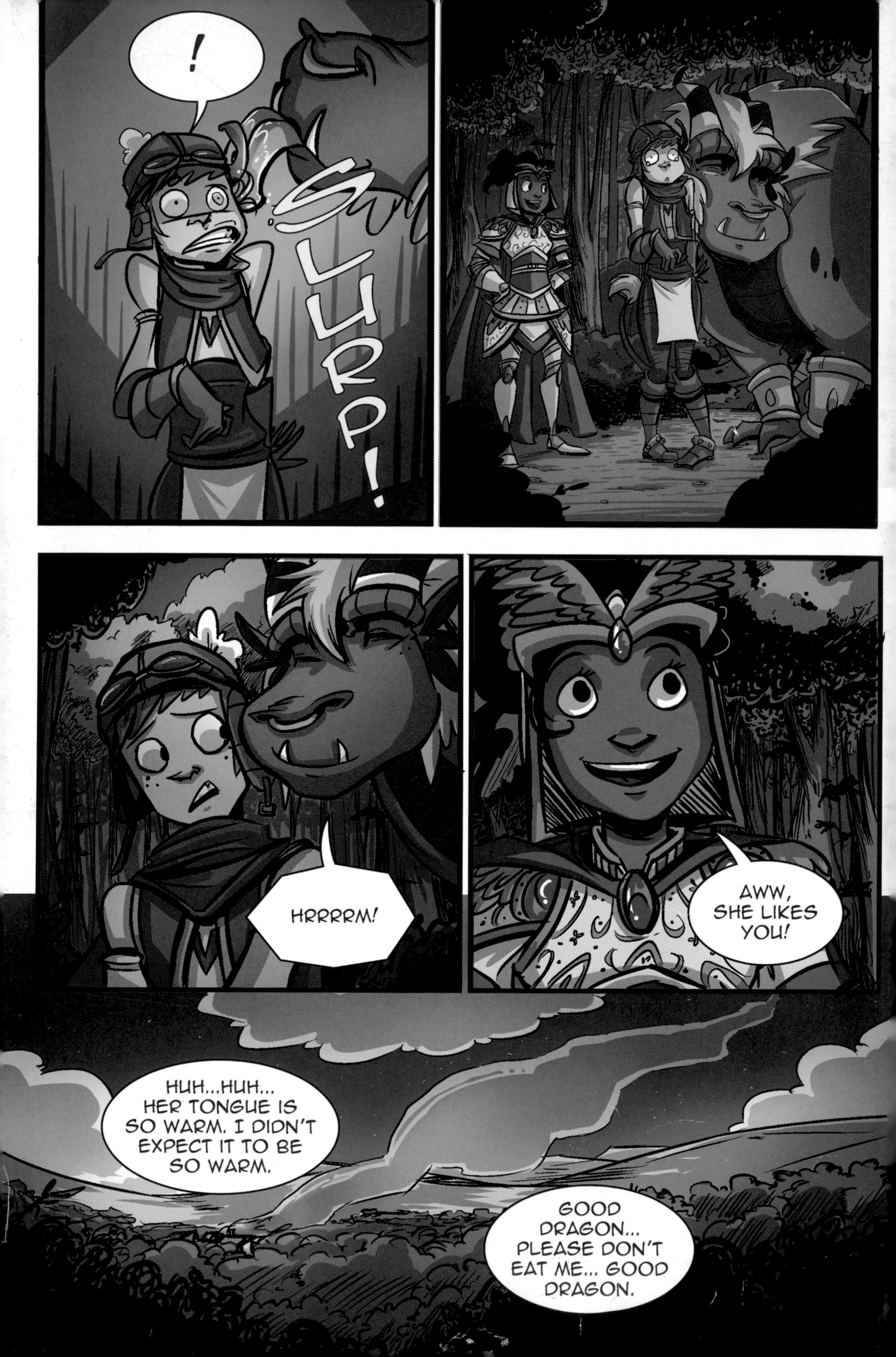
!
SLURP!
HRRRRM!
AWW, SHE LIKES YOU!
HUH...HUH... HER TONGUE IS SO WARM. I DIDN'T EXPECT IT TO BE SO WARM.
GOOD DRAGON... PLEASE DON'T EAT ME... GOOD DRAGON.

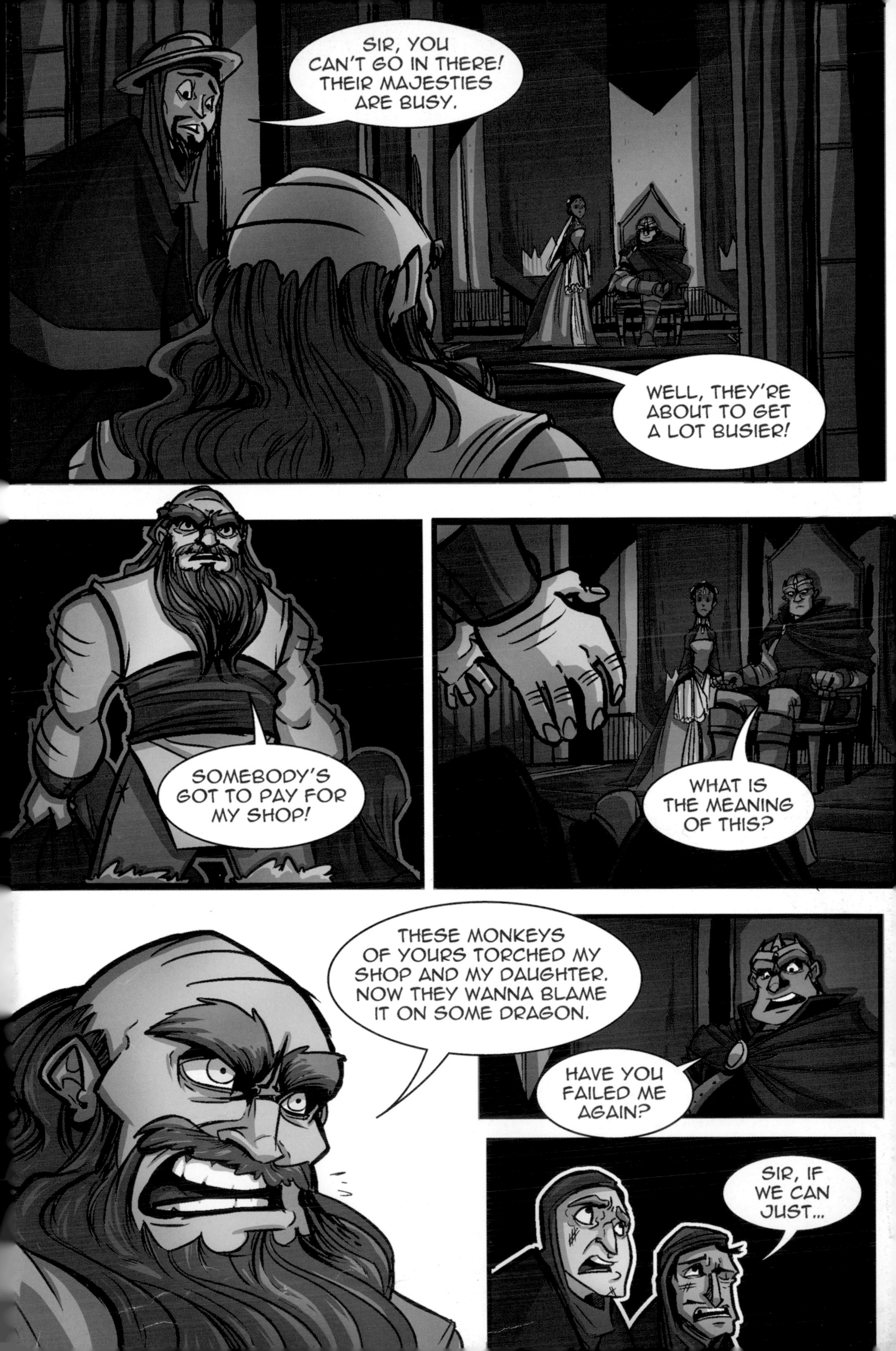
SIR, YOU CAN'T GO IN THERE! THEIR MAJESTIES ARE BUSY.
WELL, THEY'RE ABOUT TO GET A LOT BUSIER!
SOMEBODY'S GOT TO PAY FOR MY SHOP!
WHAT IS THE MEANING OF THIS?
THESE MONKEYS OF YOURS TORCHED MY SHOP AND MY DAUGHTER. NOW THEY WANNA BLAME IT ON SOME DRAGON.
HAVE YOU FAILED ME AGAIN?
SIR, IF WE CAN JUST...

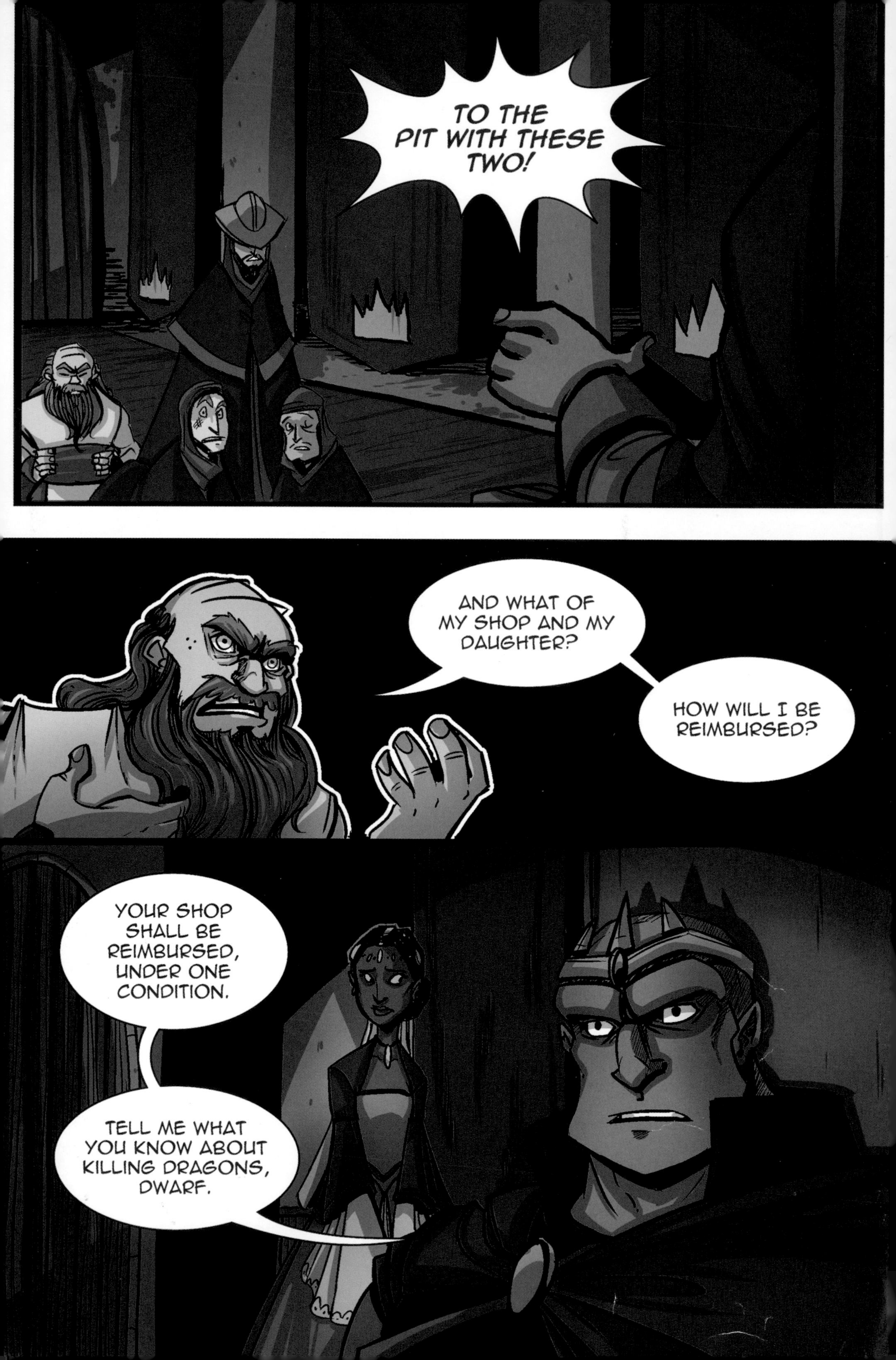
TO THE PIT WITH THESE TWO!
AND WHAT OF MY SHOP AND MY DAUGHTER?
HOW WILL I BE REIMBURSED?
YOUR SHOP SHALL BE REIMBURSED, UNDER ONE CONDITION.
TELL ME WHAT YOU KNOW ABOUT KILLING DRAGONS, DWARF.

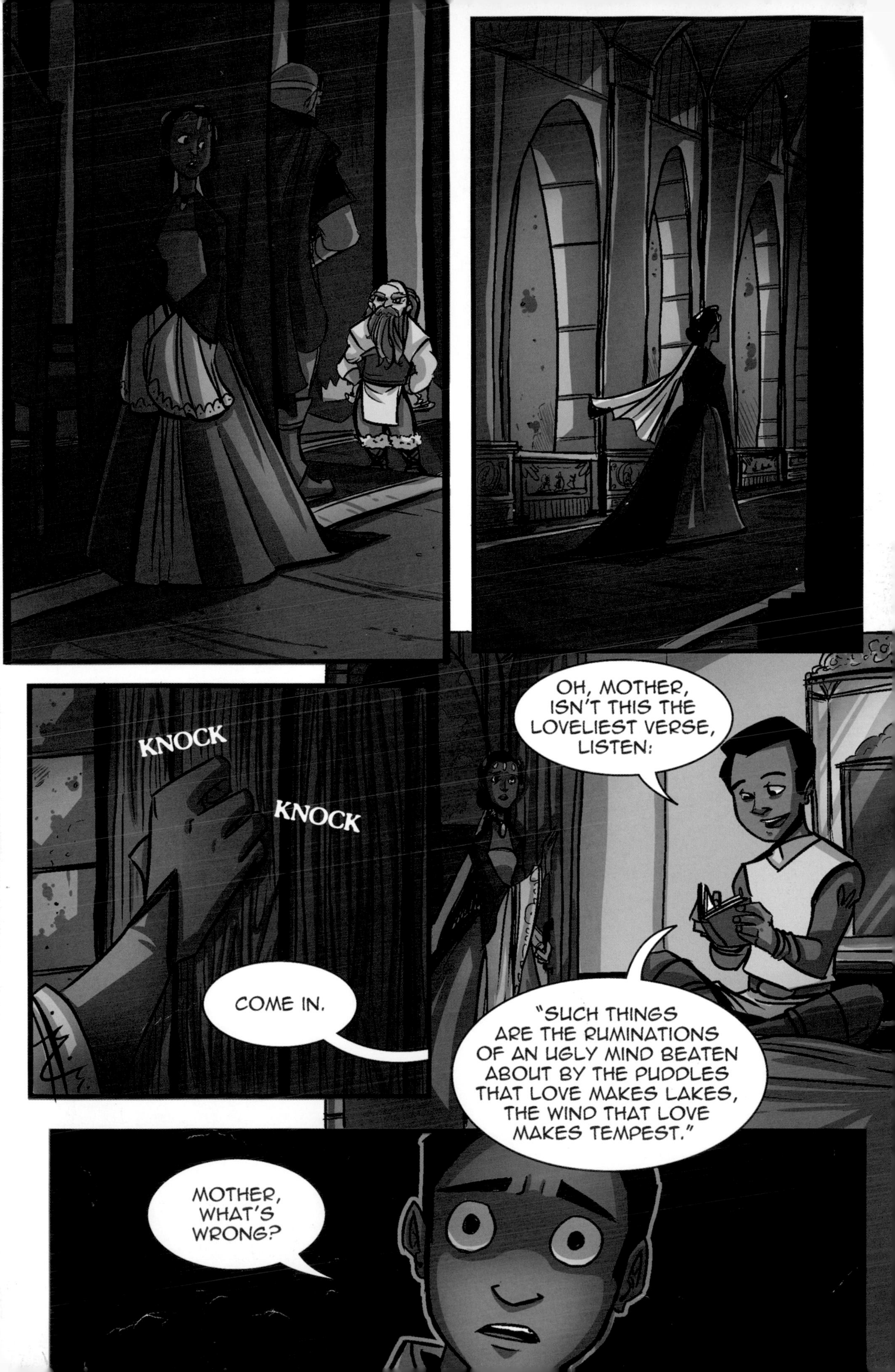
KNOCK
KNOCK
COME IN.
OH, MOTHER, ISN'T THIS THE LOVELIEST VERSE, LISTEN:
"SUCH THINGS ARE THE RUMINATIONS OF AN UGLY MIND BEATEN ABOUT BY THE PUDDLES THAT LOVE MAKES LAKES, THE WIND THAT LOVE MAKES TEMPEST."
MOTHER, WHAT'S WRONG?

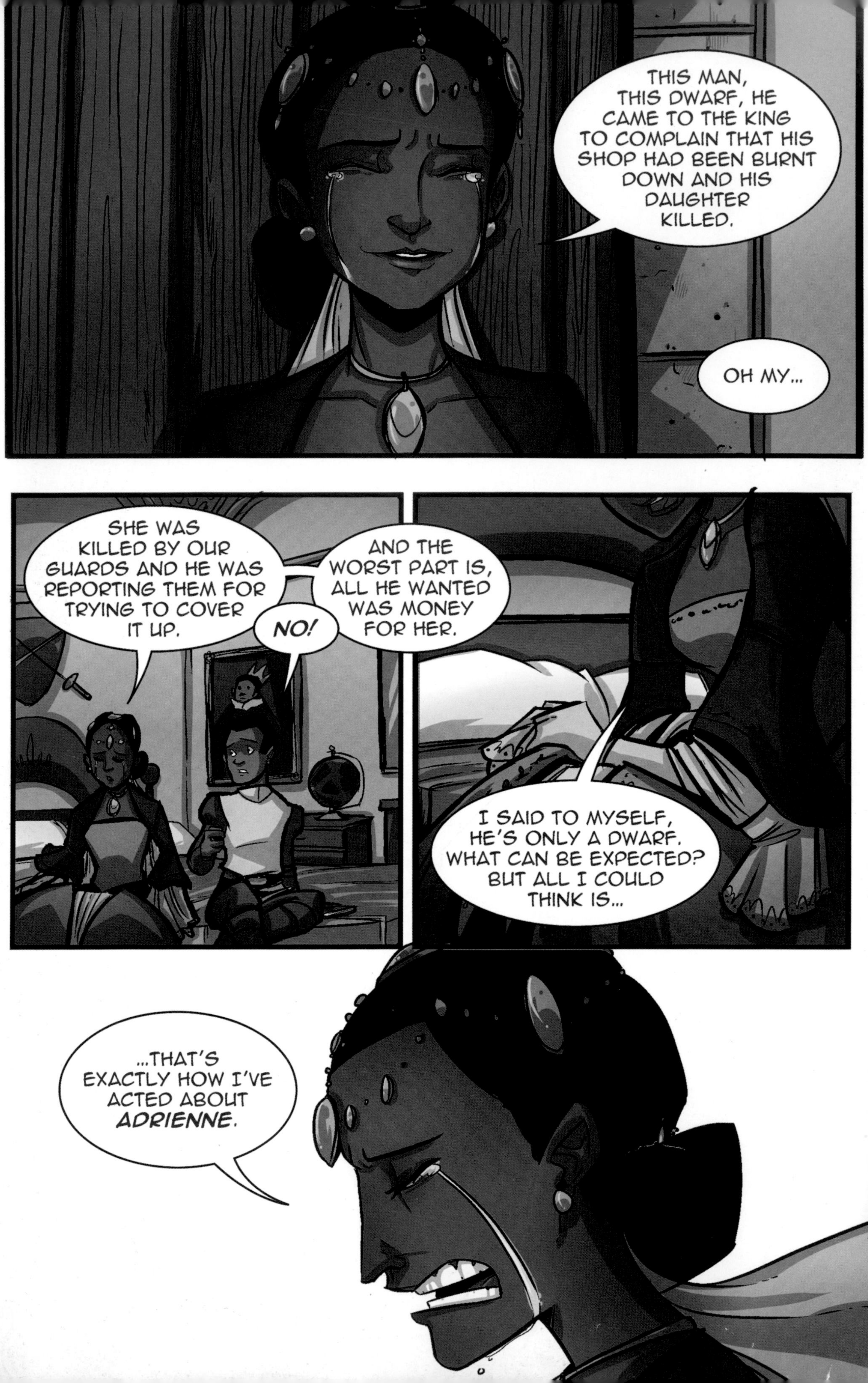
THIS MAN, THIS DWARF, HE CAME TO THE KING TO COMPLAIN THAT HIS SHOP HAD BEEN BURNT DOWN AND HIS DAUGHTER KILLED.
OH MY...
SHE WAS KILLED BY OUR GUARDS AND HE WAS REPORTING THEM FOR TRYING TO COVER IT UP.
NO!
AND THE WORST PART IS, ALL HE WANTED WAS MONEY FOR HER.
I SAID TO MYSELF, HE'S ONLY A DWARF. WHAT CAN BE EXPECTED? BUT ALL I COULD THINK IS...
...THAT'S EXACTLY HOW I'VE ACTED ABOUT ADRIENNE.

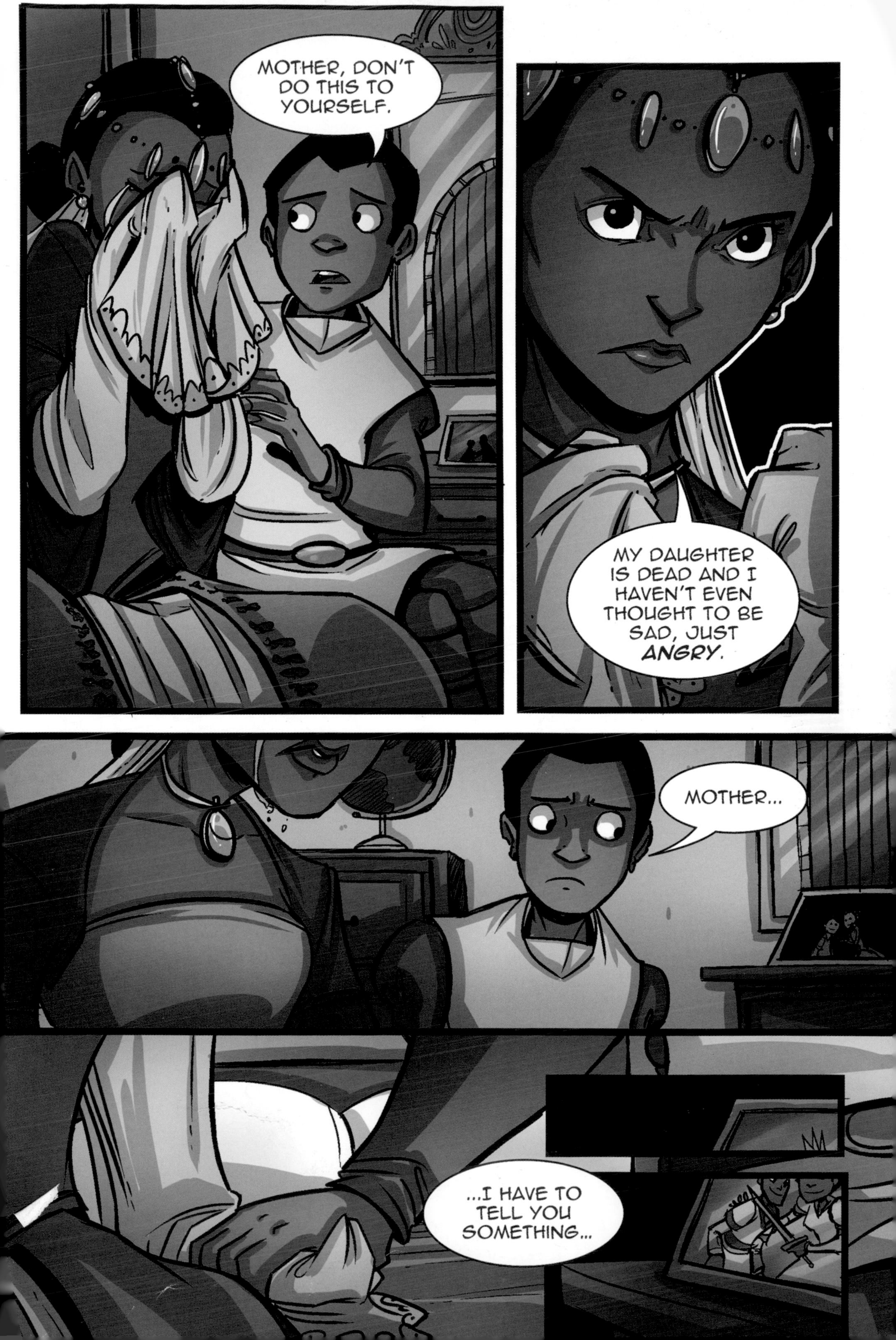
MOTHER, DON'T DO THIS TO YOURSELF.
MY DAUGHTER IS DEAD AND I HAVEN'T EVEN THOUGHT TO BE SAD, JUST *ANGRY*.
MOTHER...
...I HAVE TO TELL YOU SOMETHING...

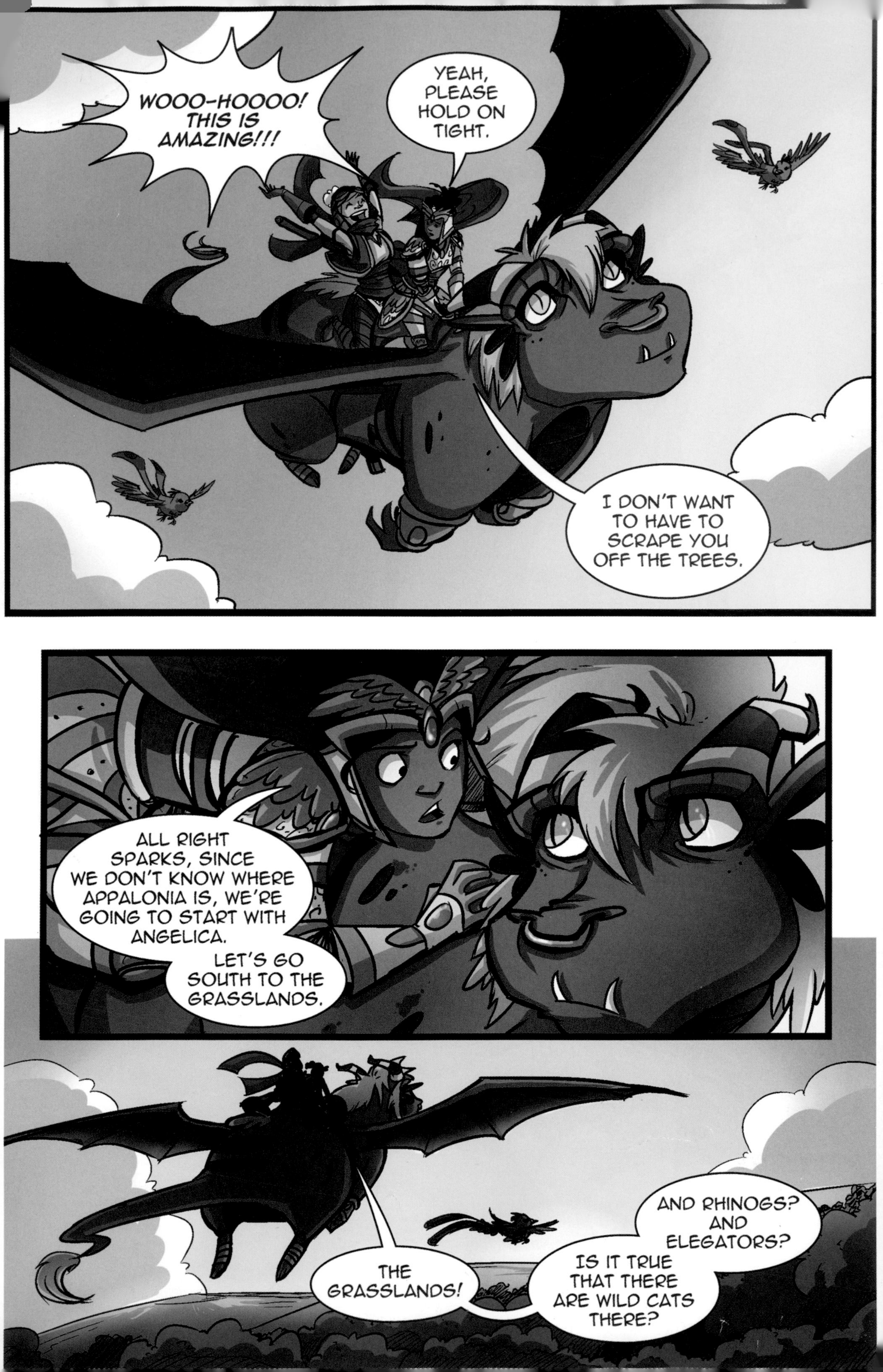
WOOO-HOOOO! THIS IS AMAZING!!!
YEAH, PLEASE HOLD ON TIGHT.
I DON'T WANT TO HAVE TO SCRAPE YOU OFF THE TREES.
ALL RIGHT SPARKS, SINCE WE DON'T KNOW WHERE APPALONIA IS, WE'RE GOING TO START WITH ANGELICA.
LET'S GO SOUTH TO THE GRASSLANDS.
THE GRASSLANDS!
IS IT TRUE THAT THERE ARE WILD CATS THERE?
AND RHINOGS? AND ELEGATORS?

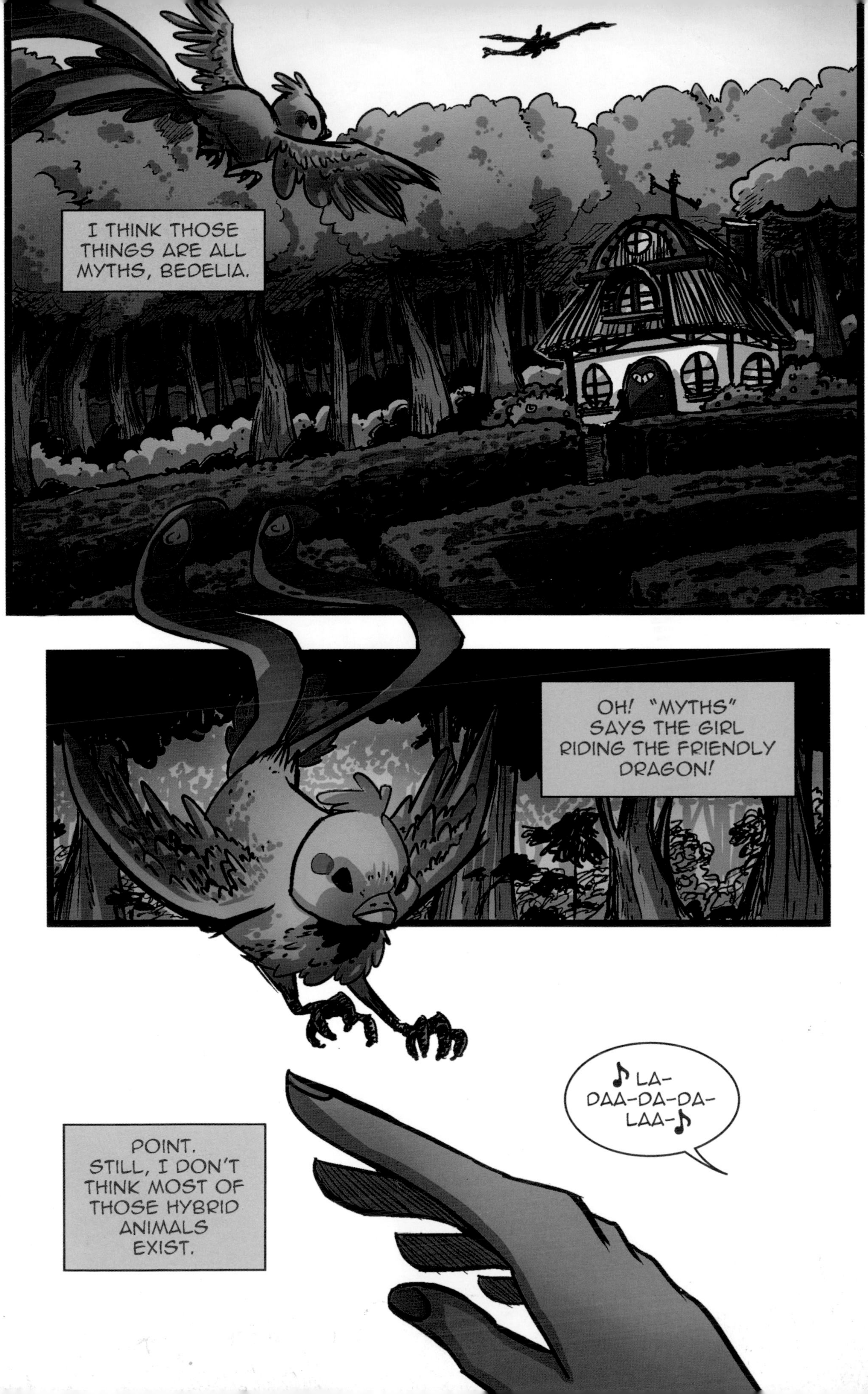
I THINK THOSE THINGS ARE ALL MYTHS, BEDELIA.
OH! "MYTHS" SAYS THE GIRL RIDING THE FRIENDLY DRAGON!
POINT. STILL, I DON'T THINK MOST OF THOSE HYBRID ANIMALS EXIST.
♪ LA-DAA-DA-DA-LAA-♪

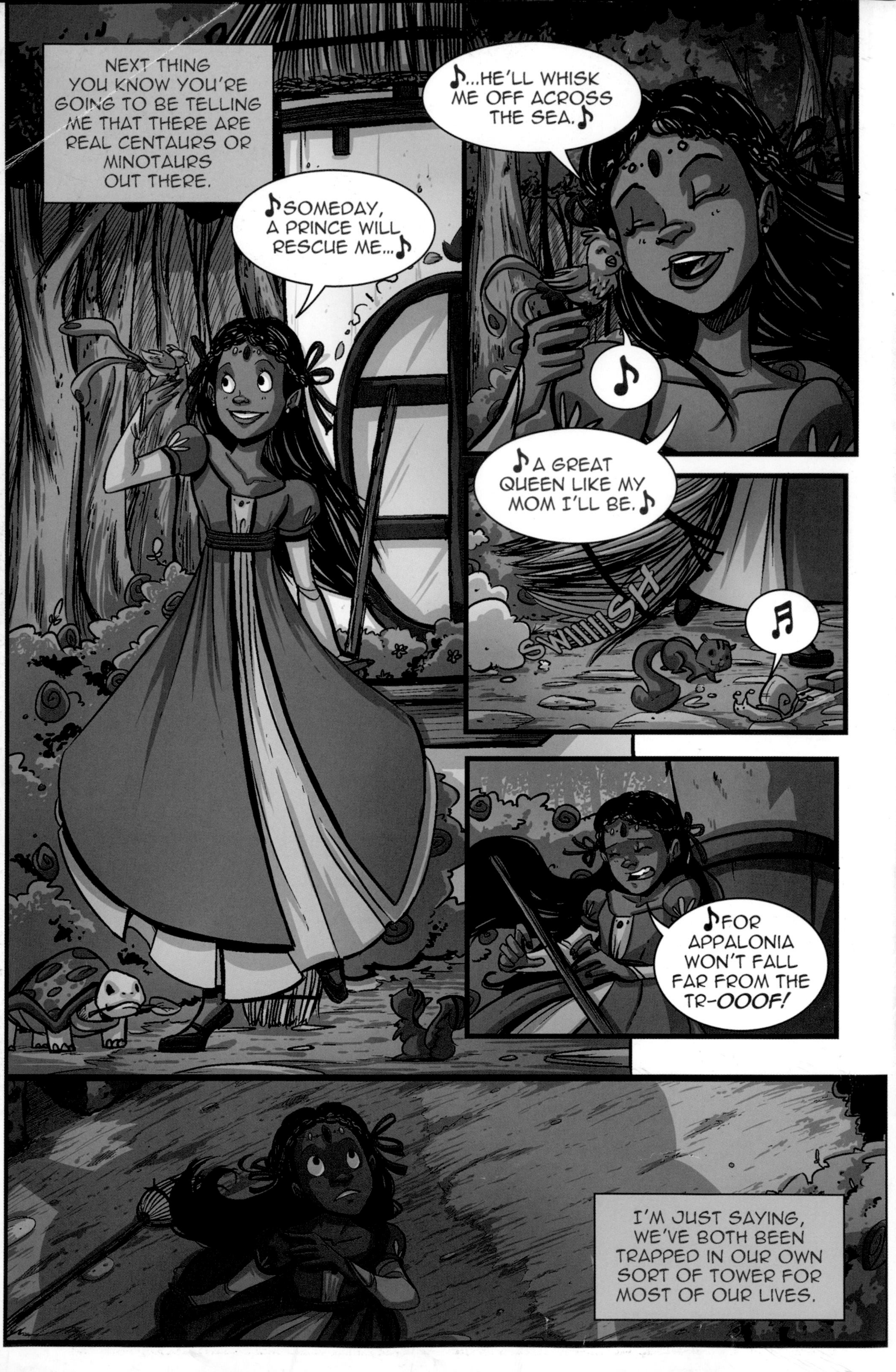
NEXT THING YOU KNOW YOU'RE GOING TO BE TELLING ME THAT THERE ARE REAL CENTAURS OR MINOTAURS OUT THERE.
♪SOMEDAY, A PRINCE WILL RESCUE ME...♪
♪...HE'LL WHISK ME OFF ACROSS THE SEA.♪
♪
♪A GREAT QUEEN LIKE MY MOM I'LL BE.♪
SWIIIISH
♬
♪FOR APPALONIA WON'T FALL FAR FROM THE TR-OOOF!
I'M JUST SAYING, WE'VE BOTH BEEN TRAPPED IN OUR OWN SORT OF TOWER FOR MOST OF OUR LIVES.

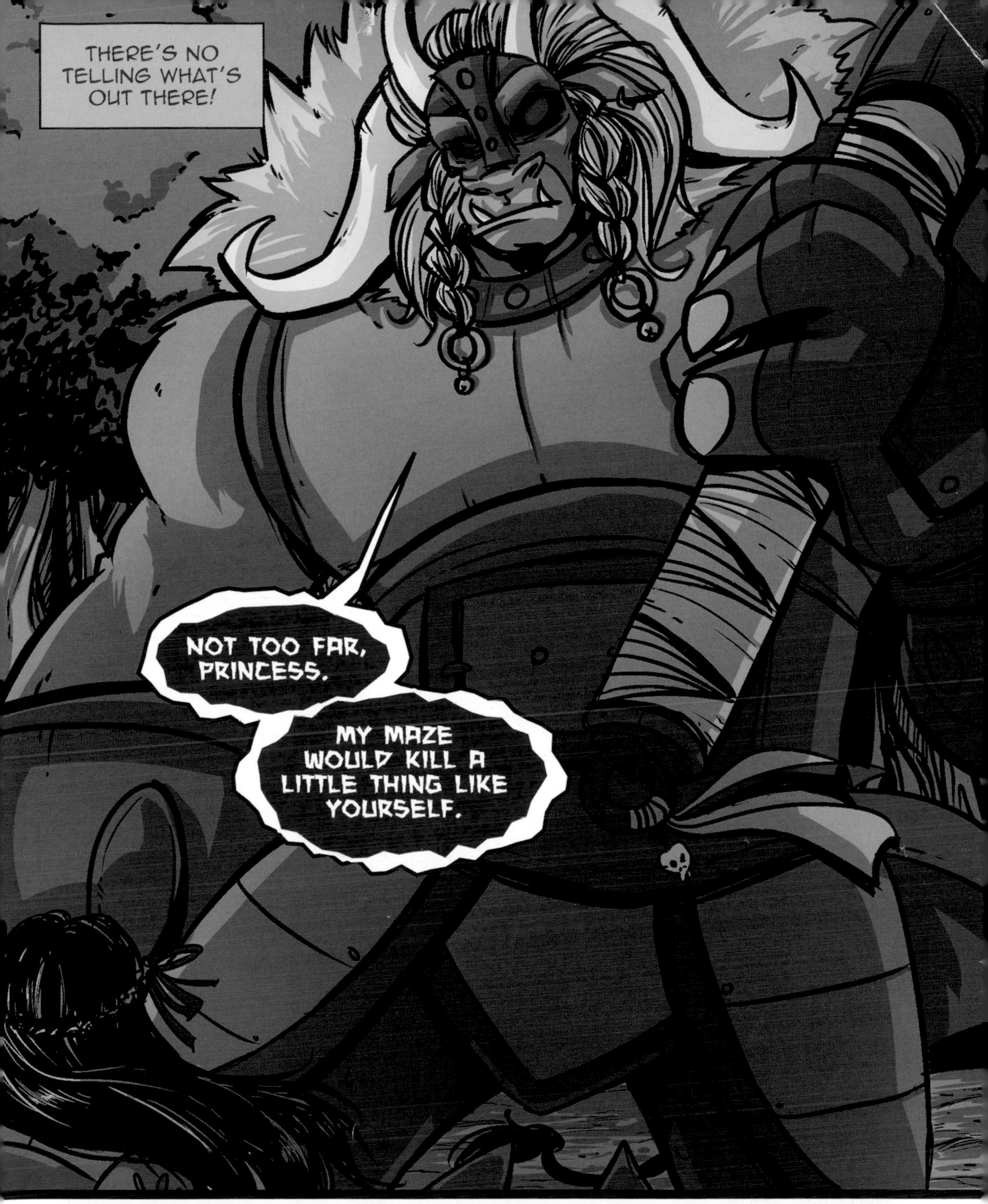
THERE'S NO TELLING WHAT'S OUT THERE!
NOT TOO FAR, PRINCESS.
MY MAZE WOULD KILL A LITTLE THING LIKE YOURSELF.

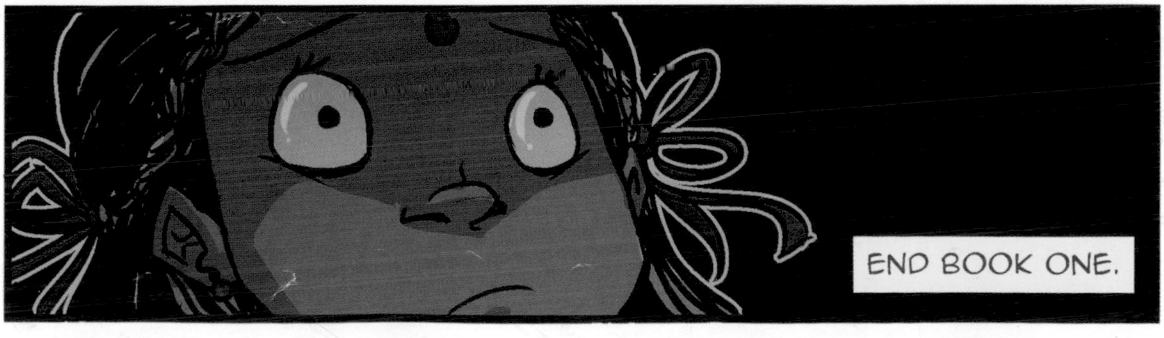
END BOOK ONE.

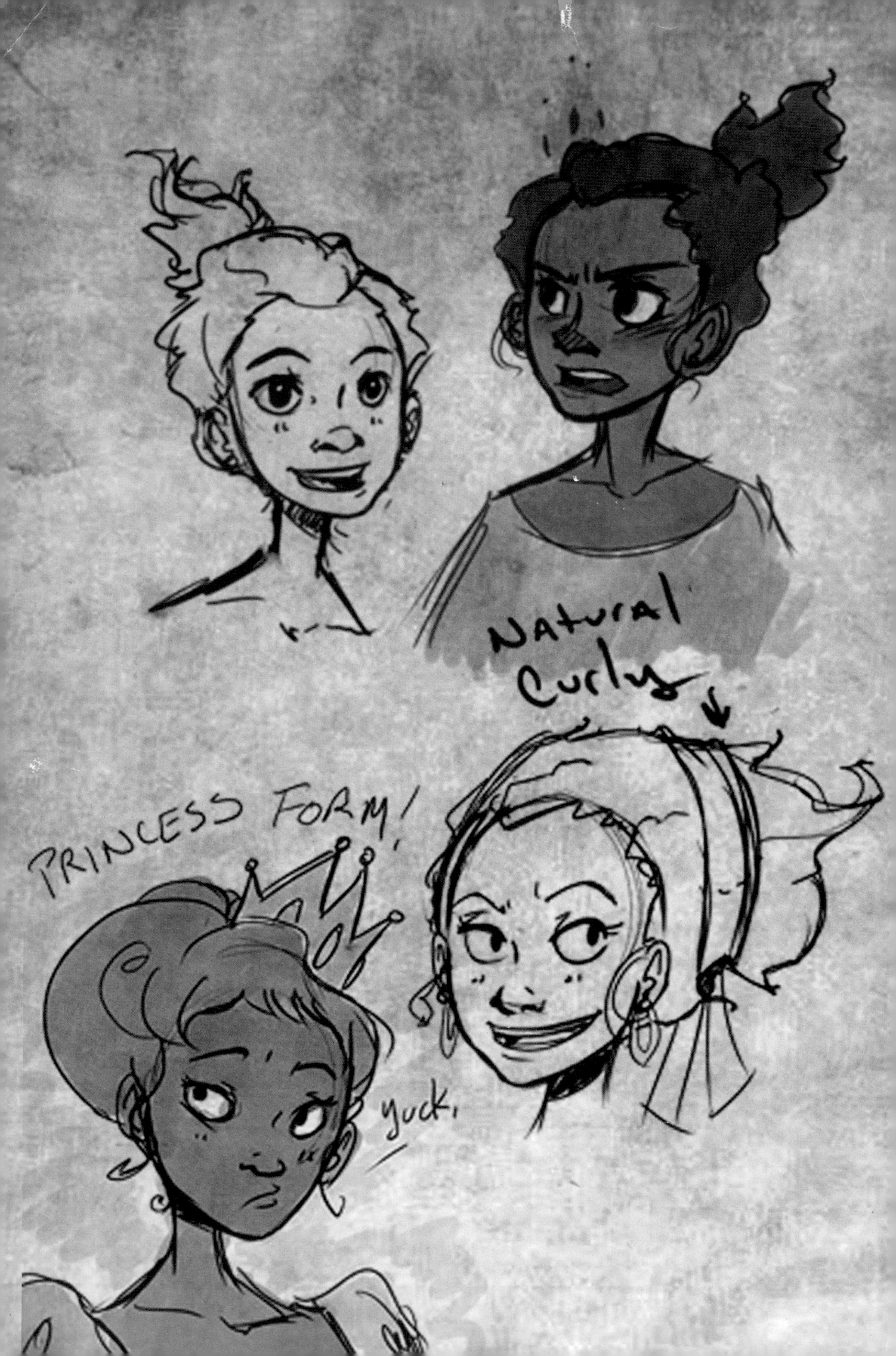
Natural
Curly
PRINCESS FORM!
yuck.

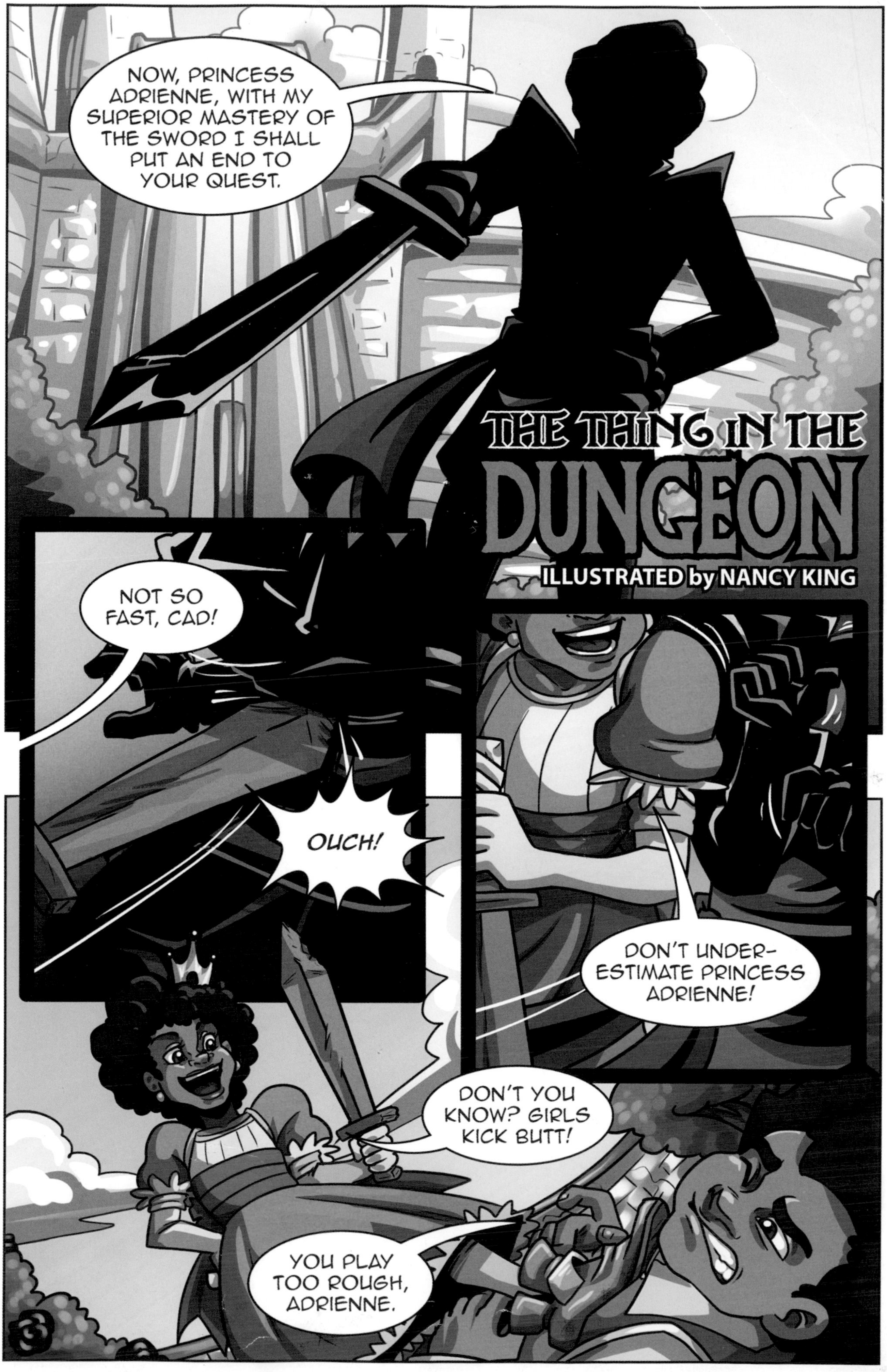
NOW, PRINCESS ADRIENNE, WITH MY SUPERIOR MASTERY OF THE SWORD I SHALL PUT AN END TO YOUR QUEST.
THE THING IN THE DUNGEON
ILLUSTRATED by NANCY KING
NOT SO FAST, CAD!
OUCH!
DON'T UNDER-ESTIMATE PRINCESS ADRIENNE!
DON'T YOU KNOW? GIRLS KICK BUTT!
YOU PLAY TOO ROUGH, ADRIENNE.

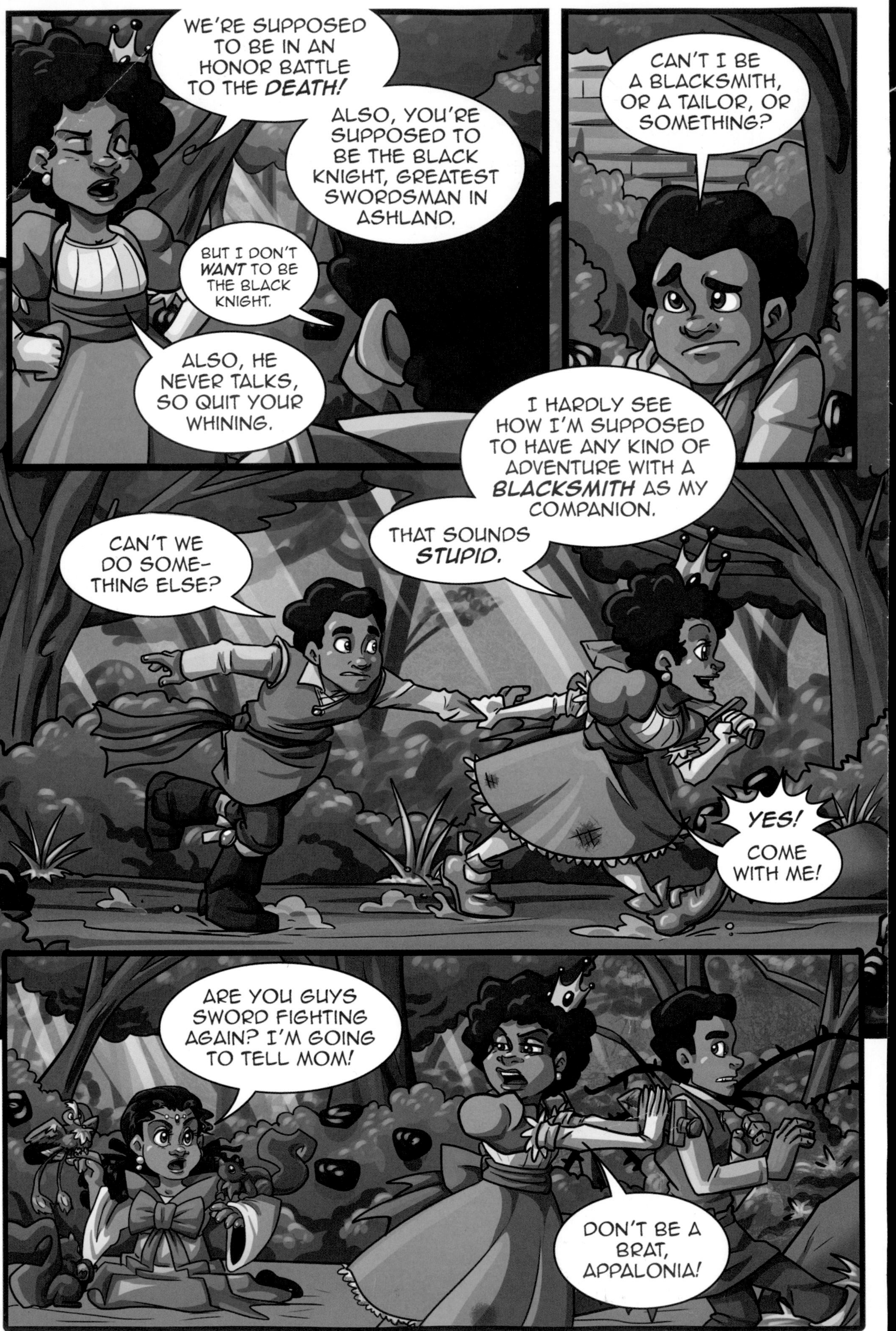
WE'RE SUPPOSED TO BE IN AN HONOR BATTLE TO THE *DEATH!*
ALSO, YOU'RE SUPPOSED TO BE THE BLACK KNIGHT, GREATEST SWORDSMAN IN ASHLAND.
BUT I DON'T *WANT* TO BE THE BLACK KNIGHT.
ALSO, HE NEVER TALKS, SO QUIT YOUR WHINING.
CAN'T I BE A BLACKSMITH, OR A TAILOR, OR SOMETHING?
I HARDLY SEE HOW I'M SUPPOSED TO HAVE ANY KIND OF ADVENTURE WITH A *BLACKSMITH* AS MY COMPANION.
THAT SOUNDS *STUPID.*
CAN'T WE DO SOME-THING ELSE?
YES!
COME WITH ME!
ARE YOU GUYS SWORD FIGHTING AGAIN? I'M GOING TO TELL MOM!
DON'T BE A BRAT, APPALONIA!

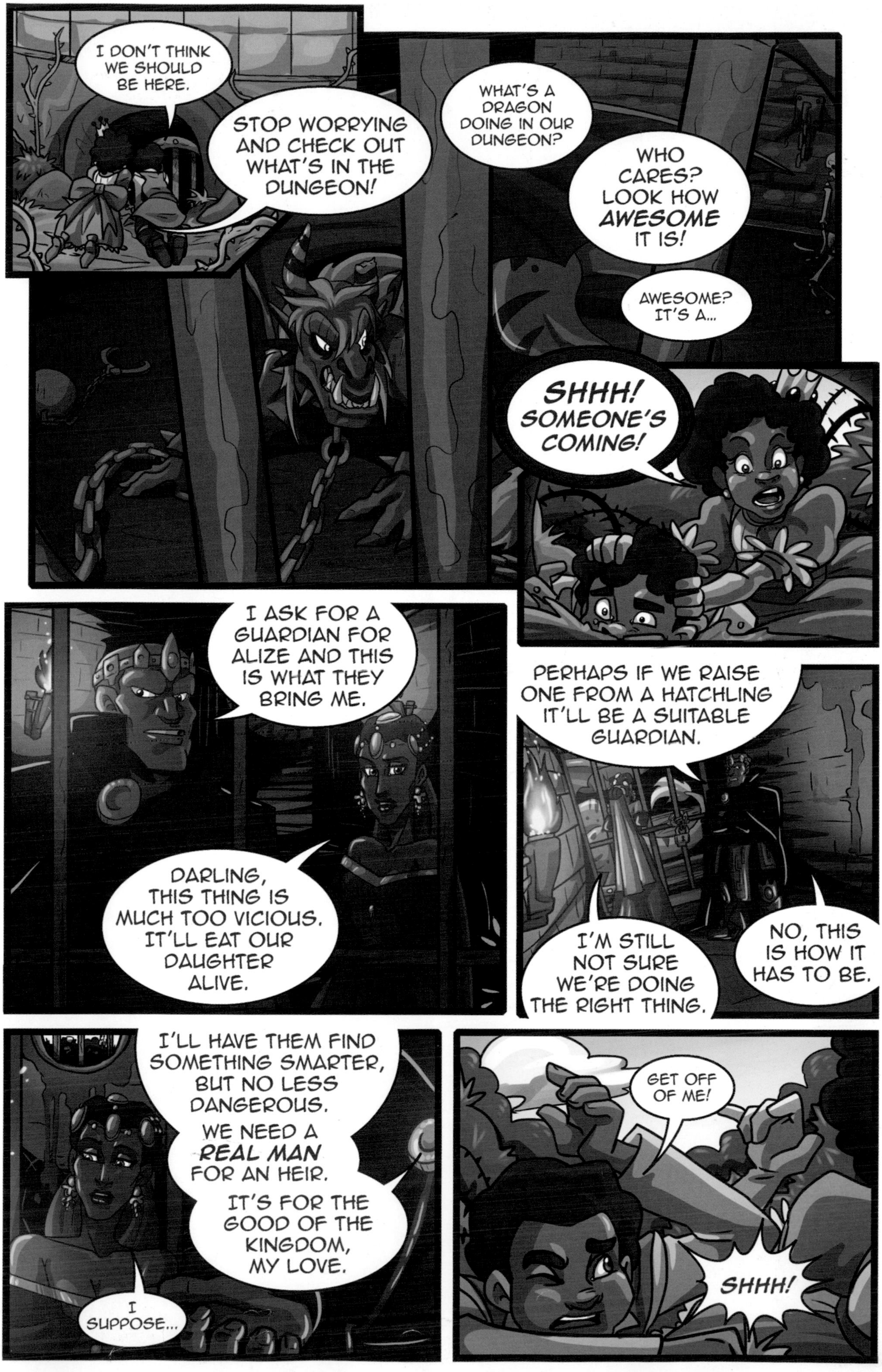
I DON'T THINK WE SHOULD BE HERE.
STOP WORRYING AND CHECK OUT WHAT'S IN THE DUNGEON!
WHAT'S A DRAGON DOING IN OUR DUNGEON?
WHO CARES? LOOK HOW AWESOME IT IS!
AWESOME? IT'S A...
SHHH! SOMEONE'S COMING!
I ASK FOR A GUARDIAN FOR ALIZE AND THIS IS WHAT THEY BRING ME.
DARLING, THIS THING IS MUCH TOO VICIOUS. IT'LL EAT OUR DAUGHTER ALIVE.
PERHAPS IF WE RAISE ONE FROM A HATCHLING IT'LL BE A SUITABLE GUARDIAN.
I'M STILL NOT SURE WE'RE DOING THE RIGHT THING.
NO, THIS IS HOW IT HAS TO BE.
I'LL HAVE THEM FIND SOMETHING SMARTER, BUT NO LESS DANGEROUS.
WE NEED A REAL MAN FOR AN HEIR.
IT'S FOR THE GOOD OF THE KINGDOM, MY LOVE.
I SUPPOSE...
GET OFF OF ME!
SHHH!

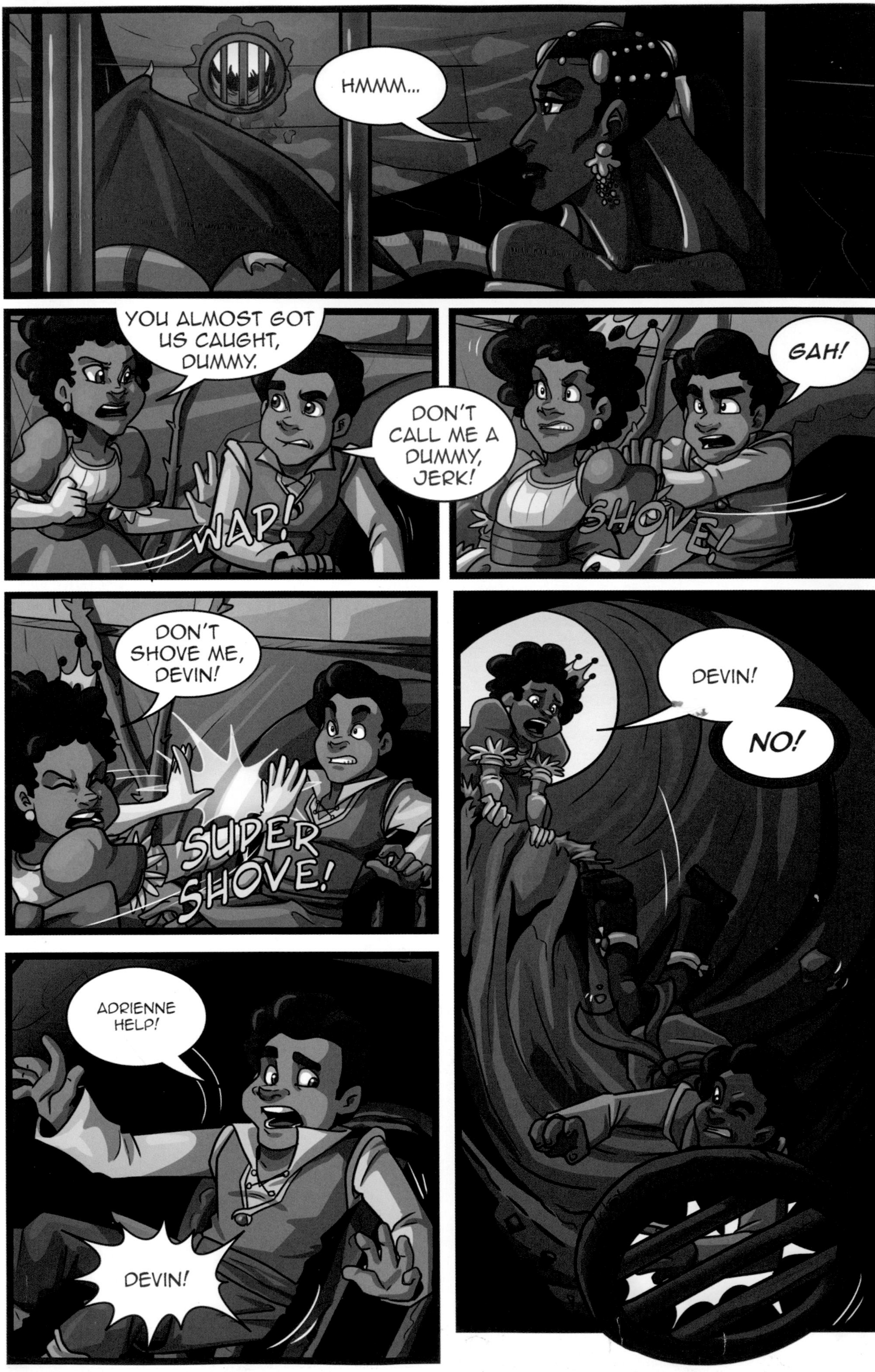
HMMM...
YOU ALMOST GOT US CAUGHT, DUMMY.
WAP!
DON'T CALL ME A DUMMY, JERK!
GAH!
SHOVE!
DON'T SHOVE ME, DEVIN!
SUPER SHOVE!
DEVIN!
NO!
ADRIENNE HELP!
DEVIN!

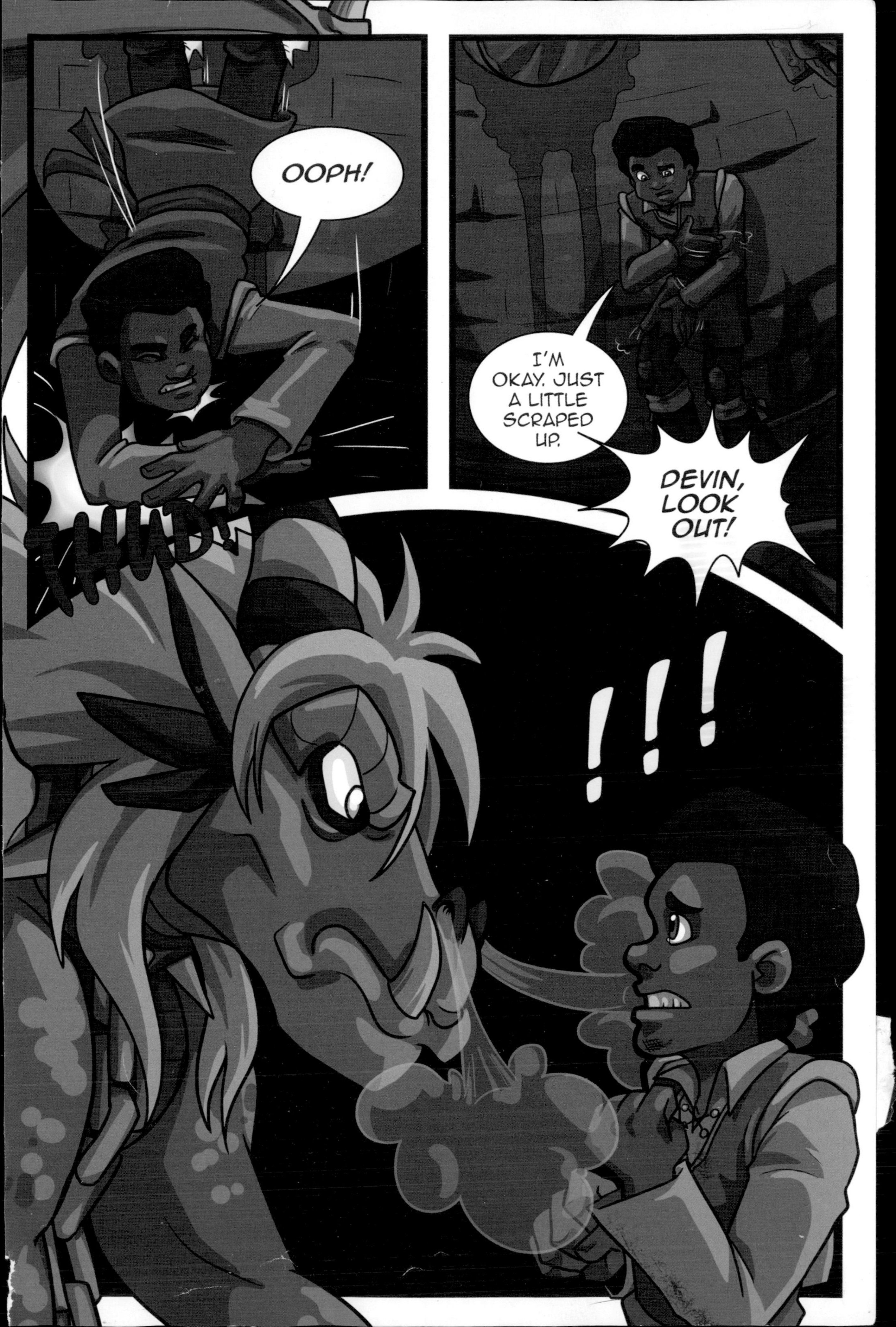
OOPH!
THUD!
I'M OKAY. JUST A LITTLE SCRAPED UP.
DEVIN, LOOK OUT!
!!!

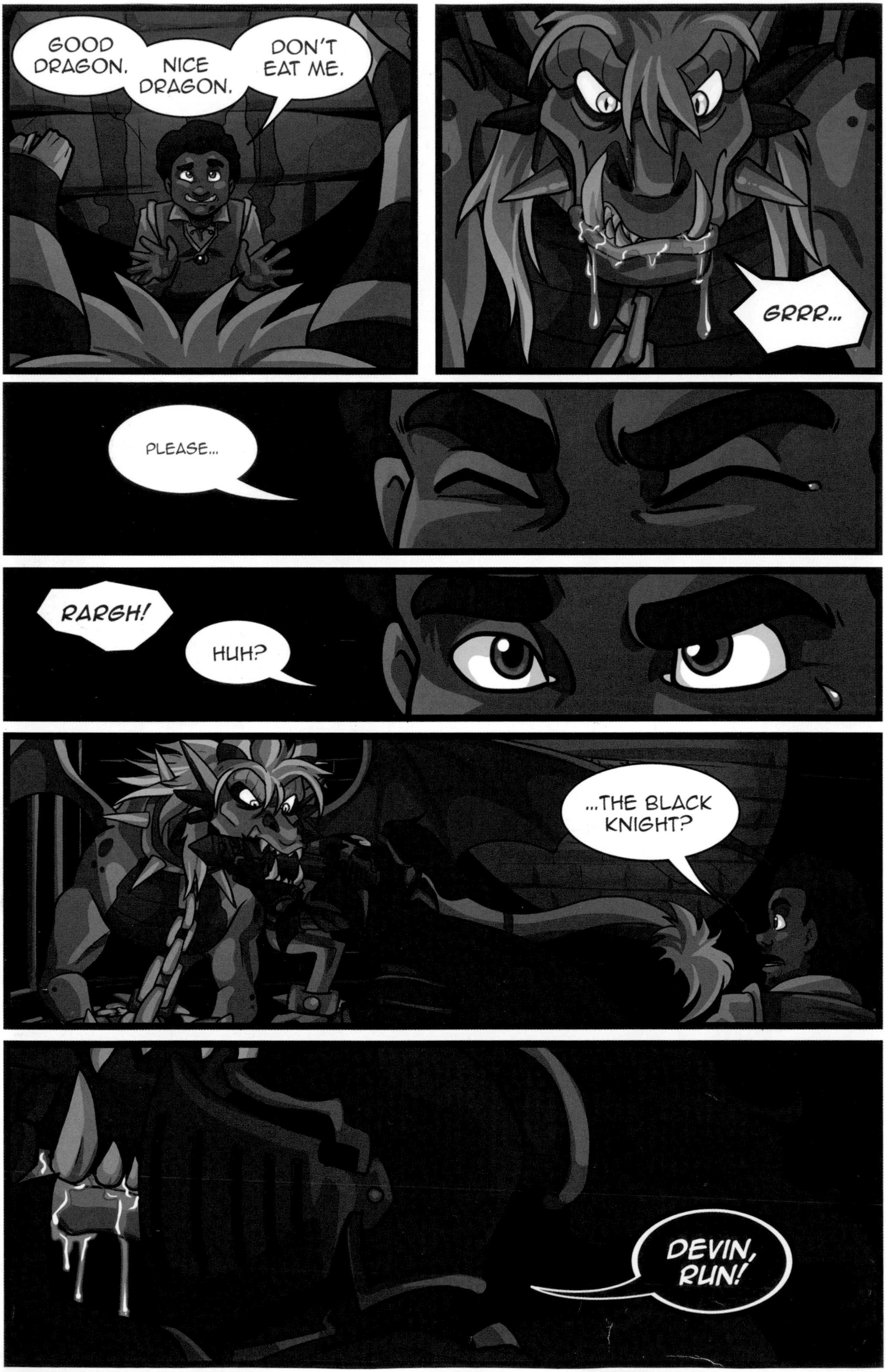
GOOD DRAGON.
NICE DRAGON.
DON'T EAT ME.
GRRR...
PLEASE...
RARGH!
HUH?
...THE BLACK KNIGHT?
DEVIN, RUN!

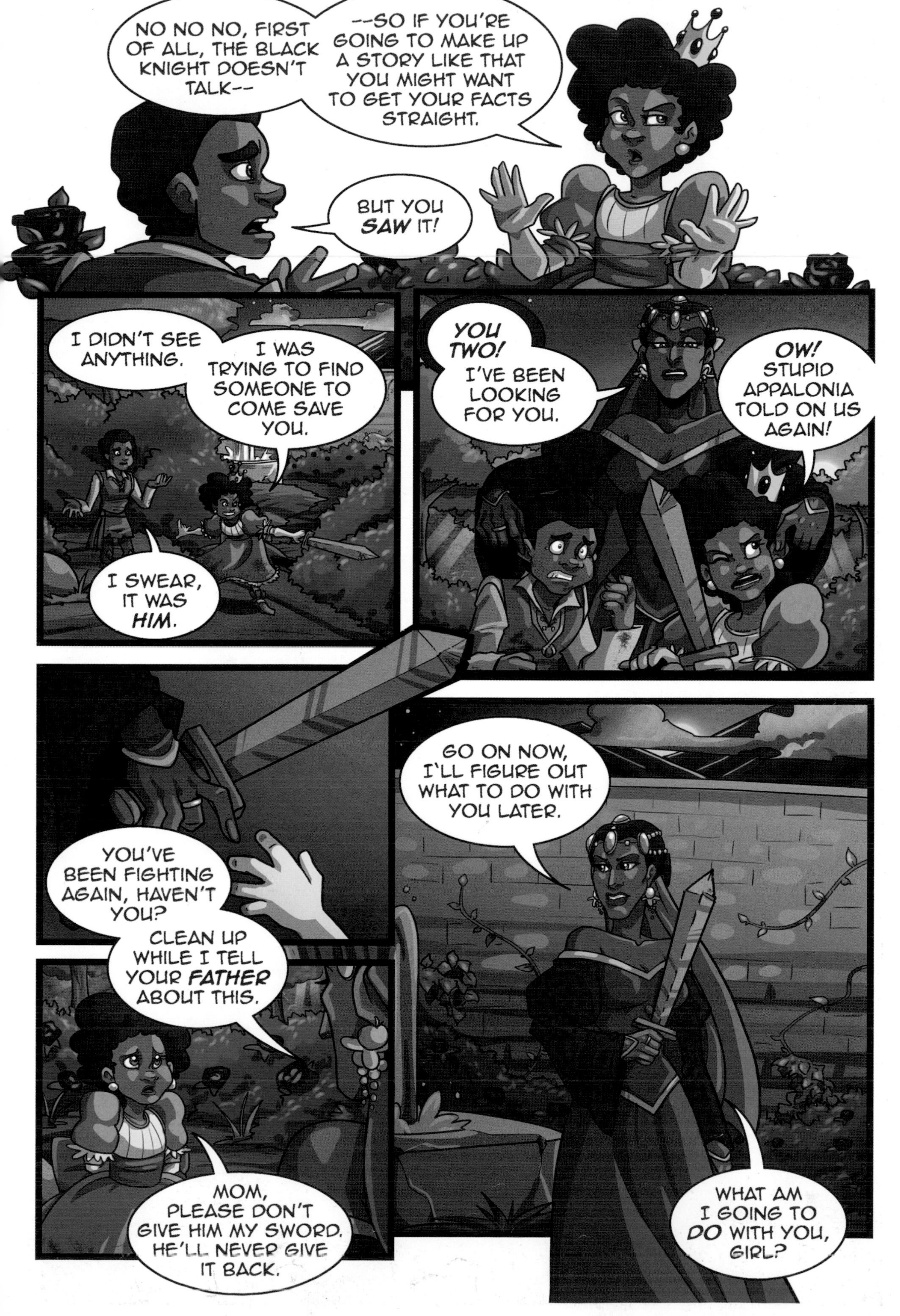
NO NO NO, FIRST OF ALL, THE BLACK KNIGHT DOESN'T TALK--
--SO IF YOU'RE GOING TO MAKE UP A STORY LIKE THAT YOU MIGHT WANT TO GET YOUR FACTS STRAIGHT.
BUT YOU *SAW* IT!
I DIDN'T SEE ANYTHING.
I WAS TRYING TO FIND SOMEONE TO COME SAVE YOU.
I SWEAR, IT WAS *HIM*.
YOU TWO!
I'VE BEEN LOOKING FOR YOU.
OW! STUPID APPALONIA TOLD ON US AGAIN!
YOU'VE BEEN FIGHTING AGAIN, HAVEN'T YOU?
CLEAN UP WHILE I TELL YOUR *FATHER* ABOUT THIS.
MOM, PLEASE DON'T GIVE HIM MY SWORD. HE'LL NEVER GIVE IT BACK.
GO ON NOW, I'LL FIGURE OUT WHAT TO DO WITH YOU LATER.
WHAT AM I GOING TO *DO* WITH YOU, GIRL?

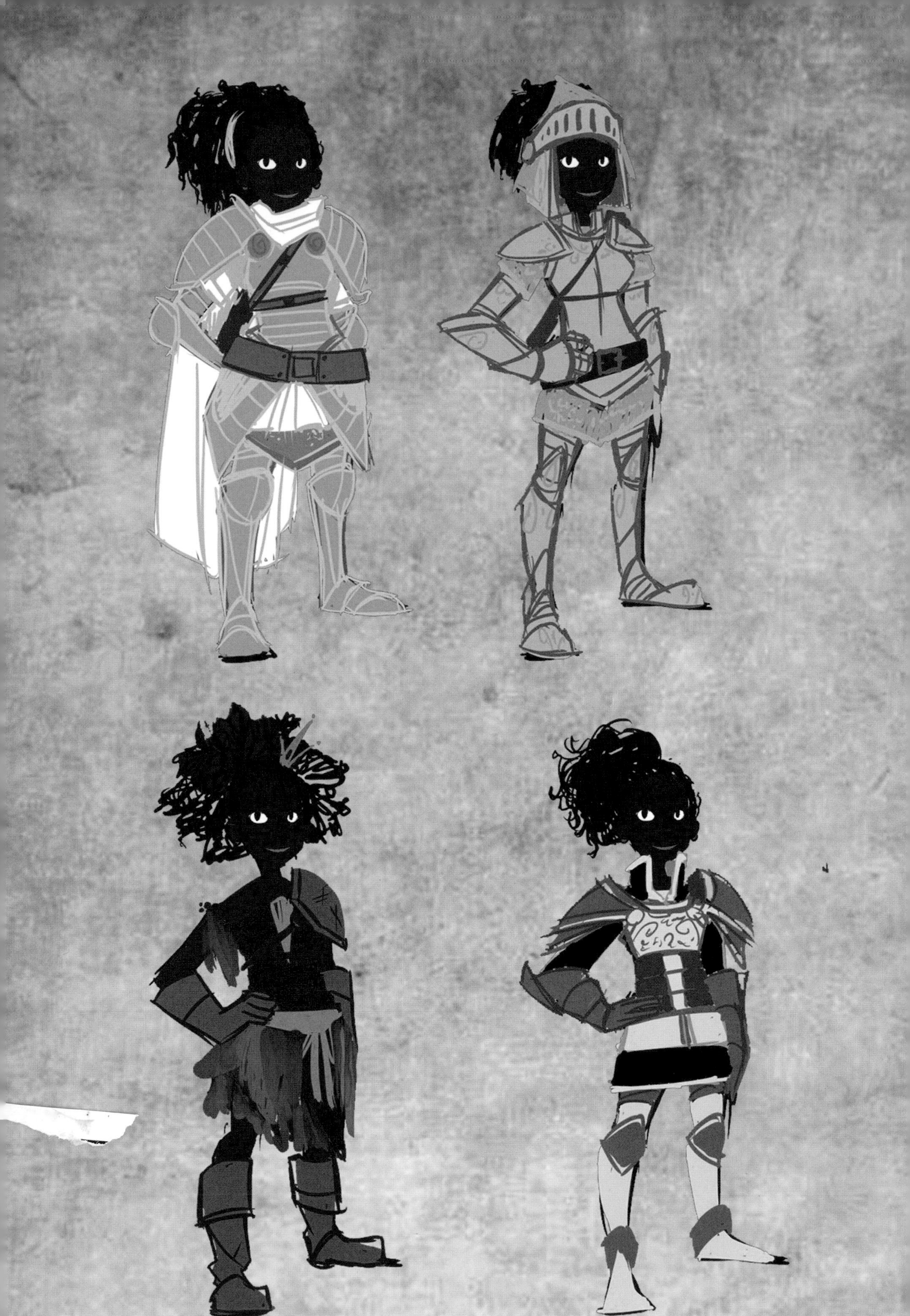

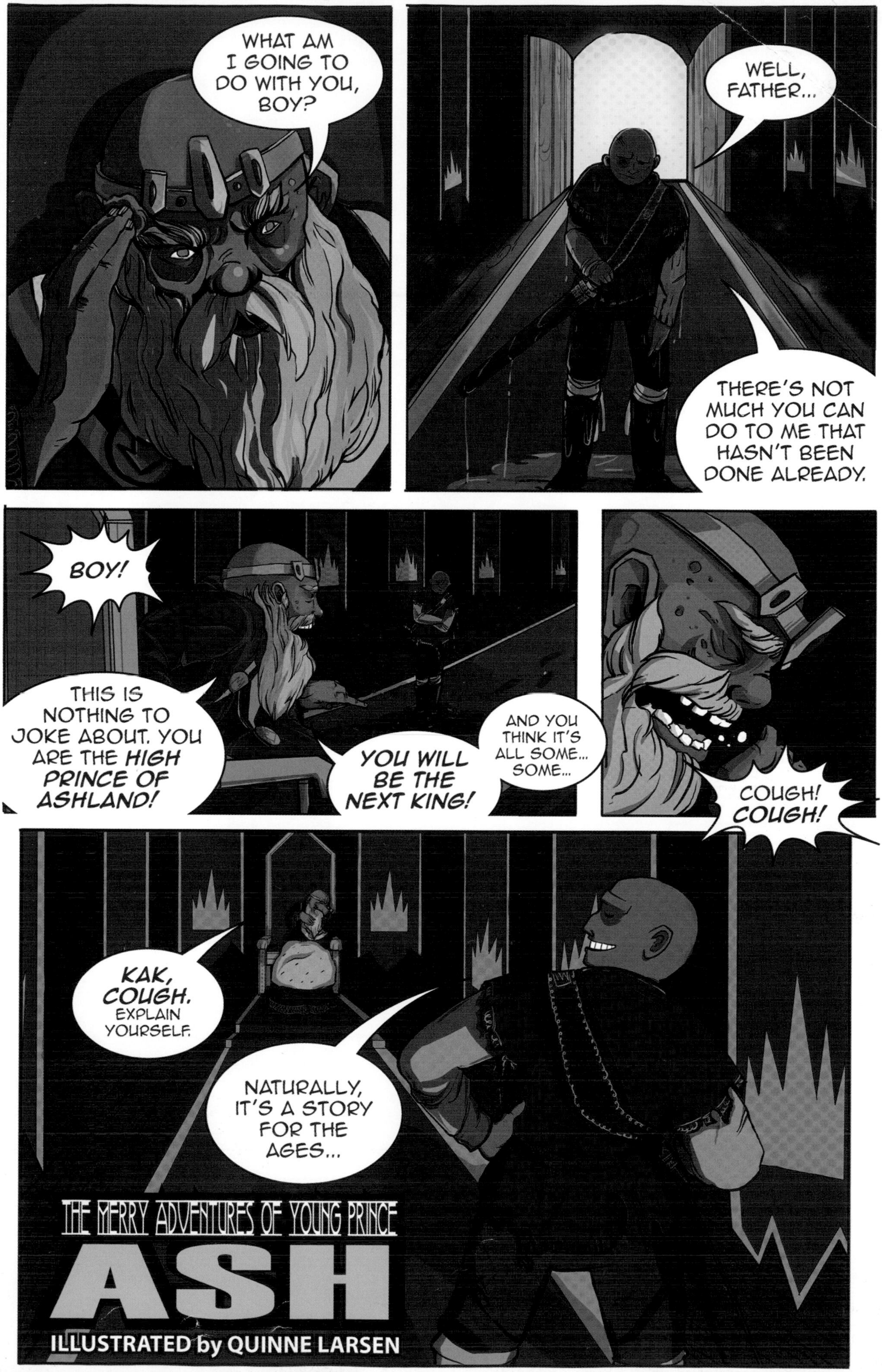

WHAT AM I GOING TO DO WITH YOU, BOY?
WELL, FATHER...
THERE'S NOT MUCH YOU CAN DO TO ME THAT HASN'T BEEN DONE ALREADY.
BOY!
THIS IS NOTHING TO JOKE ABOUT. YOU ARE THE HIGH PRINCE OF ASHLAND!
YOU WILL BE THE NEXT KING!
AND YOU THINK IT'S ALL SOME... SOME...
COUGH! COUGH!
KAK, COUGH. EXPLAIN YOURSELF.
NATURALLY, IT'S A STORY FOR THE AGES...
THE MERRY ADVENTURES OF YOUNG PRINCE
ASH
ILLUSTRATED by QUINNE LARSEN

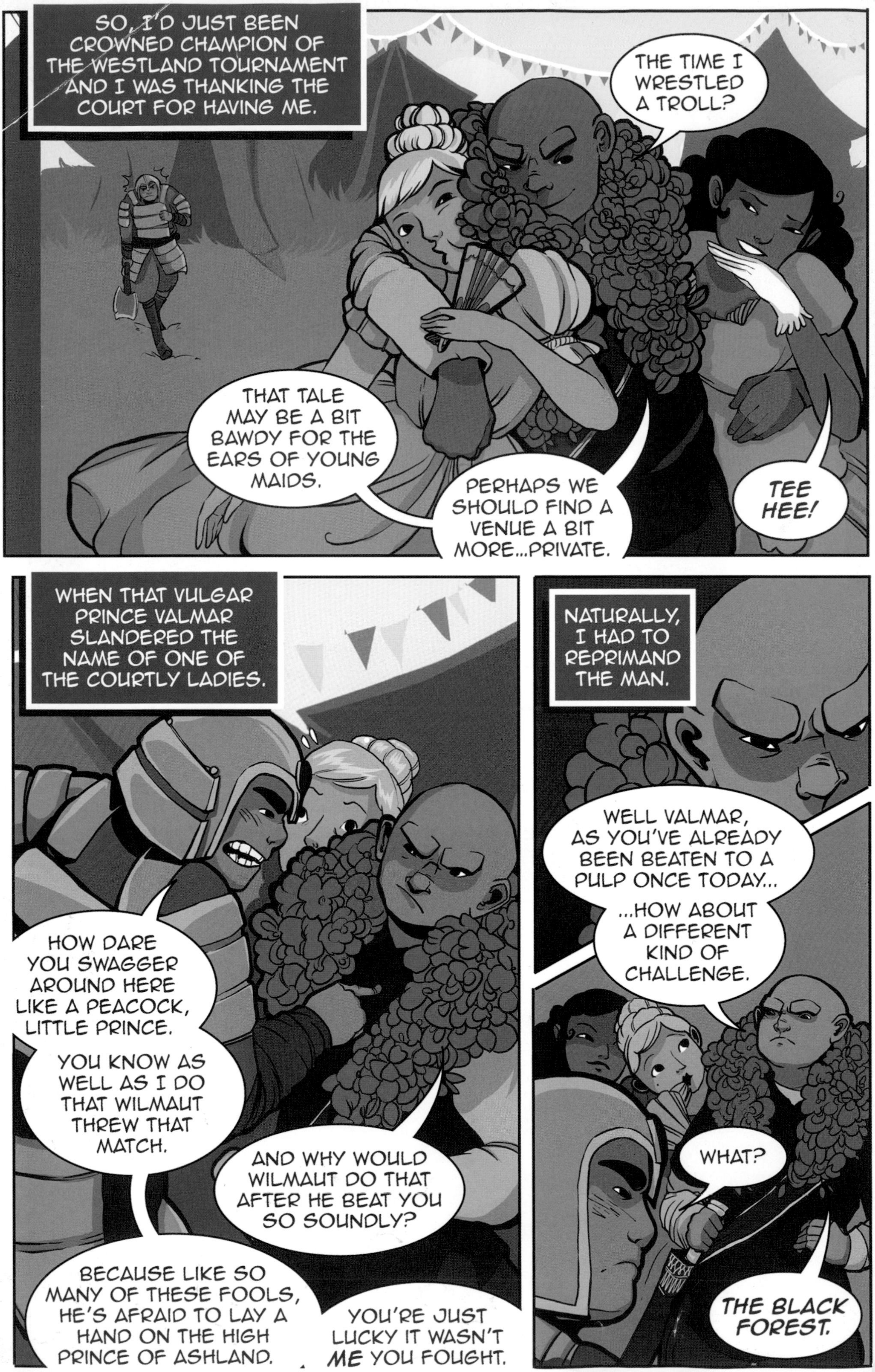
SO, I'D JUST BEEN CROWNED CHAMPION OF THE WESTLAND TOURNAMENT AND I WAS THANKING THE COURT FOR HAVING ME.
THE TIME I WRESTLED A TROLL?
THAT TALE MAY BE A BIT BAWDY FOR THE EARS OF YOUNG MAIDS.
PERHAPS WE SHOULD FIND A VENUE A BIT MORE...PRIVATE.
TEE HEE!
WHEN THAT VULGAR PRINCE VALMAR SLANDERED THE NAME OF ONE OF THE COURTLY LADIES.
HOW DARE YOU SWAGGER AROUND HERE LIKE A PEACOCK, LITTLE PRINCE.
YOU KNOW AS WELL AS I DO THAT WILMAUT THREW THAT MATCH.
AND WHY WOULD WILMAUT DO THAT AFTER HE BEAT YOU SO SOUNDLY?
BECAUSE LIKE SO MANY OF THESE FOOLS, HE'S AFRAID TO LAY A HAND ON THE HIGH PRINCE OF ASHLAND.
YOU'RE JUST LUCKY IT WASN'T ME YOU FOUGHT.
NATURALLY, I HAD TO REPRIMAND THE MAN.
WELL VALMAR, AS YOU'VE ALREADY BEEN BEATEN TO A PULP ONCE TODAY...
...HOW ABOUT A DIFFERENT KIND OF CHALLENGE.
WHAT?
THE BLACK FOREST.

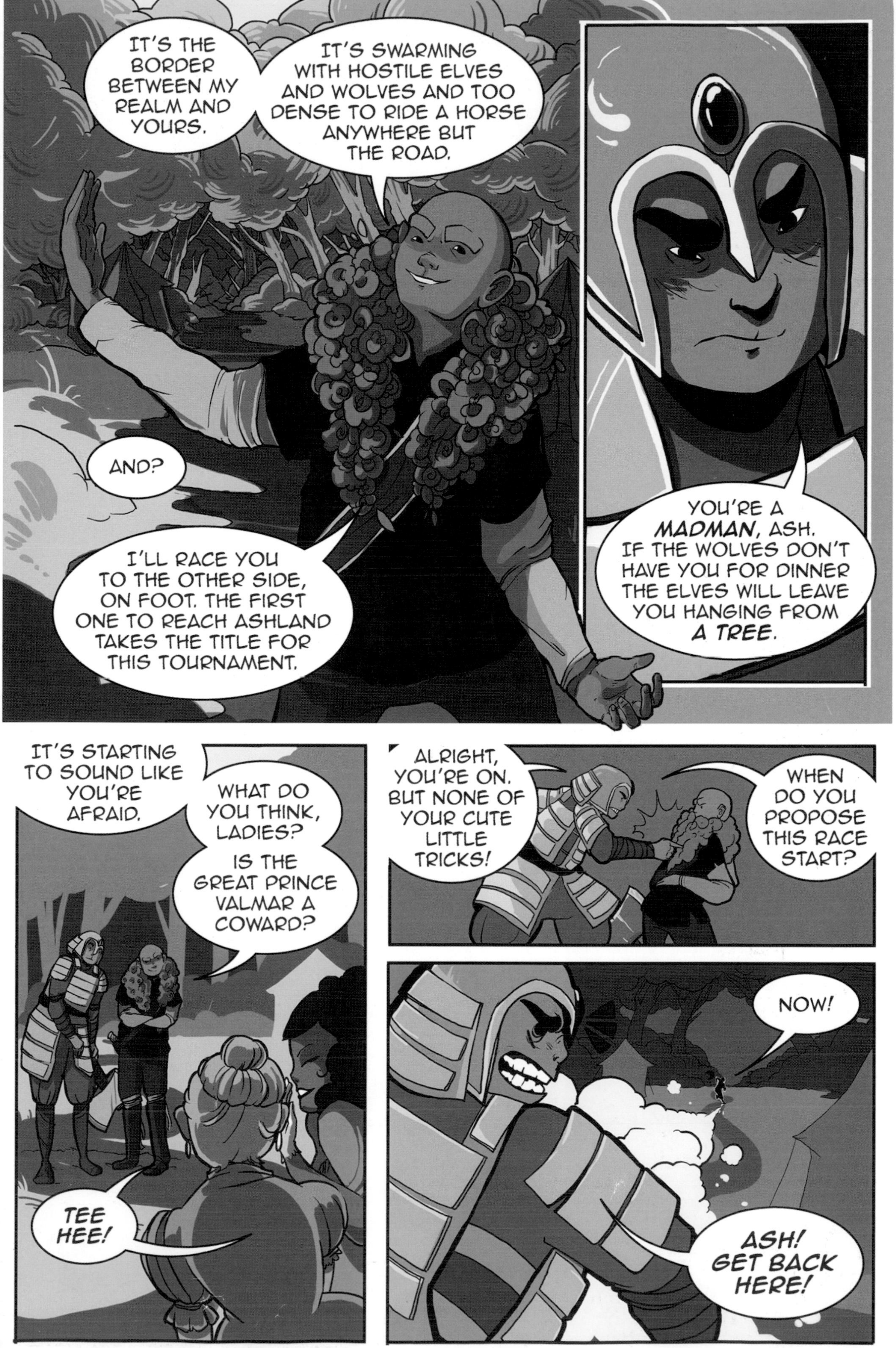
IT'S THE BORDER BETWEEN MY REALM AND YOURS.
IT'S SWARMING WITH HOSTILE ELVES AND WOLVES AND TOO DENSE TO RIDE A HORSE ANYWHERE BUT THE ROAD.
AND?
I'LL RACE YOU TO THE OTHER SIDE, ON FOOT. THE FIRST ONE TO REACH ASHLAND TAKES THE TITLE FOR THIS TOURNAMENT.
YOU'RE A MADMAN, ASH. IF THE WOLVES DON'T HAVE YOU FOR DINNER THE ELVES WILL LEAVE YOU HANGING FROM A TREE.
IT'S STARTING TO SOUND LIKE YOU'RE AFRAID.
WHAT DO YOU THINK, LADIES?
IS THE GREAT PRINCE VALMAR A COWARD?
TEE HEE!
ALRIGHT, YOU'RE ON. BUT NONE OF YOUR CUTE LITTLE TRICKS!
WHEN DO YOU PROPOSE THIS RACE START?
NOW!
ASH! GET BACK HERE!

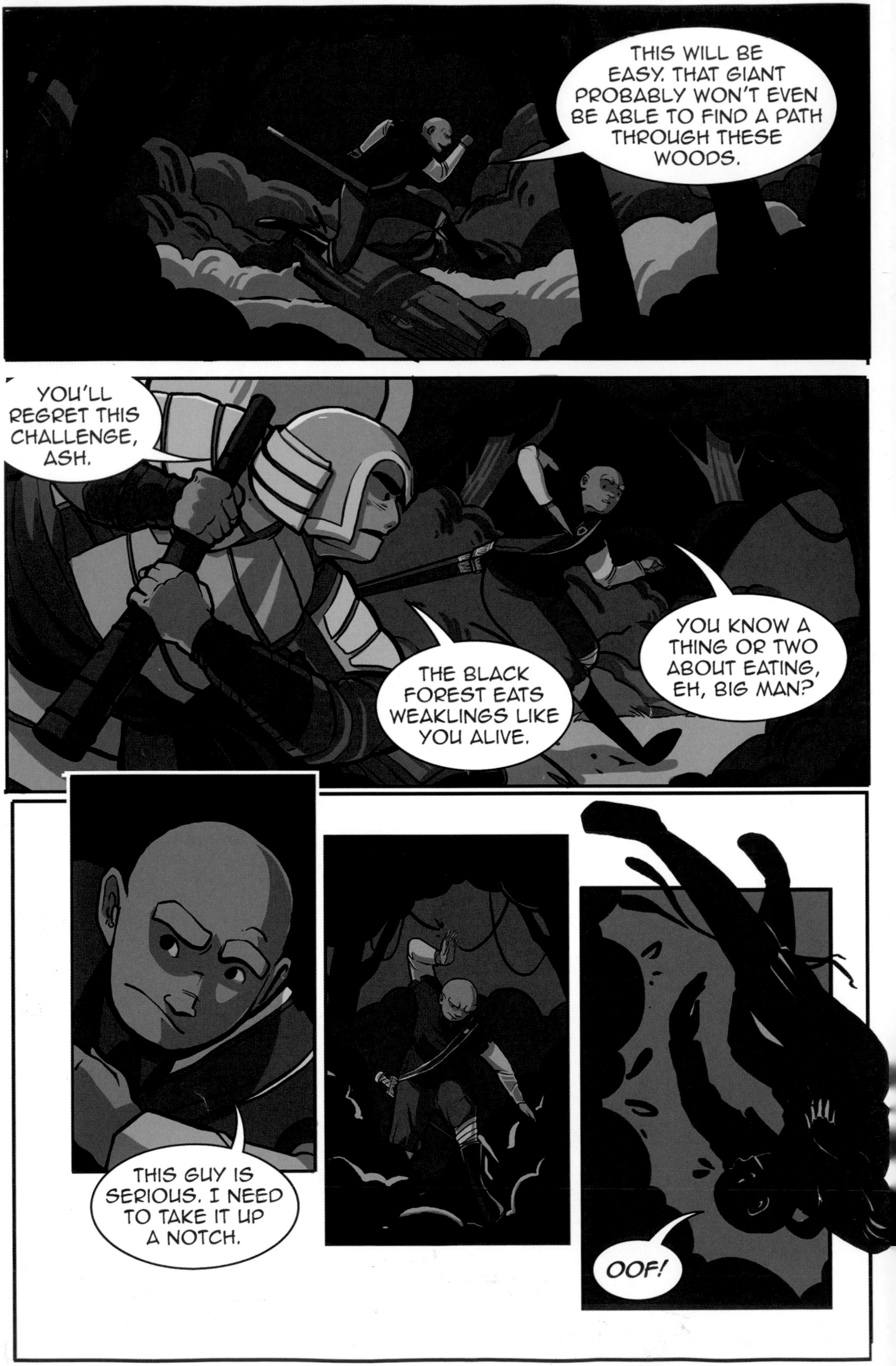
THIS WILL BE EASY. THAT GIANT PROBABLY WON'T EVEN BE ABLE TO FIND A PATH THROUGH THESE WOODS.
YOU'LL REGRET THIS CHALLENGE, ASH.
THE BLACK FOREST EATS WEAKLINGS LIKE YOU ALIVE.
YOU KNOW A THING OR TWO ABOUT EATING, EH, BIG MAN?
THIS GUY IS SERIOUS. I NEED TO TAKE IT UP A NOTCH.
OOF!

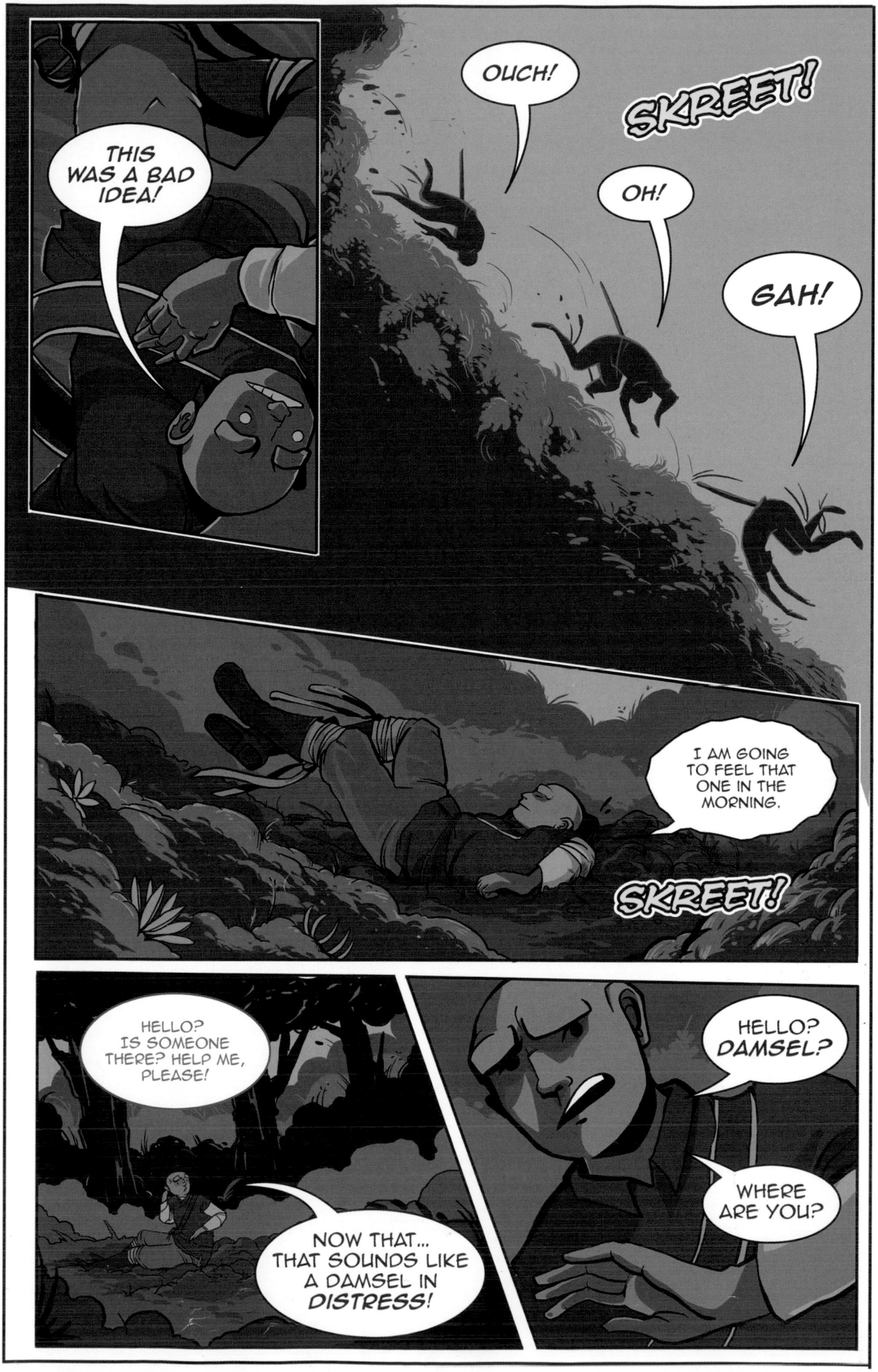
THIS WAS A BAD IDEA!
OUCH!
SKREET!
OH!
GAH!
I AM GOING TO FEEL THAT ONE IN THE MORNING.
SKREET!
HELLO? IS SOMEONE THERE? HELP ME, PLEASE!
NOW THAT... THAT SOUNDS LIKE A DAMSEL IN DISTRESS!
HELLO? DAMSEL?
WHERE ARE YOU?

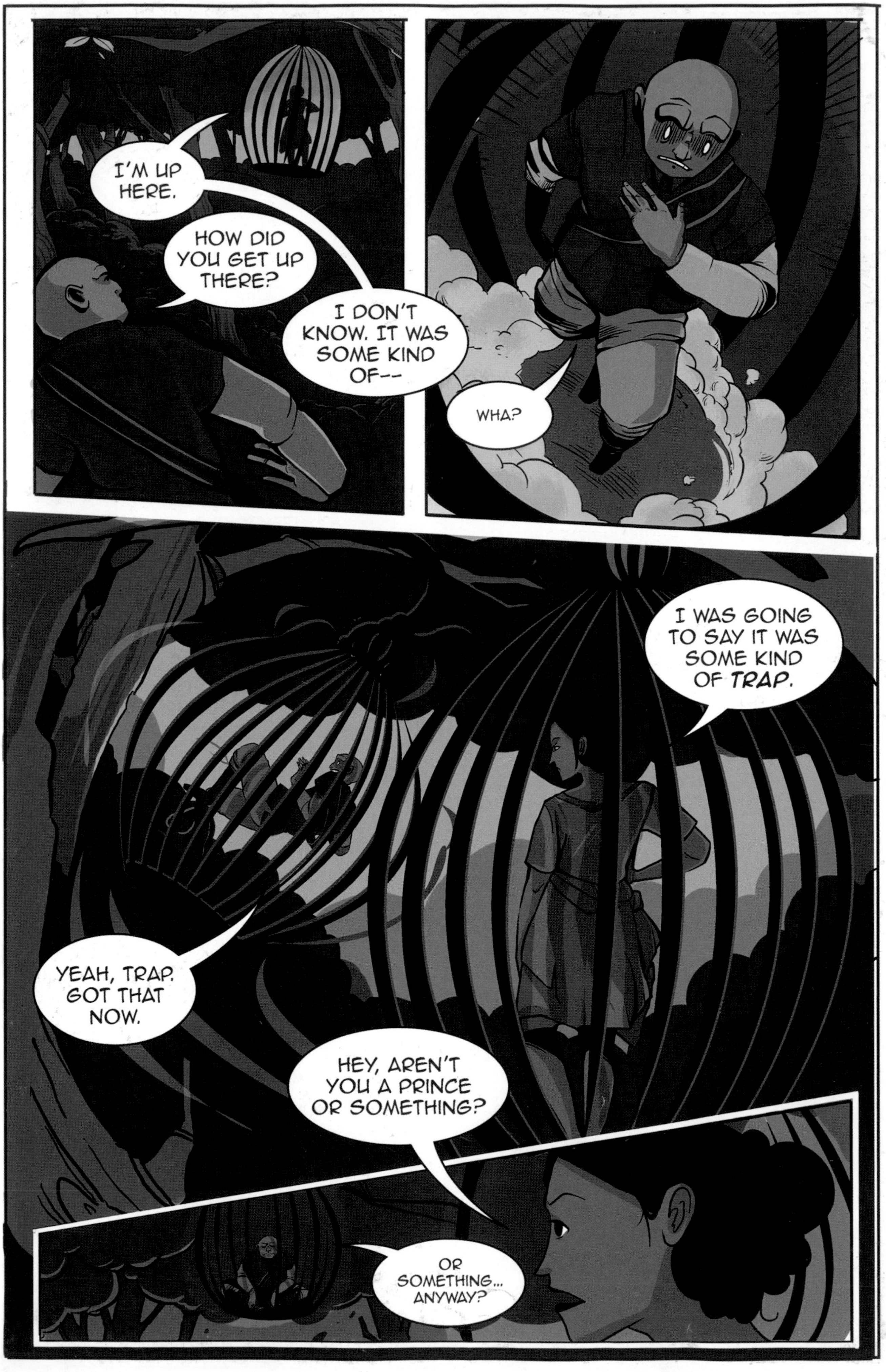
I'M UP HERE.
HOW DID YOU GET UP THERE?
I DON'T KNOW. IT WAS SOME KIND OF--
WHA?
I WAS GOING TO SAY IT WAS SOME KIND OF *TRAP*.
YEAH, TRAP. GOT THAT NOW.
HEY, AREN'T YOU A PRINCE OR SOMETHING?
OR SOMETHING... ANYWAY?

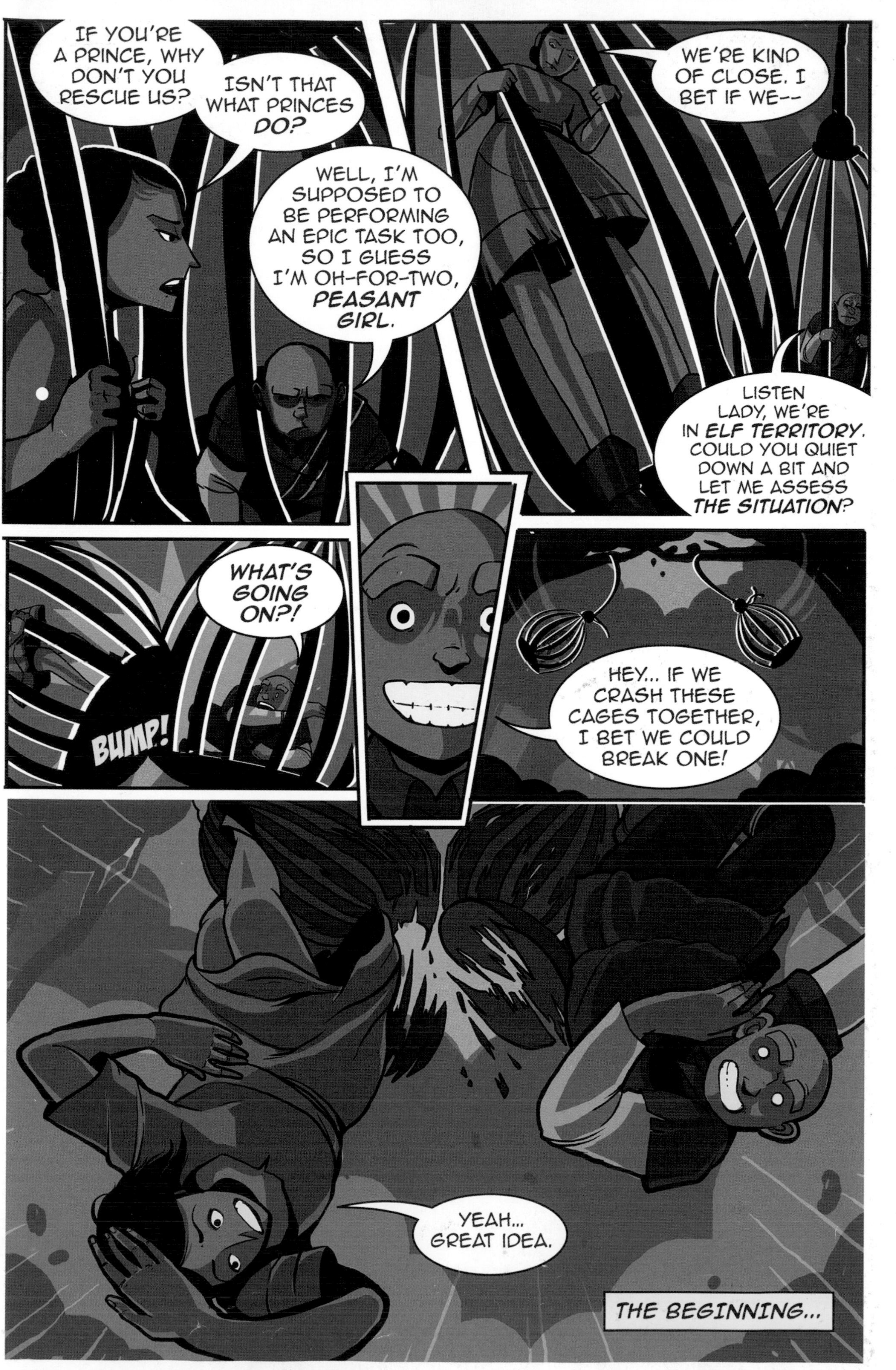
IF YOU'RE A PRINCE, WHY DON'T YOU RESCUE US?
ISN'T THAT WHAT PRINCES DO?
WELL, I'M SUPPOSED TO BE PERFORMING AN EPIC TASK TOO, SO I GUESS I'M OH-FOR-TWO, PEASANT GIRL.
WE'RE KIND OF CLOSE. I BET IF WE--
LISTEN LADY, WE'RE IN ELF TERRITORY. COULD YOU QUIET DOWN A BIT AND LET ME ASSESS THE SITUATION?
WHAT'S GOING ON?!
BUMP!
HEY... IF WE CRASH THESE CAGES TOGETHER, I BET WE COULD BREAK ONE!
YEAH... GREAT IDEA.
THE BEGINNING...

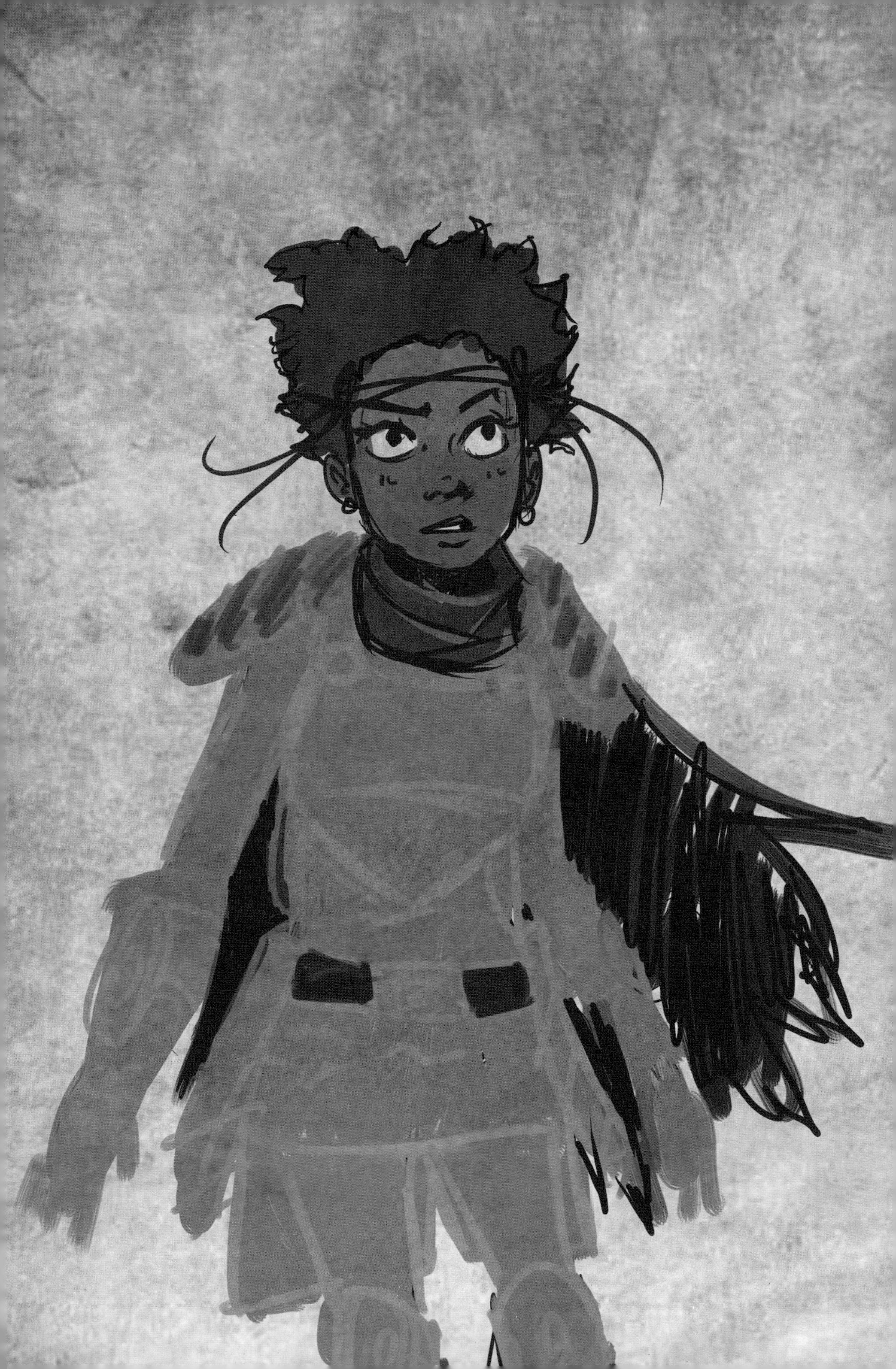

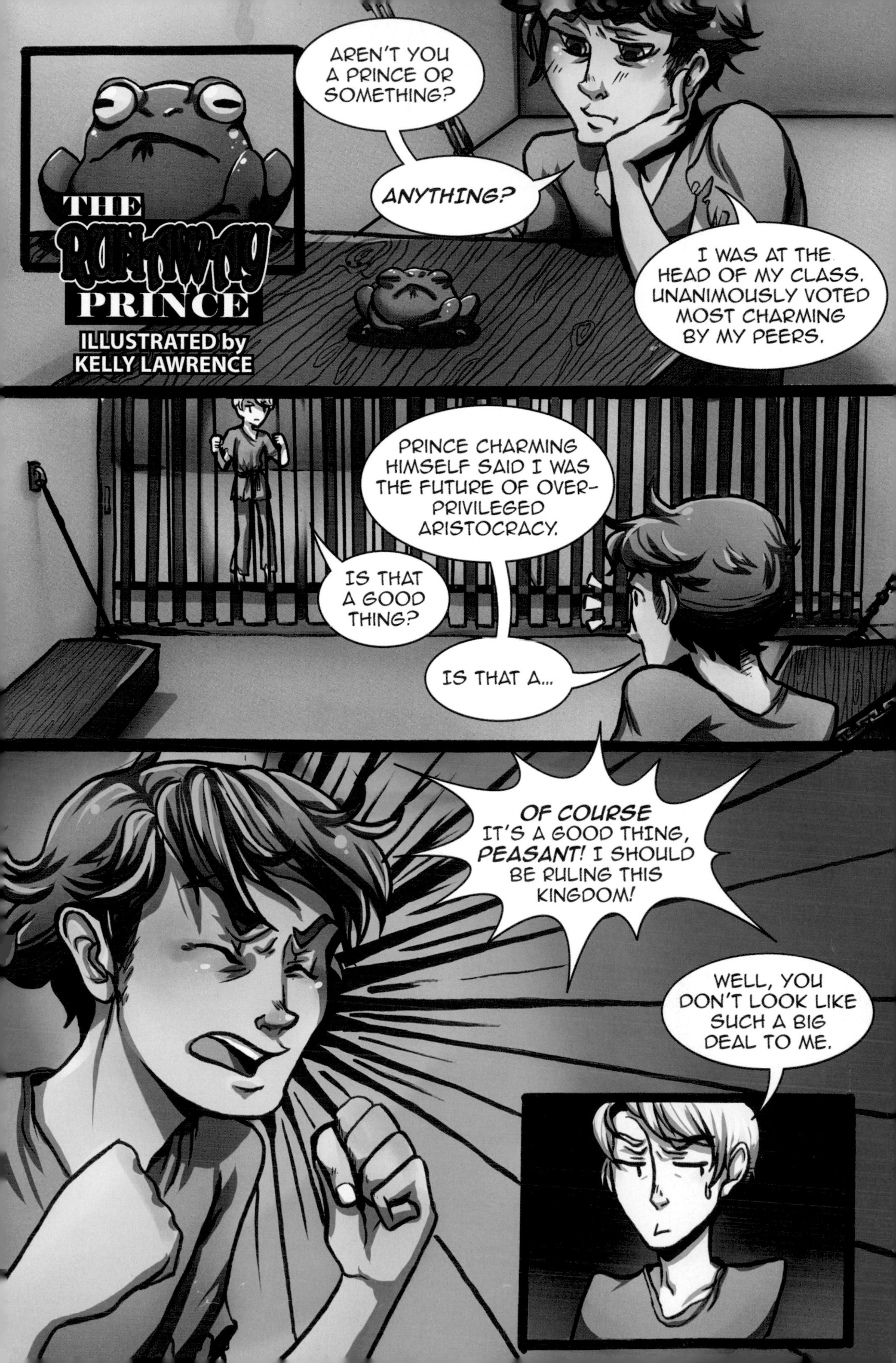
THE RUNAWAY PRINCE
ILLUSTRATED by KELLY LAWRENCE
AREN'T YOU A PRINCE OR SOMETHING?
ANYTHING?
I WAS AT THE HEAD OF MY CLASS. UNANIMOUSLY VOTED MOST CHARMING BY MY PEERS.
PRINCE CHARMING HIMSELF SAID I WAS THE FUTURE OF OVER-PRIVILEGED ARISTOCRACY.
IS THAT A GOOD THING?
IS THAT A...
OF COURSE IT'S A GOOD THING, PEASANT! I SHOULD BE RULING THIS KINGDOM!
WELL, YOU DON'T LOOK LIKE SUCH A BIG DEAL TO ME.

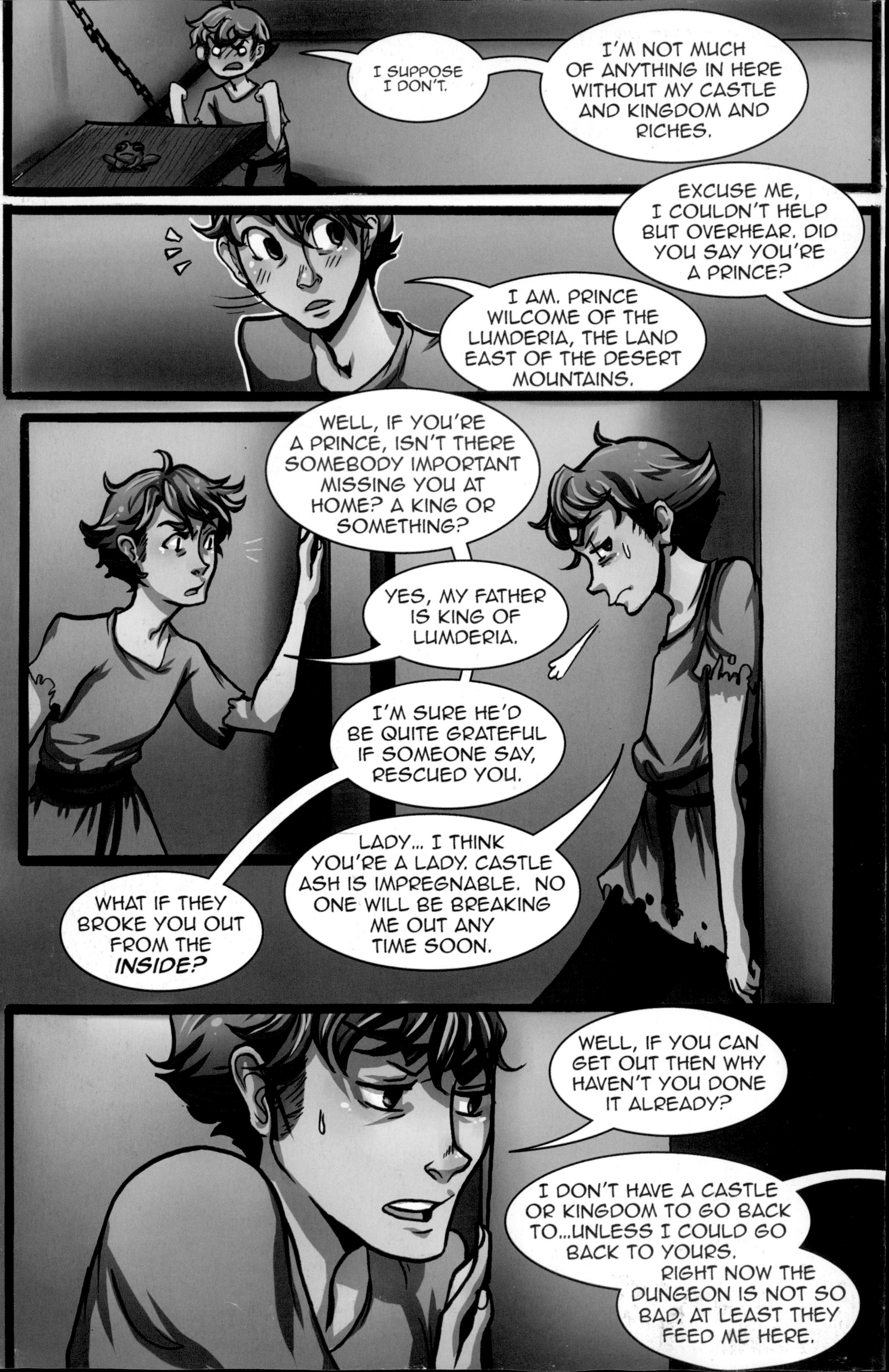
I SUPPOSE I DON'T.
I'M NOT MUCH OF ANYTHING IN HERE WITHOUT MY CASTLE AND KINGDOM AND RICHES.
EXCUSE ME, I COULDN'T HELP BUT OVERHEAR. DID YOU SAY YOU'RE A PRINCE?
I AM. PRINCE WILCOME OF THE LUMDERIA, THE LAND EAST OF THE DESERT MOUNTAINS.
WELL, IF YOU'RE A PRINCE, ISN'T THERE SOMEBODY IMPORTANT MISSING YOU AT HOME? A KING OR SOMETHING?
YES, MY FATHER IS KING OF LUMDERIA.
I'M SURE HE'D BE QUITE GRATEFUL IF SOMEONE SAY, RESCUED YOU.
LADY... I THINK YOU'RE A LADY. CASTLE ASH IS IMPREGNABLE. NO ONE WILL BE BREAKING ME OUT ANY TIME SOON.
WHAT IF THEY BROKE YOU OUT FROM THE *INSIDE?*
WELL, IF YOU CAN GET OUT THEN WHY HAVEN'T YOU DONE IT ALREADY?
I DON'T HAVE A CASTLE OR KINGDOM TO GO BACK TO...UNLESS I COULD GO BACK TO YOURS.
RIGHT NOW THE DUNGEON IS NOT SO BAD, AT LEAST THEY FEED ME HERE.

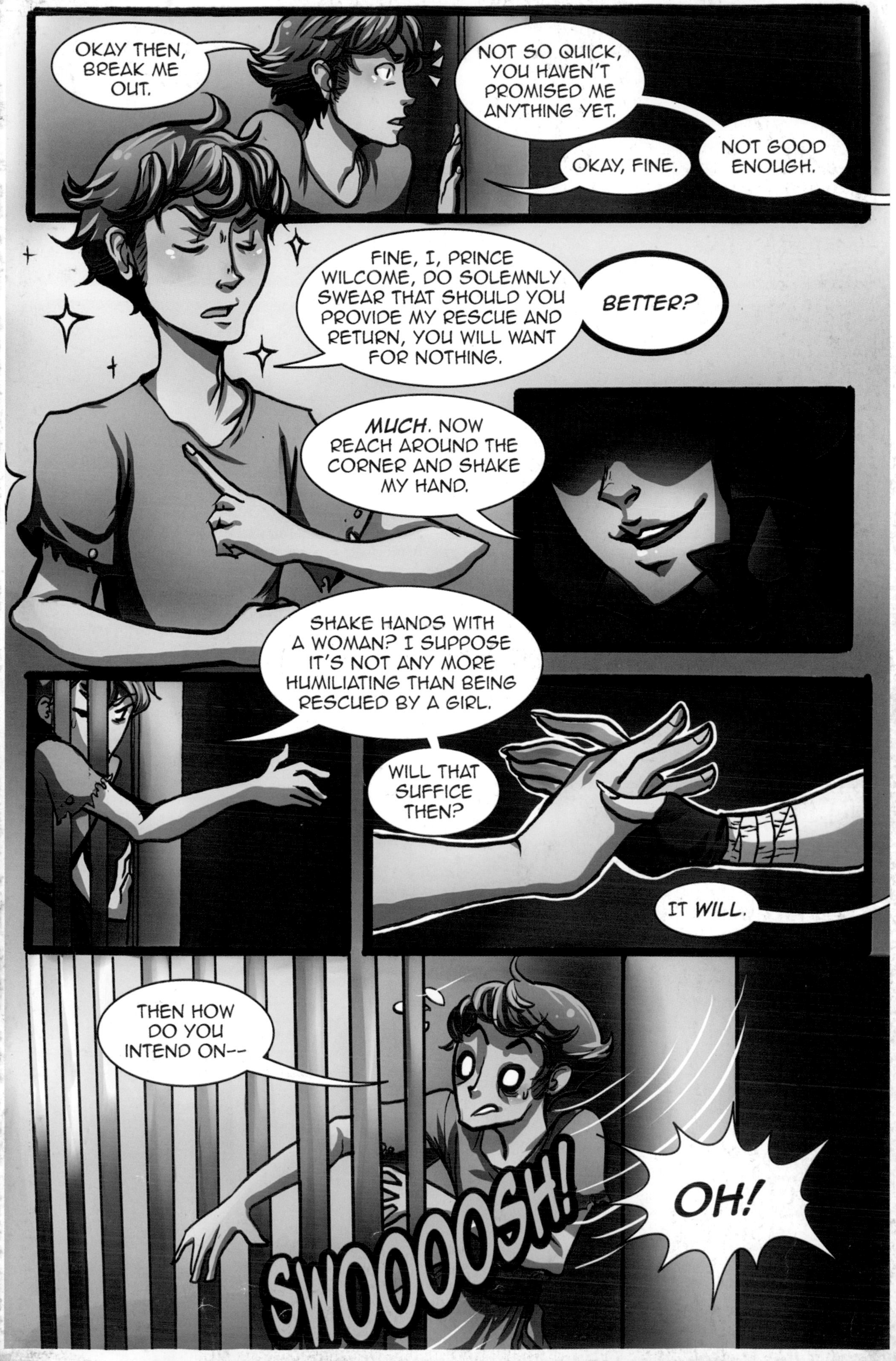
OKAY THEN, BREAK ME OUT.
NOT SO QUICK, YOU HAVEN'T PROMISED ME ANYTHING YET.
OKAY, FINE.
NOT GOOD ENOUGH.
FINE, I, PRINCE WILCOME, DO SOLEMNLY SWEAR THAT SHOULD YOU PROVIDE MY RESCUE AND RETURN, YOU WILL WANT FOR NOTHING.
BETTER?
MUCH. NOW REACH AROUND THE CORNER AND SHAKE MY HAND.
SHAKE HANDS WITH A WOMAN? I SUPPOSE IT'S NOT ANY MORE HUMILIATING THAN BEING RESCUED BY A GIRL.
WILL THAT SUFFICE THEN?
IT WILL.
THEN HOW DO YOU INTEND ON--
SWOOOOSH!
OH!

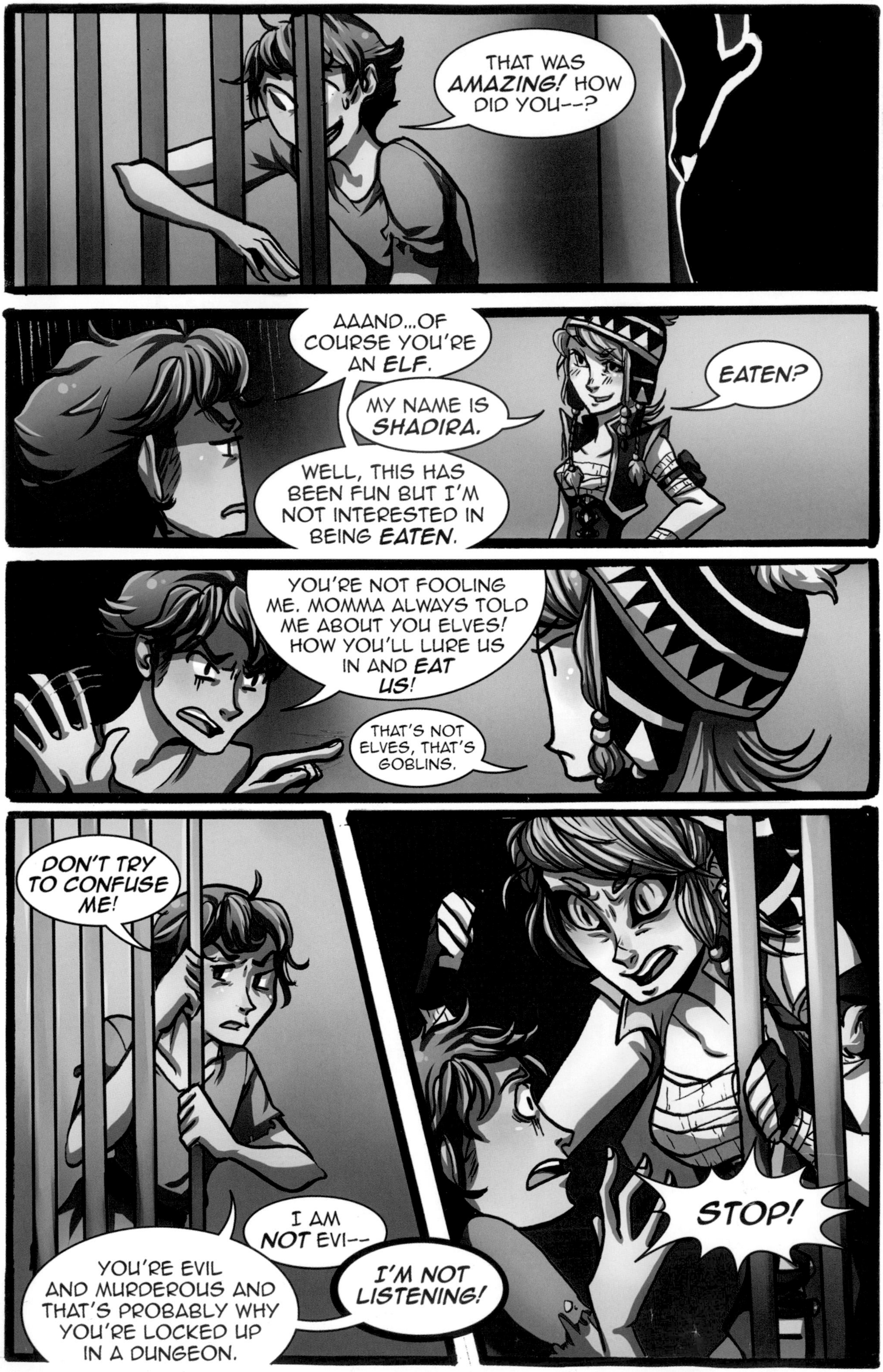
THAT WAS AMAZING! HOW DID YOU--?
AAAND...OF COURSE YOU'RE AN ELF.
MY NAME IS SHADIRA.
WELL, THIS HAS BEEN FUN BUT I'M NOT INTERESTED IN BEING EATEN.
EATEN?
YOU'RE NOT FOOLING ME. MOMMA ALWAYS TOLD ME ABOUT YOU ELVES! HOW YOU'LL LURE US IN AND EAT US!
THAT'S NOT ELVES, THAT'S GOBLINS.
DON'T TRY TO CONFUSE ME!
YOU'RE EVIL AND MURDEROUS AND THAT'S PROBABLY WHY YOU'RE LOCKED UP IN A DUNGEON.
I AM NOT EVI--
I'M NOT LISTENING!
STOP!

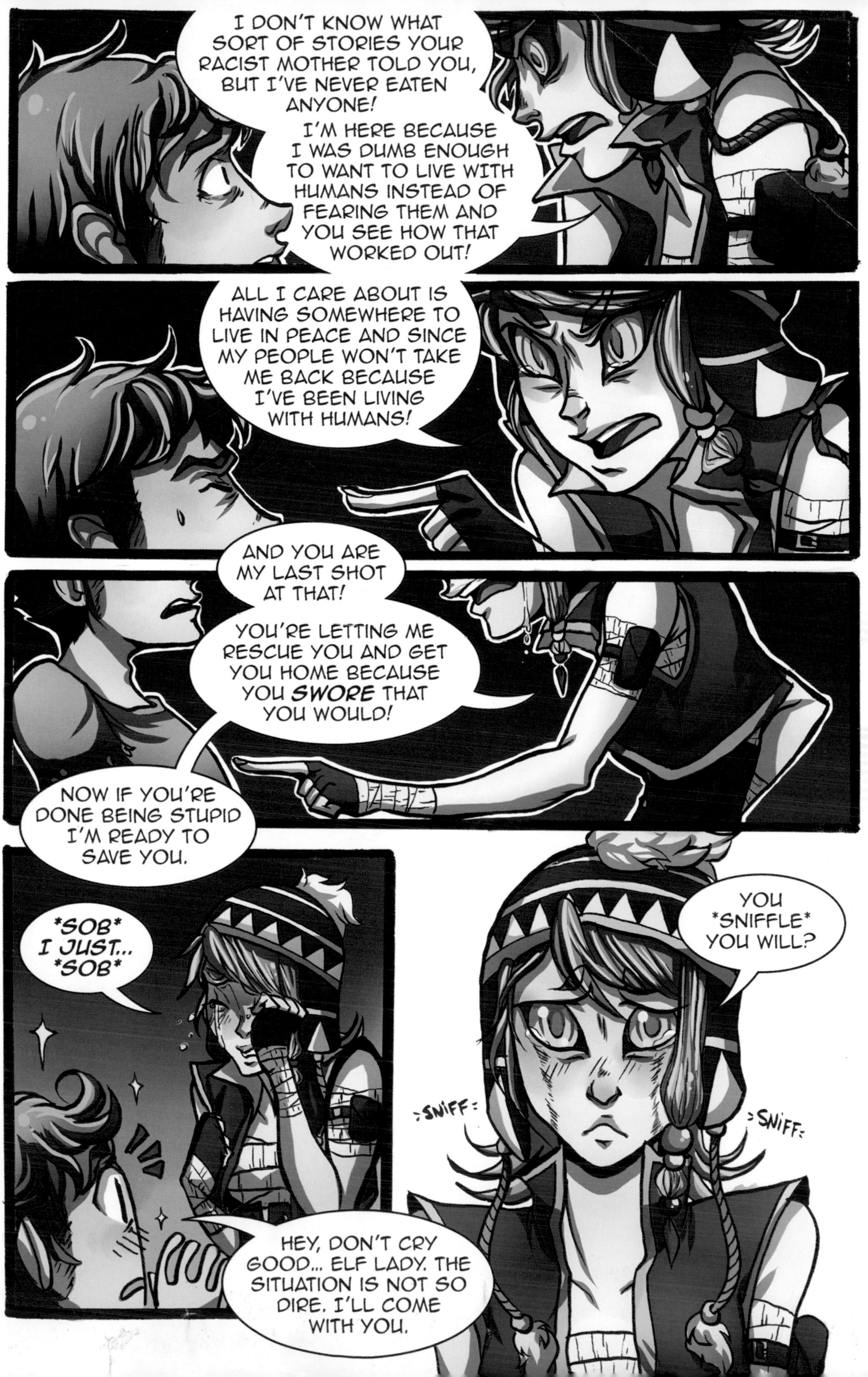
I DON'T KNOW WHAT SORT OF STORIES YOUR RACIST MOTHER TOLD YOU, BUT I'VE NEVER EATEN ANYONE!
I'M HERE BECAUSE I WAS DUMB ENOUGH TO WANT TO LIVE WITH HUMANS INSTEAD OF FEARING THEM AND YOU SEE HOW THAT WORKED OUT!
ALL I CARE ABOUT IS HAVING SOMEWHERE TO LIVE IN PEACE AND SINCE MY PEOPLE WON'T TAKE ME BACK BECAUSE I'VE BEEN LIVING WITH HUMANS!
AND YOU ARE MY LAST SHOT AT THAT!
YOU'RE LETTING ME RESCUE YOU AND GET YOU HOME BECAUSE YOU *SWORE* THAT YOU WOULD!
NOW IF YOU'RE DONE BEING STUPID I'M READY TO SAVE YOU.
SOB I JUST... *SOB*
HEY, DON'T CRY GOOD... ELF LADY. THE SITUATION IS NOT SO DIRE. I'LL COME WITH YOU.
YOU *SNIFFLE* YOU WILL?
:SNIFF:
:SNIFF:

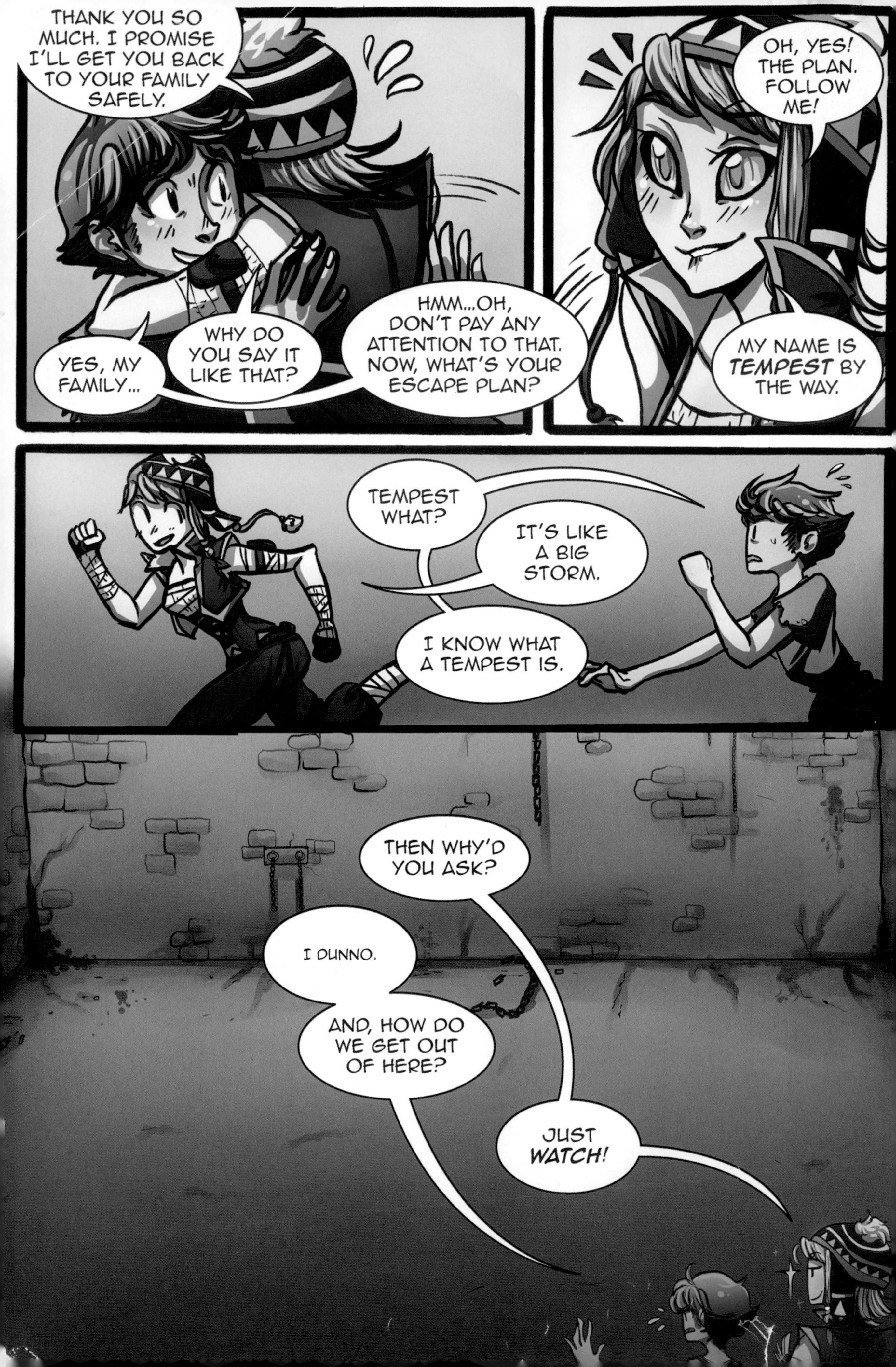
THANK YOU SO MUCH. I PROMISE I'LL GET YOU BACK TO YOUR FAMILY SAFELY.
YES, MY FAMILY...
WHY DO YOU SAY IT LIKE THAT?
HMM...OH, DON'T PAY ANY ATTENTION TO THAT. NOW, WHAT'S YOUR ESCAPE PLAN?
OH, YES! THE PLAN. FOLLOW ME!
MY NAME IS **TEMPEST** BY THE WAY.
TEMPEST WHAT?
IT'S LIKE A BIG STORM.
I KNOW WHAT A TEMPEST IS.
THEN WHY'D YOU ASK?
I DUNNO.
AND, HOW DO WE GET OUT OF HERE?
JUST **WATCH**!

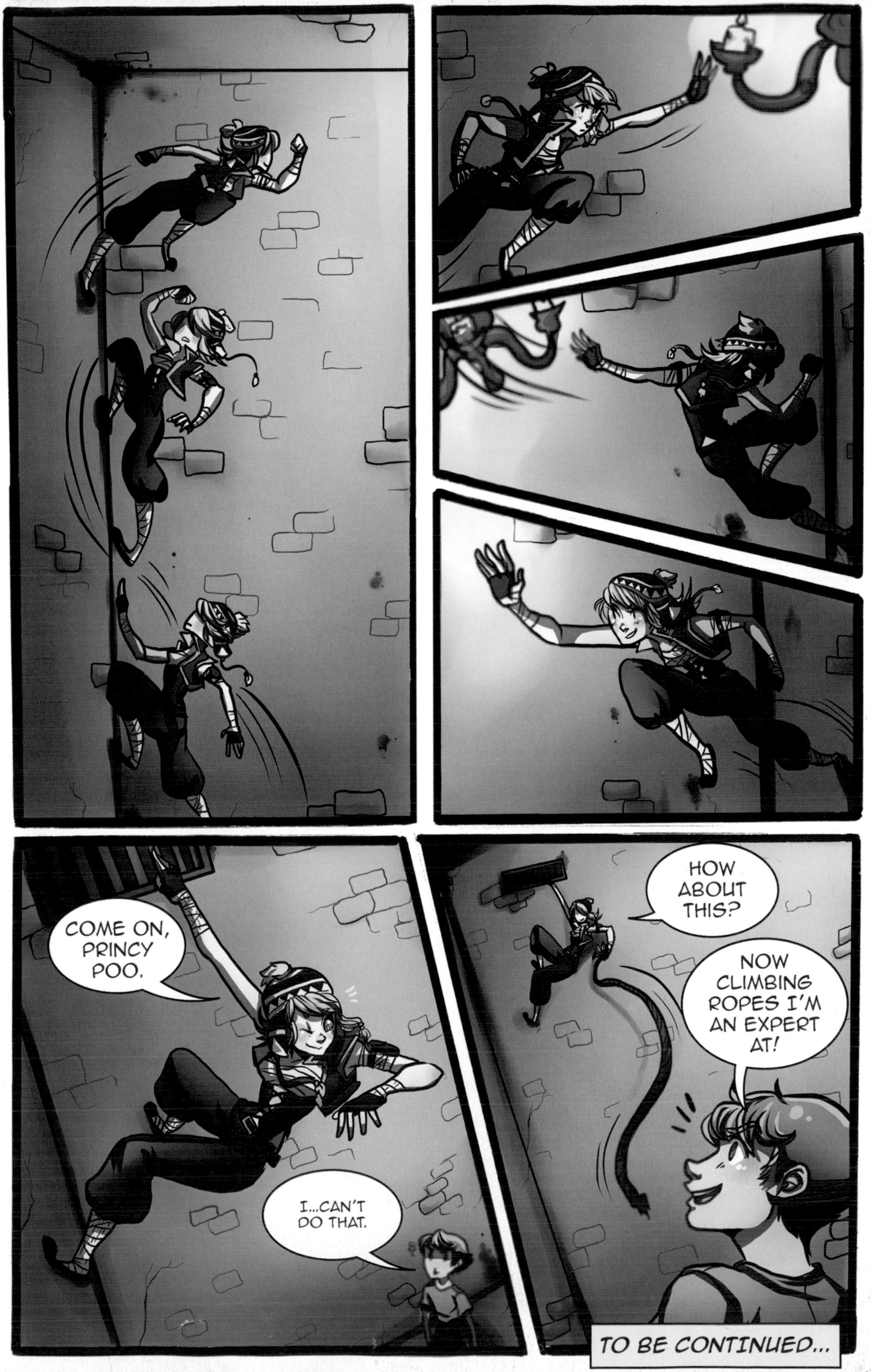
COME ON, PRINCY POO.
I...CAN'T DO THAT.
HOW ABOUT THIS?
NOW CLIMBING ROPES I'M AN EXPERT AT!
TO BE CONTINUED...

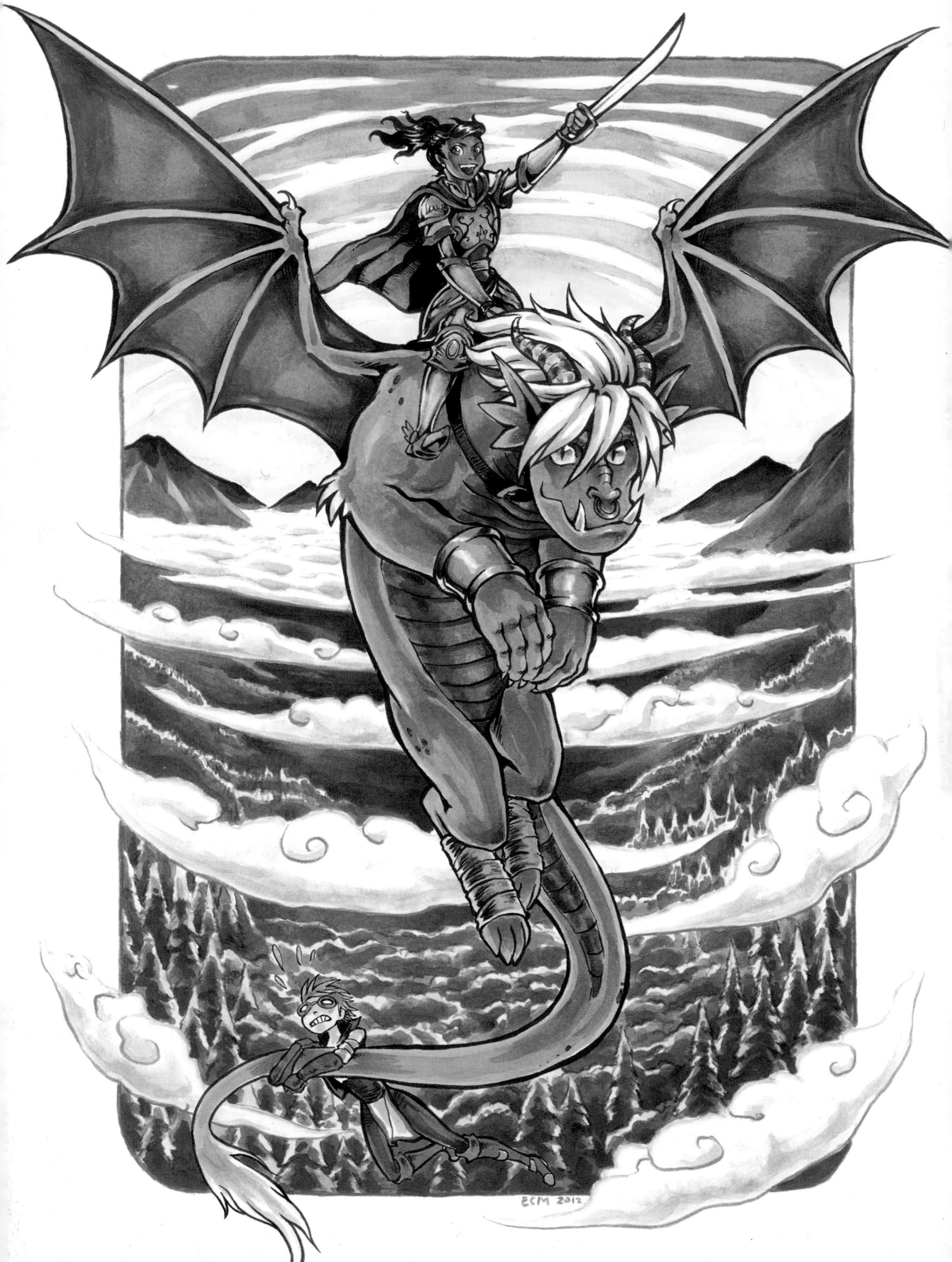
ECM 2012

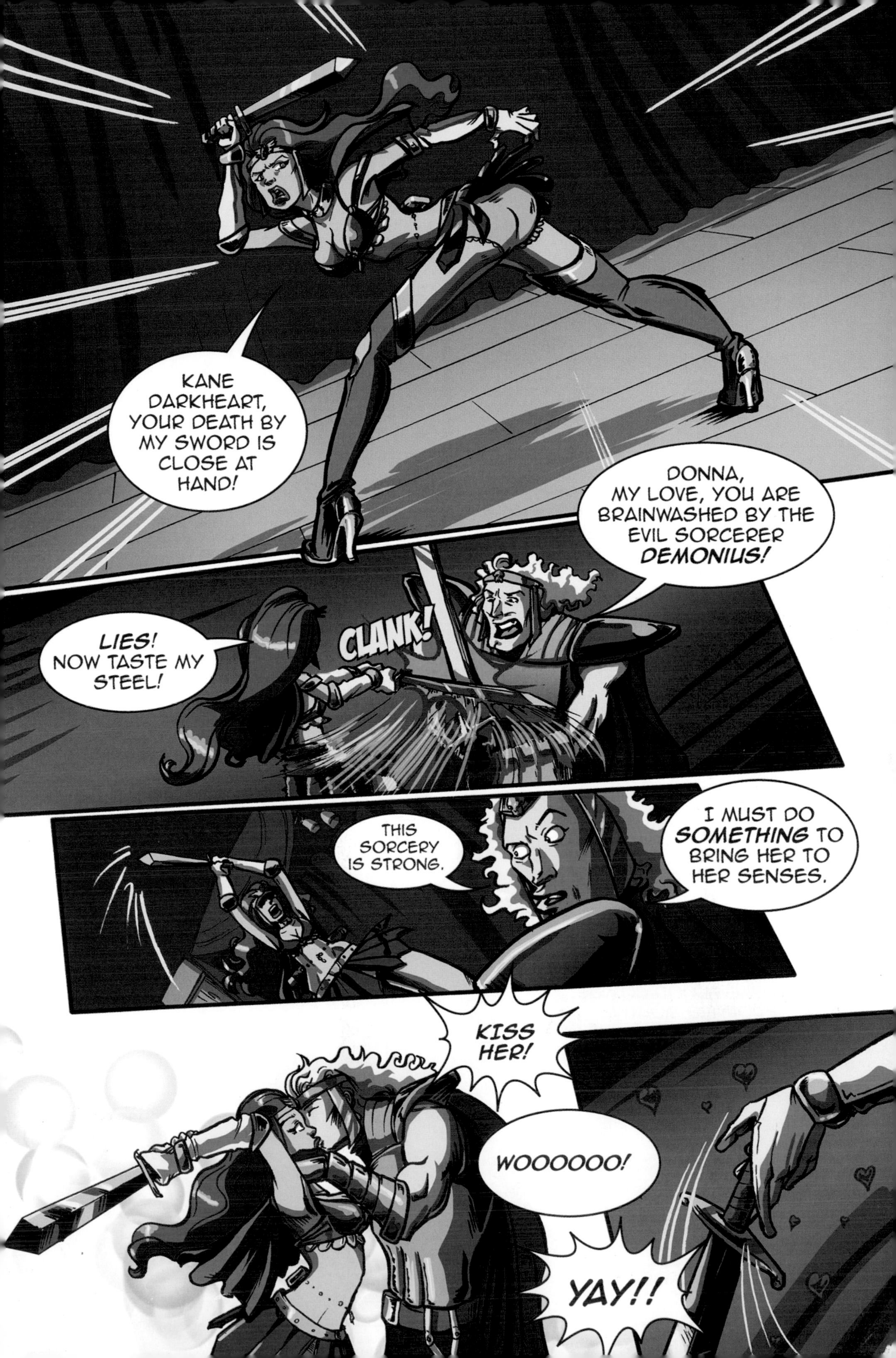
KANE DARKHEART, YOUR DEATH BY MY SWORD IS CLOSE AT HAND!
DONNA, MY LOVE, YOU ARE BRAINWASHED BY THE EVIL SORCERER *DEMONIUS!*
LIES! NOW TASTE MY STEEL!
CLANK!
THIS SORCERY IS STRONG.
I MUST DO *SOMETHING* TO BRING HER TO HER SENSES.
KISS HER!
WOOOOOO!
YAY!!

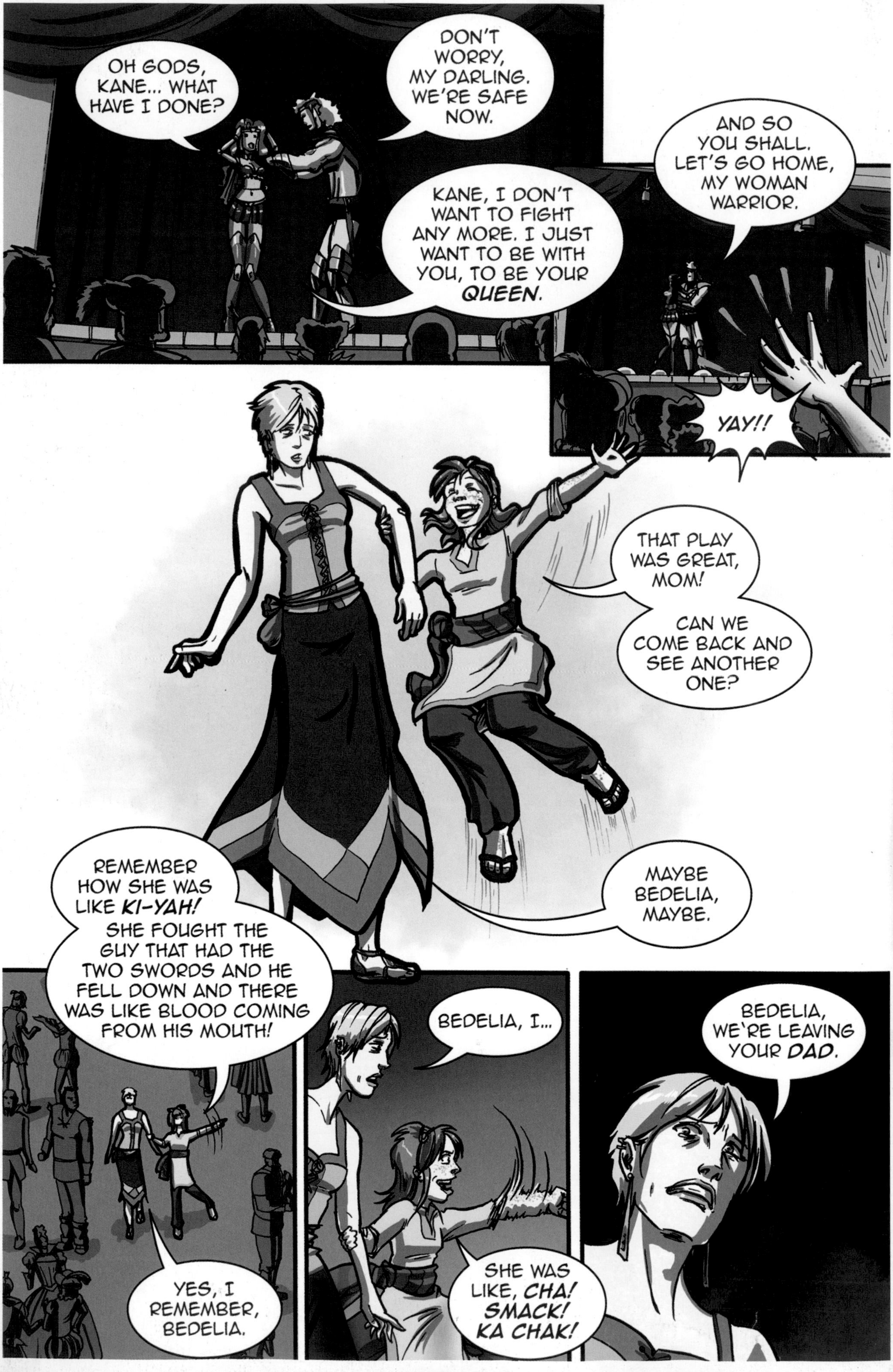

OH GODS, KANE... WHAT HAVE I DONE?
DON'T WORRY, MY DARLING. WE'RE SAFE NOW.
KANE, I DON'T WANT TO FIGHT ANY MORE. I JUST WANT TO BE WITH YOU, TO BE YOUR *QUEEN*.
AND SO YOU SHALL. LET'S GO HOME, MY WOMAN WARRIOR.
YAY!!
THAT PLAY WAS GREAT, MOM!
CAN WE COME BACK AND SEE ANOTHER ONE?
MAYBE BEDELIA, MAYBE.
REMEMBER HOW SHE WAS LIKE *KI-YAH!*
SHE FOUGHT THE GUY THAT HAD THE TWO SWORDS AND HE FELL DOWN AND THERE WAS LIKE BLOOD COMING FROM HIS MOUTH!
YES, I REMEMBER, BEDELIA.
BEDELIA, I...
SHE WAS LIKE, *CHA! SMACK! KA CHAK!*
BEDELIA, WE'RE LEAVING YOUR *DAD*.

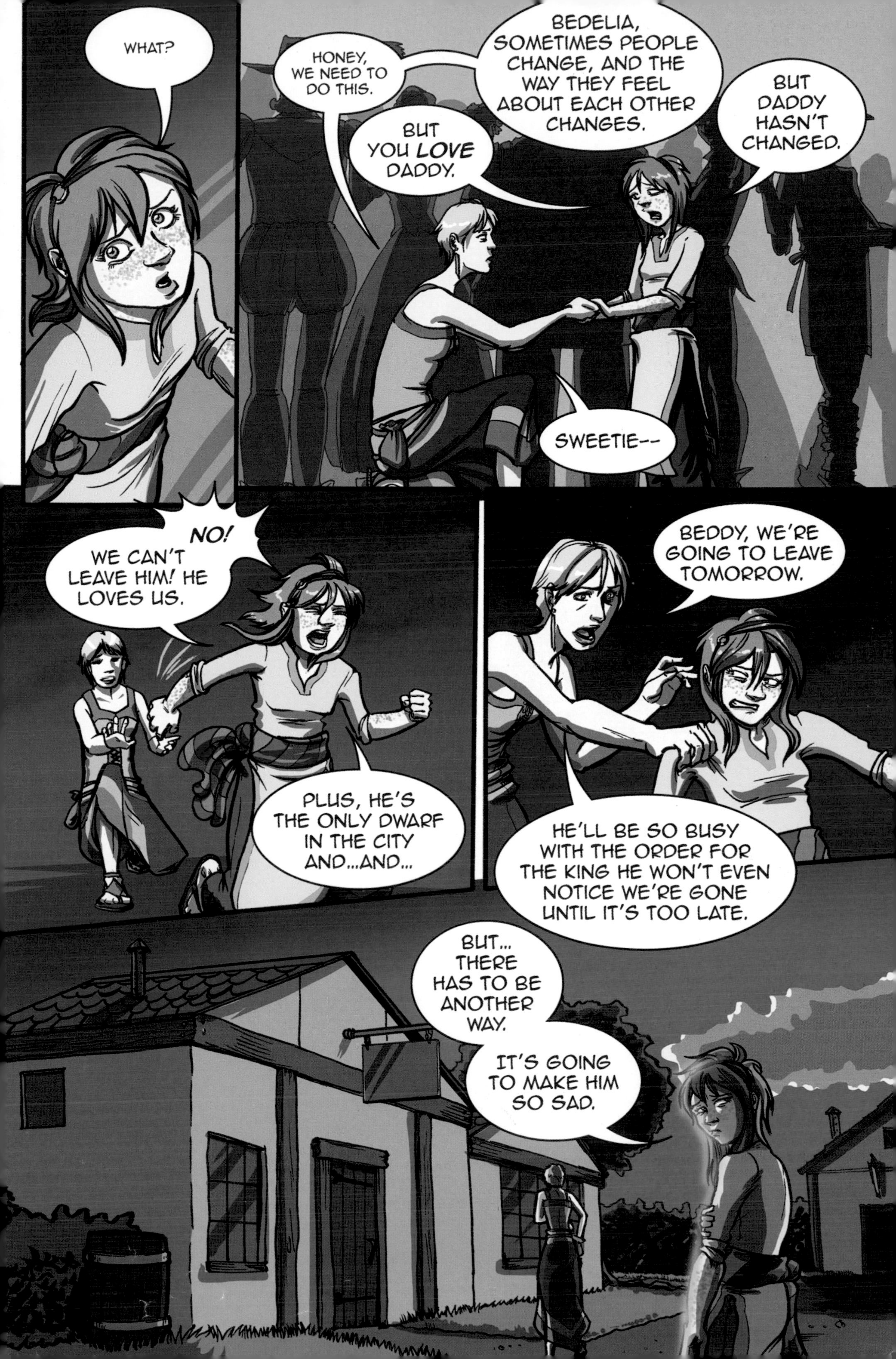
WHAT?
HONEY, WE NEED TO DO THIS.
BEDELIA, SOMETIMES PEOPLE CHANGE, AND THE WAY THEY FEEL ABOUT EACH OTHER CHANGES.
BUT YOU *LOVE* DADDY.
BUT DADDY HASN'T CHANGED.
SWEETIE--
NO!
WE CAN'T LEAVE HIM! HE LOVES US.
PLUS, HE'S THE ONLY DWARF IN THE CITY AND...AND...
BEDDY, WE'RE GOING TO LEAVE TOMORROW.
HE'LL BE SO BUSY WITH THE ORDER FOR THE KING HE WON'T EVEN NOTICE WE'RE GONE UNTIL IT'S TOO LATE.
BUT... THERE HAS TO BE ANOTHER WAY.
IT'S GOING TO MAKE HIM SO SAD.

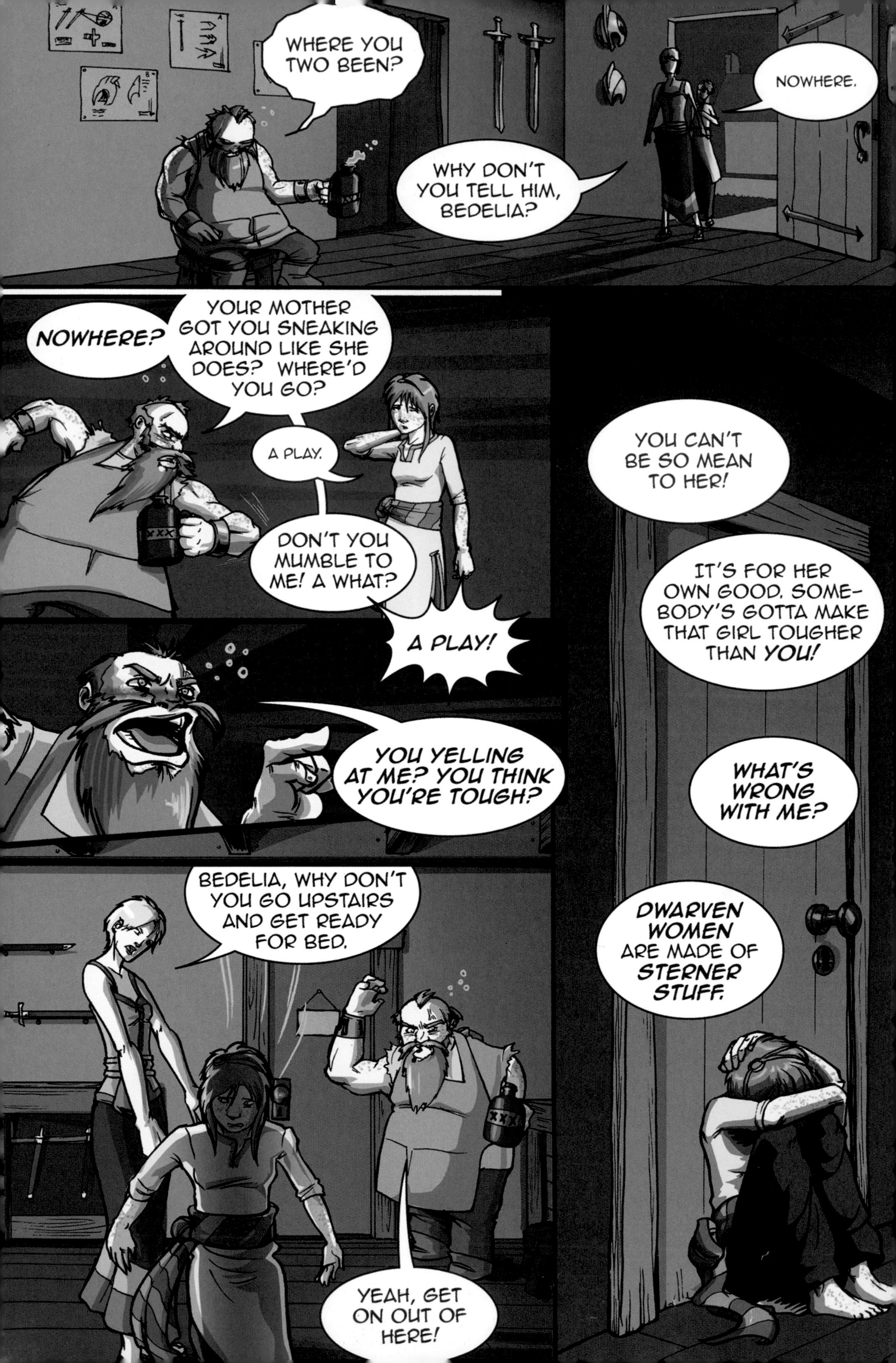
WHERE YOU TWO BEEN?
NOWHERE.
WHY DON'T YOU TELL HIM, BEDELIA?
NOWHERE?
YOUR MOTHER GOT YOU SNEAKING AROUND LIKE SHE DOES? WHERE'D YOU GO?
A PLAY.
DON'T YOU MUMBLE TO ME! A WHAT?
A PLAY!
YOU YELLING AT ME? YOU THINK YOU'RE TOUGH?
BEDELIA, WHY DON'T YOU GO UPSTAIRS AND GET READY FOR BED.
YEAH, GET ON OUT OF HERE!
YOU CAN'T BE SO MEAN TO HER!
IT'S FOR HER OWN GOOD. SOME-BODY'S GOTTA MAKE THAT GIRL TOUGHER THAN YOU!
WHAT'S WRONG WITH ME?
DWARVEN WOMEN ARE MADE OF STERNER STUFF.

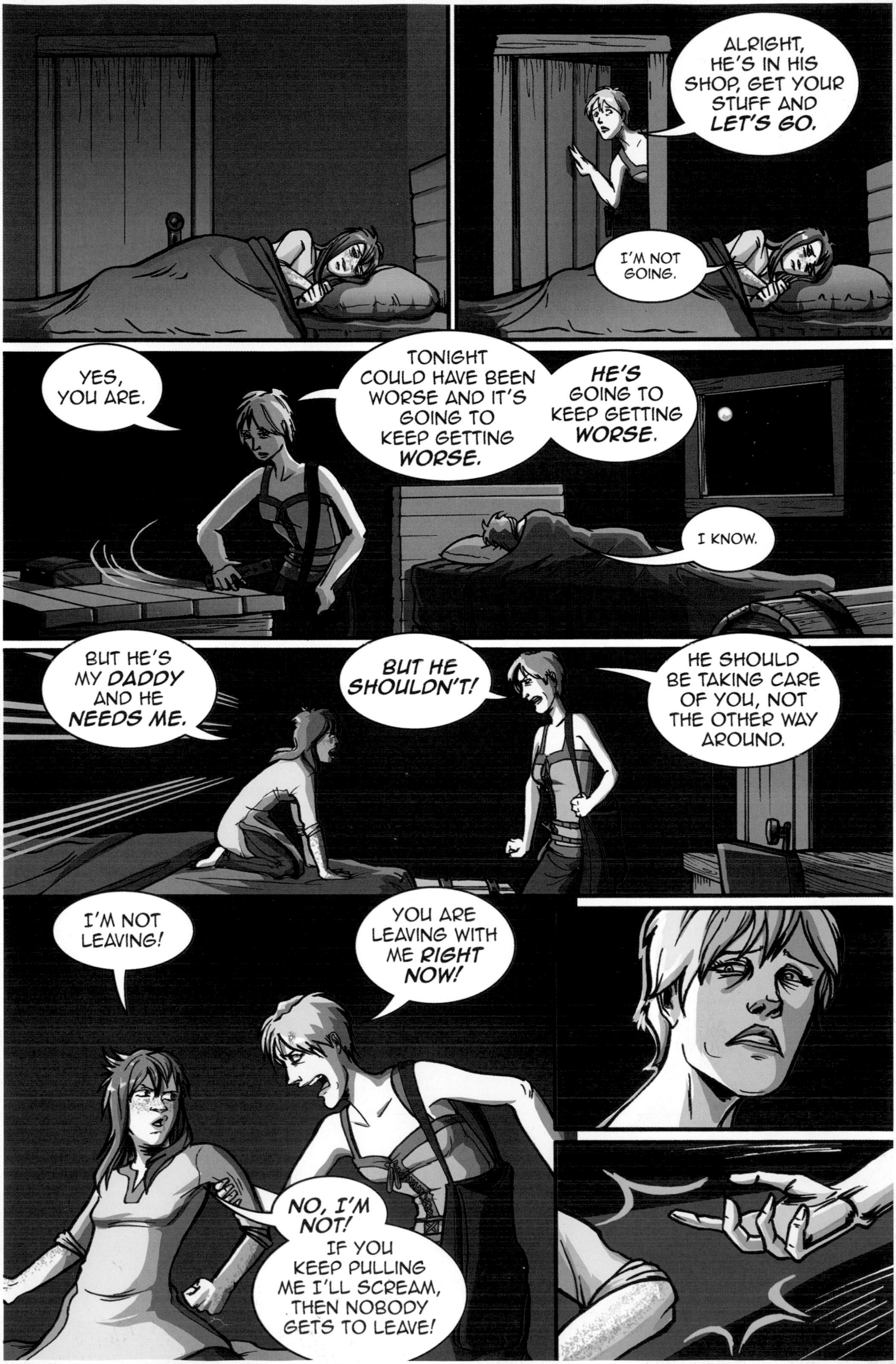
ALRIGHT, HE'S IN HIS SHOP, GET YOUR STUFF AND LET'S GO.
I'M NOT GOING.
YES, YOU ARE.
TONIGHT COULD HAVE BEEN WORSE AND IT'S GOING TO KEEP GETTING WORSE.
HE'S GOING TO KEEP GETTING WORSE.
I KNOW.
BUT HE'S MY DADDY AND HE NEEDS ME.
BUT HE SHOULDN'T!
HE SHOULD BE TAKING CARE OF YOU, NOT THE OTHER WAY AROUND.
I'M NOT LEAVING!
YOU ARE LEAVING WITH ME RIGHT NOW!
NO, I'M NOT! IF YOU KEEP PULLING ME I'LL SCREAM, THEN NOBODY GETS TO LEAVE!

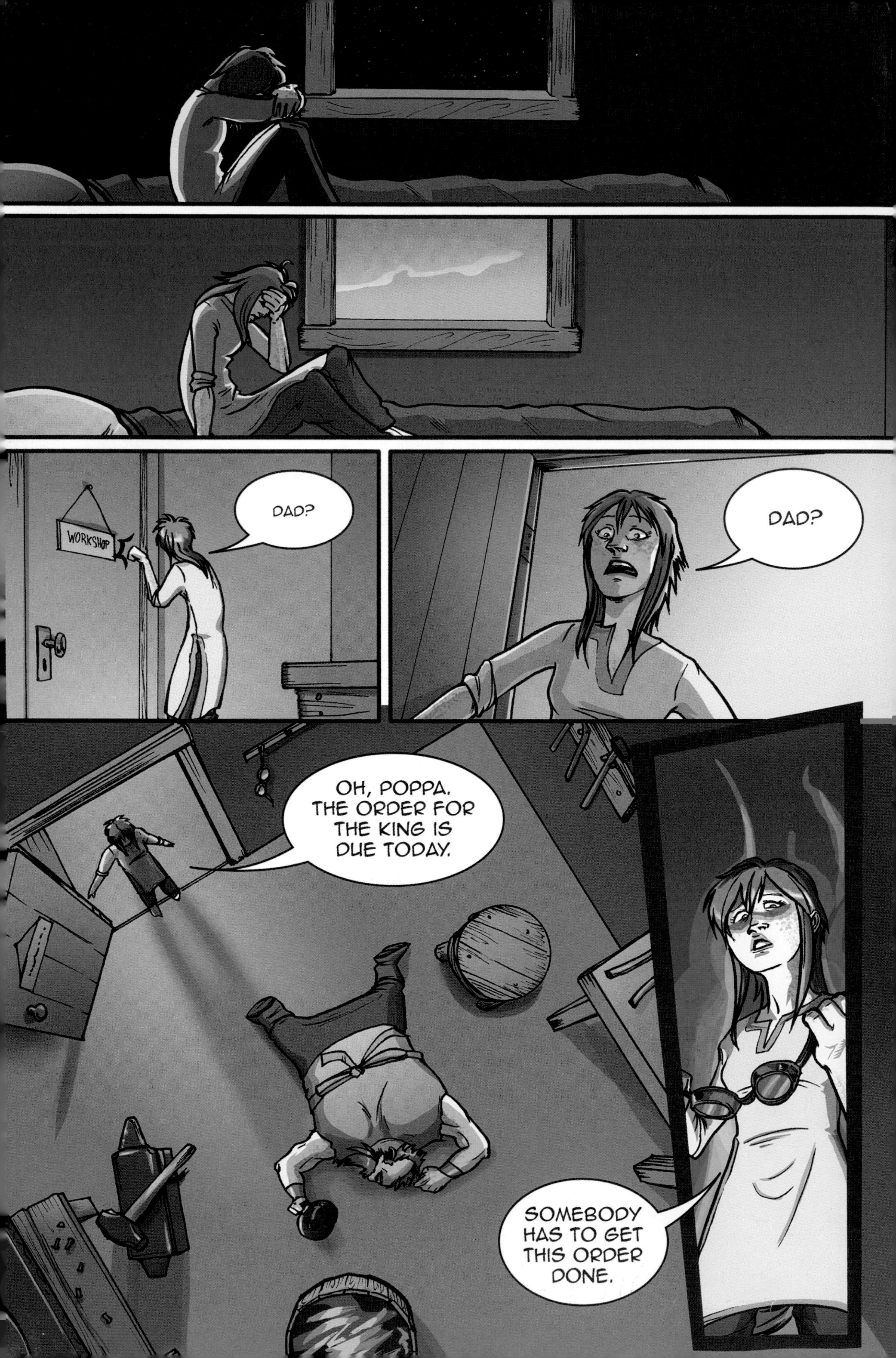
WORKSHOP
DAD?
DAD?
OH, POPPA. THE ORDER FOR THE KING IS DUE TODAY.
SOMEBODY HAS TO GET THIS ORDER DONE.

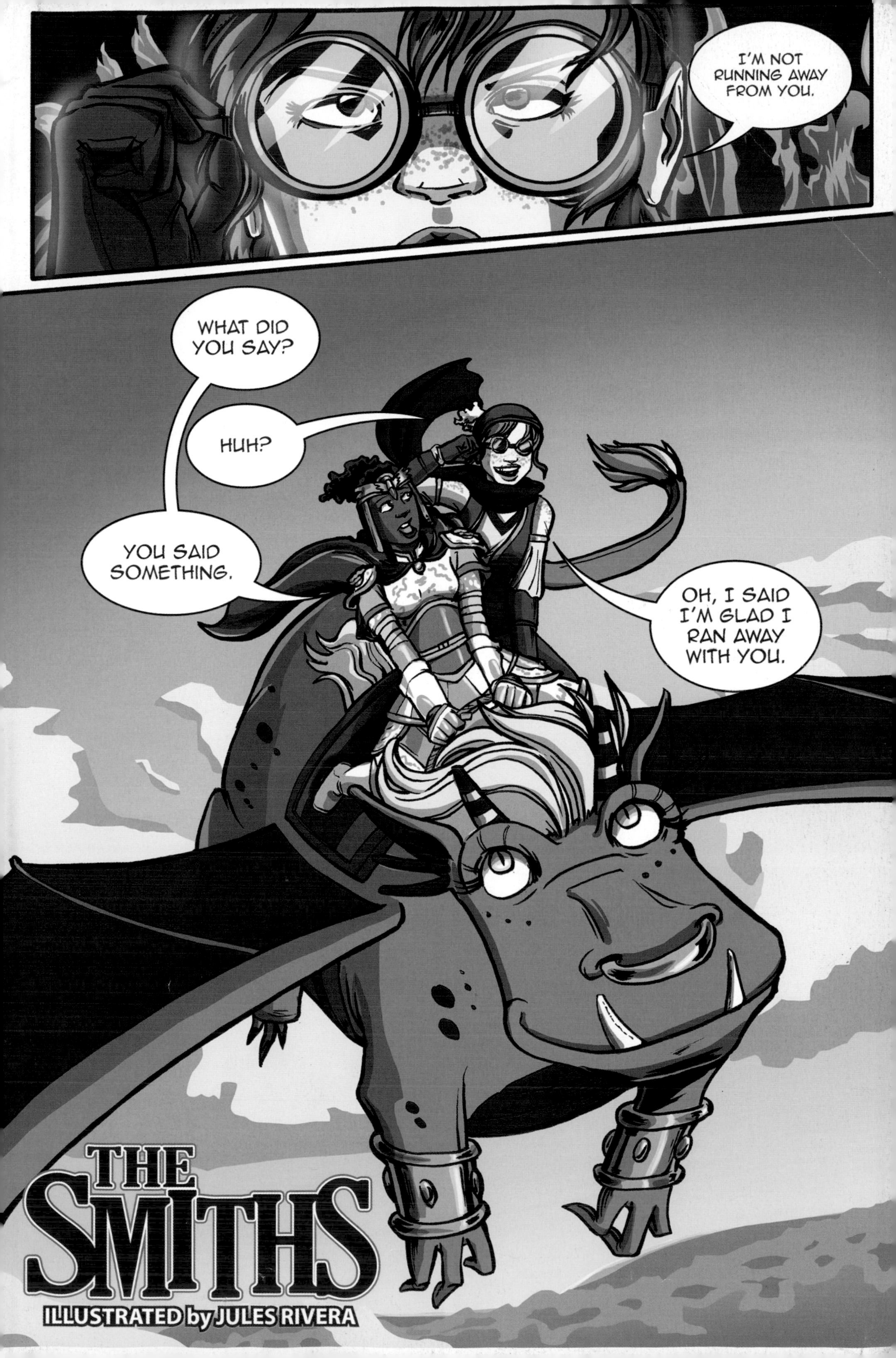
I'M NOT RUNNING AWAY FROM YOU.
WHAT DID YOU SAY?
HUH?
YOU SAID SOMETHING.
OH, I SAID I'M GLAD I RAN AWAY WITH YOU.
THE SMITHS
ILLUSTRATED by JULES RIVERA

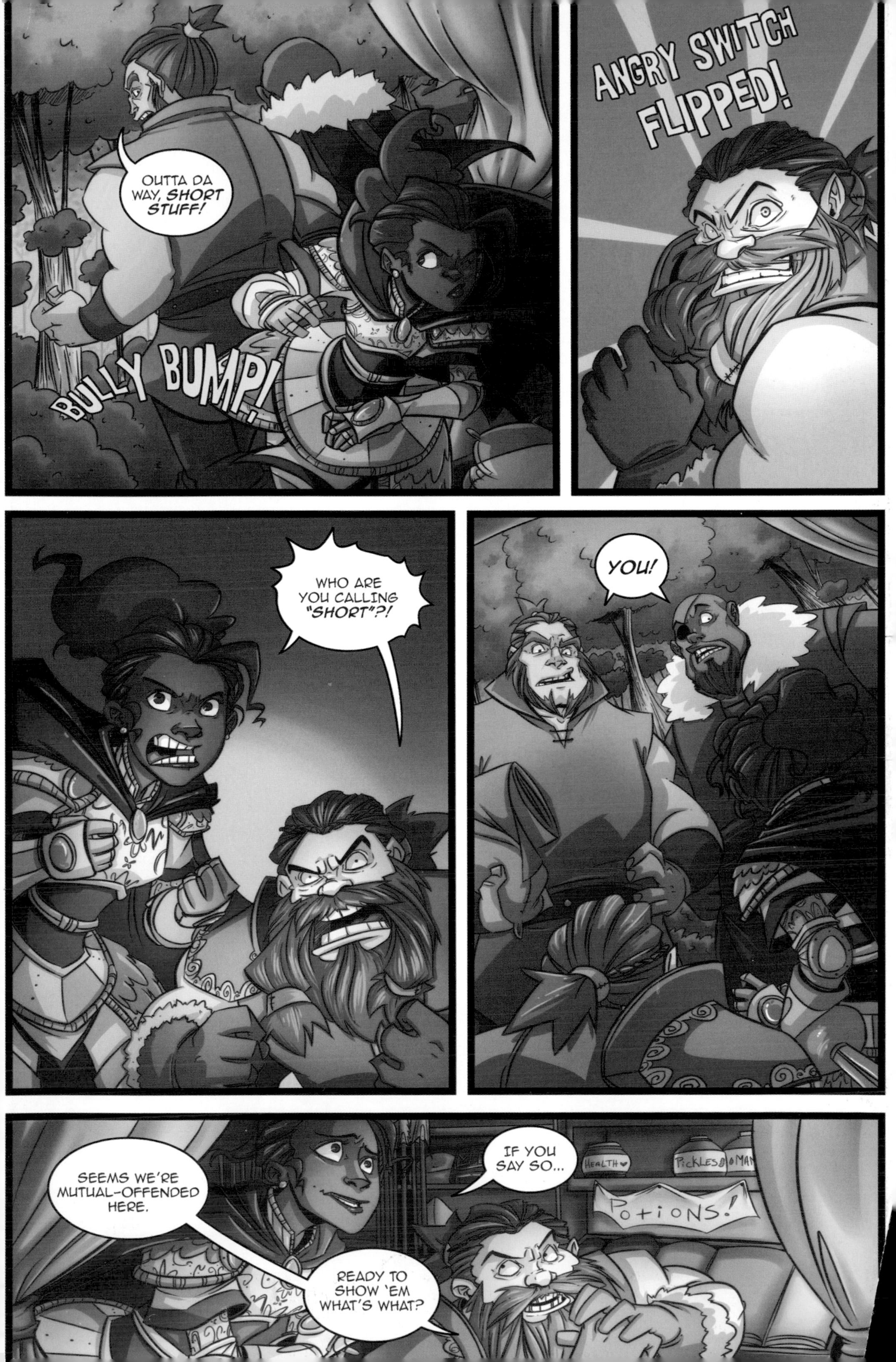
OUTTA DA WAY, SHORT STUFF!
BULLY BUMP!
ANGRY SWITCH FLIPPED!
WHO ARE YOU CALLING "SHORT"?!
YOU!
SEEMS WE'RE MUTUAL-OFFENDED HERE.
IF YOU SAY SO...
HEALTH
PICKLES
MAN
POTIONS!
READY TO SHOW 'EM WHAT'S WHAT?

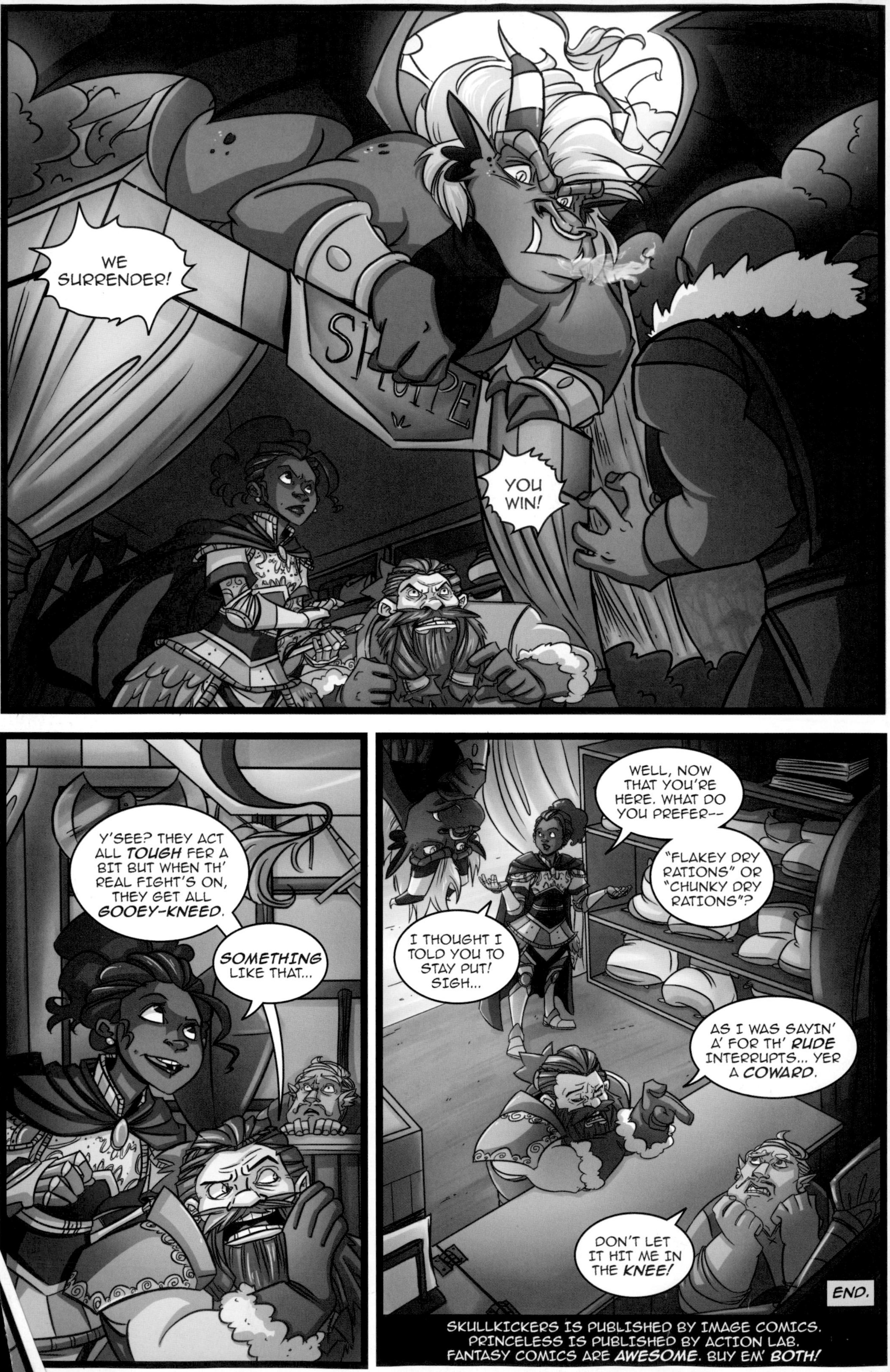
WE SURRENDER!
YOU WIN!
Y'SEE? THEY ACT ALL TOUGH FER A BIT BUT WHEN TH' REAL FIGHT'S ON, THEY GET ALL GOOEY-KNEED.
SOMETHING LIKE THAT...
WELL, NOW THAT YOU'RE HERE. WHAT DO YOU PREFER--
"FLAKEY DRY RATIONS" OR "CHUNKY DRY RATIONS"?
I THOUGHT I TOLD YOU TO STAY PUT! SIGH...
AS I WAS SAYIN' A' FOR TH' RUDE INTERRUPTS... YER A COWARD.
DON'T LET IT HIT ME IN THE KNEE!
END.
SKULLKICKERS IS PUBLISHED BY IMAGE COMICS.
PRINCELESS IS PUBLISHED BY ACTION LAB.
FANTASY COMICS ARE AWESOME. BUY EM' BOTH!

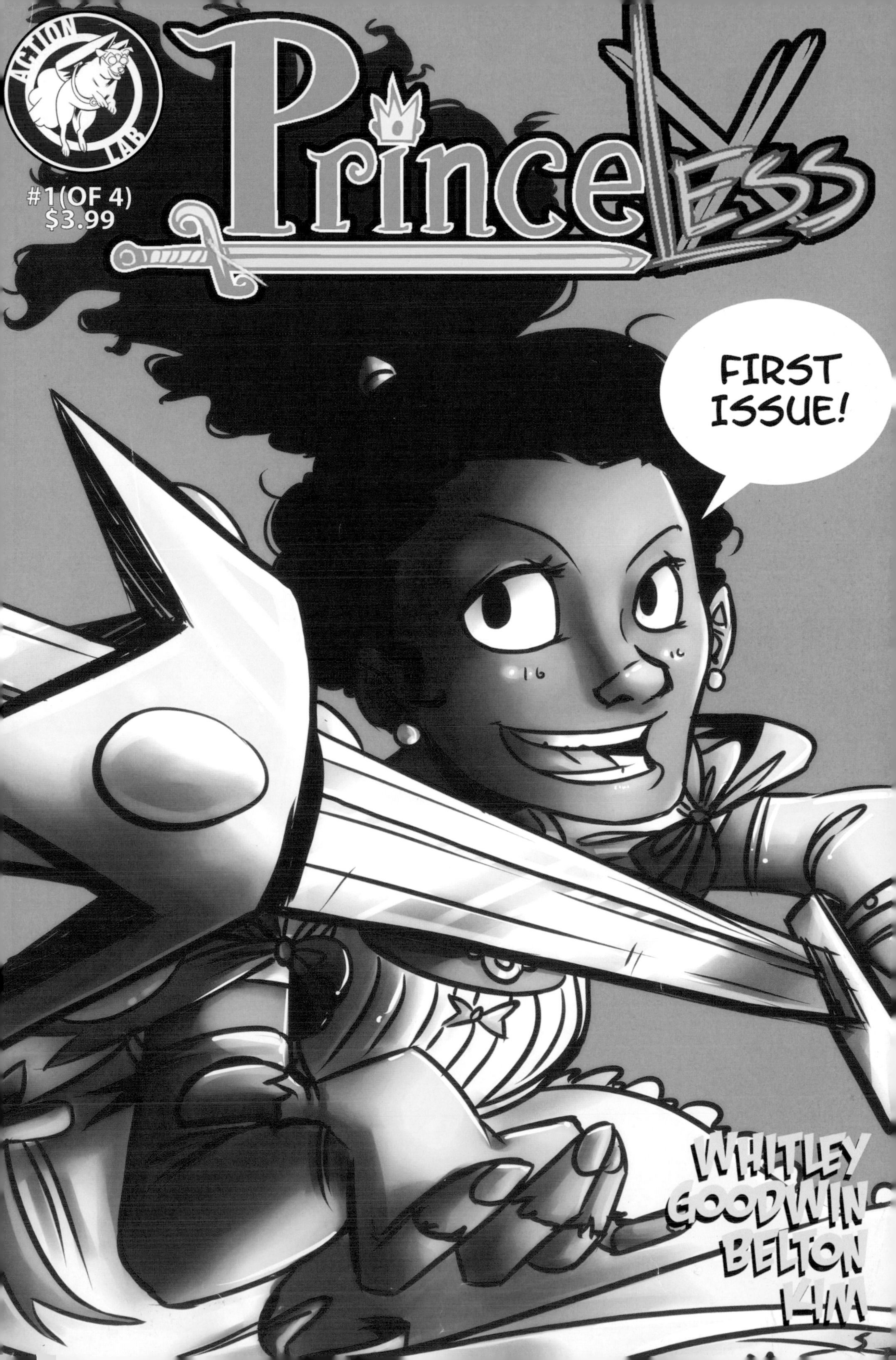
ACTION LAB
Princeless
#1 (OF 4)
$3.99
FIRST ISSUE!
WHITLEY
GOODWIN
BELTON
KIM

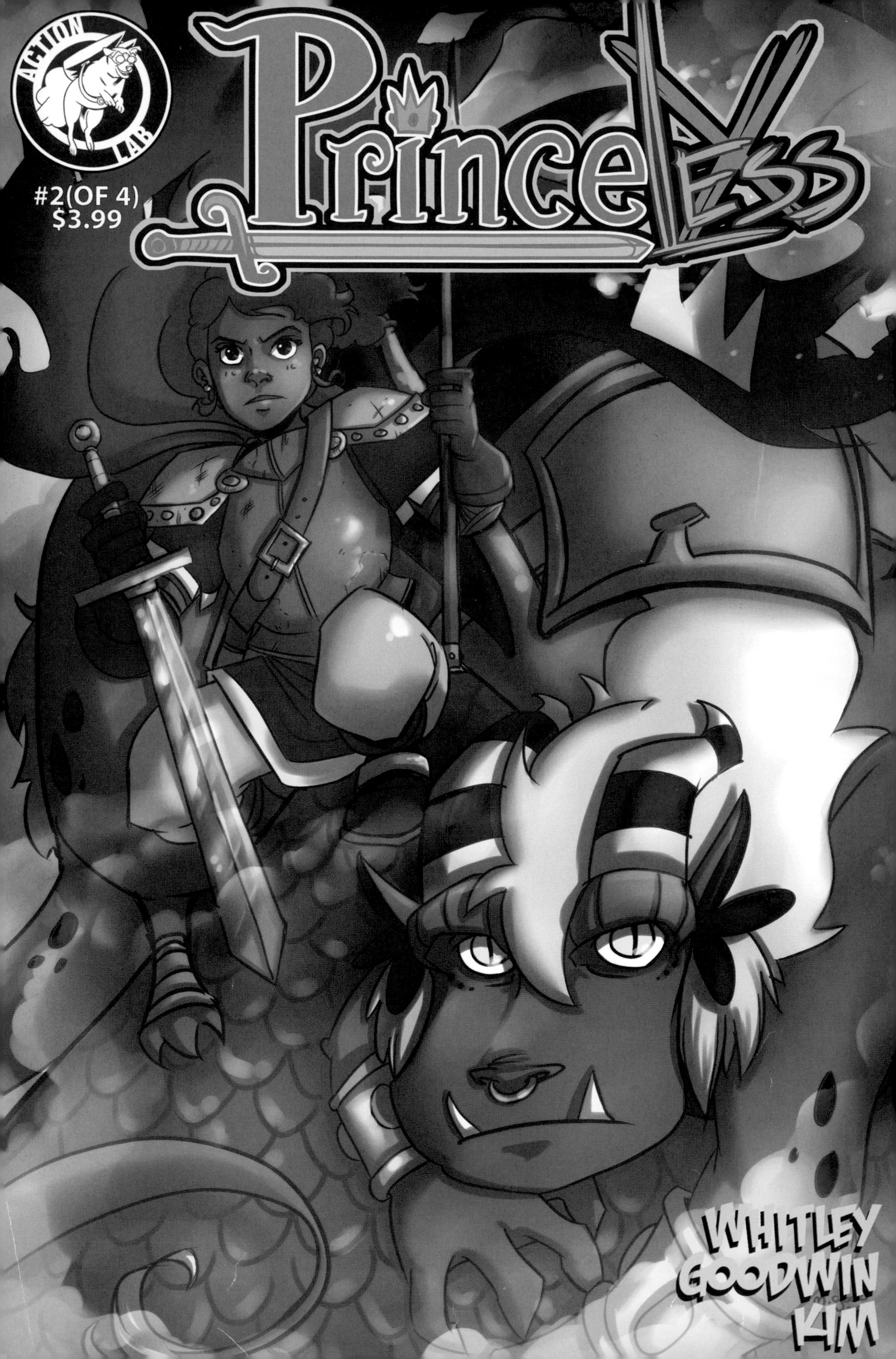
ACTION LAB
Princeless
#2(OF 4)
$3.99
WHITLEY
GOODWIN
KIM

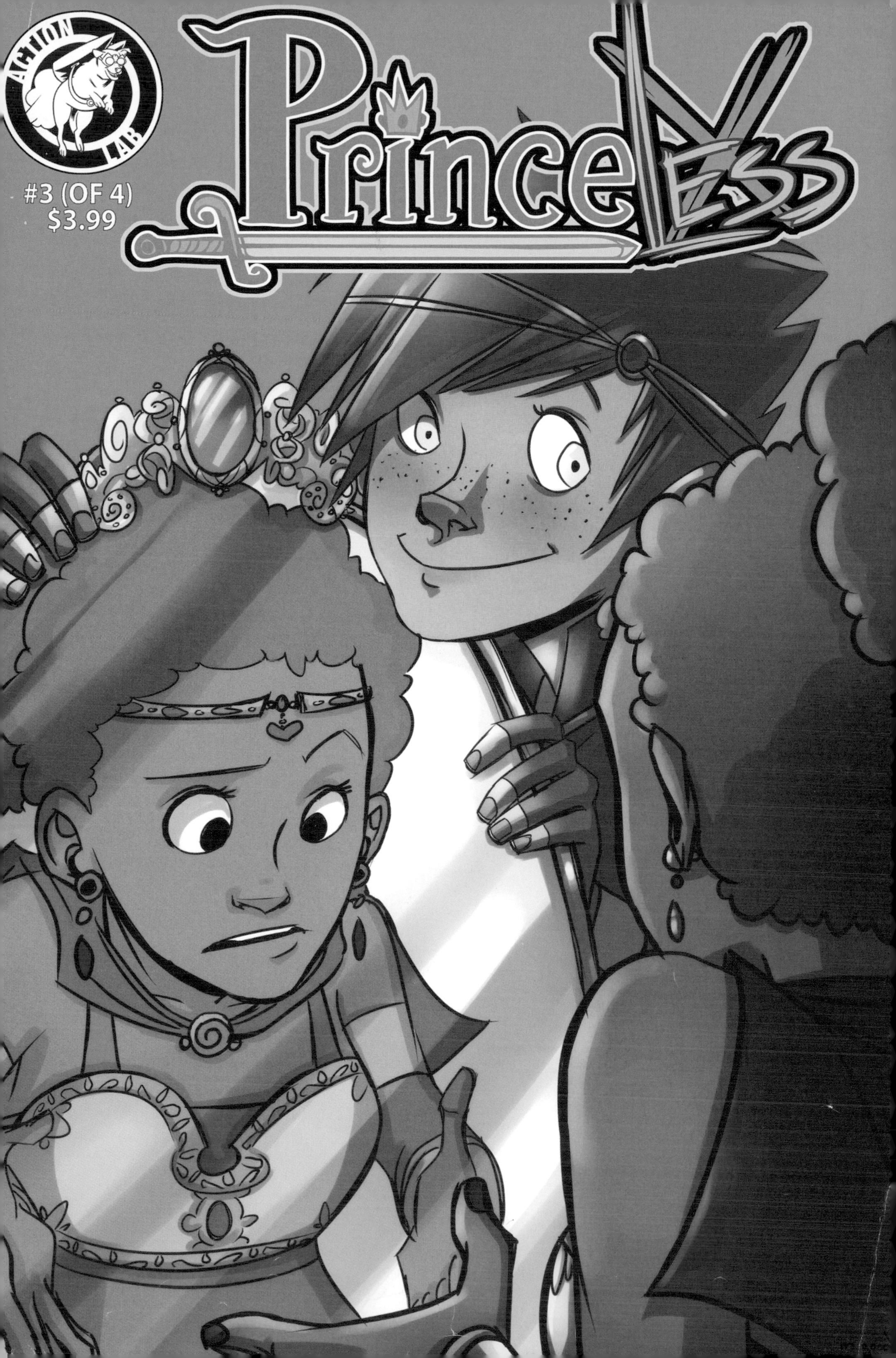
ACTION LAB
Princeless
#3 (OF 4)
$3.99

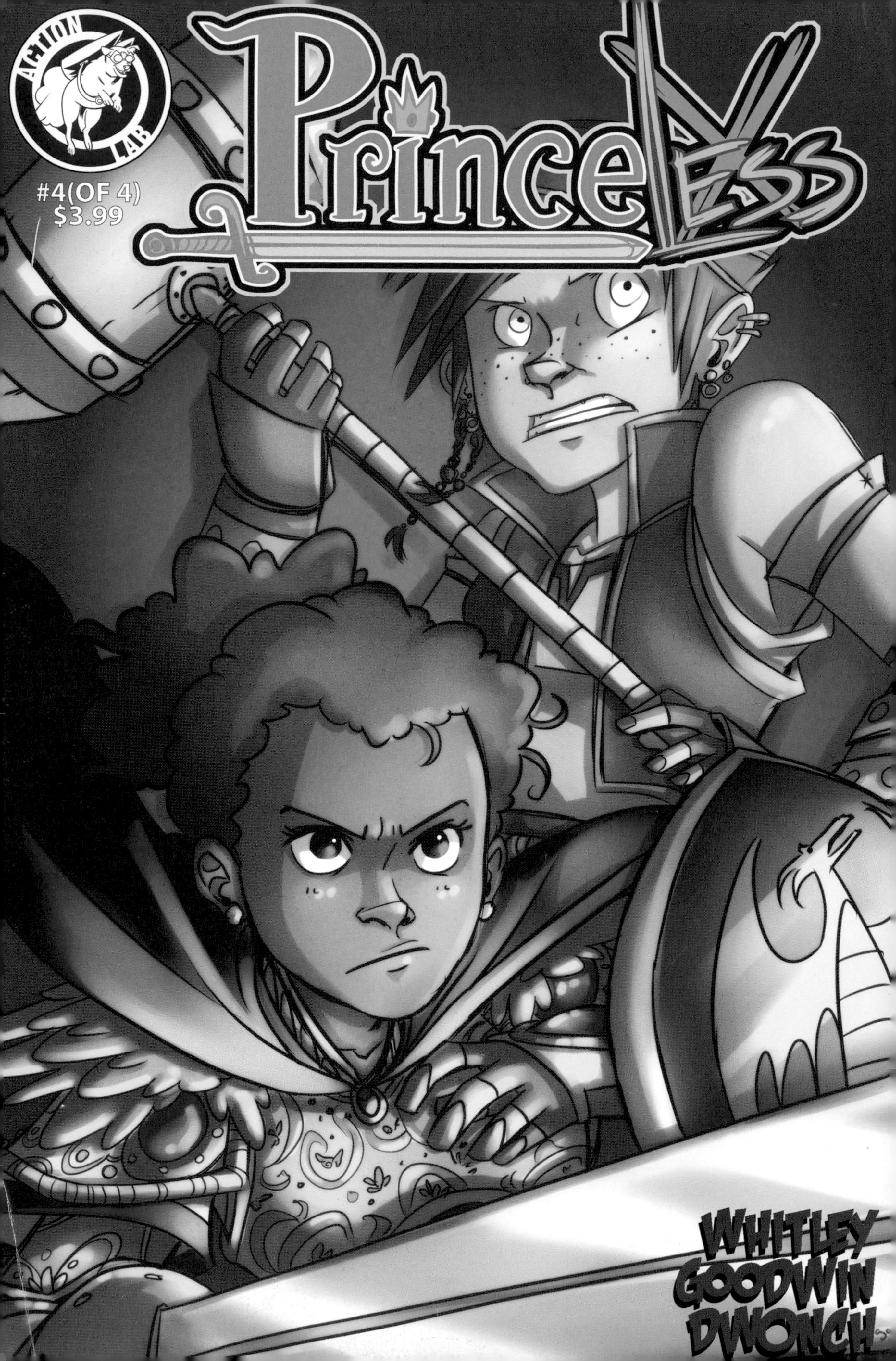
ACTION LAB
Princeless
#4(OF 4)
$3.99
WHITLEY
GOODWIN
DWONCH

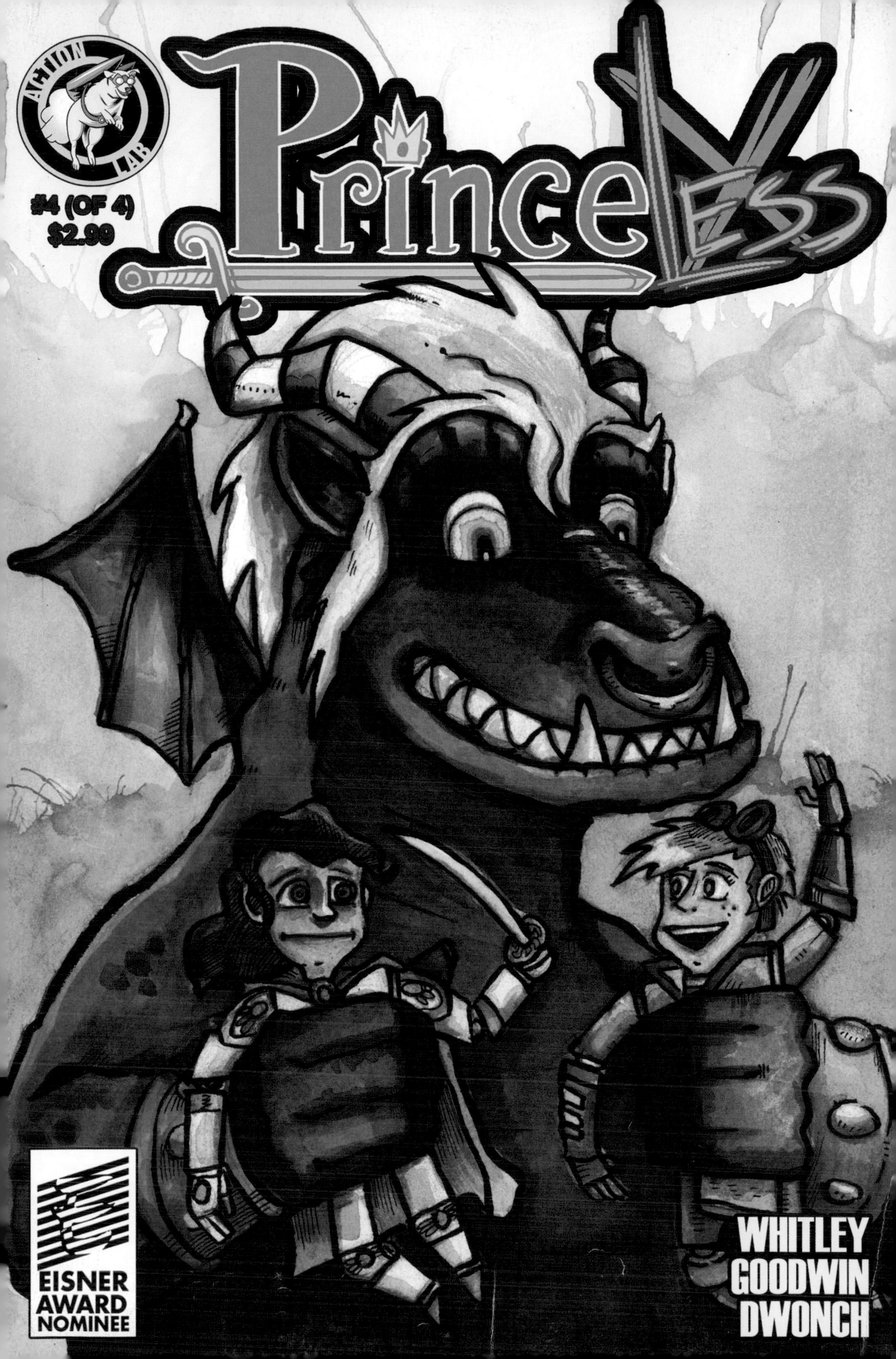

ACTION LAB
#4 (OF 4)
$2.99
Princeless
EISNER AWARD NOMINEE
WHITLEY
GOODWIN
DWONCH

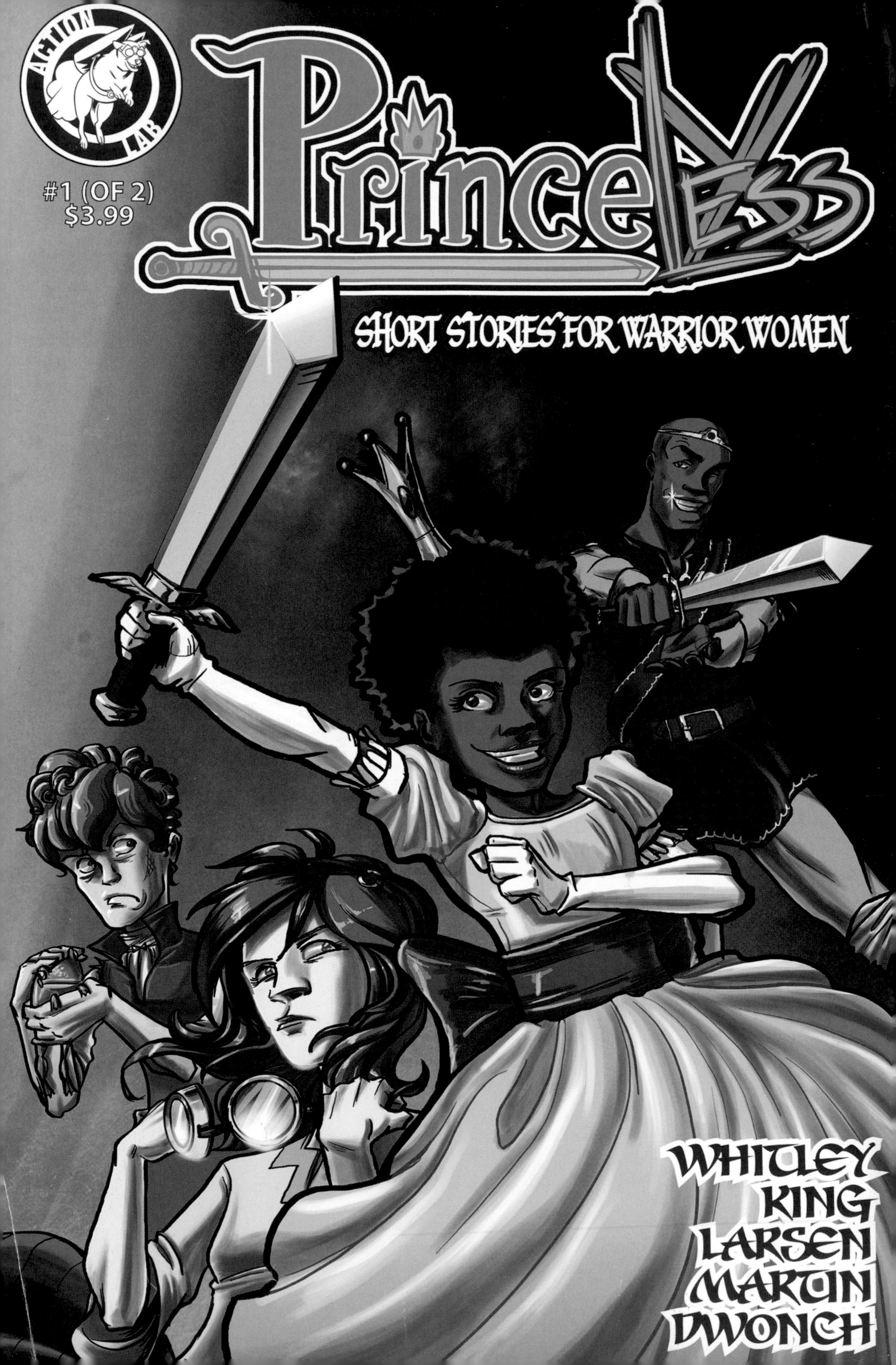
ACTION LAB
#1 (OF 2)
$3.99
Princeless
SHORT STORIES FOR WARRIOR WOMEN
WHITLEY
KING
LARSEN
MARTIN
DWONCH

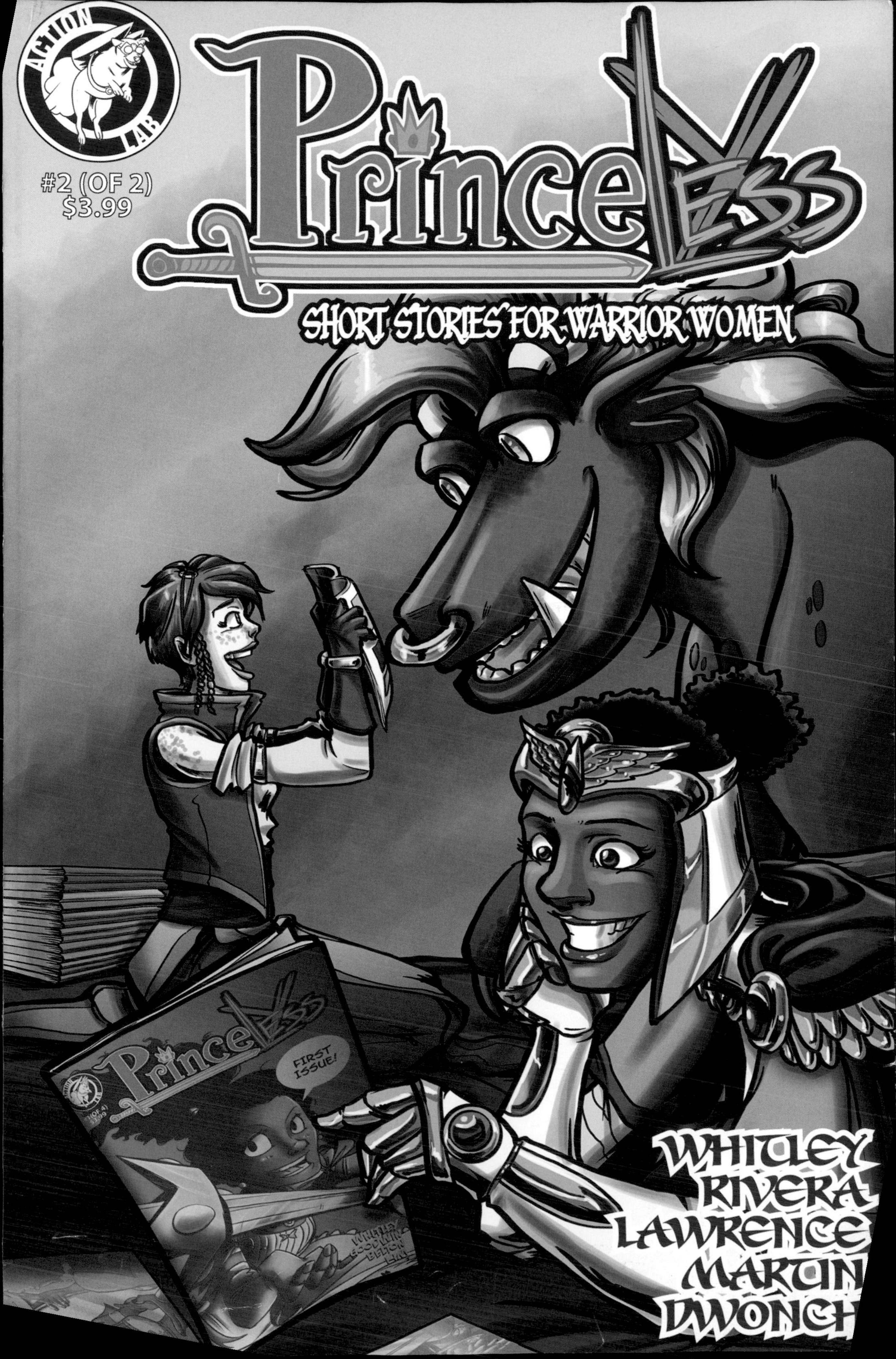
ACTION LAB
#2 (OF 2)
$3.99
Princeless
SHORT STORIES FOR WARRIOR WOMEN
Princeless
FIRST ISSUE!
WHITLEY
RIVERA
LAWRENCE
MARTIN
DWONCH

PIN-UP BY SARAH LEUVER

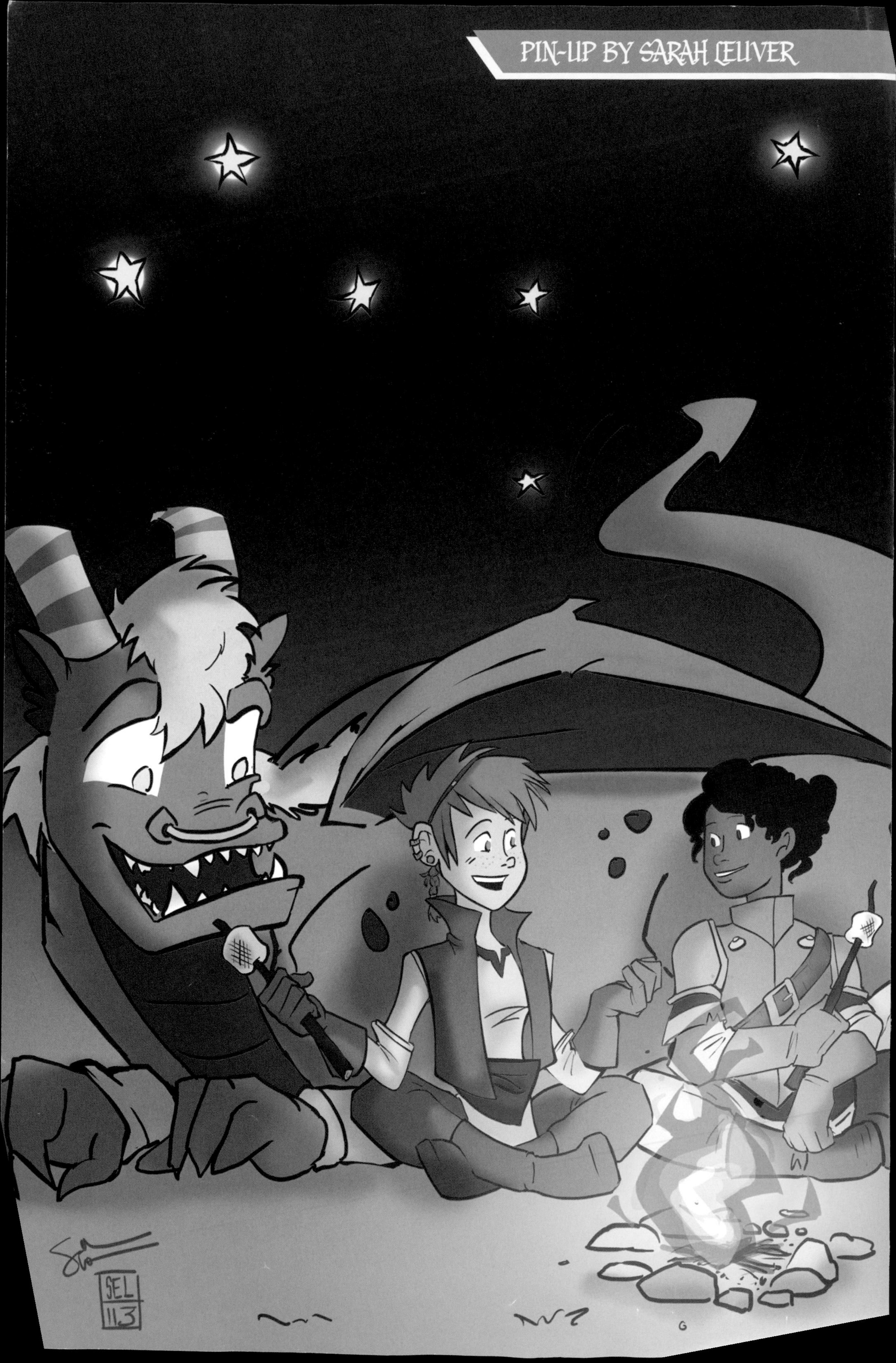
SEL
11.3

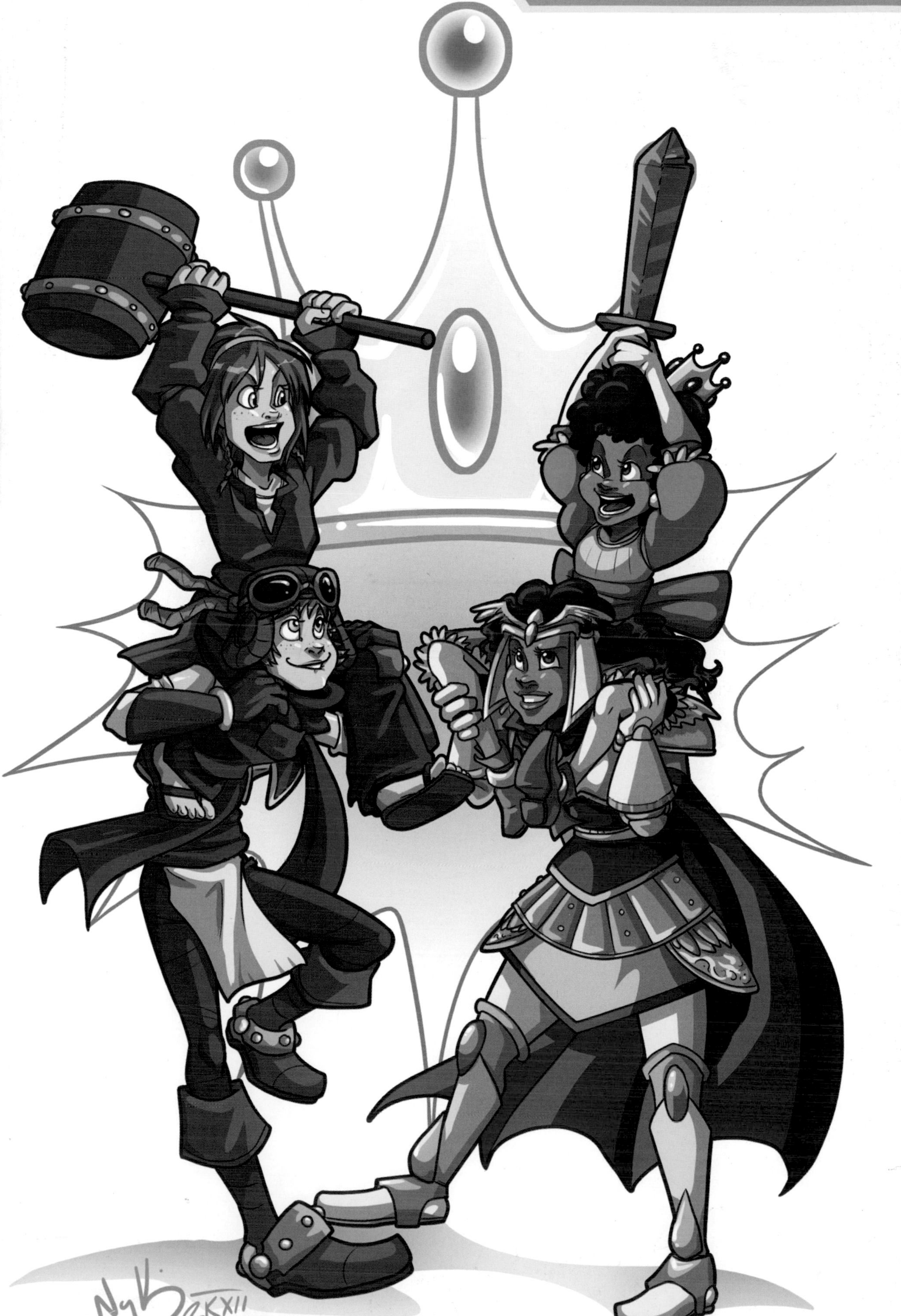

PIN-UP BY ELSA KROESE

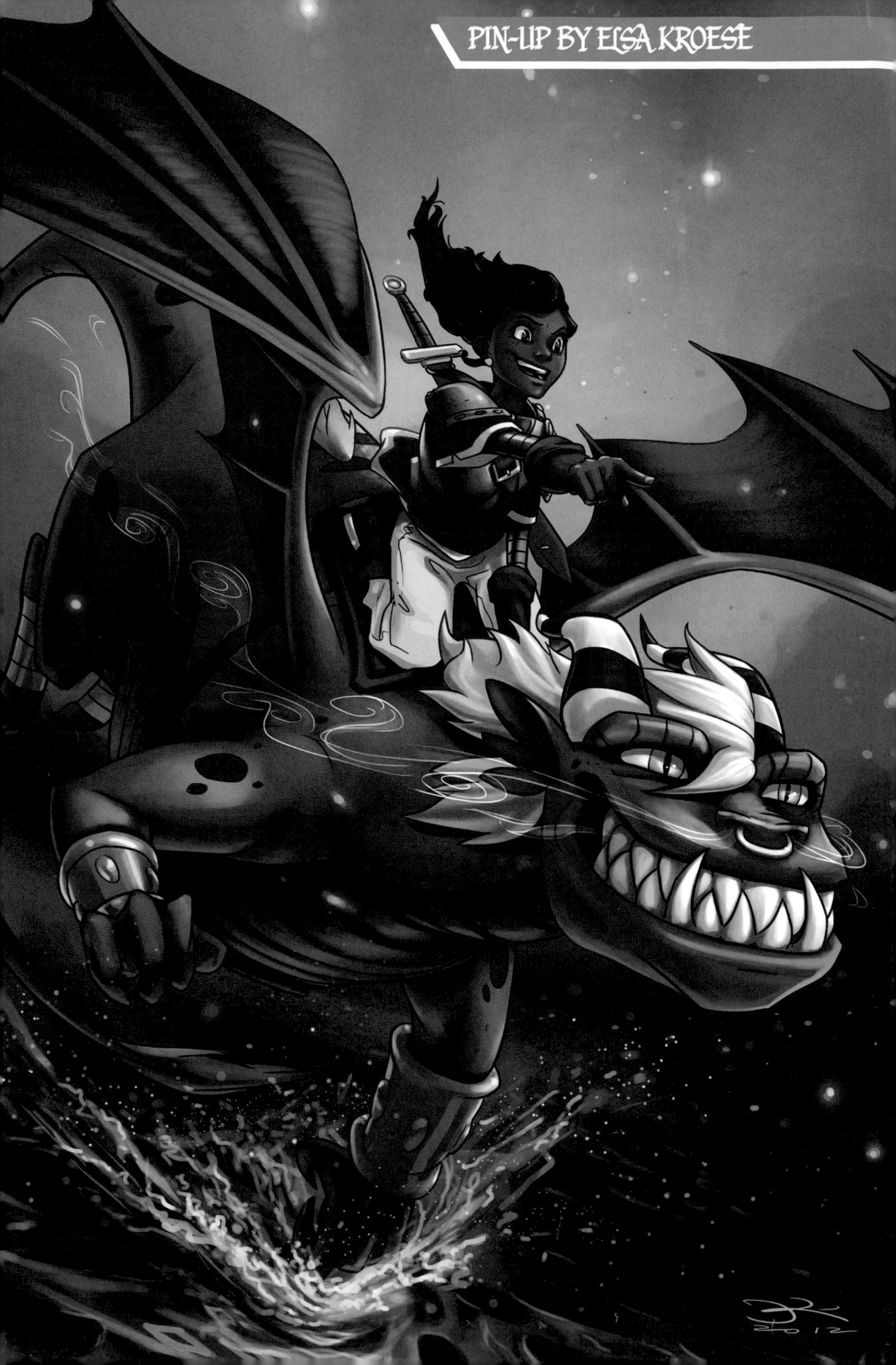

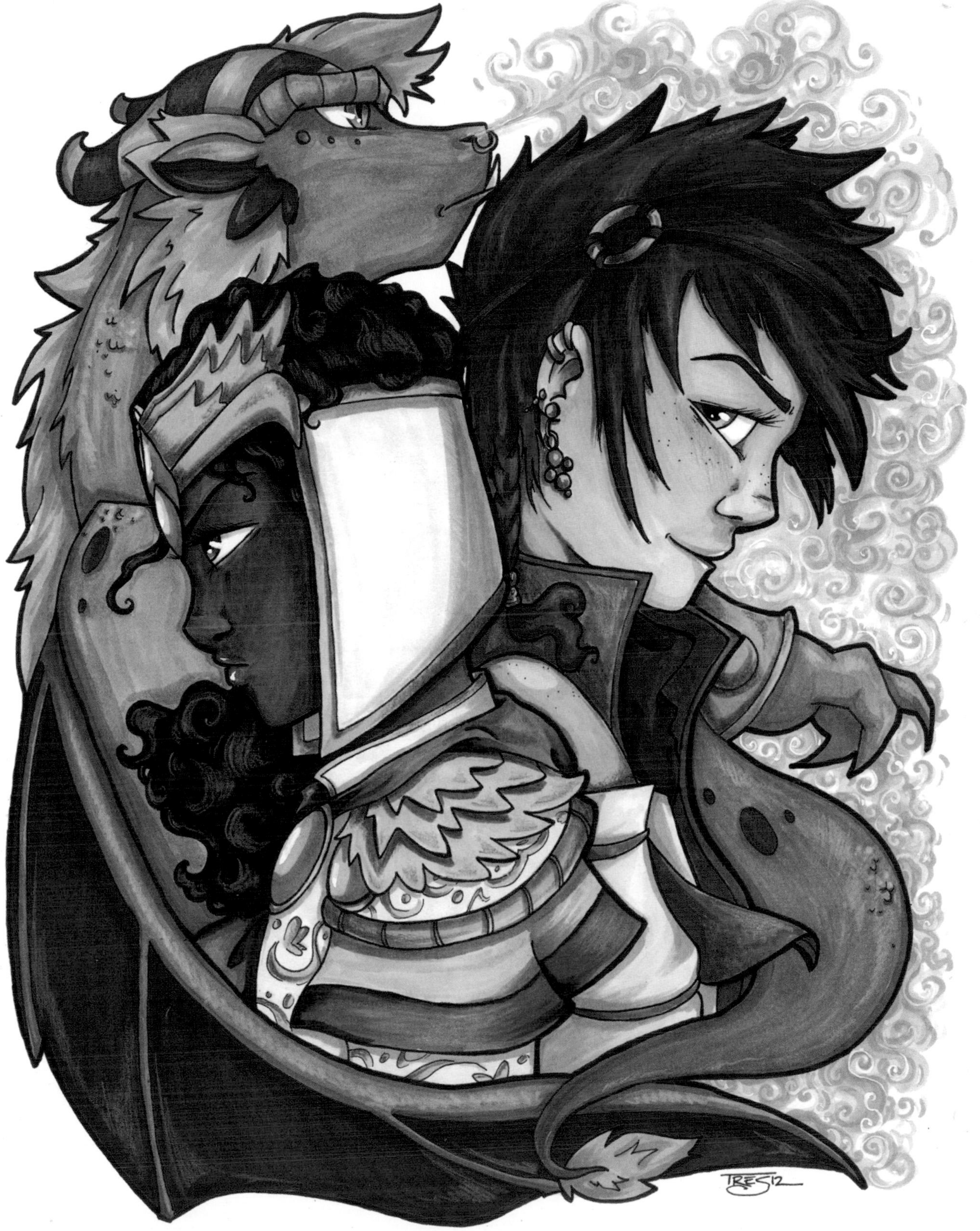
TRES '12

PIN-UP BY TRESSA BOWLING

PIN-UP BY LAURA GUZZO

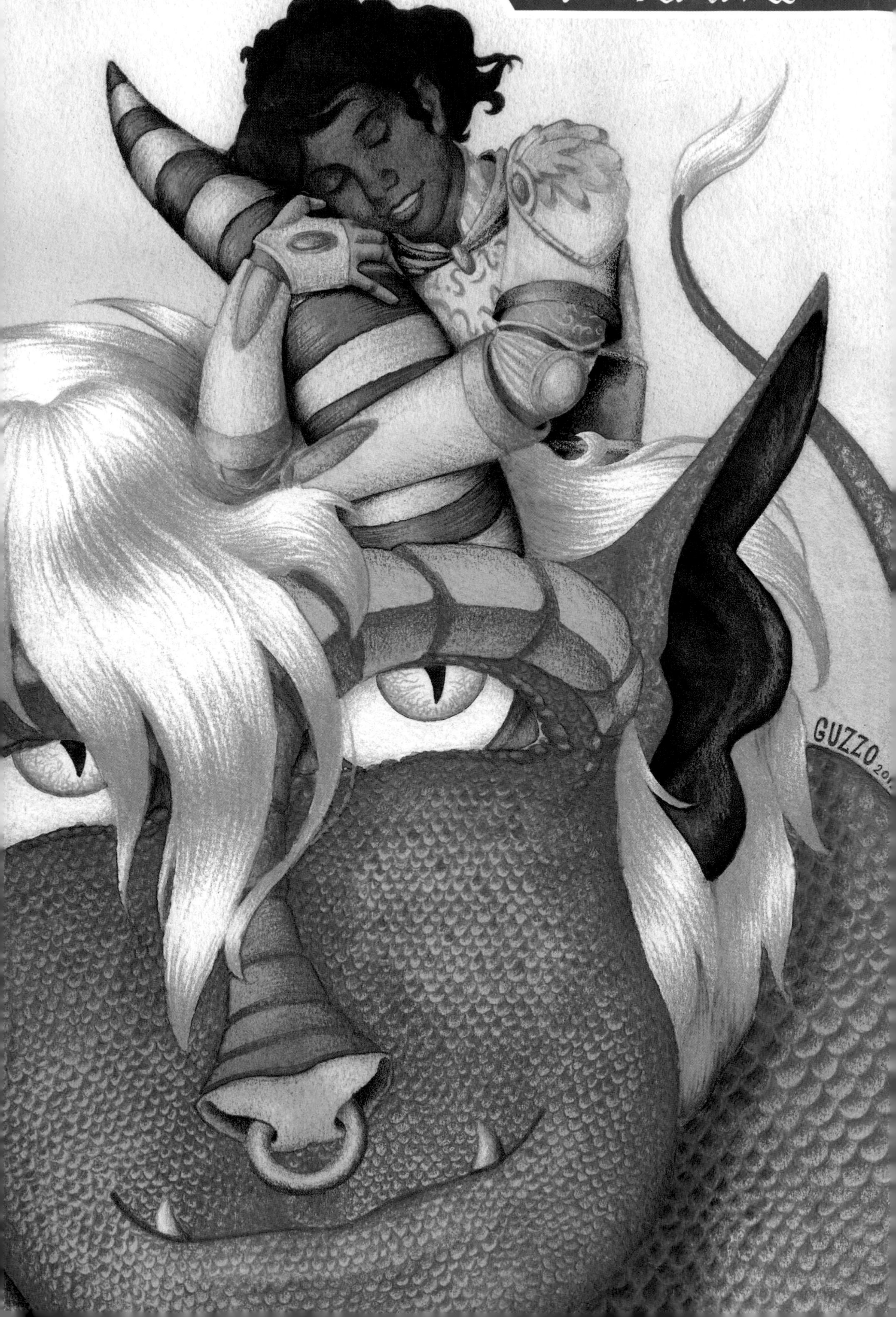
GUZZO

PIN-UP BY JANET WADE

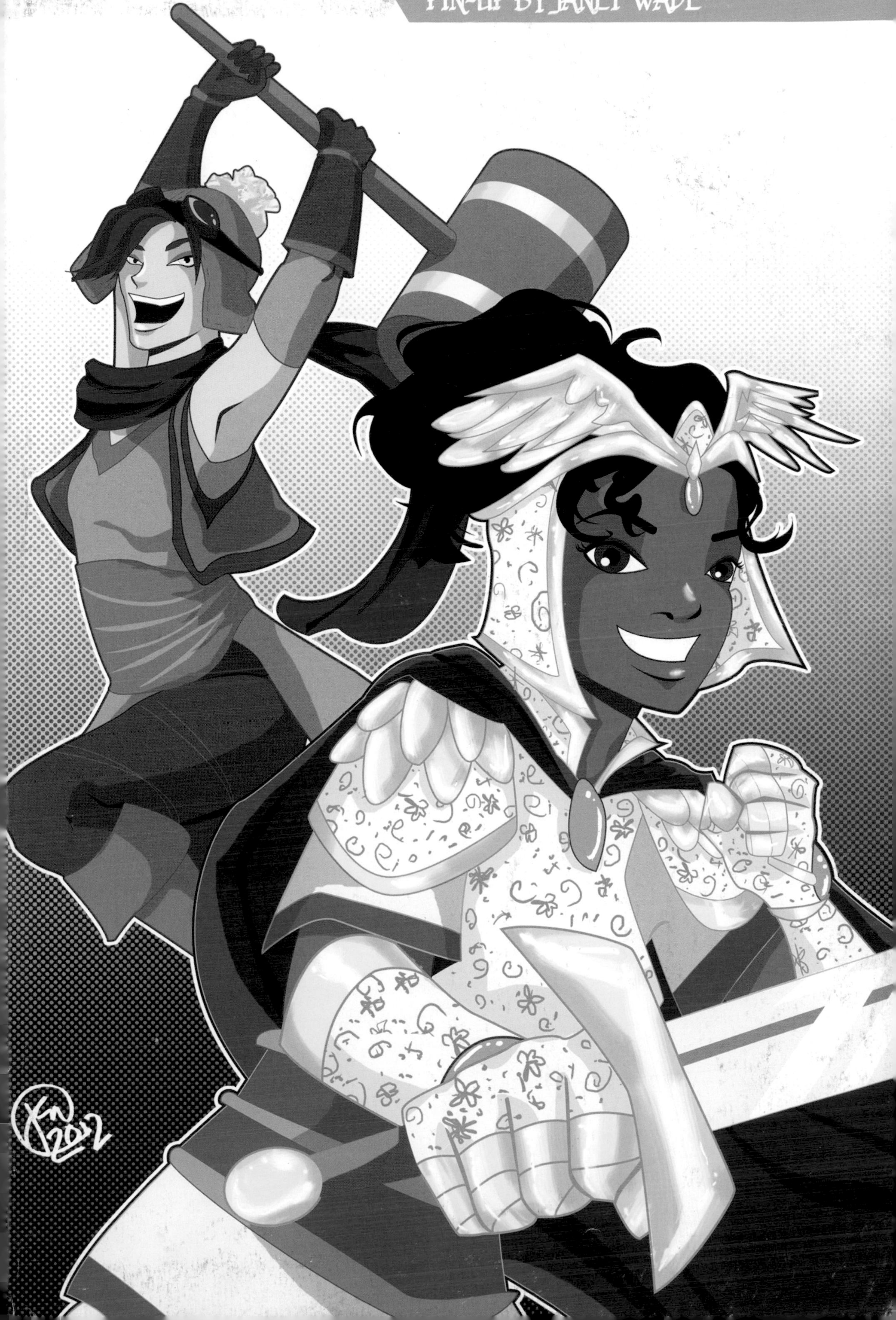

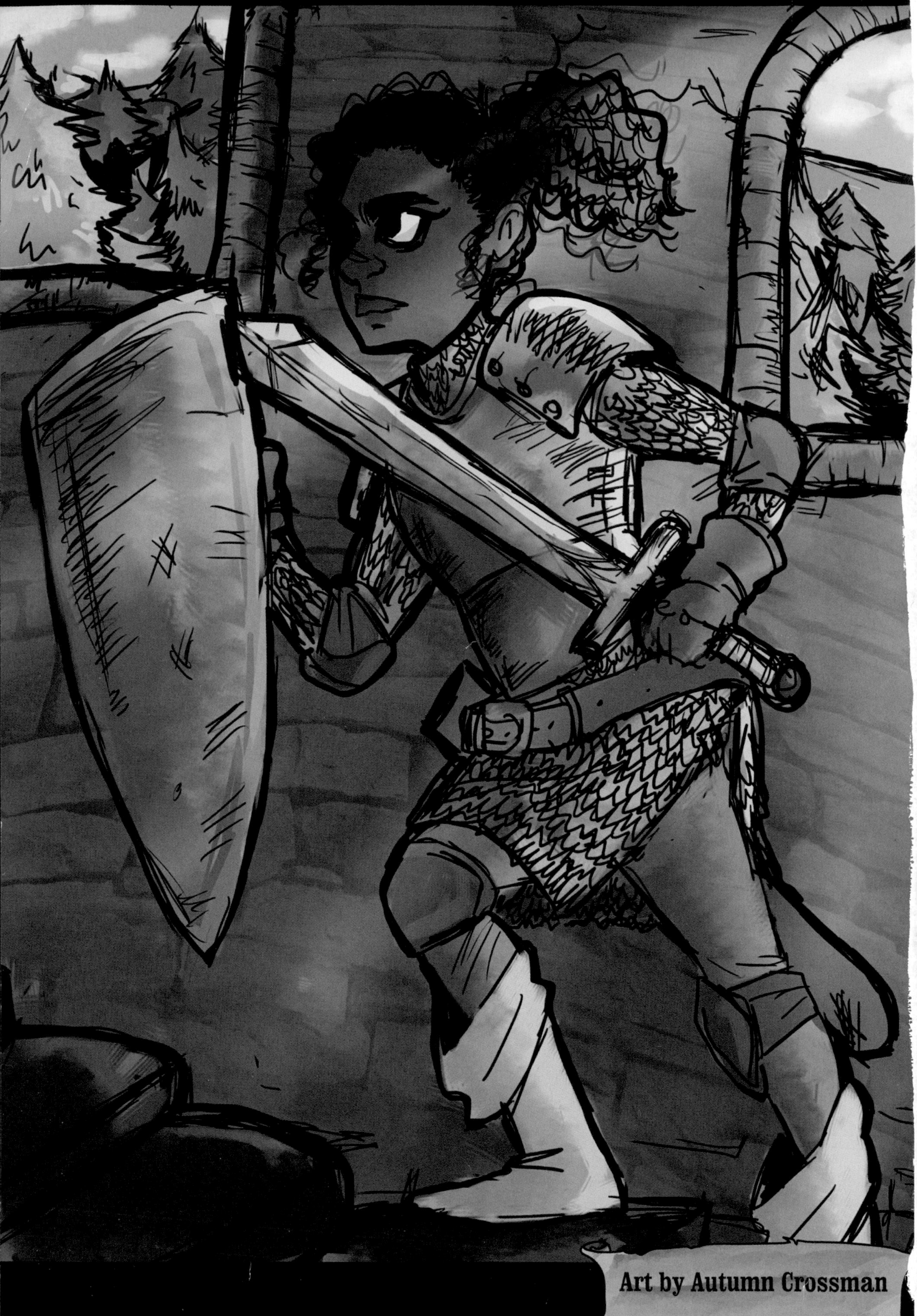

Art by Autumn Crossman